KENNETH KAPPELMANN

The DRAGON OPPRESSION

HIDDEN MAGIC VOLUME IV

THE PREQUEL

Black Rose Writing | Texas

©2021 by Kenneth Kappelmann
All rights reserved. No part of this book may be reproduced, stored in a retrieval system or transmitted in any form or by any means without the prior written permission of the publishers, except by a reviewer who may quote brief passages in a review to be printed in a newspaper, magazine or journal.

The author grants the final approval for this literary material.

First printing

This is a work of fiction. Names, characters, businesses, places, events, and incidents are either the products of the author's imagination or used in a fictitious manner. Any resemblance to actual persons, living or dead, or actual events is purely coincidental.

ISBN: 978-1-68433-738-5
PUBLISHED BY BLACK ROSE WRITING
www.blackrosewriting.com

Printed in the United States of America
Suggested Retail Price (SRP) $19.95

The Dragon Oppression is printed in Adobe Caslon Pro

*As a planet-friendly publisher, Black Rose Writing does its best to eliminate unnecessary waste to reduce paper usage and energy costs, while never compromising the reading experience. As a result, the final word count vs. page count may not meet common expectations.

For Gran

The DRAGON OPPRESSION

Chapter One

"He has returned," stated the large dragon. "You must not allow him to turn any of those who follow you. You have asserted yourself, as it should be. Don't relent now and show weakness."

The black dragon snarled toward the dragon next to him. "Why don't you stand up to Anbari? Why don't you—"

Slayne was cut off by his larger counterpart. "If you wish me to take over, I will. I have no fear."

"I don't fear Anbari. I just see you standing in the background. Why push me in a direction you yourself will not go?"

Fire dripped from the dragon's mouth, and his voice was low and filled with strength. "Try me, Slayne, and see what I do. This is your fight today, if you are dragon enough for it."

He lowered his head and turned to leave the outcropping of trees to enter the glade. The other dragon went the opposite direction and backed further into the trees to remain out of sight.

"Anbari, what are you doing here? You have no business coming back. The dragons have answered the question—they no longer choose to follow you."

Anbari opened and arched his wings and glared to the much smaller, but still powerful rival before him. "Slayne, although your tone depicts otherwise, you have not won anything yet. You have used your magic to twist the world we live to be what you want it to be. There are many powers on Troyf today that will, in the end, stop your foolish plan."

The black dragon took several steps toward his larger counterpart. Fire dripped from his mouth like beads of molten lava. "Surely you don't mean the canoks, elves, and that fool race of maneths? Do you really think they can do anything to stop my dragons?"

"Your dragons?" Anbari questioned, a slight laugh carried in his words. "The reason you gave them to follow you was to allow dragons to be free across the land, as we once were. Now you claim them as yours. Do you intend to rule over them as well?"

"I will assert my leadership as required. All races need a leader, why should it not be me?" Slayne was pacing as he spoke, but always kept his head turned to face his counterpart.

Anbari stared back at him. His voice was deep and unrelenting. "Because you are no leader. You wish to rule, not lead."

Slayne did not remove his stare. "It doesn't matter what you think, Anbari. The dragons have spoken, and they chose me. I don't want you in Draag any longer. Leave now, or I will have the dragons turn on you."

Anbari laughed. "They would not, and you know it as well as I do."

As he said the words, a dozen dragons started up the hill. Anbari watched as they slowly approached. With each step they took, Slayne's eyes grew wider and his smile deepened. He turned to stand in front of the larger and more powerful silver dragon. "You see, you naïve soul. Your time is over. You can no longer hold the dragons back. We were meant to rule Troyf, not follow. You have kept us down long enough, and now, at a time before the young dragons will hatch, we will reclaim what is ours."

Anbari's eyes locked on several of those behind Slayne. A few looked down, feeling some level of shame but not enough to move from their new leader. He felt their pain and confusion, but they chose to remain. They had been promised a world. They had been promised to rule. They had been promised things that went against everything Anbari would want his race to crave. They had been promised *power*.

He was about to speak when a noise was heard above the trees. It was the sound of leaves being kicked up by the fierce beat of large wings. All dragons in the area looked up and watched as the huge green dragon slowly landed between Slayne and Anbari. The large female dragon shook out her wings and turned to Anbari. "Are you well, Anbari?"

"I am, Hawthorne," he replied.

"Welcome, my love," interrupted Slayne. "I am pleased you have come to share in our position and demonstrate to this fool that his time over Draag has come to an end. I had decided to allow him to leave and never return, and we have a dozen dragons to ensure that would happen. Now with you by my side, perhaps a better answer is to simply end his rule in a more permanent way. Together, we can prevent Anbari from ever poisoning our world again."

There was a stir among the dragons as his words struck their ears. Hawthorne turned her head to the black dragon and then back to Anbari. She took a few steps to stand beside the black dragon who was now, standing taller, carrying more confidence than he had for this entire exchange. Anbari took a step back and began envisioning every option in his mind on how he could escape. Previously he had not considered his execution as an option, but now Slayne was taking a more defiant stance. The black dragon would not allow him to leave. Anbari represented everything Slayne wanted to extinguish on Troyf. He stared at the beautiful green dragon. "Hawthorne, you are the one who could make a difference. You are the one who can see the truth. Please don't tell me you have joined with this misguided band. Please don't fall prey to the power-hungry dragons who seek to repeat the mistakes of the past."

Hawthorne stared hard at her counterpart. She had been close with Anbari for almost her entire life, but different than all other dragons, as she was not born in Draag. She had come from somewhere outside the historic dragon lands. Her power had allowed her to join the dragons without hindrance. She had become close with Anbari. He was the strongest with magic and power, but even he was still learning. They had been provided no guidance. No teachers. But Anbari could do things no other dragon could even learn, until Hawthorne, that is. She had learned from him. She had grown with him, and now, as he looked upon her next to Slayne, she too had fallen to the power of seduction. Slayne did not need her to turn the dragons, for he had already done that. However, Slayne did need her assistance to defeat him. And now he was in a position to do that. She never took her eyes off her longtime friend. And then, she winked.

It was less than a second later when both Anbari and Hawthorne turned their immense strength directly on the dragons before them. Slayne was

THE DRAGON OPPRESSION

thrown to the side, not expecting the attack from Hawthorne, while Anbari lit up the glade knocking all twelve of Slayne's counterparts to the ground.

"*Hawthorne, don't fight,*" Anbari said telepathically. "*I don't want to hurt them. Follow my path and run.*"

Both dragons took off through the trees. Slayne recovered quickly but the other dragons who had faced the brunt of Anbari's attack were still down and scattered. The black dragon shouted to follow and attack but only two dragons rose and neither took flight. A large blue turned to his all-black leader. "They are gone. They are too strong for us to catch and defeat. You have won, Slayne. They have fled."

"But they are not dead," Slayne replied. "They are not dead."

***

From the trees the large dragon watched as Slayne and Anbari talked. To his surprise, Hawthorne entered the glade and moved beside the black dragon.

"Why are you hiding in the trees, Bjork?" a female dragon asked from behind.

The large blue dragon turned with a start. "Don't surprise me like that, and please remain quiet. I am not hiding but waiting to see if that fool can turn Anbari away. Hawthorne has joined his side. I did not foresee this. Together they could defeat Anbari now and end my visions once and for all."

The female dragon peered through the trees in amazement. "I want Hawthorne dead. I don't trust her."

He laughed. "Trust Hawthorne." His eyes narrowed. "She is far from trustworthy, but easily confused on where her loyalties should lie. She has power deep within her. I can feel it. If I can truly turn her, then I don't need Slayne."

"But they follow Slayne. The eggs have been laid. If you want to lead the young, you must hold control now. You said so yourself; Slayne can do that."

He took his eyes off the exchange in the glade before him and turned to the large female. In a stern voice, he stated, "They follow power. Right now, they only know the power of Slayne. With Hawthorne and me together, we can rule them all without question. They will follow us."

Her faced turned down at the thought of Hawthorne and Bjork together, but the female dragon did not have a chance to reply. Without warning, there was an explosion in the glade and fire erupted. Dragons were tossed aside like twigs and all Bjork and his female counterpart saw were Hawthorne and Anbari disappearing above the trees.

"The fool," stated the large dragon, as he turned and started to walk away.

"You see," the female replied. "You can't trust her. She has always been with Anbari."

***

"Where do you wish to go, Anbari?" Hawthorne asked once they had slowed the cut of their wings and eased back on their hurried escape. They had been traveling for quite some time ensuring a good distance between them and Draag, but neither actually had spoken about any specific destination.

"I am not sure, Hawthorne," he replied, but nodded down to a small clearing. "Let's land there. I wish to speak to you about what you have chosen."

She knew this conversation was coming. She had been spending all her time with Slayne. It was believed they were to be together. As Slayne had continued to grow in power, they seemed to thrive. Hawthorne was certain that Anbari did not trust her. Why would he? She landed gently next to him in the glade and her eyes were immediately locked on his. She felt his magical hands peeling into her mind. Although she could have defended against it, she did not. "You can search my entire mind. My actions are true."

"I will never underestimate anyone again, Hawthorne. The fact you know of my search is enough to tell me you can expose whatever you wish and protect that which you don't wish me to know. You are powerful and until moments ago, you were with the one who wished me dead."

She did not hesitate in her response. "I do hold the power to block; however, today my mind is yours. Search my feelings about the black dragon. Search what I believe. I may be able to block what I do not wish you to know, but I can't create false beliefs for you to steal."

Anbari nodded. He believed that to be the case, in at least the limits of his abilities. He did not believe Hawthorne's knowledge of magic was greater than his, but she was powerful, that much was certain. He searched her mind. He focused on her thoughts about Slayne, the black dragon she had been so close to in recent days. When he found her thoughts, he looked away in disgust.

Hawthorne smiled. "Now you understand, don't you, my friend? Slayne is disturbed. He is confused. I could not reach him, even now. He has poisoned many. He can change those who are young, weak, and driven. He finds the dragons that crave power and exploits that thirst for power. He teaches the minimum to give them a taste. Then he owns them. They are his, and an army he is building because of it. They use the Rock in Draag to gain their power. It is not within them like it is for him and the two of us. They must tap into the powers of Draag."

He understood how Slayne was winning them over. Giving a dragon a taste of magical abilities was a powerful tool to persuade them. He did not have that tool at his disposal. He shook his head and then stared directly into Hawthorne's eyes. "Why did you follow me?" Anbari asked. "Did you sense something in me?" He was very interested in the answer because he had worked very hard to protect his feelings from prying minds.

"Not one thing," she replied flatly. "Although I tried on numerous occasions, even those times you didn't know I was there and I received nothing from you."

Anbari was noticeably pleased with this response. "Then why did you join me?"

"She stepped closer and was almost whispering. "Because when I could not sense anything in you, I searched Slayne's feelings about you. Slayne fears you. If that dragon is scared, I want to know why."

Anbari held his smile but turned away and paced around the glade appearing to be examining the environment. He turned back. "He is scared because of the prophecy."

"What prophecy? I don't know of any prophecy." Hawthorne walked toward Anbari but stopped well short of reaching him. Her voice was much louder, and her confusion was clear.

Anbari turned and stared directly into Hawthorne's eyes. "The prophecy that states one dragon will bring complete rule across the land, pulling on all the powers ever created to be harnessed into one source."

"The dictatorship he kept speaking of when I was with him. He wishes to rule all of Troyf?" Hawthorne stated this as a question to Anbari, but in her mind she felt it was simply a statement.

"He does," Anbari replied.

"But from where is this prophecy? What creature would create such a ridiculous belief and then replay it for all to know?"

"I did," he replied. "The day the last dragon died protecting the eggs." He paused and his voice softened. "The last dragon, other than me."

"You were alive?" she replied questioning. "You lived through the Oppression?"

"No, I hatched early. I left the eggs and met one dragon—one of the original creatures of the past who was gravely injured. He told me things. He taught me a little. He told me the truth, a truth I have not told anyone."

"Can you tell me?" Hawthorne asked.

"No, I can't," he replied.

"Did he tell you the prophecy too?" she now asked, ignoring the previous response which she was disappointed to hear.

"He did."

"Who? Who is the dragon?" she asked. "Is it Slayne?"

"I don't know, but he said I am the only one who can stop him, or help him get there."

"Stop him or help him? What does that mean?" she asked. "Did he tell you anything else?"

Anbari paused and seemed to be fighting with telling her any more. However, she had just saved him, and he felt such good within her. "Nothing more but a basis from which to learn some magic, and he gave me a gift."

"A gift? What gift?" she asked, her voice gaining excitement.

"He gave me a seed. When I placed it within my talon, I could not control what I felt. I have kept it hidden ever since."

She looked at her friend and saw the pain in his eyes. "What is the seed for? Did the dragon tell you anything else?"

"No, nothing else. Not where it should be planted, what it is for. It appears like a normal acorn seed for an oak tree, but feels so very different."

She let the conversation drop and simply opted to repeat what she had just heard. "So, you are from the original eggs. You hatched early most likely through some magical influence. You meet the only remaining dragon who tells you that a dragon is going to try to take over the world and you are the only dragon who can stop him or provide him a path to rule." She looked toward Anbari who was watching her as she replayed the summary. "It sounds like a riddle. What dragon would you stop and then also allow to do this?" There was a short pause until she continued, "And the only clue you were given was an oak seedling that seems to be filled with some power of its own."

The sliver dragon smiled. "That is about it, I suppose."

She shook her head, finally stopped pacing, and took a seat next to him without another word.

***

"King Hoangis, your son is talented. I don't know if I have seen one better with a bow."

The king nodded appreciatively. "I know, King McCard. I have thought the same thing many times. Madeiris does lack patience, however, but he is young. He is still bitter about being born without wings, a trait he shares with his father."

The large maneth king smiled. "You wish to have been a flyer?" He was smiling as he said it. "You can barely walk and now you want to fly."

Hoangis smiled in return but that smile faded quickly and the serious nature he felt growing in their conversation took over. He walked back toward the Great Hall with King McCard following in his wake. Hoangis turned so he could better face his friend. "So, McCard, what brings you here unannounced?"

He stopped walking and instantly the elf king knew he was correct, and the situation was serious. "Have you seen anything odd in the forests around Elvinott?" he asked.

Elvinott was the elf city Hoangis and his father had built. It was easily the most beautiful city in all of Troyf. It was a city cut into and from the trees. Huge oaks able to be carved into houses. Branches connecting everything like veins of a body. Water flowing through springs feeding the life for the entire village. Stores, smiths, homes, and everything the elves needed was carved directly from this magnificent area of the forest. In the very center was a tremendous fountain of immense size and beauty. Then, carved from a single tree in the center of the fountain, was a beautiful flyer elf. Hoangis had created it with magic stating that someday the figure would be his daughter. The elves paid little mind to the statement as Hoangis only had one child—his son—and Madeiris's mother had not been able to carry a child again. Elves marry for life, so there was no belief that he would ever have a daughter. Regardless, it was truly amazing. A short distance from the fountain was the greatest oak in the forest. Carved into its base was one of the most intricately carved doors which took three elves nearly a year to complete. Above the door, in Elven, read, "The Great Hall." This was where the king resided and all-important matters for the elves were discussed. When Hoangis heard the maneth king's question, he opted not to answer. Instead, he turned and walked the rest of the way to this door. An elf positioned outside bowed to his king and then moved to open the door. Once they had passed, the door closed, and they were alone.

They entered a large chamber. In the center of the chamber stood a huge wooden table with enough seats around it to allow for more than twenty. The two kings sat at the corner of the far end. A fire burned to the side to bring warmth to the entire room.

Hoangis stared back toward the maneth king who returned the gaze with an inquisitive smile. His previous question did not need to be re-asked as it still hung in the air. "McCard, why do you ask this question? I must assume you have seen things of which you cannot explain."

McCard leaned back in the large wooden chair. He fit adequately well in the chair, though maneths were more than a foot taller than elves and much broader. Their bodies were covered with hair ending with a large, brilliant mane around their heads. McCard, however, was not as large as some of his Batt Line maneths—those maneths who fight and defend their village and lives. He had come from the Dimat Line, those that believed in diplomacy before brawn. Neither were better or worse than the other; they simply followed a different path, much like the elves, whereas some were born with wings and some were not. Their path was chosen for them.

McCard let the question linger a moment, then chose his words carefully in response. "Hoangis, I don't know what to think. Maybe it is nothing. Maybe it is something. The forest just does not seem right."

Hoangis leaned back and took in McCard's words. Hoangis had been king for only ten years, barely a scrap of time in an elf's or maneth's life, both typically living more than 250 years. However, he was considered wise beyond his days, and when Ku had vanished ten years ago, he rightly assumed the throne. He sat back and demonstrated this was indeed an important conversation.

"I have felt nothing to make me believe there is anything astray," he finally responded. "Nor have my scouts reported anything in our woods, but remember, our woods are enchanted. If there is something amiss in the forests, you would see it first. Tell me, what has brought this question to you?"

McCard shook his head slightly. "I don't know for sure. It is more of a feeling than a physical presence. However, we have seen changes also. We have seen bands of trolls and goblins in areas of the forest near our camp. They have never strayed this close before and in such great numbers. Then, the canoks. There is a restlessness there. Queen Daphane was supposed to visit our camp six moons ago and still she has not come."

He stopped talking and his voice trailed off as he ended. Hoangis recognized how deep these concerns were carried with his longtime friend. He would not have come if his fears were not real, and he would not be sharing this if he did not truly believe there was something wrong. He leaned forward as he replied, "McCard, we have not strayed beyond our protective forests often. I fear I would not know if things were not as they should be. Perhaps my ignorance and fear to remain has made me unprepared and unwise. I trust your feelings are true as I know you would never have come this far if you did not feel it was critical."

"I don't know if it is as serious as you feel it might be. I simply know there is an unbalance, the likes of which I have not seen before. The animals are changing, and I don't know why."

Hoangis stared at his longtime friend. McCard had been a king much longer than Hoangis, but the two had grown up together. Maneth and elves had been allies since before they had been born, and throughout history, anytime there was an issue with either nation, the other was there in support.

The elf king rose and placed his hand on his friend's shoulder. "I will send a party of flyers with you back to the maneth camp. My son will travel with you as well on foot. Show my son what you are seeing. He knows the forests as well as any, even at his young age. He might know what is happening. While you are gone, I will prepare the elves for a potential change in our world. What that change is, time will tell." McCard seemed pleased with this response but his face still showed concern. The elf king asked, "I see you still have a question."

He nodded. "Not a question, but one more thing we have seen. A young maneth, a bit of an undisciplined Batt Line attendant, claims to have seen many dragons assembling near Draag. I can't believe he traveled that far but he claims he did. He said he saw several fighting and using extreme levels of magic." He paused and then shook his head. "I don't know, my friend. We have not seen dragons across the land in so many years. We knew they existed, but to say they have large numbers forming without us knowing and waging some sort of war against each other, it just doesn't make sense."

Hoangis could feel as well as hear the tension in his friend's voice. He rose and turned away and paced around the table before turning back to the king. "Do you have any reason not to believe this young maneth?"

"What do you mean?" McCard asked.

"I mean, has this maneth ever been known to tell tales that may have been based on some truths, but are actually more about the story than the facts?"

McCard shook his head. "No, Geoff has always been honorable, to the end. His father is high up the Batt Line."

"Very well, then," Hoangis returned. "We must assume he is telling the truth, in which case we have a new enemy among us—one which only our ancestors have faced." He paused and softly stated, "I do wish Ku was here."

McCard ignored the last statement and focused on the first. "The dragons?" His tone clearly showed he questioned the quick determination. "Why do you assume they are our enemy?"

Hoangis did not pause a moment to respond. "Because I have seen it in my dreams. A black dragon leading a team through Elvinott. His direction is toward Feldschlosschen but not before his team wielding fire reduced my city to ashes sending the elves out of our home." Now he paused and stared into the fire. "I have had this dream every year on the anniversary of my becoming King and naming the great Ku lost."

McCard understood his position, but still responded in question. "King Hoangis, I have known you too long not to believe there are things I don't fully understand, but we can't assume war based on a dream. We must be sure."

"I am sure, my friend, but I will get the proof you desire."

"Where? Where will you get this proof? You cannot go to Draag."

"I can, and I will," Hoangis replied.

"I will not let you." He paused and then added, "I will not let you go alone."

"I do not intend to go alone. There are many things we have discussed, and we must address each."

McCard, pleased that Hoangis would not head on some solo crusade to Draag, nodded agreement. "Where do we start?"

"We have four key steps to take. First, you must return to your camp and inform your council that your suspicions are valid, and we will investigate further. I will send flyers to support your travel, as well as my son's scout team to walk with you. On this trek, he will investigate the surrounding forests with the maneth and determine the extent to which the expansion, if any, is happening."

"I agree, Hoangis. What else?"

"We must seek out the canoks. They are too powerful with magic to not be with us. We must find Queen Daphane immediately. She is the most powerful canok alive and if she agrees to walk with us, then the canok's strength can help us understand what's really happening."

Again, McCard nodded but this time remained quiet.

"Next, we must send a team to Feldschlosschen and Antaag. We must know where the dwarves stand. They can hold the southern border as a place for retreat if it should ever come to that. In my dreams, it has. I need to know the elves have a place to go." Hoangis took a breath and then returned to his seat at the table adjacent to King McCard. "What was the name of the young maneth who claims to have seen the dragons at Draag?"

McCard smiled. "Geoff, son of Gunthen."

Hoangis knew Gunthen. He did not know him well, but what he did know, he respected. "We must speak with Geoff as well."

"Agreed," McCard replied. "But I should state, he has grown strong and defiant. I believe in time he will move up the Batt Line as he has the traits of a leader, but now he is unrefined and not controlled."

The elf king accepted the description but did not comment further. "The last thing we must do is have Geoff describe exactly what he saw and where it was, then a team will go there."

McCard nodded in agreement. "Then it is decided. You will go to the canok homeland, you will send an elf team to visit the dwarves, and my team will return to the maneth camp to prepare for a trek to Draag. Did I capture everything?"

Hoangis's ears twitched ever so slightly. "You did, and I should be only a few moons behind you. I can make the canok homeland in one day and then another two back to your camp."

"Who is traveling with you?" McCard asked.

"I must go alone, as is required by the canoks."

The king understood but did not like the idea of his ally and friend traveling alone in times they had just determined to be unstable. However, he held his tongue, and knew there would be no changing the mind of his friend. "Then we should prepare to leave immediately, for I do believe time is critical."

"I agree, my friend. I agree."

Chapter Two

"Where are you going, Anbari?" asked Hawthorne.

"I don't know," the large dragon returned. "I don't know where to go."

"You have friends. You have those who will support you. Not every dragon wants to follow Slayne and take over our world."

"But they are scared. They have all laid their eggs. They will rest there for 200 years. Now they have but one thing—to wait. Slayne has convinced them that to wait in hiding is a waste of what they were born to do. He has them believing that to rule a world and leave it to their children is their fate."

Hawthorne pointed her head toward the ground. "There—let's land there and rest. We have much to discuss." They landed in a glade that was completely encircled with thick trees. There were possible paths through them for smaller creatures, but a dragon's only entrance or exit would be via flight. "We should be well protected here for the time being," she added. "Now..." Her tone became stern. "You need to stop with the comments that Slayne has convinced all the dragons of anything. I can tell you for sure that he has not."

"How can you be sure?" Anbari asked.

"Because I was by his side for many moons. He is desperate to bring any dragon under his wing, but he only has a handful. If we strike now, I know we will have support and will turn many. To wait any longer, however, may be too late."

Anbari did not reply but instead closed his eyes and searched for what he could see. Softly, he replied, "Slayne has more than fifty dragons before him now. They are outside Draag Caverns. He is talking to them about their direction."

"Can you hear what he is saying?" Hawthorne asked. "Because that could be helpful."

The comment drew Anbari out of his momentary trance with a smile. "No, my dear, I cannot hear what he is saying, but I do agree it would be helpful. I can only see visions of activity in areas of which I have recently been."

"That is amazing," she replied.

"I am only just learning it, but I do improve every day."

Hawthorne moved around and sat next to the larger dragon. "Fifty dragons is more than Slayne had before, but that leaves hundreds who could be turned to our side."

"Our side?" he replied. "Our side? I don't even know what our side is. We don't even have a place to go."

"That is why I stopped," she replied. "Where can we go? Where can we go to get help? All of Troyf does not want dragons to rule the land. Who can join us that is not a dragon?"

"Any race that joins us would simply be wiped out by Slayne and the dragons. They are too strong, and I will not put others in harm's way because we—I mean *I*—lost control. We must do this alone."

Hawthorne's eyes fell. "Is there truly no other race that can help us?

His voice was still low, almost lost. "There is no other race strong enough with magic to defend against the dragons." He paused, and Hawthorne saw the change.

"What?"

"Not what," replied Anbari, "but who?"

"Okay then, who?" she asked.

"Daphane."

"Who is Daphane?" Hawthorne asked.

"She is the queen of the canoks. When she left Draag ten years ago she told me to never come to the canoks for anything. I remember the words exactly when she spoke them." Anbari shrugged sadly. "I was younger then, and more like Slayne. I did not see a situation where we would ever need the magic carried in canoks. It is a different magic, one which I do not understand. I could feel the power within her, but respect it, I did not."

"Do you really think she and the canoks can help?" asked Hawthorne. "And if they do agree, what support can they really give?"

"They are strong, Hawthorne. Very strong. I see that now but did not before. It is not our magic. It is theirs, but that does not make it less. That is where we should head."

"The canok homeland? Where is that?"

"I have no idea, but I do know the name of someone who does."

Hawthorne smiled. "Who?"

"An elf named Hoangis."

"Who on all of Troyf is Hoangis?"

"I have no idea," replied Anbari smiling. "I just know that in one of my conversations with Daphane before things turned negative, she had told me if I ever needed to speak to her, I should call on Hoangis."

"How do you suggest we find this Hoangis?"

He turned and faced her. "You have a great deal of very good questions. So far, I have not been able to answer any of them, and this last one is no different. I suggest we head to the sky and see who we can find to ask."

Hawthorne smiled so large, fiery drool actually fell from her mouth and sizzled on the ground. She had to excuse herself as if she had just spit on her friend accidently. "So, your plan is to simply find some new race walking through the forest, fly down and ask them if they know where we can find a random elf named Hoangis? Keep in mind that whatever race we do find has not seen a dragon, much less a huge dragon, in their entire lifetime."

"That is basically the plan," Anbari replied.

She shook her head. 'Well, I guess as long as I understand it, that will have to be enough.

***

"Madeiris, are you okay?" shouted McCard into the trees.

The green skin of the elf prince had turned almost red with embarrassment as he broke through. "Yes, Your Majesty, I am fine. I, uh,"— he paused, then in a softer tone, finished— "fell."

The king smiled but did not comment further. "You have never been to the maneth camp, have you, son?"

"No, Your Majesty," Madeiris replied. "But I am eager to see it. Is it similar to Elvinott?"

McCard could not help himself and laughed out loud. His laughter was such that the guards walking in front and behind turned to stare for a second before continuing forward. "For starters, my young prince, please call me McCard. Your Majesty just does not fit." Madeiris nodded but did not speak and McCard continued. "Secondly, the maneth are significantly different than the elves. We hold many of the same values for life—all life in the forest—but we live much more simply. The maneth live in tents so we can move across the land at different times of the year to support our camp. In the winters, we find shelter deep in the woods protected from the weather and in areas where there is an abundance of life for us to hunt for our provisions. In the summer, we raise crops across the prairie and fields. Elvinott is a magical place that, to be honest, I don't even want the maneth to see for fear they would want to join the elves." He laughed lightly at the comment, as did Madeiris.

"If we are being honest," replied Madeiris, "other than you and a few of the elders, I have not seen many maneths. Do they all look the same? I mean, some elves have wings and some don't."

Again, McCard smiled. "No, all maneth are basically the same, other than size, that is."

"Size?" questioned the elf.

"Well, I am about seven feet tall, though I like to claim with my mane I am seven and a half. That puts me at least half a foot above you. There are some maneth over eight feet tall. There is nothing that determines who or why, just that it is."

"Do they all have manes?" asked Madeiris.

"Yes, son, we all have manes."

"Amazing," he said softly.

"I would not call it any more amazing than an elf's wings or incredible sense of hearing." He stopped and turned to face his young counterpart. "All creatures have traits which make them special. That is what we are fighting for—to keep that which makes all races different. Just because one creature may be more powerful, or more intelligent, or bigger, or able to fly, does not mean they are better."

Madeiris understood but laughed slightly.

"What are you laughing at?" McCard asked.

Madeiris blushed. "Well, when you just described what makes all creatures different, all those descriptions you used is how I have always thought about dragons, if I ever were to see one. They would be more powerful, intelligent, larger, and able to fly."

"I understand what you are implying. If they carry these traits, how can we keep them from taking over?"

Now it was the elf's turn to stop and cause the maneth king to face him. "I had not actually thought about that, but now that you say it, how can we stop them?"

"Well, son, we can stop them because we are many races together that do not want to rule. They are but one that does."

They turned and continued walking. Madeiris wasn't sure McCard had answered his question, but because the king clearly felt he had, the elf did not pursue it further.

***

Hoangis walked out into the open field. Across its vast open space, he saw the two large stones guarding the entry. He whispered a short enchantment to reveal his approach. For the canoks, it was the equivalent of a knock on the door. Although the elf king knew where the entry was, there was no guarantee he would be allowed in. The canok's homeland existed outside of the normal dimension. Passage into and out of this wrinkle in space was controlled solely by those within it. Hoangis could walk between the stones for the rest of his lifetime, and if the canoks did not wish him to enter, he would not.

He approached the stones slowly. Although he had visited the canoks three times in the past, every time the act of entering brought a subtle fear to his mind and body. He recited the words as he was taught and stepped between the boulders. Instantly the environment melted away. The field before him turned into a series of partially tree-lined paths that led to a village cut out of solid rock. What they called homes, Hoangis thought of as caves.

Before him stood two canoks, a female and a male. Their red fur glistened in the sun.

"Greetings, Hoangis, it is a pleasure to see you again," the female said.

"I feared you would not feel as such, Daphane, but I am extremely pleased for your response and allowing me to enter," Hoangis replied.

"Why would I not welcome you into our home?" the canok replied. "Have you not always been a friend to our race?"

"I have and will continue to be, Queen Daphane, but I have often been a stranger, which does not hold well for friendships to grow stronger."

She smiled and motioned for the elf king to follow. They walked a short distance and passed by several caves and other openings. She stopped to turn and enter one nearest the middle of their magical homeland. She motioned him inside and telepathically stated, *"Please go in and sit, my friend. Let me gather several others, and we will talk. As you state, you have not visited in some time and I assume this visit is due to some event or issue. Because of that, I want others to join me."*

Hoangis nodded but did not answer. He didn't know if he was supposed to answer telepathically or not, or if he even could. With that, he didn't know if any response was needed. He ducked and entered the cave which had one canok already sitting around a small fire, and an elf which Hoangis could not believe sat next to him. His immediate response was that of elation, but quickly the silence from the elf put a question in his mind.

"Greetings to you," Hoangis stated, toward the canok he did not know.

"Greetings in return," the red canok replied. "I am Stoven." He did not speak telepathically, but instead spoke for all to hear.

The elf sitting next to the canok looked away immediately as Hoangis's eyes fell on him. The elf king took a few steps in and knelt beside the canok placing Stoven between the two elves. However, the king's comment was directed completely toward his counterpart. "So, would you like to tell me how you came to be here, and what happened to you ten years ago, Ku, or should I more accurately say, Grandfather?"

Hoangis's tone appeared on the surface to be positive, but very clearly hidden beneath his words were the sounds of distrust. There was no reason for the true elf king to be here. There was no reason for him not to be in Elvinott. Hoangis knew something was wrong.

Ku swung his head back to greet his grandson. "The time dictated as such, that is all I can say."

His voice grew strong. "All you can say. You left the elves without word. You left Elvinott and for years we thought you had been killed. My father had just died and you left me in charge with no guidance. For years we looked for you and found nothing—no sign, no proof. Now I find you here, alive and with the canoks?"

Stoven rose and took a step back. "My friends, I don't know what has transpired with your world, but Ku arrived here only half a moon before you. If you have things to discuss, now is not the time. My counterparts are on their way, and we wish to speak to everyone, together. We wish to know what is happening in the world and if the canoks should be involved. As canoks, we prefer to stay outside of your world, but we also know that our home is not safe should your world falter. We live together, though we are apart. For this moment, I would ask you to hold your personal questions until we have concluded our talks."

Hoangis had no intention of holding his thoughts, but just as Stoven had finished, Daphane and two other canoks appeared in the cave. One of the canoks was young, only a pup, and clearly uncomfortable with his presence there. The other was old, possibly near the end of his life based on the pain he showed in his hind legs as he moved. Ku stared at Hoangis the entire time, but no words were said.

Daphane sensed the discomfort and didn't shy from speaking to it. "I feel that you two have much to discuss. I believed as much. I am not certain what has transpired with the elves, but for many years the canok have recognized Hoangis to be King, and yet Ku is alive and here. Clearly, questions are many. However, that is of no concern to the canoks. We wish only to know what is going on in your portion of the world today. Unless your internal separation is part of that discussion, I do not wish to hear your reasons. Do you both understand?"

Hoangis did not agree with the statement. "Queen Daphane, with all due respect, I don't understand why you are not interested in the reason my grandfather and king of the elves vanished ten years ago only to be found hiding away with the canoks. If you truly believe I can't ask about such an event, then you are gravely mistaken. I fear the canok have in some way affected this turn of events and…"

He was cut off by the queen. "Don't patronize me, Hoangis. Until this day, neither you nor I knew about the return of Ku. Our discussion on this subject is over." She paused and stared directly to the elf who sat at the same height as her. "Do you understand?" she asked slowly and clearly.

Hoangis had not heard this tone from her before. Something was amiss. He knew it, but perhaps now was not the time. "Very well," he answered, turning back toward Ku as he spoke. "But we will speak once we are done."

Ku did not respond or even acknowledge the comment. Daphane turned back to the group and began the conversation she had planned from the beginning. "Canoks and friends, obviously we have felt changes in the world as we know it. With both of you here now, it only furthers our belief that something is not correct. Therefore, before we speak, we wish to hear why you have come seeking the canoks. I wish you to be precise and without emotion. This is not an emotional discussion. It is about our world and the changes taking place, and I want to begin with you," she stated, facing Ku.

The much older elf raised his eyes questionably but did not shy from his speech. "Daphane, thank you for allowing me entrance into your world. You were the best source I could think of to direct me. There are changes in the world. I have been fighting them for over ten years. I fled Elvinott to protect them against this subtle movement of certain races fighting for absolute rule, but alas, the actions are still coming. I can't stop them, which is I why I came to you. I need your magic to forge weapons that may be used against these forces. Together, by combining the elves' inherent magic and the canoks, we can create something to help defend and destroy them. It is our only chance."

The canok seemed surprised, but not nearly as surprised as Hoangis. "Weapons?" the elf questioned. "Are you serious? You claim you left ten years ago to fight an enemy that didn't exist to anyone at the time, and after ten years you are finally in the canok homeland asking for weapons? Grandfather, I don't believe you. You are lying."

"Mind your respect, Hoangis. You have no idea what I have seen," Ku answered.

"No idea? Just how in the world…"

Daphane again cut him off. "Stop your bickering. This is exactly what I stated we would not accept." She turned to Ku. "We do not forge weapons or use our magic against other creatures. I do agree with your grandson. What is really going on here, Ku? Understand, if you don't speak the truth to me now, you will leave this place."

Ku shifted slightly in his seat. His voice was hard and unrelenting. "Daphane, you are a fool if you ignore my request. This is no time to be scared. We have to fight back before it is too late. We have to build weapons that can go beyond what our world allows—weapons that will defeat dragons and defend against the magic they are learning to wield. You must have felt it. You have to know there is evil growing in our world and the only way we can stop it is to be more powerful."

Daphane turned to the older canok next to her. Together they clearly had a telepathic conversation, but nobody in the area knew its content. She turned back to the older elf king and then without a word, he vanished.

She turned to Hoangis. "I am sorry. I know you wished to speak to him, but we sensed pure deception in his thoughts. The ability to read the thoughts of certain individuals is within our grasp, unless they have the power to defend against such a search. However, when one defends it, we must question why. I do believe he wanted these weapons, but his use was unclear. He could not remain here."

"You can send him out, just like that?" Hoangis asked.

"We did not send him out," stated the older canok. "When you are allowed in, it is by our acceptance. As you walk through our land, you are still walking through our field, in the same place but simply a different space. If we remove that acceptance, your space returns to the field as if you had never left. It takes three to refuse acceptance."

"We all agreed," broke in Queen Daphane. "He was no longer welcome."

I understand," stated Hoangis. "May I ask, what is your name and your counterpart's?" he asked referring to the young canok as well.

"You may ask," he replied smiling. "I am Tashro, and with me is my young apprentice, Werner. We are pleased to make your acquaintance."

Hoangis nodded. "I need to understand your feelings on our direction. The elves and maneth are concerned and have begun to bring our races together. We need guidance and wish to know if you will support us? We do not wish for weapons. We wish for knowledge."

"Support is a relative word," answered Daphane. "Let us begin with what you know, and we shall determine our place in it."

***

Hawthorne and Anbari soared across the sky. They had been traveling for the most part of two days. They had not come to any villages or cities. They simply saw land beneath them. Anbari had traveled the world a great deal, but his time outside of Draag was driven by not being seen. He avoided all outside contact. Others in the world knew there were dragons, but they also knew the dragons kept to themselves. Anbari's action was within those lines. Now, however, he sought to make contact, specifically with the elves.

"Look there," Hawthorne stated.

"I see them," replied Anbari.

They began a descent toward the group moving through the clearing. Anbari did not know what to expect, and what happened was one of his fears. As the group of humans saw the two beasts approach, they scattered like bugs to fire. Screams echoed throughout the area. Anbari spoke, but he did not know the tongue of those below him, so his words sounded like a roar. He landed in the clearing where they had originally seen the group with Hawthorne.

She laughed. "How did that go for you, stud? A real friendly greeting?"

He shrugged. "What in the hell were those creatures?"

Hawthorne shook her head in return. "I don't know. I heard talk about strange creatures building a village by the sea. Slayne said they are not strong and are of no concern. I have never seen one, though. Ugly creatures, that is for sure."

"I have to agree with that. What was that stuff on top of their heads? It wasn't fur. It was like strings."

Just as she was about to respond, her voice stopped and she softly added, "Anbari, one of them returns." She pointed behind her friend with her wing.

It was a man. He was tall and skinny. He wore the skin of animals for protection. No armor plating. In his hand, he held a stick that was sharpened on one end. He approached slowly, showing great fear beneath the huge creatures that could squash him under their feet, cook him with their breath, or simply lower their heads and bite them in half with their teeth. Anbari turned to face the man.

"I mean you no harm," Anbari stated, causing the man to lower his body and raise his sword.

"I am Octavius Starland," the man replied, his voice timid and broken. The human tongue meant little to the dragons.

Anbari and Hawthorne both looked at each other and clearly did not understand. Anbari turned and closed his eyes. He concentrated on the man before him. He centered his thoughts on his mind. He was amazed how easily his mind was accessible to him. The large dragon focused harder and felt his words come. He placed his thoughts in the human and then opened his eyes releasing the connection.

In perfect human tongue, Anbari replied, "I am Anbari and with me is Hawthorne. We are friends."

Hawthorne stared on in disbelief. She had no idea what her counterpart had said but it sounded like the human. "How did you do that?" she asked.

Anbari smiled. "I am not sure, but I tried to join with his mind to communicate our intentions and it just happened." He stopped and concentrated his mind on the dragon beside him.

Her eyes grew wide. "Wait, now I can feel and understand their words. But how?"

The man had heard the words as he watched the exchange. However, he had not moved his stick to his side but stood crouching down with the stick raised toward the dragons. He looked toward the two creatures before him and realized his small branch would be of little use if they wanted to kill him. He slowly lowered his weapon and answered, "What did you do to me? I felt you."

"I am not sure," Anbari replied. "I wanted you to know we would not harm you, and I tried to impart that in your mind, but some exchange took place. I now know your language and your thoughts, and might I add, it is a pleasure to meet you, Octavius. I have never met a creature like you before. I feel that you call yourself *human*."

Octavius nodded. "We are. There are hundreds of us toward the sea. We have a village. We need food. I am leading the party to get help." He turned to the forest around him and hollered, "Everyone, please come back."

A group of seven other humans slowly emerged from the trees around them. They were skinny and all dressed in the skins of animals. The two dragons had not seen anything like this before, and their stare demonstrated it. Octavius could see it in their eyes. "I know what you are thinking. We look pathetic, and to be honest, we know. However, we are desperate. Can you help us?"

If Anbari had tried to predict what would happen when he finally found another race, this was the furthest thing from it. Who would approach a dragon, a creature they had never seen before and could easily destroy them, and ask for help with no option to defend themselves? These humans were desperate, Anbari was sure of it, and desperate meant useful.

Anbari's voice deepened, as if trying to sound more powerful, and he raised his head higher above the much smaller human party. "I could help you," he scowled causing Hawthorne to tilt her head questionably. "But if I should, what could you do for me?"

The human leader was the only one to speak. "We can only give you what you see here. We have nothing more to offer."

Anbari shot fire into a nearby bush causing it to burst into flame. "Octavius Starland, do you think me a fool?"

He took a step back, and his voice now broke slightly as he started to speak, the fear in his tone carried through every muscle in his body. "By all the gods, no. We seek your help. Our race is dying, and you are the second creatures we have met. The first simply taunted us with their movements. We never actually made contact."

"Ah," replied Anbari. "Perhaps you do possess something that would be of use to me."

The small group looked at each other, but none knew what the dragon spoke about. Again, Octavius answered, "Tell me, then, what do we have? Because as we look at each other, it is clear we do not know."

"Describe to me what you saw in those other creatures who hid their movements."

The human leader appeared surprised but answered without hesitation, "There were many of them. They were in the trees and we barely could see movement. One shot this arrow at me and it split my leg so close to my..."— he paused and motioned toward his midsection— "it cut the cloth covering me. We saw only a few of them. They were slender, and fast, and"—he paused again as if fighting to say the next line for fear of not being believed— "green."

"Elves," Anbari stated, turning back to Hawthorne with a smile. His eyes fell back on the humans. "Where? Where did you see them? Tell me now."

Octavius pointed. "Half a day back by foot. Straight east."

Anbari smiled again. He closed his eyes and then blew across their faces. Octavius thought they were about to be scorched but instead, their bodies fell limp and fell to their knees. They used their hands for support making them rest before the two dragons on all fours. The human leader looked up. "What are you doing? I can't move."

Anbari blew again, this time focusing on the crude weapons they held, which were really sharpened sticks that to date had been unsuccessful in capturing any food. As the heat moved across them, the weapons changed. Their shape melted and became blurred. When the dust that had been kicked up subsided, the two dragons were gone and four weapons laid on the ground—a curved sword,

a bow, a hatchet, and a hammer. All shiny steel, a material these humans had never seen.

***

"I have but two things to say about what I just saw," Hawthorne stated as they lifted into the air. "First, let me say that was amazing, Anbari. How did you create weapons?"

He arched his wings to turn eastwardly. "I am not always sure. There is something inside me which guides me. As long as I can think it, and it doesn't change free will, I seem to be able to manipulate things."

"What do you mean, does not change free will?" she asked.

"I mean, for instance, that I can't say or do anything to make you love me." He paused his comment and watched for her reaction. She provided none and the uncomfortable silence caused the large dragon to quiver just a bit beneath the beat of his wings. "What was the second thing you wanted to say?" he added, his voice now half as strong as it had been.

She held a small smile. "Secondly, should you have given them weapons like that? Are they ready for them?"

He thought about the question. "I fear that this race of humans, whoever they are, are so far behind the rest of Troyf they will find themselves wiped clean before they have a chance to evolve. Providing a small picture of advancement to one bewildered race isn't going to change our world."

She seemed to accept the answer but was not done speaking. She pushed forward so she could turn back and look toward Anbari as she continued. "And regarding your other statement, I don't believe it."

"What do you mean?" he returned.

"You have done many things to make me love you."

Chapter Three

"Why do we get stuck with the boring work?" Tantis asked. "Everyone else is going to the meeting with the maneths. Why are we stuck going to the dwarves?"

"First off," replied Faessler, "we do what our king asks us to do, and we do it without question. There are over five hundred elves he could have selected, but he selected you and me. To say there are more qualified elves than you would be an understatement. However, he told me directly that you are the strongest of the young flyers." The large and much older elf stopped and stared down on the young flyer. "To be honest, I argued that you were not ready, but he would hear nothing of it. He said he felt something in you. I told him I felt nothing but recklessness. Your words are making me feel I was right."

The tone tied to the words struck Tantis in the heart. He was a gifted flyer, he knew it. But he also wasn't well liked by the older elves. He did not have many friends and he alienated himself most of the time. The fact that Hoangis had specifically chosen him for this mission was as much a surprise to him as it was to everyone else. The young elf knew immediately what he had to do. "I am sorry, Faessler, I meant no disrespect to you or our king. I will not let either of you down."

Faessler's tone softened, but his words did not. "You had better not. Don't prove me right."

Nothing more was said for much of the day. Tantis had never been to Feldschlosschen, the closest dwarven city to the elf's home of Elvinott. The two elves had been tasked with delivering word to the dwarves and urging their leaders to join them at the maneth camp. If they were to come, Tantis and Faessler were to guide them to the meeting. If all went well, they would only be in Feldschlosschen for a short time before they could head out. If that were to happen, they could still make the maneth-elf get together before it started. Faessler knew this but did not share it with Tantis who he knew was still angry about not being able to attend.

The older elf smiled as he thought about this, until Tantis struck him with his body knocking him into tree cover.

"What in the..." started Faessler angrily.

"Quiet!" Tantis exclaimed, though his voice was simply a raised and firm whisper. He pointed to the sky. "What are those?"

Faessler's green skin took on a new shade. "In Shriak's name, I never thought I would see the day. Did they see us?"

"No," replied Tantis. "Are those dragons?"

"Yes," replied the elf, "though I have never seen one in real life. I have only heard Hoangis speak about them."

"They are flying right back toward our home. Do you want me to intercept?"

Faessler could hear that his counterpart was trying to sound strong and powerful, but fear was clear in his statement. "No, young Tantis, for you would be of little use against those two. It will take our entire camp to even have a chance against one, but hopefully their intentions are not hostile."

"What happens if they are not?" Tantis asked.

"Then we may not have much of a home to return to." The older elf had made the comment somewhat flippantly, but the truth was carried in the words. He knew two dragons could easily destroy a home constructed of trees. Dragon breath was storied to be the hottest substance on all of Troyf. Though he knew of none that had experienced it firsthand, there was no reason not to believe it was true. "Come on," broke in Faessler again. "They have passed us now. We should move on, and quickly."

It was not long before the two reached the outskirts of a simple cave. In front of the cave stood two statues carved out of rock. The carving was intricate and showed the greatest detail. On each side of the cave entrance rested the figures of two small men with long beards and each with an axe in one hand. Etched into the stone above the entrance were the following words: *Elkenhan Yosen Demisin*, which directly translated, meant "Enter at your own Death." The older elf translated the words for Tantis who stopped when hearing what they meant.

"Shouldn't we stop and wait for a dwarf to meet us?" Tantis asked.

"No, the dwarves do not have the means or power to prevent entry except in hand-to-hand combat. We can express our intention before any such encounter commences."

Tantis still looked on hesitantly but did not speak again. Although, when Faessler took another step forward, the younger elf did not move. Faessler looked back. "Relax, my friend, it is a warning to help prevent entry, that is all. We do not have evil intentions. We will be fine."

"Have you been here before?" Tantis asked in return.

There was a long pause until the older dwarf smiled. "It truly does not matter if I have or if I haven't. We are going to enter one way or the other. Don't you agree with that?"

Tantis did not answer but realized the response was true. The king had sent them on this mission. There was no chance they would quit before attempting to complete it. Tantis may be young, but he was smart and well trained in the ways of elves.

They entered the cave and vanished into its darkness.

***

"King McCard, I am pleased to see you back so soon," stated Gunthen, the maneth head of the Batt Line. "You of course remember my son, Geoff."

The large young maneth bowed as he stood next to his father, but he could not take his eyes off the strange, green-skinned individual standing next to him."

"Of course, Gunthen," replied the king, lifting his arm in response so the two large leaders of the maneth race could touch forearms, as was their greeting. "And with me is King Hoangis's son, Madeiris. This is his first visit to our camp."

The elf's eyes moved from their wandering gaze around the camp to fall on the two maneth that had greeted them. Gunthen was large, broad, and had a very powerful demeanor though tainted with a bit of age, but his son Geoff appeared simply as raw strength. His shoulders were huge, and muscles so well defined that sweat as it rolled down his arms would turn several directions like a creek between rocks. Both maneth stared at the young elf.

Madeiris bowed. "It is a pleasure to meet you both. This city is amazing."

Gunthen smiled. "This is hardly a city, my young friend." He paused then changed his tone. "But I am surprised to see you. I would have expected Hoangis. Please don't say something grave has occurred."

Both Gunthen and Geoff saw the strain in McCard's eyes and Geoff took the signal from his father. "Madeiris, come with me. I will show you around camp. I would guess most of the maneth here have not seen a skinny, pointed-eared elf before, and you similarly have never laid eyes on the strongest race on all of Troyf."

The elf smiled at the last comment but he did honestly want to see the camp. Further, he too sensed the discussion lingering between Gunthen and McCard and realized it would be best to leave them alone. He fell in beside Geoff and the two began to move through the village, with Geoff pointing out certain things and introducing the elf to different maneth as they passed.

McCard motioned to Gunthen to follow him to his tent. "Come with me, my friend. We must talk."

The large maneth turned and walked with his king. He did not speak at first, and the silence seemed to draw out more discomfort than he was used to handling. "Tell me, McCard, what has happened with the elves? Where is Hoangis?"

The king turned to face his Batt Line leader. "Do not worry, Gunthen. Hoangis will be here shortly. He has reached out to the canoks to join us. He felt their magic could prove beneficial to us."

Upon hearing that the elf king would be joining them, Gunthen took a deep breath and then released it as if he had been holding it in for an extremely long time. His muscles that had become tense relaxed dropping his shoulders with them. "Thank all the gods. When I saw your…"

He stopped in mid-sentence to the raised hand of McCard. "There is something amiss in our world. Hoangis and I have both felt it. He feels the races should join forces and fight whatever evil is growing across our land."

"Do you agree with him?" Gunthen asked.

The king shrugged and looked away letting out a breath that spoke of many troubles carried in his mind. "I don't know. Hoangis is the elf king, but he is young, at least in his role. I do wish Ku was here." He turned back to his friend but did not speak further.

Gunthen stopped and turned to face McCard. "Tell me what you want me to do?"

McCard's face softened. "I have two things. First, help the camp prepare for a large gathering. We will need food for many. The elves have sent a party to the dwarves as well. They will join us; I am sure of it. If Hoangis convinces the canoks to come, there will be even more. We must be prepared to honor all those races should they come to stand beside the maneth. We will have a feast for all races to eat, and live, as one."

Gunthen nodded understanding but did not leave. He stared at his king because he knew there was more. "You said *first*. What is your next wish, my King?"

His voice lowered to a whisper. "You cannot do it alone, nor can you take one from the Batt Line. Should this be judged later, it would have to be unbiased. I want you to choose a maneth from the Dimat Line. A younger one. Have the two of you leave the camp at your first opportunity and find Ku."

Gunthen's eyes narrowed. "Find Ku? I wouldn't even know where to look. Ku has been missing for so long. Are you saying you don't trust Hoangis?"

McCard pressed his lips together and continued softly. "No, I am saying something is not right with the elves. I have known Ku my entire lifetime. His disappearance is suspicious at best, and Hoangis's quick rise to leadership is simply too convenient. I want to know what happened to Ku. You tell me that, and we may have some answers."

"Who do you want me to take? Alhize has proven worthy in our Lines."

The king shook his head. "No, Alhize is a good maneth, but too high and set in his beliefs. Talk to Selbee. He is only halfway up the line and still has an open mind. He can be persuaded to keep his tongue while you search. Then, continue to befriend the elves. Learn everything you can about Hoangis and Ku and what took place with his departure. Perhaps that will give us some direction."

"I will speak to Selbee immediately and prepare the camp."

"Thank you, my friend. I will be in my tent. I must concentrate on these times."

Gunthen turned and disappeared into the trees surrounding the camp, and McCard took a deep breath as he slowly made his way to his large royal tent.

***

"So, you are saying there are two types of maneth, Dimats and Batts?" asked Madeiris.

Geoff smiled. "No, we are all the same type. There is only one maneth. However, at birth, our father determines whether we are to be warriors or diplomats. Our upbringing is modeled based on that decision."

"How do fathers know?"

Geoff shook his head. "I don't know. I have never been in that position. I suppose the question is the same as why some elves have wings and others do not."

Madeiris pressed his lips together and although he did not completely accept that answer, he had no other questions on how a maneth direction is chosen. He was more interested in what it meant. "So, Geoff, when a maneth is given his title, what does it mean?"

"Well, every thirty moons we have Lines. During those times, the direction of the village is determined. We discuss where we will locate our camp, where we will obtain food, who will perform each function, what other races we will reach out to for trade or support. The Dimats, or diplomats, will sit on one side and have their opinion, and the Batts, or battle-ready maneth, will sit on the other. The two groups accent each other well, and because of this, the maneth have thrived for hundreds of years."

Madeiris smiled. "It seems complicated. Wouldn't it just be better to have your king decide?"

"The king does decide, but he has the whole village available to provide knowledge to help him make that decision. The further up the line a maneth sits, the more experience he has. Over the years, the young at the end of the line learn from the elders' experiences. It ensures that our race will always make the wisest decisions."

Madeiris nodded understanding.

"So, my pointed-eared friend, why do you carry that bow instead of a weapon with a little more girth?"

The elf turned to the maneth and smiled as he looked at the large club he held out proudly before him. Quicker than even Geoff's eyes could follow, Madeiris had removed his bow, knocked an arrow, and released it toward another maneth carrying a basket of fruit. The melon on top of the bushel was split in half. "That is why?"

Geoff smiled. "We are going to get along well. That much is certain."

***

Faessler and Tantis moved slowly through the mine. They had been traveling for nearly half a day in the dwarven mine and had not crossed any other living creatures. Although both were feeling frustrated, neither spoke to that effect. The older elf knew something was not right but did not know what it could be. Finally, he turned back to his counterpart and stated, "We are wasting our time. We are walking in circles."

"What is the issue?" asked Tantis. "We can't just give up," he stated flatly. "Do you have any ideas?"

Faessler shook his head. "I don't know. Hoangis told me that dwarves are suspicious of intruders. He said they don't have magic like the elves to protect their land, but to be wary that they may have developed some level of protection."

"What do you mean?" asked Tantis. "You mean they can fool us to believe we are not getting anywhere?"

The older elf thought a minute. "Maybe it is something like that. Hoangis also said they are very concerned about weapons. They only carry battle-axes, he said. They fear those who can kill from a distance."

"You mean like us, who use bows?" Tantis asked.

"Right," replied Faessler. "So, if I were a race in fear of other races with more advanced weapons, and I was beginning to develop some protection around it, what protection would I develop?"

"Do you think it is possible that because we carry our bows, the way through this maze of tunnels is being blocked somehow?"

Faessler stopped and turned to the younger elf. "Well, I am not sure about that, but I know for certain we have passed this rock at least three times. This tunnel is running us in circles."

He removed his bow and discarded it on the ground. When Tantis saw him, he followed suit. It was as if they had opened up the gates to a great city because the moment the second bow struck the ground free from the elf's hand, the mine wall dissolved, and twenty dwarves were surrounding them with axes drawn.

"Why do you invade our mines, you green-skinned murdering thieves? Here to steal more minerals?" The lead dwarf was short, in full armor with what appeared to be a well-defined crest etched into the breastplate and a long beard that nearly touched the ground.

Faessler stood nearly twice the dwarf's size and his arms appeared as if they could wrap the small leader in one quick stroke and turn his axe to his throat. However, he also knew a dozen other axes would be splitting his ears long before even a breath was lost from his small counterpart.

Tantis glanced to Faessler who remained calm, but he let his older counterpart speak. "I am Faessler, a lead guard from Elvinott. My king, Hoangis, has sent me to meet with your king and request his presence in a meeting with the elves and maneth. We fear changes in the land and believe that united is the best direction to ensure our lives remain as they should."

The lead dwarf studied the elf briefly but his stoic stare and look of distrust did not fade. Nor did the stares of the dwarves nearby, especially two identical dwarves that stood on each side of this leader. They were slightly taller than the leader but also younger. They also appeared more unstable. Faessler believed he could convince the leader to take his word as truth, but the twins beside him appeared to carry a deeper anger. He believed something had happened to these dwarves. The original words from the leader spoke of those who stole minerals. Perhaps the danger in the land had already reached the dwarves as well. His thoughts were interrupted when the leader spoke.

"Why should I trust you? You came to us armed. You meant to steal more of our minerals and kill any that got in your way, just like the last time." He paused and let that statement sit with the two elves. He then nodded to several dwarves that had encircled the two before continuing. "Had we not enchanted the mine, you would have done just that."

Faessler's voice was soft and caring as he responded, "My friend, we have never been to this mine, or any dwarven mine, although my king has. He has met with King Lendzion and wishes to share our knowledge with the dwarves and in turn, learn from you. Please let me only have an audience with him. If he does not agree to the meeting, we will leave without question."

"You lie," stated one of the twin dwarves moving a step closer as he spoke. "You mean to gain audience only to kill our king, the same way you killed our brethren. Do not think us fools."

"I assure you we killed nobody," Faessler replied.

The other twin joined his brother's side but instead of pushing his axe forward in defiance, placed it to his side and removed an arrow he had previously kept hidden in a quiver behind his back. "Then why was this through the back of our guard?"

Both Tantis and Faessler locked eyes on the arrow. They instantly recognized it. Not only was it Elven, but it was also from Elvinott. But more importantly, it was the King's arrow. There was no mistaking the markings.

"This makes no sense," stated Faessler immediately.

"Then you do recognize it. King Lendzion was sure it was Elven, and in your eyes, I can tell he was right."

"But it can't be," added Tantis, that comment being his first words. Faessler swung his head toward his counterpart sending a message to hold his tongue. He then turned back to the dwarves. To his surprise, there was an axe lifted to his throat. "Stop. We come in peace."

"There will be no peace," the twin holding the axe stated. "You have stolen from our mines and killed one of our brothers. Only our enchantment prevented it from repeating." The other dwarves in the area were becoming engaged with the exchange almost pushing the small twin to separate the elf's head right there. "You both must die. We must send a message to the elves that you cannot simply come in and take over our mines, and the message must be in blood."

The two elves' expressions changed. There was no way to hide it. They both could see it in the eyes of the dwarves and hear it in their tone. Both Tantis and Faessler knew they would not leave these mines alive.

"Stop!" exclaimed a voice from the back. The abrupt shout actually made Faessler cringe as he thought the dwarf was pushing through his final blow.

"Do not harm these elves until we know why they made such a move against us."

The party of dwarves immediately split into two half circles allowing the new dwarf to enter. The dwarves in the back bowed as he passed. This dwarf was equal in height to the twins, which made him taller than most of the others. He wore the same armor, but it glistened with a much more refined shine. The dwarf approached where the two elves stood, the twin still holding his axe to Faessler's throat."

"Put that blade down, Bretton. There will be no killing until we know why our Elven friends have turned to such evil. They pose no threat right now. We have them surrounded." The new dwarf studied the two elves as he spoke to his younger guard.

Faessler returned the stare. "Are you King Lendzion?" Faessler asked.

"Aye, I am the king you seek." He did not break his stare as he also introduced the three dwarves beside him. "I see you have met the leader of my guard, Krystof, as well as Jermys and Bretton. It seems you have walked into a bit of a problem today."

The older elf liked the king's demeanor. He was clearly not trusting, but open to a conversation. Faessler knew he had to make it count as he would have only one chance. "King Lendzion, let me first begin by stating again that we come in peace. Our presence here is only due to concerns carried by our King, Hoangis, as well as the King of the Maneth, King McCard. They met just one moon ago and felt a danger taking over our world. We were sent to bring the dwarves to a meeting of all races at the maneth camp." He paused and then his voice softened even further. "We came here for your help."

There was a stir among several in the circle, but none spoke. The king simply continued to stare at the two before him. He turned his eyes quickly to the twins whose expression had not changed. They were prepared to kill both elves. All they needed was the word from their king. Krystof nodded. "Strange you speak of peace but mention nothing about how an Elven arrow was found in the back of one of my dwarves. Do you think we will simply ignore the action?"

Faessler shook his head in return. "I think nothing of the sort. I don't know of any scenario where an elf would bring arms against a dwarf nor steal minerals for which we had no use. We live among the trees. We have no

THE DRAGON OPPRESSION

reason to steal. Therefore, I did not ignore the occurrence or deny the presence of the Elven arrow, but I also cannot explain it."

The king's eyes softened ever so slightly. Tantis didn't see the change, but Faessler did. The king took a step forward so he could feel the elf's deep breaths as they expelled from his belly. He stared into his eyes. "You state Hoangis sent you. Am I to believe then Ku has not retuned?"

The question surprised the elf, but he answered without delay. "No, we have not seen Ku since he vanished so long ago. As I said, it is Hoangis who sent us and who now is traveling to the canok homeland to seek their aid."

Lendzion lifted his eyebrow. "The canoks. Hoangis is going to ask the canoks for help?"

Faessler quickly amended his comment. "To be honest, my king is not so much asking for their aid; rather, he is inquiring about where they stand. He feels the evil in the land has magic behind it, and he wishes to know if the canoks will support a force against it."

"Fascinating," Lendzion stated.

"Excuse me, King Lendzion?" the older dwarf who had been referred to as Krystof questioned. "Fascinating?"

"Bretton, Jermys—put your weapons away." The two were about to argue but when their eyes met the eyes of their king, they opted to refrain from speaking. The king continued, still turned on the two elves. "I don't believe you came here with the intent to do harm. I don't know why exactly I believe as such, but my gut tells me this. However, I cannot ignore that an Elvinott arrow killed one of my dwarves. I will go to the maneth camp, but I will bring a full detachment with me. Krystof will watch over our mines, and Bretton and Jermys can lead the team. Will that fulfill the request?"

Faessler let out a short but still deep breath. "Yes, it will." He turned and smiled toward Tantis. "It absolutely will."

"Do not smile too large, elf. If I determine that your intentions are not just, you will be killed immediately. I will have a full garrison of troops ready."

"I understand, King Lendzion. Do not fear. You will find all with the elves is as it should be, and we will stop at nothing to determine the source of that arrow."

The elves were guided into the mine without further discussion. Though it was clear many of the dwarves did not agree with this direction, especially the two young twins, none would ever speak against their king. The two elves were given a bit of food but before they could eat their rations, the large dwarven troop was assembled and headed back toward the mine entrance with the two elves weaponless and surrounded in the center. However, they were next to King Lendzion which Faessler believed was a strong sign of trust, even with their weapons seized.

Chapter Four

"Hawthorne, did you see it?" Anbari asked.

"I did," the large dragon stated as they began a slow descent toward the trees.

Anbari narrowed his eyes. "I am sure I saw movement. It was quick, almost as if pushed by the wind."

"I will circle down in the direction it was headed and perhaps we can cut it off." She paused, waiting for approval but thinking about how to phrase her next comment. When Anbari did not reply, she added, "Should we be fearful of whatever it was?"

Anbari ignored the comment. He was tired of searching for a city he had started to believe did not exist. He wondered if the human had tricked them into this wild direction. But now he had seen something. Now he had seen an elf. He was sure of it. He lowered his head and dove.

Hawthorne saw the change and quickly angled the direction she had suggested. If the path of whatever they had seen was true, they would pin it between them in only moments. As Hawthorne first broke the upper branches of the trees, the first arrow struck. She roared in pain, but it was more from the unforeseen shock. The arrow had struck in a path directly to her heart, but the impact was minor and with a quick twist, it fell harmlessly to the ground. She swung her head in the direction of the arrow's flight to see her counterpart with one talon holding down a struggling elf, his bow harmlessly tossed aside.

"I cannot believe my eyes," shouted the elf. "Dragons! Outside Draag? What are you doing here?"

He was speaking Elven but somehow Anbari understood it. It froze Anbari for a moment as he realized he was changing. Something within him was growing, and it was not under his control. In Elven, Anbari replied, "How do you know about Draag?"

"Because I have been there, you fool."

"Hoangis?" stated Anbari proudly. "You are Hoangis. Hawthorne, we have found…"

He was cut off by the deep scowl of the elf held under his weight. "I am not Hoangis, and he is not the rightful king. I am Ku, and Hoangis has stolen my throne at a time when I was seeking support for our city. If you wish to seek the king of the elves of Elvinott, then you have found him."

Anbari stared hard at the elf who was struggling to get free with no success underneath the full weight of perhaps the largest dragon on all of Troyf. The dragon's confusion was clear in his eyes.

Softly, Hawthorne whispered, "Anbari, perhaps you should remove your weight and allow the king of the elves to stand. Whether he is the one we seek or not, we should not hinder a king as such."

Anbari blinked out of his trance and released his talon but did not speak or apologize. Daphane had specifically told him to seek out Hoangis. She had said nothing of Ku. Perhaps she did not know Ku existed, he thought. But how? Canoks and elves had been friends longer than Anbari's life. He lowered his eyes to the elf before him. "Tell me, Ku, why would the most powerful canok I have ever known not tell me to seek you out? Why did she tell me to seek out Hoangis?"

Ku stared back at the dragon showing no fear. His speech was immediate and confident. "Because, over the last ten years, the canok have migrated toward the dragons. One dragon in particular. That dragon has confused the canok queen. That dragon cannot be trusted, and because you seek out Hoangis and are aligned with Daphane, you cannot be trusted either. Now leave me. You have the numbers and the strength, and we have nothing."

"Is that dragon who has partnered with the canok queen a black dragon?"

Ku had begun moving away but turned back immediately upon hearing the question. "Why yes, all black, whose strength is consumed by his arrogance. Do you know him?"

Hawthorne stared at Anbari and then back to the elf. Anbari, his large silver wings stretched out, created an ominous sight before the two. His voice was cold and hard. "If you are standing before me against the black dragon known as Slayne, then I will stand with you. If Daphane has turned and aligned with him, then she may no longer be trusted."

The elf took a step closer. "Not only has she aligned with him, but I also just left the canok homeland. I was there with Hoangis and he fooled her into believing I was the source of the evil taking over our world." He paused when he said it, as the irony of speaking to a dragon about stopping a dragon onslaught struck him. Anbari nodded for him to continue. "He convinced Daphane to banish me from the canok homeland. I fear my elves have been turned by Hoangis and now will stand beside whatever he and the canoks have joined. Can you help me find allies?"

Anbari glanced toward Hawthorne and then back to the elf. "We can, as our mission is truly the same. We, like you, need allies."

The three seemed to revel in this companionship for a moment but Anbari quickly stopped when he realized his previous direction was now no longer possible. In short, he had nowhere to go. He held his stare on the elf. "Ku, this is Hawthorne, and I am Anbari. We are traveling together to find any race that will stand beside us should this evil attempt to wage war. Our direction was to your homeland, but now I fear we must make another choice. What was your plan?"

Anbari had released his grip and the elf now stood. After brushing himself off, he explained what he knew. "There is a gifted magician that legend says can enchant objects to take on powers within them."

The large dragon appeared skeptical. "What do you mean, take on the power within them?"

I mean if something is created by magic, then this magician can enhance that magic. I believe that if I can create, or more accurately, find someone to create, a magical weapon, I can then take that weapon to this magician and end up with something that can bring fear to those who may have other intentions."

"Who is this magician?" asked Anbari, his tone clearly showing interest but also surprise. He knew he was growing strong with magic in ways he did not understand, but he had never heard of a creature that would be doing the same.

"I cannot say at this time," replied Ku, turning away as he answered.

"Why not?" Anbari returned, his tone growing stronger.

Ku turned back to face the large dragon. "Because I do not know you, and you are a dragon. Perhaps you are at the center of the evil I have felt. Perhaps you are that which I plan to defend against."

That satisfied Anbari and he glanced toward Hawthorne to see her small nod. "I will respect that for the time. I will, however, travel with you to seek this magician."

Ku nodded. "Thank you for the respect, but before we find the magician, we have to learn how to fashion the weapon to take to him."

"I might know someone that can help with that," stated Hawthorne, looking toward Anbari.

The large silver dragon smiled. "Wait, my dear, creating a bow or spear out of a branch is one thing, but truly fashioning a magical weapon is beyond my reach at this time."

She smiled. "Not you, Anbari, but I do believe that strength is within you and you just don't know how to retrieve it. But I heard Slayne speaking of a strange legend he had learned about from another dragon—the one called Bjork. Bjork told him about a creature of immense power, the level of which he had never felt before. He had met him outside his lair while traveling through the Gar Swamp, a lair he later came to learn nobody had returned from before. His name was odd." She paused and lifted her eyes into the air with both Ku and Anbari hanging on to her every word. She stuttered a bit when she began again. "It, it, it...it was like Taibu or Taiju, or something."

Ku appeared skeptical but Anbari did not. He had not heard of anyone with this name or any new power, but he did know one thing: Bjork had gained some power. He had felt it the last time they were together. Hawthorne did not know him, but Anbari did. He also knew that Bjork wished for power, so if he was telling Slayne, then the Gar Swamp should be their next destination. "Then let's head to the Gar Swamp," he stated. "Does anyone know where that is?"

Ku smiled. "I can lead us there, but are you sure we want to go running after a rumor?"

Anbari now smiled broadly. "With no other plan or idea, I think I am as sure as I can get."

"Fair enough," Ku replied, finding no argument against the reasoning. He had no direction to go. He simply knew he needed these dragons if he ever was going to put his plan into motion. He had put all his hopes into gaining the magic from the canoks. When he was banished from their camp, he was out of options. He knew how lucky he was to run into two desperate dragons. Although he held no hope for an all-powerful Taibu, at least now he was protected, and traveling by flight would save his tired legs from the pain he was starting to experience. In moments they were in the air and headed in the direction Ku pointed. The Gar Swamp was only a half day away.

***

"So, tell me, Hoangis, why have you truly come, and what do you know about your king?" Daphane's voice was not cold but soft, like a mother speaking to a child.

"I don't know anything about Ku. As I said, the first I have seen him in ten years was when I walked in here. My distrust about him not returning to Elvinott is high, but he is my grandfather and my mentor. Prior to his departure, I, like all elves, would have followed him anywhere. Had he walked into Elvinott prior to my leave, he would have instantly returned as king."

"And if he heads directly there now, in your absence, what will happen?" The female canok shifted slightly to become more comfortable curled on the ground.

The comment struck Hoangis deeply. He had not thought about where Hoangis would go. His voice was much weaker as he considered the depth of the question and answered, "I suppose it would be as I just said. His return would be considered a great thing for Elvinott. He would return as King, and whatever his direction would be the direction of the elves."

Stoven, Tashro, and Werner all appeared to be in a conversation with Daphane, but no words were spoken. Daphane then turned her eyes back to the elf. "We feel you should tell us why you are here. We will provide you the support you need, but you should return home to ensure whatever intentions your former king has are not carried to your elves."

Hoangis shook his head. "No, I will share the details of why I am here, but my goal is not to return to Elvinott, regardless of what we know or don't know about Ku. My goal is to bring you with me to the maneth homeland. We are bringing all races together to discuss what actions we can do to protect our world. Something is amiss. We don't know what it is, but both the maneth and elves have felt it. I have sent elves to meet with the dwarves and hopefully do the same. We need the canoks' help. We need you. Will you join me?"

The words stuck like daggers to the four canoks. Daphane immediately turned her lips down and did not wait to speak to those beside her. "The canok do not get involved in the outside world. It is yours to defend and control. We will provide support in travel or help one in need, but we will not choose sides in a war."

"A war?" replied Hoangis. "Let me assure you, this is far from a war. This is a change in our world. Animals are not acting as they should. There is magic amiss which we don't understand. We need everyone united if we are going to stop it."

Daphane did not respond as quickly this time and again all four seemed to be in conversation. The pause was uncomfortably long for Hoangis and he wanted to speak again, but as soon as he was to begin, Stoven broke in. "If we were to join you, what would be our role?"

"Your role?" inquired Hoangis. "Your role is simply to share what you know or feel."

Again, there was a long pause during which Daphane stood and paced before turning and approaching the elf. "What Stoven is asking, to be more direct, are you interested in our use of magic?"

"Magic?" the elf asked. "We are only interested in knowledge. We want the canok involved so should this progress, we are united in our actions."

"A very good answer," Daphane replied.

"Does that mean you will join me on my trek to the maneth homeland?" Hoangis asked.

There was a very short discussion before Daphane answered, "Tashro, Werner, Stoven, and I will join you. We are offering no commitment in any form, but the canok do wish to hold all the knowledge they can, and if something is amiss in our world, as you believe, then this knowledge will help guide the canok in their future direction."

Hoangis smiled and nodded in appreciation. "When may we leave?"

Daphane turned and walked out without further conversation. Stoven stepped forward. "We will leave as soon as our queen is ready. May I prepare anything for you while we wait?"

Hoangis shook his head. "No, I am ready whenever you four say it is time."

Stoven nodded understanding. He turned to walk out following the others who had already left the small cave. Then he stopped and turned back. "Tell me, Hoangis, what are your actions should Ku return to Elvinott in your absence?"

Hoangis pressed his lips together. "I do not know. Many questions his actions have brought. Why was he here instead of with the elves? Where has he been for more than ten years? Remember, he is my grandfather. He is my blood. My family. I could not speak against him. It would go against everything I know and believe."

The canok seemed satisfied with the answer and continued out of the cave without further comment. The elf sat down and closed his eyes.

A voice suddenly broke through the elf's mind, but from where, he had no idea. *"You are the key, Hoangis. You will create the balance. Defend against the humans. Take the boy."* Then, the voice was silenced.

***

"The preparation is coming along fine, my King," stated Gunthen. "I have my son tending to the elves and ensuring their comfort. Did I hear correctly, that both dwarves and canoks may be joining us?"

"You did hear correctly," answered McCard, his voice showing the same unspoken concern.

"May I ask, then, how you plan on having this meeting? Our lines are not sufficient to hold…"

The king raised his hand. "I have thought about this for some time. I believe this should not be a meeting, it should be a Feast of All Races. We should amend our lines into a great circle and allow for all to speak equally. A circle has no head, but only connections. We are not maneth, or elf, or dwarf. We are one."

Gunthen smiled. "I will get Geoff. He and his friends can make it so."

McCard nodded. "And food. We need more food than we have ever prepared. Tell them to prepare as they have never done before. Tonight must be focused on our action."

Just then there was a stirring on the outskirts of camp. Maneth voices shouted across the glade toward the king and Batt Line leader. "King McCard," hollered a maneth voice. "An army of dwarves approaches from the southwest. They appear to be leading two prisoners." McCard and Gunthen hustled over to where the guard stood pointing to a small mass headed directly toward their camp. "Do you wish my team to take a defensive position?"

"We do not," answered Gunthen. "Lead a group of two guards out to greet them. Verify their intentions. I believe they are here via our invitation. Why they have prisoners is another question, but one we shall answer upon their arrival. Lead them in." He paused while two other guards were called over. Then Gunthen spoke to all three. "Heed your steps well. We are assuming they approach as friends. Should you decide otherwise, protect yourselves and return immediately. I will have support at the ready."

McCard nodded that he agreed, and all three guards immediately set out on foot to intercept the dwarven party. Those in the camp watched with anticipation. Madeiris and Geoff had been motioned over during the discussion and Gunthen explained the new arrangement of the lines the king wanted in place. However, he had both individuals stay while they watched the maneth group meet the dwarven party.

As the two groups drew within what appeared to be a range where speech could be exchanged, both McCard and Gunthen recognized a change. The maneth party stopped and began stepping backward slowly. The dwarves were in full armor and difficult to see, but they looked different somehow. McCard could not place it, but he could tell there was a difference. Maybe in height, or demeanor, but something.

Gunthen's voice carried an instant level of concern. "What's going on?"

McCard turned to his friend and warrior leader. "Get them out of there. Those are not dwarves as we know them." He turned to the elf standing next to Geoff.

Madeiris, whose Elven sight was better than any maneth, answered the unasked question. "They are not mining dwarves, or if they are, they are different. Their skin is not in shadow, it is simply darker. The prisoners with them appear to be Eltakian elves." He paused, then in a raised voice, hollered, "Oh no. They are going to…"

Before he could finish his statement, the dwarves severed the heads from the two elves which they guarded. They then turned on the maneth guard. The guards pulled their clubs but not before a hatchet was embedded between one of their eyes. The other two turned and ran back toward camp. Gunthen shouted commands to those in the area. Madeiris grabbed his bow and let bow fire fly toward the dwarven party. Even from this distance, his mark was true on the first three arrows. Two dwarves went down and a third took an arrow in the leg. The two remaining maneth guard were still on a path directly back to their camp while at the same time Gunthen, Geoff, and about twenty other maneth were on a path directly toward them. Although the dwarven party outnumbered the maneth, the quick accuracy of the arrows stopped their initial pursuit.

Spread out to avoid group shots having an effect," shouted Gunthen. "Geoff, lead a team to the left side, and I will take the center to protect our guards. The rest, go right."

The instructions were followed without hesitation or response. Madeiris moved in behind, then stopped and set for additional bow fire. His mark was exceptional and the dwarven numbers were now even with that of the maneth. When contact was made, it was like an explosion of metal on wood. A maneth club, though made of wood, is almost as durable as the strongest metal. Fashioned from only certain trees, one club may take a year for a young maneth to complete. They are with them for life and to date, none had ever been broken. The battle was fierce. When the guards who had retreated met the other maneths, they turned and entered the battle without hesitation. In only moments, all had subsided and the dwarven party of dark dwarves was eliminated.

Madeiris joined the group and as his eyes scanned the area, he shouted to his new friend, "Geoff, your father is hurt."

Geoff turned toward the elf and saw his father's head, with blue blood encrusted throughout his mane, resting in the elf's hands. "Father!" Geoff shouted.

Gunthen looked up. "Damn lucky throw," he grumbled. "I am fine, son," and turning to Madeiris who still held his head, "and you too, elf."

The elf smiled and released his head grabbing under his arm as the maneth tried to stand. "Don't move too quickly. You have lost some blood."

Gunthen's lips turned to a smile. "With comments like that, if I didn't know better, I would think we were bonded for life."

Geoff walked up as the comment was made. "A maneth bond with an elf," he added laughing. "That will never happen."

Madeiris added, "No way!"

"Both of you shut up and let's get back to camp. We need to figure out who these changed dwarves are. They are not from Feldschlosschen."

They nodded but Madeiris paused. "If you don't mind, I have to do something first." He reached inside his armor and pulled out a small pouch. He reached in the pouch and pulled out some dust and spread it across the elves that were killed by the dwarves. He closed his eyes and said a short prayer which none of the maneth could hear. He then expanded and spread the dust over all those deceased, including the entire dark dwarf party and two maneth guards who had also fallen in the battle. As he turned and approached those who were watching intently, the bodies either appeared to vanish into the air or melt into the ground in a dark haze.

"What did you do?" asked Geoff.

Madeiris's voice was hollow and almost not his own when he finally replied, "Elves hold all life at the highest. When those are passed, we have a special ability to aid in passage. That is all I did. I provided a path for the souls to take."

"But some simply vanished where others seemed to be swallowed by the land?" questioned Geoff. He turned to head back to their camp with the others who also were listening right in tow.

"Yes, how you live your life determines your path. Elves can only aid in passage, not choose the direction. We each own our path."

The young maneth could feel the pain carried in the elf's voice and did not pursue it further. He was, however, fascinated by his new mysterious friend and would most likely ask more questions later when they were alone. He knew this recent event with the mysterious dwarves who committed an unprovoked attack would be of dire concern for everyone, and when the party reached King McCard, that fact was brought full circle.

"What happened, Gunthen?" McCard stated, placing his hand on the large maneth's chest to stop his steps. "For all the gods, you are injured?"

He sighed and let out a painful breath. "I am fine, my King. A lucky shot, that is all. The dwarven party was defeated."

"They were dwarves then?" McCard asked.

"Yes," stated Gunthen, "but they were different. Their skin was dark, and they were taller. I have never seen dwarves like that. They still carried battle-axes as their primary weapons, but that was the only other similarity. Their speech was different as well as their tactics. They did not ask questions. They waited until we were within range, and then they attacked. They killed the two elves without thought, as if they were bait."

"Bait?" repeated the king softly. "What does this mean?"

Gunthen knelt down as he was out of breath and in pain. "I don't know, my King, but we must assume the dwarves have been compromised. Something has changed them, and they cannot be trusted."

McCard took that statement without comment. He began a slow walk toward his tent. Gunthen was back on his feet though his steps were slow and unstable. Geoff and Madeiris were keeping the slow pace in the back. The king stopped and turned toward the elf. "Madeiris?"

"Yes, King McCard," the elf replied.

"When Hoangis arrives, please bring him to my tent. We have much to discuss."

"I will," he replied.

"And we must assume the party Hoangis sent to Feldschlosschen did not meet with success. If you wish to return to Elvinott and put together a team to help them, I understand. I will also provide you a garrison of maneth for you to take directly from here. Feldschlosschen is an easy walk from here. You could make it in less than two moons."

Madeiris was surprised at the king's direction toward him as if he were the leader of the elves. Although he was the king's son, he was young and never had been treated as such. He thought for what seemed like an eternity before he finally replied, "No, I will wait for my father to return. He should be here soon and together we will decide a direction. I don't know what has happened to the dwarves, but if they did run into trouble, the elves on this trek are two of the best. They will know how to handle it best to ensure their safety."

McCard nodded. "Very well," he replied, then turned to Geoff. "Do as your father asked and organize the arrangement of the lines. We will have a feast for all races to become one. I only hope it is not too late for the dwarves, but because of what we saw, we now know for certain there is evil in our land. The time to act is now."

The last comment created a stir among those around and Geoff did not hesitate to bow to his king and then move swiftly to carry out his order. Madeiris opted to assist so the elf followed his lead. Gunthen remained standing beside him, but still clearly unstable. His voice cracked slightly as he spoke. "Thank you, my King, for sending my son away. Now, please get me to the med tent."

McCard recognized the situation and motioned to two nearby guards to assist. Together the small group walked to the medical tent. Gunthen was still losing blood from his wound, and his dizziness told the true story. He was injured deeply and simply did not want his son to worry. Once at the tent, the two large maneth stared at each other and McCard motioned for the guards who had guided Gunthen and carried much of his weight to leave.

The king placed his hand on his longtime friend's shoulder. "You are not well, are you, my friend?"

Gunthen nodded. "The pain is immense, my King. I do not wish my son to..."

"Stop, Gunthen. Your son is strong. If it is your time, he should be with you."

"I cannot stand." As Gunthen said the words he fell to one knee.

"Kessel," stated McCard, hollering into the tent. "Please come."

Immediately an older maneth appeared, observed the situation, and as quickly shouted to the others inside. Within a moment, the nearly unconscious body of the large leader of the Batt Line was being carried inside the tent. They stopped when Gunthen motioned to his king.

McCard leaned in close. "What is it, my friend?"

"Watch over Geoff," and Gunthen closed his eyes.

***

"Are you sure this is the right place?" asked Anbari.

"I am sure this is the Gar Swamp," stated Ku.

The two were silent for a long period just looking across the marshy landscape. Hawthorne finally broke the silence. "Then where do we go?"

The question was simple and short, and it was immediately apparent none of them knew. The swamp was large, too large to simply wander looking for a creature with immense power, as Hawthorne had described. They needed guidance, but from where they would get it, none had any idea. "Let's continue walking this direction." Ku pointed as he spoke. "I am certain that the further we go into the swamp, we will find someone or something that can help us."

They were on foot now to ensure they did not miss anything. Although travel by flight would have been faster and much more efficient, with the thick cover on the ground, they all knew anyone who wanted to hide would be able to. Even walking presented its own problems, especially for the large dragons. However, just as they began to calm and find a good pace, all three froze in their tracks.

"Did you see that?" asked Hawthorne.

"Yes," replied Anbari.

"What?" Ku asked. "What did you see?"

"Someone or something is watching us. Directly ahead." Hawthorne moved to the side as she talked to approach from a different angle.

"Wait," replied Anbari. "I do not sense any evil intentions."

"Sense evil intentions?" questioned Ku. "You can sense what other creatures are feeling?"

"No," he replied immediately, then stopped. "Well, I never could before, but I definitely feel its presence is not planning an attack."

Anbari closed his eyes and concentrated. Moments later, he stated, "*Com ooted ray oot rataj.*"

The other two stared at him in disbelief. The words he said meant nothing to them. However, as soon as they were said, the bushes in front of them began to stir, and before them emerged a creature the likes of which none had seen before. Its skin was that of scales and it walked on two legs, but it appeared it would be happier in the water than on land. The creature stared at Anbari. "*Com ooted ray oot rataj.*"

Anbari turned to the two beside him. "I don't know how, but I can *feel* his language. I learned his language just by joining his mind. When we saw him, I channeled my thoughts toward him, we connected, and I know what he knows."

"That is amazing, Anbari," stated Hawthorne. "Can you teach me?"

Anbari simply stared on in disbelief. "I would love to if I understood it myself."

The creature took a few steps closer as the two were talking, and Ku reached out and tapped Anbari's side to alert him. "He is coming closer."

The creature stopped when he heard the elf speak. Anbari lowered his head. "*Com to isten ritel.*"

"What did you say?" asked Ku.

"I said we are friends. Let me try something." The large dragon closed his eyes and focused on the creature. It turned directly toward Anbari with a level of fear. It slowly began fading into the trees, and then stopped suddenly. Its eyes lifted and its glassed-over stare melted into one of understanding. Anbari's head fell slightly as if exhaustion had just set in, though he had not moved one step.

The creature turned to the others and in a perfect, ancient dragon dialect, stated, "I am Kalcall. I am a gar. I oversee this region of our home." The gar's eyes were wide, and it was clear he did not understand how he had just spoken.

Both Hawthorne and Ku looked on in amazement. Ku, though not fluent in the language, did understand the basics as it was fashioned from ancient Elven, born at a time when all creatures spoke the same. Hawthorne simply shook her head in disbelief. "How did you do that?" she asked in the same Dragon tongue.

Kalcall nodded. "May I ask you the same question?"

Anbari lifted his head. "I don't know. I simply felt I could do it, and I did. That is all I can say."

"This gift will help the gar grow with those not of the swamp. I thank you."

"You don't need to thank me, my new friend, for we are here to seek your help." Anbari paused a moment before continuing. "We seek the presence of one known as Taibu or Taiju. We are not sure of his name, but legend states he may be able to help us. Do you know of any named as such?"

The gar stepped back, almost in fear again. His voice cracked and it was clear he was uncomfortable with the discussion. "His name is Taiju, and I do know of him. However, I cannot help you. He is protected."

"Protected?" questioned Ku. "What does that mean?"

Kalcall turned his head toward the elf and studied him briefly, taking in all that he was. The gar did not seem surprised at the presence or appearance of dragons, but the elf was different. There was something off in the way Kalcall acknowledged Ku. Both Anbari and Hawthorne saw it, but neither spoke. The gar turned away from Ku and answered his question toward the two dragons. "Taiju lives within our swamp. He keeps the environment constant so our lives can prosper. He protects us, and in return, we protect him."

"We mean him no harm," stated Hawthorne in a very soft and caring tone. "We seek only his knowledge. Just as he protects you, we feel he may be able to help guide us to protect our entire world. If our fears are true, in time, nothing will remain due to the evil taking over the land."

"Evil taking over the land does not concern the gar. Our swamp is not a place anyone wishes to rule."

Anbari shook his head. "You are wrong, Kalcall. A dragon behind this evil is where we learned about Taiju's presence. He will come."

Hawthorne added, "You also have to realize you are a race on this land. For a creature to rule over the land, they must possess power over all creatures, regardless of where they live." She still spoke with a soft tone trying to draw the gar into her meaning.

Still the Kalcall did not relent. "No, we do not fear a takeover. What happens to those outside of our swamp is of no interest to us. We have gone unnoticed for thousands of years, and we will continue as such."

"But you are not unnoticed now," interrupted Ku. "We are here, and behind us others will follow, and when they do, they will not greet you with conversation. Fire will be the first thing you feel, and the last."

Anbari did not agree with the direction, but it was done and there was no taking it back. Further, it did seem to have an effect. The gar stepped back slowly and looked to each of the dragons and then back to Ku. "No, you are trying to scare me. You want me to make a decision that goes against everything the gar have done since time began." He turned to Anbari. "He does not speak the truth. You are a dragon, and you are here. Dragons will not attack us here in the swamp."

Anbari's voice took on the same soft tone as Hawthorne's had previously. "I cannot say what the other dragons will do, but to trust that they will not do as the elf implies would be foolhardy. They will come for Taiju, that much is certain. I don't understand yet what role he plays, but we learned of his existence from one of the dragons at the source of these changes. If he brings just one dragon with him or more than fifty, I cannot say, but he has many. In time he will have hundreds. There are eggs."

"Dragon eggs do not hatch for centuries," stated Kalcall.

"As I said," acknowledged Anbari, "he has more than enough dragons following him now to destroy the entire swamp and everything in it. The eggs will establish his dynasty to ensure dragon rule forever."

Hawthorne cringed at this and directed a comment to her counterpart. "Anbari, are you serious? The dragons are going to take over the land and then have the younglings establish their rule forever?"

"It is what makes sense. Why else would they take these actions? Many of the dragons draw their power from Draag. With the eggs hidden and their power flowing from there, why else would they fight to hold onto Draag so tightly? The eggs are hidden deep within its caverns. Slayne has organized the dragons that follow him and they will protect it at all costs. Our only hope is to find those races outside of the dragons that can defend against them. We have to be the ones who lead the dragon young to the side of good."

Hawthorne and Anbari had completely taken their minds away from the gar and were speaking directly to each other. "Are you saying this will be a two-hundred-year war while we wait for the young to hatch? There is no way we can…"

Anbari cut her off. "No, this will be a very short war. We have to defeat all the dragons so when the young awake, they will only have our influence."

"Defeat them?" she questioned. "Do you mean kill them all? How can we do that? How can you even think to do that? These were your friends long before they became confused with who to follow. You can simply destroy them?"

He did not like her tone and the direction this was going. He also knew this was not the time nor the place. Again, his voice was soft. "No, we have to destroy those who lead or come up with a plan that will defeat them. I believe if we destroy the head, the rest will fall."

Hawthorne seemed satisfied with that response but did not speak as the gar now interrupted, "I believe you, Anbari."

"You what?" the large dragon asked.

"I said I believe you. I sense passion in you. I don't believe you and Hawthorne would be having this discussion if the truth wasn't behind it, and I sense you are both against death." He paused and saw both dragons' bodies fall just a little down at the relief. "But I cannot take you to Taiju, because I have never seen him. In fact, I don't believe any gar has."

"Then we have wasted our time here," issued the clearly frustrated elf.

The gar heard the tone but continued speaking as if the interruption had not occurred. "What I mean to say is, I can guide you to the entrance to his lair, but from there it will be up to you."

"His lair? Is he a dragon?" asked Anbari.

Kalcall smiled. "I cannot answer that, for I have never seen him. The only thing I have ever been told is that you never want to meet him." The three were caught off guard by the comment but did not address it further.

Ku interrupted. "How far until we can get there?"

"Just follow me," stated the gar. "I can guide you there within the next half day."

***

"I have felt a tremor growing," stated Bjork.

"A tremor?" Slayne replied, his eyes lifting at the comment. "I thought you said there would be no issues. If I got rid of Anbari and turned the remaining dragons to my side, we could fly through Troyf with our rule. Now you feel a tremor?" The last comment was said with a level of displeasure Bjork was not used to hearing from anyone, much less his pupil.

"Watch your mouth, Slayne. I have taught you the ways. I have presented you gifts you have only begun to understand. I told you to kill Anbari, and you did not. I told you not to get involved with the female Hawthorne, and you could not resist your desires. There were several other dragons I could have chosen that would have respected my direction, but instead I went with you, and because of that, you have muddied the water in what should have been a short offensive across Troyf. Now, you have work to do."

Slayne was taken back by these words of defiance. He had been told to ignore Hawthorne, but he could not. She was beautiful and he had felt something in her, but to be asked to kill Anbari—that was not his fault. Anbari was his friend long ago, but he was also growing with some hidden strengths. Anbari was stronger than Slayne, the black dragon knew it, and so did Bjork.

Bjork frowned. "Stop your idiotic thoughts about how you did not fail. I can feel your arguments growing. Let them pass. The damage is done, but don't fail me again."

Slayne lowered his head. "What would you have me do?"

"There is a mass growing in the maneth camp. I feel Daphane, the queen of the canoks, will be joining them. You must go to the camp, you must sneak in, and you must take her."

"Take her?" Slayne questioned. "You want me to bring her here? To you?"

"No, you fool," Bjork replied. "You must take her."

Slayne's eyes hardened showing some level of fear. "I cannot…"

"You can and you will." Bjork leaned forward and Slayne could feel the dragon breath on his face. "You dug this hole and now we need help. We need the offspring of a bond between the strongest canok ever to walk Troyf and a young and talented dragon, like yourself."

"If you need a talented dragon, then why don't you do it? Why don't you go to Daphane?"

Bjork gritted his teeth together causing balls of fire to drip from his mouth and almost land on Slayne's talons. "Because, you fool, they don't know about me. I need to remain in the background to continue to organize this plan. You are the soldier. Now, I am growing tired of your constant arguments, so either do as I say or I will find someone who will. My need for you is growing shorter with each comment. Evidently you do not wish to rule all of Troyf as King."

That last statement changed Slayne as the words passed his master's mouth. "I will do it, Bjork. Do not fear, as I am dedicated to our plan."

"Good," he replied. "I knew you would be. Now go. Find the maneth camp and wait for Daphane to arrive. When she arrives, go to her at night and put the new plan into action. Do you understand?"

"I do," replied Slayne. "I will go now."

Just as he was about to leave, Bjork's eyes opened wide. "Damn!" he shouted.

"What?" Slayne asked looking back.

"Anbari is on the move. He is seeking out..." He stopped and shook his head. "How did he learn about Taiju?"

"Taiju?" asked Slayne. "Do you need me to change my plans?"

The large dragon turned back to Slayne who still sat waiting to begin flight to the maneth camp. "No, boy, you have your direction. I will have to handle Anbari, as you should have handled him so many moons ago."

"Is Hawthorne with him?"

His face showed pure anger. "I will be handling both of them. Keep that female dragon out of your mind. She will taint you and destroy you. She makes you weak. The best thing I can do for you is to kill her."

Slayne's eyes hardened, but he did not speak. He had already heard the message. He was too far committed to this plan to leave it now. His destiny was confirmed. He was headed to the maneth camp, and if he was successful in his mission, he could never turn back.

"Now go," stated Bjork. "And do not fail me again, as I will not be so understanding in the future."

Nothing more was said between the two. Slayne opened his large black wings and took off through the trees toward the center of the wooded plains. He was not sure where the maneth camp was, but he was confident he could find it. He was not sure why, but he could feel it. The minute Bjork had told him there was a tremor, he too felt it. He was gaining power. He knew he was, and he liked it. He thought about Hawthorne, and then with a snide tone, he stated to himself, "You should have joined me, you fool. I would have protected you. I will find a female that will join me and show you and all of Troyf how to rule as King and Queen."

Bjork watched the black dragon fly away and then paced around trying to determine his next step. He had no intention of facing Anbari. "I need another dragon to go to the swamp. One who is strong and loyal. Who can I find?" He thought. "Who would be strong enough but as stupid as Slayne? Who?" His eyes widened as his mind connected with his answer. He opened his wings and headed to the air opposite in flight to his black counterpart.

Chapter Five

"McCard," shouted Geoff. "Another dwarven party approaches. They too appear to have prisoners."

The king came running to his side. "Damn, has there been any word on your father?"

"No, my King. He remains in the med tent."

"Then you will need to lead a full garrison to intercept. We will not make the same mistake again."

"Understood," replied Geoff. Though young, he was well-respected, and his father was one of the greatest battle leaders the maneth had ever known. He had learned much from his father and was ready for more responsibility. He immediately began shouting out orders and in only moments, he had a team of twenty-five maneth ready to move in formation toward the oncoming dwarven party. All had clubs drawn and ready, and Madeiris and four other elves joined the group in the rear, bows with arrows knocked at the ready.

"Break into two parties, separated in the center," shouted Geoff. "Hold your shields high should any battle-axes be thrown. Your shield will protect you, but hold it strong. Should it be knocked free, you will be exposed. Wait for them to declare their intentions. Do not attack unless they do first. Should that happen, release all you have."

The maneth and elves understood the direction and marched forward. The elves knelt and prepared to fire, but followed the lead, waiting to see what the dwarves would do. When the dwarven party drew closer, Madeiris recognized the prisoners and shouted forward, "Geoff, the ones in the center, the prisoners, they are from Elvinott. They were sent to meet the dwarves."

"Halt!" shouted Geoff, directing his voice toward the party ahead of him. "Dwarven party, what are your intentions, and why do you have two elves as captives?"

King Lendzion pushed through his lines. "King, wait," stated Bretton. "We don't know…"

He was cut off by the king's hand. "There is something amiss here, but I see maneth and elves working together ahead of us, defending their camp. I don't see a secret ambush or attack."

"But they are in attack formation. They mean to…"

"Then if I am wrong, tell Krystof he is the new king."

The comment stopped Bretton in his tracks, but the dwarf still did not reduce his guard. His brother Jermys moved to the opposite side and both twins prepared for a direct offensive.

"I am King Lendzion of the Dwarves of Feldschlosschen. I have come in peace at the request of these two elves, however, my trust of the elves has been damaged and I want to know that the maneth have also requested our presence."

Geoff lowered his shield and took several steps ahead of the troops. "I am Geoff. With me is Prince Madeiris of the elves of Elvinott. We too seek peace and only ask for your support and knowledge. Will you release the elves with you?"

The king hesitated a moment. If Geoff was lying and had evil intentions, his first goal would be to get the elves clear of the dwarven guard so any attack could occur without fear of killing their own. However, if he was telling the truth, then the elves were not lying about the elf that stole from their mines and killed one of the dwarves. He glanced over to Jermys and saw him ready to attack. He swung his eyes back to Bretton standing in the same pose. He shook his head. "To Keabda's grace I pray I am right. Faessler, Tantis, please come forward." The two elves were guided to stand beside the king. "Walk with me." He turned to his troops. "All dwarves stay back and hold here until I signal."

"I cannot let you walk alone," stated Bretton. "I will stand by your side."

Lendzion was about to protest but after letting out a short sigh, he understood the need and allowed it.

The four walked toward the maneth and elf party where Madeiris had come to stand beside Geoff. When they arrived about ten steps from each other, the elf prince was first to speak. "Thank you, Faessler and Tantis. Thank you for convincing the dwarves to meet. We must all share our knowledge if we are to defeat this evil."

The words were a relief to all parties. Trust was in short supply and none knew what to say to convince the others of their intentions. Lendzion heard the words and answered in a strong tone, "We have much to share, of which I am certain these two elves will fill you in as we prepare. My dwarven party is tired and hungry. We would like to enter your camp as friends, if you will allow us?"

"Absolutely," answered Geoff. "We have many questions for you as well. We are waiting for King Hoangis and possibly canok representatives, but we have planned a great feast for tonight. Preparations are on their way, so please, wave your dwarves in and we will set them up in our camp. Thank you for coming, King Lendzion. Your presence here is crucial."

The groups were called in together, and as one large party they returned to the maneth camp. Most of the dwarves had not seen maneths before nor the same in return, so the amazement of both parties to the others' presence was significant. Even the very young maneth were much taller than the oldest of dwarves, but in very little time, both sides were learning a great deal about the other.

It was drawing very close to the start of the feast and there was still no sign of the Elven king or any canoks. Madeiris was growing concerned, and questions of sending a scouting party after them or having the feast without them were discussed.

"The problem with a search party," started Madeiris to McCard and Lendzion, "is that I would not even know where to send them. I do not know the location of the canok homeland so all I could do is send a party back to Elvinott to ensure plans did not change and he returned there."

"And if we have the feast without him, then we lose a great deal of insight and knowledge," added McCard.

Lendzion nodded. "We must have the feast as planned. I know Hoangis. If he can be here, he will. Without him, we have his son. Although missing some of the years, I do hold Madeiris to be very well balanced and wise. He will provide great knowledge even in Hoangis's absence."

Madeiris nodded in respect for the kind words, but inside he was very nervous. He was the only son of Hoangis, but Hoangis had only been king for a short time. That means Madeiris had been in his role as prince for the same amount of time, and had never been asked to take a leadership position of this magnitude. He prayed his father made it back, but he recognized that the feast did have to go on.

"Then it is settled," stated McCard. "At nightfall, the Feast for All will begin, and a new age of life on Troyf will begin with it."

"An age where all races work together for the betterment of all," added Lendzion.

The exchange was powerful and made all the leaders feel like great things were about to happen. However, Geoff stood in the background staring at Lendzion wondering what that first small attack from the dwarves had meant, and why had it not been mentioned to the king. However, he also knew all would be shared later, but until then he would keep watch over the dwarves and their actions while in the maneth camp.

***

As the sun fell below the tree line, horns sounded. The different races assembled in the middle of the forest and made their way to their seats. The tables were set in a semicircle instead of their traditional lines. At the open end of the circle were several other tables tying the two ends together. At those tables would sit the kings, or in the elves' case, in the kings' absence, Prince Madeiris would sit. The congregation made their way in first and took seats as assigned. There was food already spread, but none started while they waited for all to enter. The maneth outnumbered the others, but all races had a strong showing and were mixed in their seats showing the direction the leaders wanted. The words they used were integrated as one.

There was a long pause after the majority were seated. There was much conversation, in most cases in Elven as it was the most common tongue. However, often Dwarven or Maneth words were echoed through the woods. Silence suddenly engulfed the area until again, horns broke through signaling the arrival of the kings. King Lendzion and his top dwarves entered first and made their way through the circle. They walked along the tables wishing positive thoughts to many along their way before finding seats up front. Next came Madeiris and four flyer elves. The winged elves had been a favorite of many in the camp as they had not seen them before. Now, having them sit up front only furthered the amazement. Then came McCard, Alhize, and Geoff sat in for his father who was still in the med tent. McCard followed King Lendzion's lead and walked the entire circle of tables, stopping at every maneth and almost all other visitors, to introduce himself, learn their names and interests, and simply be there for them. He spent a great deal of time with Selbee. Both Gunthen and McCard had already spoken to the large maneth who was quickly moving up the Dimat Line. Selbee had already learned about the king's request to join Geoff to find Ku and determine what happened with the true Elven king. McCard was creating this feast under the guidance of trust, but deep in his mind he was concerned on what happened with Ku, what the new race of dark dwarves were and why they attacked, and what was really happening at Draag. He buried his worry deeply as he stood at the front.

"My friends, we have come together for a reason we don't fully understand, but we all agree that together is the way we will fight for our world. Alone we are not as strong. With the rulers of each kingdom here, we are to share our thoughts and fears. All information, no matter how difficult to say, must be spoken openly and not judged. The fact that you are here now demonstrates that you and your kingdoms wish to be part of the solution. I thank you, King Lendzion, for bringing the dwarves here." He nodded to the dwarven king and then turned toward Madeiris. "And Prince Madeiris, I thank you for joining me on our trek from Elvinott to bring the elves before this group, and our thoughts are with your father for a safe return as well. And hopefully he will bring another race—the canoks—to join this feast and share their knowledge of our world. This is a time for celebration and sharing. We will begin with a prayer and then eat the wonderful food my maneth have brought before us. Then, we will talk about all that we know and all we have seen and believe."

With that, everyone around the huge tables bowed their heads, each said their own prayers to their respective gods, and the Feast of All began. The food was received well, and the celebration was at its highest. When the final courses were brought forth, McCard slammed his club on the front table and all eyes swung to him. The area became deafly silent.

"My friends, much talk has already occurred during our meal on what we have seen these recent moons. In an effort to begin these discussions, I will issue what I know." He paused and coughed slightly more from searching for the correct words than actually any tickle in his throat. "Just today, my camp was attacked." A stir broke across the group as many were not aware of the strange attack which took place from the dwarven party with the blackened skin. "That is right," the king added when he recognized the instant concern. "A party of more than twenty dwarves approached our camp. When we met them in the field to the south, they attacked. Our response was quick and decisive, and in the end they were defeated, but at a price to us as well."

Lendzion could take no more of this. He stood up interrupting the king the of the maneths. "This is preposterous. No dwarves would attack the maneth…"

Lendzion paused for a moment and Bretton, the twin who had been acting as the party leader, stood and added, "Unless he was provoked by the maneth the same way the elf entered our mines, stole from us, and then killed our guard."

Madeiris now stood. "Just wait a minute, no…"

"Are you sure of that?" questioned a female voice from the tree line.

All eyes swung to the source. "Daphane?" questioned McCard. "You are here?"

"I am, Your Majesty." Her eyes panned the area. "And, Your Majesty," she repeated to the Feldschlosschen king. "It seems there is much distrust in the air for a party built on the idea of one. I can feel it all around."

McCard nodded to the queen of the canoks and the king of the elves standing beside her. Behind the two of them were another four canoks, their red coats shining in the moon's light. "It is only distrust if there is no explanation."

The queen of the canoks proceeded forward and took her place at the table prepared for her should she arrive. Hoangis approached his son and the two hugged deeply. The king placed his hand on his son's shoulders and softly stated, "Thank you for taking my place. I am sure you were an honorable representative."

"He was, King Hoangis," McCard replied, though the comment was not directed at him. He turned to Daphane. "Can I ask what distrust you feel?"

She did not address the question. "Please, continue with your discussion. I believe there was a comment on an elf that killed a dwarf and a dwarven party that attacked the maneth. Perhaps I can add a former elf king that had less than honorable intentions." Madeiris swung his eyes toward the canok then toward his father. There was a stir across the participants that continued for a long time. Geoff glanced to King McCard and then to Selbee. She had to be speaking about Ku, he thought. When he saw Selbee, they both knew they were thinking the same thing.

McCard interjected, "We must investigate these one at a time and determine the force behind them. The honorable queen of the canoks has stated she feels distrust among us. The words we have said confirm those feelings are real. We cannot have distrust if we are to be one true nation. We have to understand what is happening in our world to explain these strange occurrences."

Nobody spoke for what seemed to be too long, until a voice from a lone maneth broke the monotonous silence. "I believe I have knowledge of each event which brings this distrust, if my interpretation of the queen's words is correct."

McCard was startled by Geoff's outburst. He was the son of the leader of the Batt Line, and although he sat in his father's place now, his actual seat was well down the line. It was not his place to speak, but his words were such that all eyes and ears were focused on him. The maneth king nodded his direction. "Please, Geoff, if you can bring this into perspective, then do."

"I believe the queen just mentioned a former elf king. I have only known of two Elven kings in my lifetime. Hoangis, who sits with us now, and Ku, whose place he took many years ago under unusual circumstances. In my discussions since his arrival with my new friend Madeiris, he explained the strange past involving Ku, his mysterious disappearance, and everything surrounding it. I then heard stories from a dwarf named Jermys who sits beside us as well." He pointed toward the twin who sat drinking his ale.

"I believe I can trust him as his words were true and thoughts pure. He simply wants to stop evil in the land. He told me about a mysterious imposter that entered the dwarven mines to steal some of their minerals. When he was confronted, he was quick and precise with a bow and killed one of their guards. The arrow was Elven, from Elvinott to be exact, but I am not sure even Jermys knows of its origin. However, I am sure that Jermys does not know the arrow was fashioned for a king. It has particular markings and a craftsmanship beyond any typical make. It seems reasonable to me that the imposter at the dwarven mines and the Elven king with less than honorable intentions who visited the canoks are one and the same." He paused and his voice turned deeper and stronger. "The former king of the elves, the one known as Ku, is behind both of them."

There was a stir in the crowd and Daphane lowered her eyes showing she would not argue the summary. McCard stared at the young maneth and asked, "And how does the dwarven party tie into this?"

"I believe that if this evil could reach out and touch a king of the elves, then couldn't it infect a band of dwarves? I mean, yes, these were dwarves, but they were changed. Their skin was black, and their anger was not in control. They had a very simple mission—make those against them know they exist. They were not here to fight us. They had no plan and were easily stopped, but we do know one thing because of this exchange: They are here."

Lendzion did not like the words being stated against the dwarven race, but he held his tongue when Jermys raised his hand signaling he was going to speak. "I too have spent a great deal of time with Geoff of the maneths. We have shared all we have seen, felt, and experienced. There are many changes in the forests, the mines, and across our land. We cannot ignore these changes. I know the elves who brought us to this feast feel that no elf would attack the dwarves, but I also feel no dwarves would attack the maneth. However, we all know that these things did happen. The question we need to answer is, why?"

Hoangis stood. "Is the question *why*, or is the question *who*?"

This caused a stir among the group. McCard turned to his longtime friend. "Based on what we just heard, I believe we know who. Ku."

The elf king shook his head. "I spent time with Ku, as did these canoks." He motioned his hands over to where the five canoks sat. "I felt or saw nothing in him that leads me to believe he has the power to change dwarves. I do believe he went to the Feldschlosschen mines, and the pain I feel for the lost life at his hands is indescribable, but I believe he was sent there. I believe his actions are being controlled by another. I believe he is a willing participant, but he is not the source."

This direction seemed to be accepted by most, even the dwarves who previously had already found the former elf guilty and the target for this group to attack. Daphane now spoke, "Hoangis speaks the truth. I felt distrust in Ku. I felt a passion for power flowing within him." She paused and took a small drink of water. "But I did not feel organization. He was acting on a specific plan—a plan he hid deep within him and out of my reach to understand. My counterparts and I should not have banished him from our homeland. We should have held him and pursued his true desires sooner, but that is not our way. When trust is not there, we remove that entity from our world. We wish you to know, we do trust you." She said it to all races before her and although they were just words, they did hold a great level of meaning. Trust was something canoks did not hand out often, and to receive it in such a large order was truly significant.

"Then who?" asked Jermys. "If not Ku, who is behind this?

There was a stir again among those around the tables. A clear discomfort was growing, especially from those lower in the hierarchy of the races. The kings and leaders recognized the seriousness of the situation, but they did not hold a fear. Those lower in ranks were not free of the tension being created with each word. McCard panned those before paying particular attention to the young maneth and clearly saw the discomfort. He stood. "I would like to ask, do you believe it could be the dragons? They are known to be with magic. They are known to be strong. They are…"

He was cut off by Lendzion. "That is preposterous. The dragons have not left Draag since before most of us were born. I have never even seen…"

This time Daphane stood on her hind legs placing her front legs on the table causing the dwarven king to stop in mid-sentence. "I have been to Draag. I can tell you with a level of assuredness, there is discontent. There is a division on the dragon ranks. I have felt many things, and most of all, I have felt unsteadiness there. Upon my last visit, I left in haste as I was unsure of the direction. The reason I joined the elf king in this visit today is because I do believe if there is evil in the land, it could have originated with the dragons."

"You have been to Draag?" replied Geoff in amazement.

The canok smiled at the response. After all she had just said, the young maneth could not get beyond that simple statement. "Yes, my young friend, I have. While there I met many dragons. There was one I felt was pure, but I also felt extreme power within him. His name was Anbari. If he turned to evil, the power he carries would be difficult for even a united front to defend, but impossible for any of us alone." She looked down to her canok counterparts and appeared to be in conversation with only their small group. She then turned back to the mass of eyes before her. "It is difficult for me to believe even the canok homeland, hidden as it is, would be free from the dragon's reach should they choose an offensive."

This created a huge stir among the participants. Lendzion, who had remained standing, replied to the last comments. "If what the queen states is true, we must reach out to the dragons to determine their intentions."

"We need to first validate that what she says is true," stated Hoangis.

"How would you suggest we do that?" Lendzion shot back.

"I have been to Draag," stated Geoff. "I explored the forest on my own. I was trying to find additional food in areas we have never been before. I saw dragons. I saw dragons fighting. I saw their strength."

"Yes," Interrupted McCard, pleased that Geoff offered his information. "Draag is the key. We must send a party to Draag and determine the dragon's intentions."

Again, there was a stir. "Who would you suggest?" asked Jermys, breaking the mixed discussions among the groups at the tables.

"I will lead the party," replied a strong voice from the side.

"Father," exclaimed Geoff, standing and moving toward the maneth who walked up unnoticed.

They lifted their forearms and slammed them together the way they had done since Geoff was very young. "I am well," Gunthen said softly, his comment directed to his only son. To the group he reiterated his first comment as he walked closer to the tables and his king. "With your permission, I will lead a group to Draag. I too have been through the Draag Forest before. I am confident in the direction and what to expect. Though I have never entered the caverns, I will be able to lead us to determine what we need to know."

McCard stared at his battle leader. "Are you sure you are well enough?"

"I am, my King."

"I will join you," answered Lendzion, causing an even larger stir.

"I beg pardon, Your Majesty," answered Gunthen. "But it would be difficult to ask a king to follow my lead. Further, this trek could very possibly take us into unfriendly..."

"Do not presume to know what I am capable of, young maneth." The title was interesting because Gunthen was over 200 years old, but as Lendzion eclipsed that by another 50 years, everyone let the address stand. Gunthen continued, "I have been the leader of our kingdom for my entire time. I am skilled in battle, but most importantly I can navigate through any mine. If you are going to enter the caverns, you will want me with you."

"My King," stated Jermys, with Bretton right on his side, "my brother and I will go. You are too valuable to our..."

"Nonsense. You will go back to Feldschlosschen and inform Krystof he is the acting king until my return. He will need your support to defend our mines. Should we determine there is a force at work here, then he will need your expertise to be successful."

"But," started Jermys before Lendzion raised his hand directly before him.

"You are not challenging your king, are you, Jermys?"

He was about to protest again but when he heard the words and saw the king's eyes, he knew the decision was made.

"I will join you as well," stated Tashro, the oldest of the canok's alongside Daphane. Daphane and him had been in some sort of telepathic conversation prior to him speaking, but now all eyes were focused on him. "We wish to see what has occurred as well."

Hoangis turned his head to his son appearing as if he were going to nominate Madeiris to join this party. However, when he turned back to the group, he added, "Like Daphane, I have been to Draag. My knowledge would prove useful. I will join this party placing my son as temporary king of Elvinott."

McCard's eyes widened but not nearly as wide as the elf prince's which nearly burst from his head. "Father," stated Madeiris, "you cannot..." Hoangis shot a stare his direction that caused the prince to stop and bow in respect. "Yes, Father. I will not let you down."

There was a reluctance in McCard's next words, but he too could tell each decision was made. "Very well, then it is decided. Gunthen will lead Hoangis, Lendzion, and Tashro to Draag Caverns to seek out knowledge on whether the dragons are behind the recent changes we have seen in our world. Upon their return, we will pass word to all nations on their findings." He paused as he noticed a change in the canoks. "Queen Daphane, is there something else?"

She was startled at the address. She looked down then moved her eyes back across the group. "We have felt something else, toward the North Sea. Perhaps nothing, but perhaps another race that is able to lend support. I was discussing with my counterparts that upon our return, we will pass that direction and investigate what has caused these tremors we feel. Should we find anything worth noting, we too will pass this information forward."

"Very well," McCard replied, "but please be careful. The existence of another race could very easily be the source of evil in the land. Perhaps it is not the dragons and you are walking into the nest of our fears."

"I can assure you we will be on the highest alert. That is why it is best that the canoks take this journey. We will feel the presence of others before they know we are there."

McCard nodded and turned to address the entire group, those who had been assigned or volunteered for a mission still standing in front. "My friends, as I said when we began this Feast of All, evil could be at our doorstep. As I stand here now, I do believe we will determine what is happening and who is behind these changes. I am thankful to everyone who is here, but especially for those who are about to undertake what may be a very dangerous task for the betterment of all. You will have our support and prayers, and may your gods travel with you."

The maneth around the tables slammed their clubs down matching what was typical for the completion of their lines. Others shouted and exchanged hugs. McCard sat back and watched. It was clear to him they were no closer to knowing what was happening on Troyf, but it was also clear they had a plan to find out. Perhaps that would provide hope, or maybe something to offset the fear of the unknown. Whichever, he knew it was a step in the right direction. He looked down to Geoff who stood next to his father, their wrists locked and bent around each other in warrior fashion. Madeiris was deep in conversation with his father, the elf king, most likely trying to talk him out of this endeavor, McCard thought. Then he saw the twin dwarves, knocking down large mugs of ale in conversation, and the dwarf king sitting to the side deep in thought. Finally, his eyes fell to the canoks, the large and powerful queen staring back at him.

"Do you trust all of these here with us this night?" she asked him telepathically.

McCard did not know how to answer but something within told him simply to think his reply. *"I do, but to what level, I cannot say. I believe they are here for the right reason, but all seem to have some level of trouble in their own house."*

The canok nodded so it was clear she heard, or felt, his response, but she did not speak further. With each passing moment, many more disappeared into the camp, knowing that the next morning would signal the start of something bigger than any of them had ever experienced.

Chapter Six

Slayne had flown directly to where he believed the maneth camp would be. He landed in a clearing and closed his eyes. He felt the presence of many, but most of all, he felt the presence of canoks. He opened his eyes and looked around and then froze on a direction. "There she is," he said out loud though nobody was around to hear. "I will wait for nightfall, and then you will know what it means to be the mother of a revolution."

***

Stoven, Werner, Tashro, and Tyne, and the young canok Werner who had been asked to join their party upon their leave, all sat in their tent with Daphane secluded in her own.

Stoven swung his eyes to his older friend. "Tashro, are you sure you want to make this trek? I would be fine to go in your place."

"I know you would, Stoven, but our queen asked me specifically. I don't know why she chose me, but she did."

Werner lifted his head. "She said she foresaw other plans for us, whatever that means."

Tashro smiled as he heard Werner's disbelieving tone. "I know what you are saying. She said we all had our destinies, and—"

He was cut off when Daphane burst into the tent. "We must leave, tonight."

The canoks jumped to their feet. "What do you mean?" asked Stoven.

Daphane's face appeared as hardened steel. "There is a presence near, blocking my thoughts but I know it is near. It is coming for us. We are bringing danger to the entire camp."

"A presence?" questioned Tashro. "What kind of presence?"

"Enough with the questions," she replied, her tone exact and demanding leaving no room for further discussion. "Tashro, go to the camp and seek out McCard. Let him know I had to leave tonight to ensure the passage to the north. You stay in camp and continue on your journey tomorrow. Be strong, my son, for I feel great danger could be in your future. I feel a tremendous disturbance in the canoks' way of life. We must move quickly." She paused and turned to the rest of the pack. "Prepare to leave at once. Do not delay. I will be back with my provisions and then we will leave without delay."

She darted out of the tent leaving the blank stares of the stunned canoks temporarily frozen in place.

Tashro was the first to speak. "Let's not delay. I don't know what is going on any more than you, but I learned a long time ago, you trust her feelings. She has tremendous power and when she senses something, she has yet to be wrong. I will speak to the king and try to connect before you leave. He may choose to speak to her and get to the bottom of this." Tashro followed suit and darted out the flap in the tent.

Stoven looked to the others. "I guess we get things together and go."

"I guess we do," answered Werner.

They hurriedly gathered their things as Daphane again broke through the flap of the tent, this time with only her head breaking the plane. "Are you ready? It is time to…"

Her voice trailed off as she was slammed to the ground and pinned. The canoks inside could not see what had happened, but they knew something had hit her. The tent buckled under the weight of something. Daphane issued a few words the other canoks knew to be some sort of spell but they had no effect. The canoks could not see what had her pinned down other than a black shadow around her belly. Her eyes turned white with fear and she was lifted up in the air. Within a moment, she was gone into the night.

"What was that?" shouted Werner.

Stoven had fallen to the ground when the tent had been struck and was struggling to get up. Ignoring Werner's comment, he issued several directions. "Come with me, all of you."

They followed the old canok out the tent and stared into the sky. "Do you see her?"

Although the moon was full, it was still the center of night and the trees absorbed much of the natural light. "I do not," answered Tyne.

"What happened?" stated Tashro, approaching from behind and following their gaze into the sky. "What was that?"

"We don't know," answered Werner. "But it was strong, and it took our queen."

Two maneth guards came running. "We heard the commotion. What happened?"

Tashro answered. "Our queen has been taken by something with great strength and speed."

"And the ability to fly," added Stoven.

The two maneth guards looked worriedly at each other. "Taken where?"

"We don't know," answered Tashro. "We don't know where, or why, but we must find her. Please go tell your king and have him bring the leaders together. I wish to speak to them."

In very short order, all were together in King McCard's tent. "I am sorry your queen was not safe in my camp. Please, tell us what happened."

"Yes," added Hoangis, with Madeiris, Gunthen and Geoff, and Lendzion by his side. "Please tell us everything."

The canoks replayed the event and it was Hoangis who showed the most distress. His eyes were wide and his mind clearly full. He was about to speak, when McCard directed a question to him. "Could a flyer elf have done this?"

"A flyer elf?" Hoangis questioned, causing both his face and Madeiris's to instantly turn saddened. "No, none of what was described is within even our strongest of flyers." He paused a moment expecting the follow-up question of why, but when it did not come, he continued as if it had. "Queen Daphane was powerful with magic. Not a magic as you and I think of it, but magic. As Tashro stated, she felt something powerful before the attack. We must assume that what attacked her felt the same. I have only seen one creature in my lifetime that could have created an act like this, with the speed and strength to enter a camp and take her as such."

"What creature?" asked Tashro.

"A dragon," he replied. "Only a dragon could move with such precision. I don't know why a dragon would want her, but we must assume there is some strategy there."

"What do we do?" asked Stoven.

"We stick to the plan," Tashro responded. "We have no idea where she was taken, but the only stronghold we know the dragons maintain is Draag. We already have a party leaving tomorrow."

"I will go with that party," Werner stated. "If our queen is there, I will find her."

"No," replied Tashro. "We have too large a team as it is, and you will follow our queen's orders. Further, she felt a tremor to the north. There is equally as good a chance she was taken there. We will need all of you together if we wish to free her."

Werner was about to protest again but he couldn't argue with the logic. They didn't know where she had been taken so the more ground they covered, the better. "Very well, Tashro, I will respect the direction."

They talked further and then broke for the night. McCard quadrupled the guards on all boundaries and then finally was able to sleep. Word had spread fast and with that the fear that had been pacified hours ago now flooded back to all in the camp. Although only half the night remained, it still was the longest night of their lives.

***

"Tell me, Draketon, why do you act like such a child? I thought you were one of the more mature and powerful dragons who swore their allegiance to Slayne."

The large red dragon smiled. "Bjork, don't try to play on my emotions. Slayne is your puppet. I can see that. I will not do his or your bidding, but I can't argue for what Anbari has done. Although Slayne may not prove to be a great leader, I am pleased that you showed us a vision into Anbari's plan to make the dragons the servants for the other races. The fact he believes a dragon's power should be used to serve others is not what our fathers had planned."

Bjork smiled. "You are correct about many things, but one I must ask you directly. Slayne is not our future. I need a strong dragon with a true vision of the world. Slayne wants power. Slayne wants to rule. I need, or should I say, *we* need a dragon who is willing to lead. We don't need to destroy other races or beat them down to servantship. We need to live as one with them. I made a mistake with Slayne, but I don't believe I have made that same mistake with you."

The red dragon lifted his eyes clearly showing immediate interest. "Yes, Bjork, yes. That is what the dragons were intended to do. I know it."

"Then we have but one thing keeping us from that."

Draketon held his smile and interest. "What? What do you see?"

Bjork stepped closer. "It is the same dragon we have already mentioned, the same dragon Slayne refused to eliminate. As long as Anbari lives, the way the dragons were supposed to live is in jeopardy. We have to kill Anbari."

The red dragon lost his smile and stepped back. "You want to do exactly what I said we cannot do. A ruler kills those who are in their way. A leader brings them to his side."

Bjork turned his smile into a sarcastic laugh giving Draketon the message that he was so young and naïve it made the larger dragon break into laughter. "Don't be a fool, Draketon. Of course we will bring every dragon to our side, but Anbari is too clouded, too far gone. If we allow him to live, he will end up destroying all that dragons are. I have foreseen it the same way I was able to show you his intentions. He cannot be turned. He will use his ever-growing power to cloud the minds of those around us, and in the end, the ones who turn will be us. We will be so lost that we become servants to every race, which is not what our fathers intended. We will blindly follow like a bandicoot after food."

The red dragon paced in a small circle and then turned back to face him. "What are you asking of me, Bjork?"

The dragon smiled in return. "We have a unique opportunity. I know where Anbari is right now and he is unprotected. He is walking with a counterpart of mine, an elf. They are in search of a magician named Taiju. The elf will help you. I need you to find Anbari and destroy him. I will help you extend your power so with the elf by your side, you can be successful. This is our one chance."

"Why not have Slayne do this? He is the one who wants to rule. This would be a natural step for him to place himself on top of the dragon ladder."

Again, Bjork laughed. "We already answered that question. Slayne is not our future; you are. I have sent Slayne away on another mission. I have saved this mission for you." He reached out his talon and touched the dragon before him. "Do you feel it?" Bjork asked. "Do you feel the power flowing within you? By doing this, you will assert yourself ahead of Slayne."

Draketon opened his eyes wide as if being struck by lightning at Bjork's first contact. He could not speak and wanted to roar. Bjork removed his talon causing Draketon to drop his head. The red dragon lifted his eyes to the powerful dragon before him. "What was that? That was amazing!"

"It is what is at the tips of your wings and through your body. All I did was harness it. You and I can bring out the inherent strength in every dragon to lead Troyf into our future. When the new eggs hatch in two centuries, we can teach the young to follow. We can be the teachers of our world."

Right then when Draketon blinked his eyes, Bjork knew he had him. The red dragon lifted his head high. "Where is Anbari?"

"Very good, Draketon. Very good."

***

"Here is the opening to Taiju's lair," stated Kalcall pointing. "This is as far as I can take you."

Anbari stared at the small cave entrance that seemed to go straight down into the marshy swamp waters. "How do you expect us to fit in that?" the large dragon asked.

The gar smiled. "You asked if I could bring you to him. That much I have done. The rest is up to you."

Hawthorne stepped forward. "Can you tell us what to expect should we be able to traverse this path?"

Again, the gar held his smile. "As I said, I have no knowledge of anyone who has entered and left, nor do I know anyone who has entered in the first place. I only know that I have been told Taiju is there."

"That's helpful," stated Ku, already recognizing he was the only one who could fit inside the tunnel before them. "I do not wish to go in alone."

Kalcall nodded. "I must leave you now. I wish you luck in your endeavor, but you should know, I have no belief I will ever see you again."

With that, the gar darted off at a pace that defied what his body should be able to do, at least on land. Anbari turned to his two counterparts, holding his stare on Ku. "You wanted us here. You had this plan to help us stop the evil which is beginning to engulf our land. You are the only option."

Ku stepped up to him. "I may be a lot of things, but unintelligent is not one of them. There is no way I am going in an unknown cave alone. A cave which we have been told nobody has ever emerged from. Either we find another way in, or we change plans."

Hawthorne nodded in agreement. "We have to stick together, Anbari. It is too hard to find friends we can trust in today's world. Too many forces against two dragons working alone."

Anbari did not want to agree but he could not argue with the statements. "Let me at least look inside and see if there's anything that can help us—perhaps an idea about another entrance."

The large dragon stretched his head out toward the opening to peer inside and the moment his head broke the plane of the opening, his body contorted and changed. He roared as if in pain and then was silenced. There was a bright flash and then he vanished.

"Anbari!" shouted Hawthorne.

"What just happened?" echoed Ku, moving toward the opening but not daring to cross it.

"I am fine," came his voice from inside the cave. He walked to where he could be seen, and a reduced version of the dragon stood in the opening. His size was roughly 30% of what it used to be, but other than that, he was exactly as he had been. "Come through the gateway. It is enchanted with magic to allow all to pass comfortably. The transition is a bit of a shock, but otherwise harmless."

The two looked at each other and clearly were hesitant to move forward. Ku gestured to Hawthorne that she was welcome to go first. She looked to him and then back to Anbari. "Come, Hawthorne, you will be fine."

THE DRAGON OPPRESSION

The large female dragon gingerly took a step forward. She reached out her nose and immediately upon contact with the opening, the same burst and change occurred sucking her through to stand next to her counterpart, equal in reduced size.

"Come on, Ku. Let's waste no more time," Anbari hollered.

The elf king slowly took a few steps forward. He reached his foot out to cross the plane and then pulled it back quickly, but nothing happened. He looked at both dragons who still stood in front of him and reached out his foot again, this time breaking the plane further. He stepped down on the ground inside the entrance. Again, nothing happened.

Anbari smiled. "It is magic driven at allowing all the ability to enter, regardless of size, but you already fit, so no magic is necessary." Hawthorne pushed back a small laugh. Ku, on the other hand, relaxed the fear he was feeling replacing it with a mild elation that he could simply walk in. Once inside, the smiles vanished as they recognized they were inside an underground passageway created or guarded at least in part by very strong magic. Magic Anbari knew even he could not touch. The three looked at each other and although Ku was considered a king, all eyes were looking for direction from the large silver dragon.

"Since there is but one passage, I suggest we go this way." Anbari said in a somewhat lighthearted tone, but even at his level of confidence, the slight hesitation for the unknown was clear.

Hawthorne took a step forward as she asked, "What exactly are we doing here?"

Anbari turned to Ku. "This is more your area. This is what you said you needed to stop the evil."

The elf fell in behind the two. He had removed his bow as he was not hiding his discomfort and fear. His voice was weak because he truly was not sure if their reason for coming made any sense. "At this time, we have no way for my elves or any other race to defend against the dragons, but the three of us know that the dragons are forming an allegiance that will in some way assert their rule over our land. I believe that if we can learn how to fashion a weapon, or weapons, that carry with them some magical power, we can take those weapons where the power within them could be expanded. Perhaps they could become strong enough to demonstrate to the dragons that they cannot just assume all races will kneel to their power. The weapons we create will bring respect to all who wield them, thus creating a world of harmony. We can bring balance against the dragons."

Anbari heard the explanation and did accept it was a stretch, but he had no other plans, no other allies, and he needed support. If Ku knew a magician with such power, he needed to turn this magician to his side. He also needed to bring Taiju, whoever he was, to his side. Every day he could feel himself growing stronger, but he also felt Bjork and Slayne growing stronger. He needed help, and he needed it soon. Anbari was less concerned about the potential for weapons and more interested in the magicians that could fashion them.

Hawthorne concentrated on Anbari and said telepathically, *"Are you sure this makes sense? What can a weapon do against Slayne and a hundred dragons?"*

To her surprise, Anbari heard her question and answered accordingly. *"The idea has many gaps, but the principle is true, and we need help. We need the help of powerful magicians. We need to meet Taiju, and we need to meet whoever else Ku plans to take these weapons to. The weapons, as he calls them, are but a path to meet those who may possess what we need to defend our world."*

Hawthorne understood and did not take the conversation further. Anbari motioned to the group. "Let's continue down this cavern and see where it takes us. Please be on alert. I usually can sense what lies ahead and here I feel nothing."

Chapter Seven

The next morning the maneth camp had lost the elation from the night before, and the kidnapping of the queen of the canoks seduced all thoughts. There was much activity, but almost all surrounded the preparation for those teams heading out on their missions. The canok party had already assembled early and left before others came around. Werner, Stoven, and Tyne would not rest with their queen having been taken, Tashro remained in the camp through the night, but his direction was along a different path. The three were headed to the North Sea to investigate the presence Daphane had felt and ensure that whoever was residing there was not behind her kidnapping. It did make sense to Stoven, one of the stronger canoks with magic, that if she had felt them, they very easily could have felt her, which would have made her a target to protect discovery of their actions.

The dwarves had bid all well and under the guidance of Jermys and Bretton, they headed back to Feldschlosschen with their king remaining to join the party to Draag. Madeiris and the elves too were headed back, only their direction was Elvinott. Flyers had already left and were assuring safe passage. The remaining elves fell in behind the path cleared by the flyers. Hoangis, as arranged the night before, stood next to Lendzion and watched his son lead his Elven party home.

The two kings were joined by Tashro and Gunthen with Geoff and McCard in their wake. McCard was first to speak. "This may be the most high-ranking team ever assembled. Are we foolish to send all our leaders into such a potentially dangerous place?"

"Foolish is not the correct word," answered Lendzion. "Desperate, is what I would use. We have to determine what is happening and bring that information back. What we find may not be believable unless it is from our own mouths. We chose ourselves for this mission for the right reasons. We have to be successful."

All seemed to accept that answer and after a brief moment of silence, Gunthen added, "Then I guess to delay any further makes little sense. I have asked for provisions for each of us, and they should be ready now. Let's gather what we need and be off. We will be heading a different direction from the others. I have sent out a team of maneth to ensure our safe passage. They will be able to trail ahead of us for the first day until we reach the Ozaky River, then we will be on our own. We will need to traverse the Ozaky and then make our way through Draag Forest until we reach the caverns. With the gods watching our path, we could make it in less than five moons, that is if we don't run into any issues along the way."

Hoangis sighed. "Having no issues occur is highly unlikely considering the tragedy last night. We must be ready for anything."

Nobody had mentioned the kidnapping the night before until the elf king alluded to it. A deafening silence engulfed them as they prayed for Daphane's safety, but all realized it was probably already too late. Although none said it, all knew there was only one flying creature that could have taken her. To have a dragon attack so openly, and be unconcerned about every race meeting together in one place, sent a very strong message to those at the maneth camp. That message was as plain as if it was written in stone before them: *You will do what I say, when I say it, or I will make you do it by whatever means I choose and you cannot stop me.*

***

"Don't make another sound, Daphane," stated Slayne. "I do not wish to cause you any more pain, but I will."

The canok remained cowering in the corner of what appeared to be an ice cave. She tried to telepathically send a message to Werner or Stoven and her mind was filled with pain as if a dagger had been thrust into it.

Slayne laughed. "You are in an enchanted area. You will have no abilities here."

She tried to stand in defiance but realized she couldn't. She was exhausted. This was the first she had opened her eyes since being taken. She lifted her head and spoke to the black dragon directly. "Why do I hurt so much? What did you do to me?"

He remained standing above her with his eyes locked on hers. "A pity you don't remember. What has occurred over the last five days in this very room will change the world as we know it. You, Queen Daphane, are the vessel of that change."

"What do you mean?" she asked, her voice weak and cracking.

"I mean the young you carry now in your belly, *our* children, are going to ensure dragon rule forever. They will destroy the canoks and bring strength to the dragons. You are not only responsible for the death of your race, but the death of every race on Troyf, other than the dragons, that is. You will forever be known as the mother of dragons."

She placed her paw on her belly and instantly could now feel the life within her. "No!" she exclaimed. "It can't be."

"But it is, Daphane. It is just as I have said. You will have a litter of offspring that I will train. They will be strong with canok magic and dragon magic. They may become the strongest creatures on Troyf. They will stand by my side and together we will rule. No creature will be able to defy us."

The canok cringed as she rubbed her belly. "I will carry these for many moons. You took me from a group of all races on Troyf. They will find me. These offspring will be powerful, but they will stand by my side. This evil will actually be your undoing."

"You are such a fool," replied Slayne. "I have enchanted the conception. The birth will be in five moons, and on the sixth moon,"—he paused and beads of fire dripped from his mouth and his voice deepened— "you will be dead."

"You don't have the power to enchant my young. No creature has that power."

Slayne was caught a bit off guard by the return, but he covered it well with a smile. "Perhaps you will bear witness to my power in five moons, then you will provide me the respect I deserve."

Daphane did not like his confidence. She had never had any young, so she did not know what to feel or expect. She could tell something was different. How could Slayne have gained so much power? She stared at his smug grin and knew. Her voice was cold and hard, and struck the black dragon deeply. "There is someone else behind this, and you are simply taking credit. This is beyond your abilities; you know it, and I know it. Who hides behind you to dispel their evil work? You are but a puppet."

Slayne roared and shot fire across her face causing her to fade away from the heat. "I am nobody's puppet. I, like you, am not working alone, but I still will rule this land. It is my destiny."

"Your destiny is to die at the hands of a real dragon, true of heart. I can feel it now."

"You are a fool. All dragons can see the time of their own death. Do you think I would be so confident if mine was impending? Stay in your cage for five moons, and then give birth to my offspring. They will watch their mother die to stand by my side, and then destroy all your friends."

He paused and then opted to change direction. I will return with some food. You will eat it to keep your body and our children well. You will not be able to contact any other canoks with your magical mind words. This entire area is protected. There is no escape. Understand that it is your destiny, not mine, that drives this process." He turned and walked out of the ice cave.

Daphane moved to the back of the cage and curled up in the corner. She laid her head on her legs and closed her eyes.

***

"What do we do from here?" asked Hoangis. "Swim?"

"There is no way we are swimming," stated Lendzion firmly. "The water is no place for a dwarf."

Gunthen smiled as he looked across the vast opening of Lake Ozak. He knew where they were. He had traveled this area many times. "It would be nice if the mining dwarves could have mined some tunnels underneath the lake making land travel possible, but fortunately for us, Gnausanne is but a half day from here. There we will obtain a boat worthy of our needs. The lake is really not the issue. It is the rapids on the other side that we will need to prepare for."

"Rapids?" replied the dwarf king hesitantly. "Why on all our kingdoms would we risk traveling through rapids?"

"Because if we don't, it will take us another four to five moons to reach the outskirts of Draag. The rapids will dump us right in the forest." Gunthen understood the king's fears, but he would not allow questioning of his direction. He knew when this team was assembled that having a non-king lead several kings would lend itself to conflict. This was something he would not allow to fester. "Regardless, we are heading by foot to Gnausanne today. We are already well into this journey and replenishing our supplies, getting a good night's sleep, and possibly sending a few ales our direction all seem like good decisions."

Instantly the dwarf king's eyes took on a new softness. "Ales definitely sound like a good direction."

They turned along the water's edge, and then Gunthen led them back into the tree line to aid in protection. They had run into no other life since starting. The maneth didn't know what to think. It was possible to never cross another creature's path, but highly unlikely under normal circumstances. However, as he was deep in thought, a black arrow zipped by his head. The small group saw and heard it and instantly had their weapons raised and were diving into the thickest area of tree cover.

"What was that?" asked Hoangis, bow in hand. The elf king was skilled with a bow, not to the level of his son, but he could always hold his own when tested. He scanned the nearby trees for movement and saw nothing.

The arrow had struck a tree several steps behind Gunthen. He slowly moved back, reached up to grab the arrow, and upon making contact, a second arrow sailed in, its sharpened tip actually catching the maneth's fur before imbedding in the same tree. The maneth pulled and removed the first arrow and dove back into the tree. "I am not sure how many may be there, but their site is limited. Much of me was exposed and they still could only shoot relatively high." He paused and took a minute to study the arrow. "I do know who this is, however."

All eyes swung to him where they saw the maneth finish studying the arrow and then toss it to the side. "Who?" asked Lendzion.

"Goblins," Gunthen replied.

"What is our plan?" Hoangis asked. "I may have seen movement in that direction"—he pointed through some trees further away from the water—"but nothing definite, and nothing I would be able to hit."

Gunthen surveyed the area quickly. They were in fairly thick tree cover which seemed to become even more thick the further away from the water they went. The arrows were definitely shot from deeper in the trees. He turned back to the others. "Tashro, you are without a weapon, can you fight?"

The canok moved forward. "I will not have any trouble with goblins," he stated flatly, "and I can provide you some additional details. "There are eight of them. They are one hundred steps in that direction,"—he lifted his front leg and pointed— "and they are sitting down, not expecting you to attack, but to retreat."

Gunthen stared at him, not knowing if he should discard the comment or trust it as fact. He had heard stories of canoks and their magical abilities, but he had never seen it, other than some telepathy. He nodded appreciation. "Very well, then now we know their numbers and where they are. Based on the shots already taken, they clearly have limited sight on us so we should go on an offensive."

"An offensive?" questioned Lendzion. "Why don't we just go around?"

Tashro ignored the comment from Lendzion and didn't allow Gunthen time to answer. "Yes, an offensive. I don't feel like being trailed all the way to Draag. Gunthen, I can go alone to the far side and I will not have an issue handling any that head that way. That will allow you three to pin them in against me." He paused realizing he was far from in charge of this expedition. He was probably the lowest in rank, if canoks held rank. "If that is acceptable to you?"

"If you are sure you can handle them on your own, it is exactly my plan, but I was going to be in your position. It is your call." Gunthen stared at the canok showing incredible respect. The maneth had no idea the level of warrior he had with him on this journey. He assumed Hoangis was good with a bow and had had to use it at times, and Lendzion was also a king so he gave him the benefit of the doubt. However, Gunthen thought he would have to keep Tashro under his wing to protect him. Now he was considering putting him on point.

The canok didn't answer but darted off with incredible speed in the direction he had specified. Gunthen nodded to the others. "King Hoangis, stay just behind me and be prepared with your bow. I will attack the group directly, but I will need your bow fire to also draw their attention. King Lendzion, you bring up the rear and take out any who should slide by and verify that no others are coming from behind."

Both kings nodded agreement and Hoangis still remained with bow in hand and arrow knocked. They moved slowly in the opposite direction of Tashro and when they reached a small break, Hoangis pointed and whispered, "There, over by the rocks below the oak. Looks to be seven."

Gunthen followed his point and could barely make out slight movement of several black figures huddled down. "Damn, your eyesight is true. Are you sure there are only seven? Tashro specifically stated there were eight."

"There is a lot of cover. One could be hiding, but I am sure I only see seven now."

Just then there was a scream from behind them and Lendzion was on the ground, a goblin arrow in his leg. The goblins that had been hiding ahead of them jumped at the scream and turned full bow fire in their direction. Hoangis returned the fire with incredible speed giving the impression there were several elves firing. His accuracy was true considering the tree cover and two goblins went down quickly. Gunthen spun at Lendzion's scream and saw the eighth goblin closing in with his dagger raised. The maneth leaped through the brush to land between the goblin and the dwarf king and with one swing of his giant maneth club, the goblin's head exploded. Arrows whistled by the maneth's head as he swung back to see Hoangis backing up from the remaining goblins. There were four remaining as the elf king had dropped another. Gunthen slid in behind the king and stood in a face-off of four against two, all with weapons drawn. Three of the four goblins had arrows knocked and pointed directly at the maneth and elf.

Gunthen was fairly sure his armor would stop the goblin arrow, but they were very close, and he did not wish to test his theory. He stepped next to the king and spoke to the goblins before him. "What do you wish to take from us, goblins?"

They looked at him with a questioning gaze. Their bodies were obese and dirty. The armor they wore was broken and in some cases, missing. They carried many different weapons, most likely stolen from the bodies of those they had killed or found dead. Gunthen had no idea if they understood his language, but by the looks on their faces, he would soon find out.

"We wish to kill you, take all your provisions, and most likely eat you when we are through," stated the largest goblin, in what Gunthen and Hoangis took to be a mixture of Elven and Dwarven tongue but able to be understood.

Gunthen glanced to the elf and saw the determination in his eyes and knew his thoughts were the same. They would take them down before ever giving up their weapons. Gunthen started to speak and then stopped. The goblins looked around, seemingly confused. They immediately became tense and began spinning around pointing their weapons different directions. They appeared in a panic.

"Now, take them down. They cannot see you."

Gunthen recognized the voice although he also knew it was in his head. He had no idea if Hoangis heard it as well, that was until he saw the elf unleashing two arrows within moments of the message ending. The maneth leaped forward and finished the other two only to see Tashro standing a short distance behind them. The canok smiled, nodded, and then collapsed with his whole body falling freely, not using anything to break his fall.

The maneth hollered to the elf, "Help Lendzion. I will tend to the canok."

It was several hours later when Tashro finally started to stir. Gunthen had started a fire and Hoangis had worked on preparing Lendzion's wound. He would walk with pain for quite some time, but the wound would heal. The canok was another story. None of the three knew what had happened to Tashro nor how to help him. When he started to stir, immediately a level of elation came to each of them, but none as much as Gunthen. He felt he was in charge, and having one of his team injured and another one possibly brought down had made him question what he was doing. Now that the canok was moving, he had hope they could continue.

"Tashro," Gunthen stated sitting by his side. "Can you hear me?"

"I can hear you just fine, Gunthen," he replied, his voice showing signs of weakness, but stronger than the maneth would have expected.

"What happened?" Hoangis asked, moving in next to the maneth.

He slowly sat up and let out a deep, long breath. "I am not sure. I was moving in and preparing my spell, then all of the sudden they jumped and attacked. Because of the change, my spell was more difficult to use and if not for you reducing the total number, I most likely wouldn't have been able to do it at all. Regardless, it took everything I had. My queen could have handled this group without issue, but I am simply not that strong."

"Not that strong?" returned Gunthen. "You saved us, Tashro. From identifying them, their numbers, and location, and then completely debilitating them so we could attack. Thank you, my friend, that is all I can say."

Hoangis nodded as well. "Yes, Tashro, you did extremely well. We were outnumbered and already down one. We needed your assistance."

The canok nodded but then stopped. "Down one? Is Lendzion injured?"

The dwarf limped over. "Down but not out, my friend, and only because of you three. I am sorry," he stated, turning mostly to Gunthen. "You asked that I guard the rear, and all I did was watch forward. I never imagined there would be one from behind."

Gunthen smiled. "You performed well, Lendzion. To be honest, I would have done the same. When Hoangis only saw seven, I should have reacted immediately, but I didn't. Trust that I won't let the team down again."

"Nonsense," stated Hoangis. "We all acted well. We learned the magical strength carried in one of our friends, and we defeated our first obstacle together."

No other comments were made. The small group rested in silence for an unknown amount of time allowing both Tashro and Lendzion to gain some strength. Gunthen finally broke the silence. "We can still make Gnausanne by nightfall if we leave now and remain free of further interference. I would prefer to give it a shot and rest for the night in the safety of a room in the gnome city."

Lendzion nodded. "The safety of a dwarven ale in hand and some of that gnome chocolate does not sound too bad either."

The second comment, though meant to be lighthearted, ignited the group into a stir and within moments, they were looking toward Gunthen for direction. "I guess we will leave now, then," he stated to their questioning gazes. As they started to walk, he turned and raised his hand to the group motioning them to stop. "So, to be clear, the thought of staying in a safe room, free of the elements and attack, did not create any incentive to go, but the idea of having an ale created immediate action? Is that what I am to understand?"

"Basically," replied Hoangis. "I am not even enthralled with the idea of having an ale, but even I have to admit the idea is a significant improvement from the last several days of old water and bread."

Gunthen smiled. "I am not arguing about it. I am just trying to understand what motivates this group."

All three were staring back at him with smiles of their own. Lendzion tried to hide his growing smile and replied with a soft attitude meant to be in jest. "Great, now if you would discontinue stopping, maybe we could actually get that ale before the tavern closes."

"Understood," replied Gunthen. "Try and keep up. I am not sure those little legs can match my stride, especially with an arrow wound displayed so openly."

Lendzion was going to reply, but he also recognized keeping up would be a struggle for him so acting tough now would come back to bite him. His only response was, "I will do my best knowing there is ale in my future. That is all I can promise."

They all liked that answer and fell in behind Gunthen with Tashro taking up the rear.

***

"So, tell me, Geoff, why again are we searching for the former elf king?" asked Selbee.

"Well," the large maneth replied, "it seems our king does not have a good feeling about how Hoangis came to power and the lack of information around it. Combine that with Daphane expelling Ku from their homeland, and then the mysterious disappearance of the queen; we need to find some answers."

"Okay, but Troyf is huge. How do you know where to look?"

Geoff glanced to his counterpart from the Dimat Line and understood his concern. "I know, but I spoke to McCard and he has a theory. He believes that the canoks may be involved in Ku's disappearance. He believes that Hoangis visiting their homeland caught them in some alliance with the former elf king. In an effort to remain separated, they created the false expulsion not just kicking him out of their homeland and creating this belief of wrongdoing by the former king, but creating a trust and alliance with us. We have to find Ku and determine the truth. We will trail the canoks north and find out where they are headed and why."

Selbee nodded understanding. "But we sent one canok with our group. Isn't that a danger?"

"McCard and I spoke to Gunthen before their leave. Trust will not be something he shares with Tashro. He will watch the canok closely and limit what he knows about our plans and what we learn."

"That sounds good," replied Selbee. "What is our first step?"

"We are going to track the canoks as far as they go. If they return to their homeland, then we will see if we can pick up Ku's trail from there. That is the last place he was known to be. From there, we will see what comes our way."

"But won't they be able to *feel* us?" Selbee asked. "I thought they could sense when others were close."

"They might, but just fill your mind with the belief we are following to lend aid. If we overtake them or are noticed, then we simply say McCard sent us to be their support or backup."

Selbee nodded. "Sounds good. So, is there anything additional I need to know?"

Geoff heard the sarcasm in his friend's voice. The fact Geoff had referenced multiple conversations with McCard that did not include Selbee did not sit well with the Dimat maneth. Selbee was not as far up the line as Geoff was on the Batt Line, but he was not at the end either. Geoff placed his hand on Selbee's shoulder as they walked. "Don't worry, my friend, there is nothing you do not know. McCard spoke to me alone because I was there. Had you been there, it would have been reversed."

That seemed to satisfy him and together they continued through the trees. They walked for the better part of the day occasionally finding signs of the canoks, and then going for long periods with nothing. Deep into one of those periods, they realized they most likely had lost the group, either by their own failed tracking or the canoks blocking their trail from any followers. Either way, as they took a break in a small clearing, they looked at each other knowing the answer.

"So, you are the tracker, do we give up on the canoks?" Selbee asked, the first part of his statement clearly carrying a level of displeasure.

"I think we continue on the course toward the North Sea. If the rumors are right, we will find something there. Even if we don't find the canoks, we may absolutely find some answers."

"Fair enough," replied Selbee, "but what if we get there and find nothing but water?"

Geoff didn't like this line of questioning and his counterpart's constant negative tone. He turned to look directly at him, and his voice was strong, not leaving anything open for further comments. "Then we have a short rest on the shore, maybe catch a fish or two, then turn and head to Elvinott. We will find Ku. I promised our king as much."

As expected, that satisfied the conversation and they both arranged their packs, grabbed some food and water, and then prepared to continue.

***

"So, we are not going to the North Sea?" inquired Stoven.

Werner turned but continued walking. "No, we are going to our homeland."

"Do you not wish to save our queen?" Stoven replied, his counterpart Tyne stopping now to hear the answer.

"Our queen is dead, and if she is not, she will be soon. We must prepare our nation for what is before us." Werner had already changed their direction prior to the last stop so they had already left the path toward the North Sea.

"Dead?" Stoven questioned. "You don't know that. Why would the dragon have taken her if all he wanted to do was kill her? It makes no sense. He could have killed her at the camp."

"He wanted something from her. He will get it, and he will kill her. Accept her fate the same way we know she has. We must get to our home and warn them about the changes in the world. It is time to remain where we are safe. These evil actions cannot touch us in our world. We know that."

There would be no more discussion on the subject. They were fairly equal in stature, though Werner was younger than Stoven, he had asserted himself the leader. It was going to be his way, and neither Stoven nor Tyne would

THE DRAGON OPPRESSION

change their direction. At their current position, they would be at the canok homeland the next day. Stoven decided he would hold his tongue until they arrived and determine if the other canoks agreed with leaving their queen alone to die.

Chapter Eight

"There is something ahead, in the light through the doorway," stated Anbari, still in his reduced form so he could travel through the caverns.

"What is it?" asked Hawthorne.

"I don't know. It moved too quickly. Did you see it, Ku?"

The elf swung his head back toward them. "I didn't see anything in this foul place. I am starting to wonder what we are doing here. What can this Taiju do for us?"

Anbari nodded understanding at the elf's frustration. He had the same concerns. They really had no reason to be here. He had never heard about this Taiju and even learning his name was suspicious. "None of us knows what he can provide. We can only hope it is exactly what we seek. We have no other direction." He paused and stopped walking. "My real concern is what is alive ahead of us, and why did it hide?"

This caused all in the party to feel the tension carried in his voice. "Let me lead the way. I will determine what we need to protect ourselves against. If I say to leave, don't worry about me, and exit here the exact way we came. I assume we will return to normal the minute we exit the cavern. If I am not able to leave at the same time, you both continue to Ku's next destination. I will either return to Draag or continue my search for someone to support us."

"That is ridiculous," stated Hawthorne. "I will wait in the Gar Swamp exactly where we entered until you return. Ku may do whatever he feels is correct."

There was a short break which made the elf feel he should also speak. "That's right. We have found each other through fate. We need each other. I say forget about retreat. We will face whatever is here together."

That statement caught Anbari by surprise, and he was pleased to hear that he had not misjudged the elf. Whoever this Hoangis was, it was clear that Ku was the rightful leader of the elves. "Very well, and thank you."

He turned and slowly walked forward. He issued a few short enchantments, not knowing if they would work, but they should identify any life inside. As he broke the plane of the opening, instantly curses were heard to his side.

"Goddamn it!" shouted the weak voice. "What dwarven hell have I been…"

He stopped shouting and rolling on the ground when his eyes caught sight of Anbari, and the dragon issued a few more words. The creature rolled back to his four feet and stated, "You ist dragon smallist world."

"What?" questioned Anbari, trying to understand the strange creature's words.

"U ist pigmee is dragn."

The words were broken and Anbari had no idea what was being said. "Who, or what, are you?"

The creature smiled broadly. "Fehr is me."

"Fehr?" said Hawthorne softly from behind. "Aren't you a cute little guy?"

Anbari swung toward her with a frown. "Cute little guy?" he questioned. Turning back to the creature, "I don't understand you. Will you touch my wing as I say these words? It may help us communicate better."

"Fehr frade not is me. Wing ss good."

Anbari lowered his wing toward the creature and immediately upon contact, the dragon writhed in pain. Hawthorne reached out her neck, placed it against her counterpart, and pushed him away. The small creature on the ground stood without moving, only smiling at the exchange. To Ku and Hawthorne, it appeared the creature was killing Anbari. Ku knocked an arrow and was about to let it fly when the two broke connection.

Anbari fell to the ground. Hawthorne moved next to him, and Ku kept his arrow locked on the small creature. "Anbari, are you okay? Did something happen?"

Anbari was breathing deeply. "That creature may have the emptiest mind I have ever encountered. There was nothing there but long stories of triumphs and battles. It was like being sucked into a vacuum. Thank you for pushing to separate us. I am not sure there would have been anything left of me had you not."

"Wow!" exclaimed the creature. "I understand you both. I understand tons of words. I can say many, many things. This will be a story I will tell my friends." He stopped when he said that. "If I had any friends," he stated softly.

Hawthorne turned to the creature. Speaking in ancient dragon, "Do you understand me?"

"I do, most beautiful dragon I have ever seen."

She could not help but smile. She switched to Elven. "Do you understand me now?"

In perfect Elven he replied, "I do, and you are still the most beautiful dragon I have ever seen, even in this crazy speech."

"Turning to Anbari, Hawthorne asked, "So just by touching him, you were able to pass all these languages to him?"

"I told you I am getting better at such things, though I don't know how."

"Amazing," stated Hawthorne.

"I have to agree with her, Anbari," interrupted Ku. "That is amazing. However, are you all right?"

"I am," replied the dragon, getting back to his feet. "Now, turning to the small creature next to him, he asked, "So tell me, Fehr, what are you and why are you here?"

He smiled. "Oh, what a great story. Let's sit so I can tell you." He rustled over to a corner stone and jumped up as if he was on a pedestal. "So, let me begin by saying I was born to one of the most wonderful families of bandicoots to ever live. I had twelve brothers and sisters and we were such a loving family. We did everything together. I remember one time as a young boy, one of my brothers took me during the night and set me next to a tigon trap. I rolled during my sleep into that trap and if I had not moved quickly, I would have been killed. We laughed about that one, I tell you. Then, there was another time when I was trying to catch food and another brother told me he had scouted ahead in the area and it was loaded with figs. I went running ahead directly into a party of dwarves. Imagine my surprise as they unloaded their hatchets on me. Lost my tail but escaped. Oh boy, did we all have a laugh about that one."

Anbari raised his wing causing the Fehr to stop. "Please, my new friend, not so much old detail. Why are you here?"

Fehr frowned slightly at the interruption but then returned to his smile as he realized another story was being requested. "Oh, what a great story that is. My brothers and I were playing a game and it was my turn to run and hide. Another brother told me about this great place, a cave. He led me to it, and we were both to go inside. However, something happened and after I went in, my brother never did. Then, when I tried to leave, the doorway was blocked. I could see my brother running away, but there was something blocking me. I called to him but he kept running. I assume the force field blocked all sound because he did not slow down. But don't worry, I have kept a full record of all that has happened since I have been in here. I am sure I have won the game because nobody ever found me, though I am certain they are still looking."

"How long have you been here, handsome?" asked Hawthorne.

"Oh yeah, handsome," he replied. "Good call on that one." He carried a huge smile now. "I am sure I have not been here more than fifty or sixty years. I kind of lost count after forty or so." He paused and flexed. "But look at me. I have stayed in shape. When I do get out and catch up to my family, they will barely recognize me. I am a road warrior. I am a…"

Hawthorne now interrupted him. "You have been here for fifty years?"

"Maybe sixty. I am not sure." He looked worried. "Is that a problem?"

"No problem at all," replied Anbari, not allowing the little guy to speak more. "Can you answer me one question about this place?"

"Shoot, Baby Dragon. What do you need to know?"

"Baby Dragon?" Anbari repeated.

"Well, you are like miniature size for a dragon. What would you have me call you?"

"Why don't we start with Anbari. This is Hawthorne and with us is Ku, king of the elves."

"Wow, king of the elves. That is super excellent. You must have some great stories."

Ku nodded but let Anbari continue. "I am sure he does, but right now, we would like to know that since you have been here so long, you must know your way around pretty well?"

"Absolutely, I do. There is no place down here I do not know."

"Then you would be able to lead us to someone else who is here, and then lead us out?"

Instantly his careless smile turned to a small frown. "Well, there is nobody else here that I know of and there is also no way out."

That hit all three of them as if they had been shot by an arrow. "Wait," answered Anbari. "Are you saying you have explored all these caverns, every corner, and there is nobody else here?"

"That is exactly what I am saying. Is that bad?" asked Fehr.

"Bad?" interjected Ku. "Bad? Are you serious? You mean we are trapped here?"

"We are not trapped. There is ample food and water. It is great fun exploring. There are minerals and other trinkets you can keep. And I even found a room with a door and a hallway. I usually sleep there and when I get up, I walk the hallway to the end but there is a door that is locked, and I can't get through. I have tons of shiny stones and jewels. Do you want to see them?"

"What do you mean, a door you can't get through?" asked Anbari.

"I mean a door I can't get through," replied the bandicoot. "Am I saying a word wrong? You walk up to a door. You turn the handle. It does not open. It is a door you can't get through."

The three looked at each other and had to accept the accurate description. "Very well," answered Anbari. "Would you be interested in taking us to this door?"

"You mean join you on your mission?" asked Fehr.

"I am not sure we are on a mission, but yes, join us as we try to get through the door."

"Yes, yes, yes. I would love to join you on your mission."

"Very well," replied Anbari. "Can we leave at once?"

"That sounds perfect, Baby D. You guys follow me."

"Baby D?" whispered Hawthorne.

"Hey!" shouted Fehr as he began walking out the door. "Pretty Hawthorne dragon, why don't you join me up front? I can tell you more about myself."

"No—" she began to say but was cut off by Anbari.

"That sounds great, Hawthorne. Ku and I will be fine in the rear. You go up and spend time with our new friend."

She glared at the dragon beside her. Softly she said, "From this point forward, I may call you Baby D." Turning her speech toward Fehr, "I will be right there, Fehr."

"Great," he replied. "I want to tell you about the time I go my foot caught under a goblin's cart full of rocks and how I escaped by pretending I was dead."

"That sounds very interesting," she replied, still glaring at Anbari.

Ku, who had been quiet most of the time and had not shown any level of humor previously, added, "And Fehr, don't leave anything out. Hawthorne always tells us how she hates short stories. She wants all the details."

Hawthorne's tail snapped sideways slapping Ku across the face even harder than she intended, but she still didn't apologize.

They walked for nearly half the day. Anbari imagined these caverns must be tremendous in size. He believed they had walked so far that they most likely were no longer under the Gar Swamp. He wanted to ask their new friend how much further it would be, but since Fehr had not stopped talking since they began their trek, he didn't want to interrupt and end up taking Hawthorne's place up front. Frequently the dragon would turn her head back toward the two behind and glare, but then be drawn back to the bandicoot when he noticed Hawthorne turning away.

Anbari was amazed at the light carried through the caverns, though there was no chance it was from the surface. Magic illuminated the walls and although he could not feel its presence, he knew it was there. He also believed whatever created it knew Anbari was there. They continued walking until without warning, Fehr turned around, "Here it is?"

Anbari looked ahead and saw nothing that they had not seen for the last half day—barren walls emitting some sort of light and no doorways in any direction. "What do you mean, here it is?"

He smiled. "That was what I was wondering. It took me years to see it the first time."

Anbari moved forward and as he did so, Hawthorne moved quickly to the rear, completely unconcerned with anything that was being said. "Are you saying there is a room here and we are in it?"

"Not here," he replied pointing. "Through that doorway."

Anbari followed his direction to see a solid wall. "I see no doorway."

Fehr shrugged. "Maybe you will see it when I walk through it to the room I sleep in."

The bandicoot took several steps toward the wall and then vanished, as if he had walked directly through rock. Anbari followed his steps exactly and when he reached the wall, laughter echoed off the walls from Ku and Hawthorne as Anbari slammed his head against solid granite.

"Really, Baby D, don't you think you should see the door before you try to pass through it?"

Anbari was slightly embarrassed by the occurrence, but he was growing exceptionally furious by the continued use of the name Baby D, and that was carried more in his response than the bruise on his forebrow. "I don't understand. I can't feel anything about this wall."

Fehr suddenly appeared. "So, you can't see it yet, huh, Baby D?"

"Everyone, please stop calling me Baby D," stated Anbari firmly. "And no, I can't see it nor can I pass."

"I guess you will need to wait forty or so years like I did, Tiny Winger," Fehr replied, causing Hawthorne to laugh out loud.

"I don't intend to wait forty years to find an answer to this. Tell me, Dwarf Bait, what did you do immediately before you saw this doorway appear the first time?"

"Dwarf Bait?" questioned Fehr. "Well, that is just rude."

"Answer the question, Fur Ball."

"Listen here, Jr. Scales, I don't care how big you used to be. You are in my house now and there is nothing you can do to me because I can just go into my room and you can continue to slam your head into the wall trying to get me. Now sit your mini dragon butt down and we can talk. Otherwise, I am not speaking again."

"You know what, Goblin Dinner, I truly like the idea of you not speaking again. Let's see how long that will last." Anbari sat down and motioned his friends to do the same. He whispered a few words and a small amount of food appeared in front of them, all but Fehr. As Anbari ate his portion, he issued several grunts of pleasure with each swallow. The bandicoot wanted to shout out in anger but held his tongue, refusing to break his threat of silence.

Anbari smiled halfway through his meal. "Hawthorne, I sure do wish one of us had a story to tell. I could use a good adventurous tale."

Fehr heard that and twisted in discomfort.

"Yes," replied Hawthorne. I heard several today. It is a shame there are no more. I guess we will have to go to sleep without any additional stories."

Both dragons turned to Ku to continue the taunt. Although the elf was clearly not as versed in the sarcastic nature of the discussion, he fell in line just fine. "Yes, I was so jealous of the stories I know Hawthorne was hearing this entire day. What I would give to hear those tales."

"All right. All right!" exclaimed the bandicoot. "You win. I will tell you more stories. Let me get comfortable and you may all hear about my adventures."

"No," stated Anbari. "Either you tell me about the first time you found the hidden room, or you do not speak. That was the deal."

That wasn't really the deal, but the dragon was banking on the need for Fehr to be able to tell stories to outweigh any discussion about the hidden doorway conversation.

"Fine, if that is all you want to know," Fehr replied. "I will tell you, but it is not my best story."

Anbari smiled. "I am even happier to hear that it is not your best story. In fact, I am hoping it is one of your shortest."

Fehr shrugged but did not address the comment. "Well, to be honest, I was tired of roaming these caverns. I had not seen any other living creatures for as long as I could remember. All I wanted to do was get out and see my family, but there were no other doorways to the swamp. I kept going back to the one I entered, but I was not able to pass. So, I aimlessly walked. What I did not understand was that every morning, no matter where I slept, I woke up here, right in the center of this cavern. I would walk to the furthest end of the cavern and fall asleep, but when I awoke, I was here. Sometimes I would stay awake all night, but eventually the next day I would fall asleep, and when I awoke, I was here. I would even—"

Anbari interrupted him. "Okay, we understand. No matter what you did, you awoke here."

"Right," replied Fehr. "Impressive you picked that up so quickly. I had several other examples I was going to give."

"Yes," Hawthorne stated. "Impressive indeed."

"So, then I decided since I always ended up here, that I would just plan to sleep here each night. I would spend my day exploring, then come back here to sleep. But the days went on and on and I became lonelier and lonelier and eventually I wanted to find someone to talk to. I found myself praying for that. Then, in the course of a dream or something, I found this doorway. It was locked, and night after night I would dream and see this doorway, but I could never open it. Then suddenly, when I said my prayer again, it opened. When I awoke, the door was there and from that point on, I could pass."

"Interesting," replied Anbari.

"Does it mean something to you?" Hawthorne asked.

"It might." Anbari knelt down and closed his eyes. He concentrated his mind on nothing but the doorway. A doorway he could not even see. He said a short prayer and then opened his eyes. There was nothing there but a brick wall and his friends who were watching him intently. He took several steps toward the wall at the point where Fehr had passed and again closed his eyes. His first step was not timid or slow, but he stepped forward as if he was walking through air, and he was. He vanished through the wall.

"Anbari!" shouted Hawthorne.

"Cool," echoed Fehr. "The munchkin dragon did it." Fehr leaped through behind him.

Anbari stuck his head back through appearing to be passing through solid rock. "It is a leap of faith. There is a wall there unless you completely believe there is not. When someone dreams, they are free to believe things that their conscience will not let them when awake. You need to close your eyes, clear your mind, and envision a passage. If you can do that, you can join us."

Hawthorne and Ku looked at each other and it was clear there was skepticism. However, they had just seen their friend pass so they knew there must be some truth behind it. Hawthorne went first. She knelt down as Anbari had done, cleared her mind, and stepped forward. She too passed unhindered.

Ku shook his head. He was more uncomfortable than the others, but he could not argue what he had just seen. He stood in front of the wall where they had passed, closed his eyes, cleared his mind, and envisioned a passage, then stepped forward.

The pain on his forehead erupted as he struck the wall. "What the…"

"Relax, Ku," replied Anbari. "That was me striking you with my wing. You passed. Just do it again."

"Not funny, Baby D," Ku replied, proud of himself for carrying the title forward as he easily passed through the barrier.

Once through, all eyes scanned the area. Fehr had been accurate in his description. There was a single room, almost like a cell, at one end of a long hallway. The hallway ended with another door. Anbari had already checked the door and it was locked. There were no carvings or pictures on the walls. It was simply a barren corridor. The large door marking what had to be the exit stood on old, rusty hinges that appeared to have been unused for eternity.

The elf scanned the area, looked at the others, and stated, "So, we made it into the secret chamber, now what?"

Fehr darted down to the room at the far end. "This is where I typically sleep now. I have dreams of going to that door, but nothing ever changes."

"What?" asked Anbari. "You dream about this door?"

"Yep," he replied lightheartedly. "Every night, the same dream."

"I can't believe I am going to ask this, but will you tell me about it?"

A huge smiled crossed the bandicoot's face. "Absolutely, Bab…" he did not finish the Baby D title upon seeing the dragon's immediate glare. "Absolutely, Anbari, I will be glad to tell you about my dreams." He took a deep breath and then let it out as if he needed to gain strength. "So, as night fell in the secret chamber, I began to settle in. I stretched my legs…"

"Hey, Fur Ball, if you plan to make it through this night, I suggest you get to your dream." Anbari was actually smiling now, as were Hawthorne and Ku.

"Okay, okay, don't get your scales in a ruffle."

"I am not even sure what that means," replied Anbari.

"Well, it means to not…"

"Fehr!" exclaimed Anbari. "The dream. Our ability to get out of here may depend on it."

The bandicoot coughed and then cleared his throat again. "So, it was time to sleep, and I rested my head on the small cot in the room over there. Every night when I close my eyes, I have the same dream. I wake up with a glaring headache. I walk into the hallway and approach the door. Right before I reach the door, a black dwarf blocks me. It attacks and kills me with a plan to eat me." He paused and then lightheartedly added, "And then I wake up right here. It happens every night and never changes."

Anbari smiled and turned to the others. "Everyone, make yourself comfortable, we are going to rest here for the night. I will take the small room, and everyone else, find where you want to sleep out here."

The others were surprised by this statement, but they were tired and the thought of bedding down for the night appealed to them. They pulled out their food, had some idle talk, but in very short order, were lying down and fast asleep. Anbari curled up on the floor in the small room at the end of the hall. He had pulled the door shut and was secure inside. Slowly, his eyes closed, and he was asleep.

Chapter Nine

How am I to find this lair where Anbari has gone? Draketon thought to himself. *What if I can't defeat Anbari?* "And where am I?" he stated out loud, though nobody was around to hear him.

Draketon stopped and listened. There was nothing but faint sounds of water and creatures living in the swamp moving in the distance. The Gar Swamp was very large, he knew it, but there had to be a way to find them. He had to find this Taiju that Bjork has talked about, but he had no clues, no help, and nowhere to turn. He continued to walk.

The water under his feet gripped them with every step but he could not fly for fear of missing a clue to where they might have gone. He had not spent much time with any elves, though he had a seen a few in his time at Draag. He had no thoughts positive or negative about elves, but he also had no belief that an elf would be useful in a fight against a dragon as strong as Anbari. However, Draketon did believe in one thing as much as any other: if there was a clash between good and evil, right and wrong, good would always come out on top. He had been shown by Slayne and Bjork what Anbari wanted. Anbari wanted to destroy any race that would stand against the dragons. If they would not fall in line under his rule, he would destroy them. Then, he wanted all the dragons to fall in line behind him because he was the most powerful. He believed all would follow, and they probably would have if Bjork had not shown the vision of Anbari wiping a dwarven village from existence and turning the dwarves to a blackened evil. He burned the dwarves with his breath but with magic kept them alive. They felt an allegiance to him for saving them, no matter how twisted it seemed.

Draketon could not fathom how Anbari could have done that horrid act, but what he did know was that he couldn't let it continue. During his flight to the Gar Swamp, Draketon had come to understand he had made the right choice. He had to stop Anbari. He did not care if he ended up with any additional power or not, but to stop a holocaust was the true direction for his life.

Suddenly, a voice appeared behind him. "I don't believe it is a coincidence that I see three dragons in less than one moon. Should I assume you are with the others?"

The voice startled Draketon causing him to turn and shoot fire across the water's surface. Kalcall dove under the water and then resurfaced. "Hey, dragon, I mean you no harm." He was backing up as quickly as he could.

Draketon lowered his eyes on the creature. "What do you mean, three dragons? And how did you learn our ancient language?" The gar moved several steps back and was going to turn and run before a wall of fire again shot across his path stopping him where he stood. He slowly turned back to face the red dragon, who now moved a few steps closer. "I said, what do you mean, three dragons?" repeated Draketon.

Kalcall's voice was choppy and broken, and he feared he was about to be scorched to his death, but he also knew he had no option but to answer. "Earlier yesterday, I met two other dragons and an elf. They were looking for something, and I helped direct them. That is all. Because I had never seen a dragon, nor spoken their language, and the next day you show up, logic says you are together."

Draketon smiled. "Yes, I seek my friends. I was to assist them in their search for Taiju. Did you lead them to him?"

Kalcall relaxed. "So, you know about their mission. Then I will be glad to help you the same way I helped them, though I don't know if I actually helped since nobody has ever returned from where they planned to go."

Draketon was about to demand the location and then he stopped. "Wait, are you telling me that no creature has ever returned from where you sent them?"

"That is correct. Once a creature crosses the plane of the doorway, they have never been seen again."

Draketon smiled, speaking softly. "Then perhaps I don't need to find them. Perhaps the job is already done."

"The job?" questioned Kalcall.

"Yes, I was to help them find Taiju's lair, but not join them in the final quest. If they have already found it, then there is no reason for me to continue." He saw the concern on the gar's face. "However, if you feel they are in danger, perhaps I should go after them."

Kalcall softened his stare. "To be honest, I do not know if they are in danger. I only know that no creature has entered the lair and ever been seen again."

Draketon hesitated. He wanted this gar to believe he was there to help, but he didn't want to enter the home of this unknown magician and be trapped forever. If Anbari was truly trapped, then his job was done. The dragon could no longer lead. The large red dragon had two goals: Determine what he would tell Bjork if he did not destroy Anbari, and determine how he could leave this gar without causing further suspicion. "Why don't you take me to the entrance of this lair. I will wait there and determine my next move. Should I decide to enter, that would be my choice. My hope is that they will emerge from the lair before I have to make that decision."

"Understood," replied the gar. "However, you are actually at the doorway." He pointed his webbed arm toward the well-hidden cavern entrance. "If you enter there, you are in Taiju's lair."

This caught Draketon a bit off guard, believing he would have some distance to plan his direction. Now he had to define his next steps immediately. "Perfect. I will rest here, gather some food, and then make my decision. Hopefully in that time my friends will have returned."

Kalcall understood but he did feel there was something off with the dragon. However, he also knew if Draketon wanted to end their discussion and in turn end his life, he could with one breath, so he did not push any further. He simply nodded understanding. "Very well, then I should be off on my patrol. Good luck in your quest."

"Why, thank you, Kalcall," he replied. "But I do have one more question before you leave. My friend's name is Anbari. I assume that is one of the dragons you met?"

"Yes, Anbari was the one who taught me your language. He was truly powerful."

Draketon did not like hearing the description but continued without further comment. "He was traveling with an elf whose name escapes me. Did you happen to catch it?"

The gar smiled, pleased he would be able to help with some additional information. "Why of course. His name was Ku."

"Ku?" questioned Draketon. "Are you sure?"

"Why yes, I am very sure. Anbari was traveling with an elf named Ku and another dragon who called herself Hawthorne."

If hearing Ku was a surprise, when the gar said Hawthorne, Draketon's eyes narrowed tightly on the creature before him. Hawthorne was with Slayne. Draketon knew that. They were together. Slayne talked about it all the time. *Bjork has them all fooled*, Draketon thought. *He has infiltrated Anbari's life. The dragon has no chance.* "I have not seen Ku or Hawthorne for a long time. It will truly be nice to be reunited with them."

Kalcall nodded but did not speak further. Draketon sat down outside the cavern opening and stared toward it. He noticed the gar had not left and turned back to him. "I am sure your work is critical. Please, go and protect your swamp. I will remain here and meditate on my next move. For now, I do not believe that entering the cavern will provide my friends the best support. Your guidance has been truly helpful, and I am very appreciative of it. Thank you, my new friend."

The gar liked this response very much. He started to head out and then turned back. "And thank you, *my* new friend. I will not enter the cavern with you, should you decide to go, but if you need anything else, please don't hesitate to ask."

Draketon understood and bid him well as the gar vanished into the trees, sending up small splashes with each marshy step.

I will stay here for one full moon and then I will bid this horrible place farewell, as I bid farewell to Anbari as well. Draketon smiled at the thought and then rested his head on the ground. *I don't need to go after you, Anbari. Bjork has Hawthorne and Ku in place. I just need to relay that you are most likely trapped forever or dead. Either answer ends your reign of terror.*

***

"What in all of Troyf is that?" asked Selbee, his eyes fixed on something on the far side of a large field. They had expected to crest the top of a hill and see nothing but the North Sea, but instead, they saw something they were completely unprepared for. "Do you think they could have taken the canok queen?"

"It is one of the most decrepit villages I have ever seen. I can see from here that the construction is so poorly put together that even a strong wind could level this outcropping of life."

"I am not a warrior," replied Selbee, "but there is no line of protection. It is as if they want some race to come in and level their work."

"A band of goblins could destroy this city. They can't be behind the kidnapping of the queen, but we need to understand who and what they are. We should proceed."

"Are you sure? We are but two. Even a weak village with many can resist a visit from two. Further, look at their heads and bodies. Have you ever seen skin that white? They have no mane and most don't carry weapons. What if they capture us and make us their slaves?"

"Are you serious? If they try to capture us, we will just leave. What are they going to do to us? We are beasts. Look at their buildings. Do you really think they have weapons that could hold us?"

Selbee seemed skeptical but when he looked closer at the group, busy building what appeared to be some sort of small rock wall, he had to agree. They slowly emerged from the tree line that protected them from view. As they drew closer to the small village, there was no reaction, until one individual swinging some sort of axe saw the two approaching and yelled something. The words were foreign to Geoff and Selbee, but they immediately caused a stir. Within moments, at least thirty of these creatures were standing outside their camp with weapons drawn.

Geoff looked back to Selbee. "Are you sure we needed to worry about this group?"

"Oh my, no," he replied. "What are those things they hold, sticks? And look how skinny they are."

"Keep your club to your back," Geoff stated. "Do not draw your weapon or show any sign of threat. We wish to speak to them, that is all."

"Understood," Selbee replied, "but isn't that odd coming from you?"

Geoff understood the source of the comment. A Batt Line warrior telling a Dimat not to fight went against all principles, but this was an extreme situation. "Yes, I never thought I would see the day, and please don't tell my father."

The two smiled and stopped about twenty-five steps in front of a wall of odd figures.

"Greetings," stated Geoff in the Maneth tongue.

The group stared blankly at him and then back to each other. There was a shuffling in their ranks causing Geoff to want to reach for his club, but he did not. The line separated and four of the creatures broke through and stood at the front. They were as skinny as the rest but in their hands, they each held a weapon much beyond that of the others. Their weapons were composed of shiny, polished metal. A bow, a curved sword, a hammer, and an axe. The four men stood strong and proud.

The one with the sword stepped forward. "I am Octavius Starland. Do you mean to attack us?"

Geoff and Selbee glanced to each other. Geoff answered pointing to himself. "Geoff." Then he pointed to his counterpart. "Selbee." Then he pointed to the creature who had spoken. "Octavius?"

The creature smiled. "Yes, Octavius." He turned to those around him smiling. "We are pleased to meet you, Geoff and Selbee."

The two maneths had no idea what they had said other than they were smiling, and they repeated their names.

"What do you want to do next?" said Selbee smiling. "We know each other's names. Do you want to try to learn their language over the next fifty moons and ask them if they have seen an elf named Ku?"

"Good point," replied Geoff. "Maybe it is worth a long shot."

Their conversation between each other had made the group uncomfortable, but when Geoff turned back to them with a smile, the leader seemed to calm. In Elven, Geoff repeated, "I am Geoff, do you understand me?"

They looked at him without speaking or acknowledging. Then in ancient dragon, Geoff repeated, "I am Geoff, do you understand me?"

Immediately the one who had identified himself as Octavius lifted his sword. Returning the speech in dragon, he stated, "How do you know this language? A creature infected me with it many days ago. I don't understand how I know it, but I do."

Both Geoff and Selbee instantly drew their clubs. "What do you mean, a creature?"

"I mean a giant winged beast that blew fire and could have destroyed us. It used magic to create these weapons we hold. It is something I have had nightmares about ever since."

"Nightmares?" questioned Geoff.

"Dreams that bring fear to me and those around. This creature could destroy us," Octavius answered.

Geoff was pleased he was able to communicate, though in a language he struggled to understand. All maneth had been taught every language known as a child. Ancient Dragon was one of them, but it was one he had never used in conversation. "Don't be afraid of us. We are not with the winged creatures. We are seeking friends. We fear the winged creatures as well. They are called dragons."

It was clear only Octavius could understand his speech, as the others continued with their weapons drawn, and not just the other three in front, but the larger group holding sticks and rocks. Octavius turned to the group and shouted again in a tongue foreign to the maneths. "These two have seen the same creature that crossed us. He calls them dragons. He is seeking allies against them."

Whatever Octavius had said brought a level of calmness to the group behind. Geoff had not understood it, which showed clear on his face. When the human saw this response, he quickly repeated, "I simply told them what you had said. It appears you and I can communicate, but we have to translate to the others. We are human, and this is our city we are building."

He nodded understanding. "May we join you in your camp? We have many questions about the dragons, your experience with them, how you came to understand their language, and the origin of the weapons you hold. We are maneth, and we are friends."

Octavius lowered his weapon to his side. "I have no reason to trust you. However, we are desperate. We are trying to build a colony to protect us. We are here to build the greatest city in the land and we need allies. Please don't make me a fool and destroy us."

Geoff and Selbee glanced at each other and then back to the human. "We are here as friends," Geoff replied. He motioned to the maneth next to him. "With me is Selbee. He is one of our higher-ranking diplomats. Together, we will speak to you about all we have seen and what we are trying to do."

Octavius relayed something to his men and then they opened a passage for the maneth to pass. Geoff and Selbee slowly started making their way toward the city. Geoff was instantly uncomfortable as this was an extremely vulnerable situation. Should they opt to attack, the two maneths would be surrounded.

However, as they began walking between the groups, several stepped up and reached their hands out. Geoff looked strangely at the first who had done it and Octavius whispered, "He wishes to welcome you by shaking hands."

"Shaking hands?" the maneth questioned.

Geoff reached out his paw and gripped the human's hands. He violently shook it almost ripping the human's arm out of its socket. Octavius laughed. "No, my new friend. A bit easier. Just up and down."

The human who had started the exchange pulled his hand back in pain and actually cowered backward. Geoff appeared apologetic. Octavius walked up to him and took his paw in hand. Gently he lifted it up and down. "It is our greeting. It is our way of saying welcome."

The embarrassed maneth glanced back to the original human who still stood several steps away. He reached his paw back out to him. "Please," he stated in his Maneth tongue. "I am sorry. I am very pleased to meet you."

The human stepped forward and gingerly reached out his hand again. He repeated Geoff's words not knowing what he was saying, mimicking the maneth sounds. "I am very pleased to meet you."

Geoff smiled and they shook hands. Everyone cheered and both Selbee and Geoff exchanged handshakes and welcomes with both groups not sure what they were saying but feeling good about it regardless. They entered the small village, and to the human's credit, although it did not look like much, they had everything needed. They had homes, a smith, a council center, and stores to get food and provisions.

Octavius led them to a large tent in the center of the village. "We have much to discuss. This is where we hold our council. It should provide us the privacy we need. I am sure our discussions will be long as translating between each other will prove difficult. Is there anything I can get you before we talk?"

Geoff and Selbee both nodded that they were fine. Octavius motioned to three other humans to join him and he sent the rest away. The three humans and two maneth entered the tent and proceeded to fill each other in on what their current direction was, with Geoff and Selbee severely limiting what they shared.

***

The canoks looked on at the three questionably. A large older red stepped forward. "There is no way Stoven speaks the truth. Werner, you chose to return here instead of continuing to attempt to rescue our queen?"

"I did," Werner replied without hesitation.

There was a stir among the canoks surrounding the three who had just returned. "Why would you do that?"

"Our queen is dead," stated Werner. "And if she is not dead, she will be."

There were growls as several in front stepped even closer, their teeth showing through their tightly pressed mouths. The canok continued, "You don't know that. You don't know..."

"I know what dragons can do. I have seen firsthand how they can turn and without care scorch everything you love. That dragon came into the maneth camp, a camp filled with its enemies, and without fear it grabbed our queen and carried her off. No canok magic could stop them. She is the strongest of us and she was helpless. We do not even know where the dragon took her."

Tyne took a step away to separate from his counterpart. "I have not seen what dragons can do, and I will not continue to be led a direction because of fear. I will go search for our queen. I sensed two maneth were doing the same as we traveled. They are probably on the north shore by now. If they found something, they could use our help, if it is not too late."

"I will go as well," stated Stoven. "We must at least try. If she has been killed, we will bring her body back to our home for its final rest."

"You may find where he took her," interjected Werner, "but even together you will be no match for one dragon, much less more. We could send every canok and we would not be a match. We need to focus on becoming stronger with magic." Werner paused and turned directly toward Tyne and Stoven. "If you run into a colony of dragons, you too will die."

"I would rather die than live knowing I did not try," replied Stoven, with Tyne shaking his head at the comment.

"I sense no deception in young Werner's voice," interrupted an older female canok, stepping up from behind the group.

"Dantowin, it is your sister they left behind. It is your sister Stoven and Tyne are willing to find. It is our queen."

"I understand, Raynold," the female said to the large, older canok who had been speaking. "But a wise canok looks at all facts. As I said, I sense no deception in Werner, so he believes that which he says. Because of that, we have to conclude that what he says may be the truth."

"But how can both directions be the truth?" asked Raynold.

"Because they are independent of each other," replied Dantowin. "We can continue to strengthen ourselves with magic while a small party seeks my sister." She knelt down appearing to be tired. "As I consider the options, we must continue to strengthen ourselves, regardless of any support we provide for my sister. For if what Werner believes comes to be true, we will be without our queen, without her power, and her wisdom will be sorely missed."

Raynold lowered his head in respect. "I understand, Dantowin. Do you feel as I do that Stoven and Tyne should leave at once for the northern shore?"

"I do, if the pack agrees?" She lifted her head to those in the area and then closed her eyes sending a telepathic message to all canoks in their homeland. In moments, she opened her eyes. "They do."

Raynold nodded to the two canoks who had already begun preparing to leave. Within moments, they were back out the passage and standing in the field.

Stoven glanced back to Tyne. "Why do you think Werner did not wish to search for her?" he asked.

Tyne shook his head. "I don't know. I felt he was hiding something, but each time I felt I was about to grasp it, it was lost."

"I as well. Perhaps he is not as he should be?"

Tyne did not know what that meant but let it sit. The two canoks turned and began heading north, away from their homeland and toward the North Sea.

Chapter Ten

The dragon woke at the sound. "What was that?" Anbari stated out loud, though there was nobody around to hear him. He glanced around the cell and remembered where he was. "Well, that didn't work," he stated, again speaking loudly, even though nobody heard.

He rose from his coiled sleep position and stretched his wings as far as he could in the cramped quarters. He was still a fraction of his normal size. The magic that created this change must be extremely powerful. To be able to hold him in this reduced state for such a long time without any signs of failing was truly amazing. He stood as tall as he could, but his head still did not reach the ceiling. It was as if each room he went into adjusted his size to fit, maximizing his size for the dimensions of the room. Amazing, he thought.

He stepped through the door and re-entered the long hallway. He did not notice at first, but after only a few steps, his head dropped, and he realized what had occurred. "Hawthorne?" he shouted. "Ku? Are you here?"

There was no answer. Suddenly, he stopped, as fear slowly filled his mind. He knew he had been here before. Not the night before with his friends, but in this hallway, alone. And when he was here last time... His thoughts stopped and he swung his head around to greet the deep black eyes of Slayne.

"Well, we finally meet again," the black dragon hissed, with balls of fire falling on the ground.

"We do," replied Anbari, his voice strong and mind clear. "I remember."

Slayne did not acknowledge the response and immediately drew back his breath and released a wall of fire the likes of which Troyf had never seen before. Anbari stood strong and held his ground. He did not offer any defense or offense. He just stood and let the flames bounce across his body. He did not fade back or cringe, because he knew they were not real.

The black dragon vanished and the large door at the far end of the hallway opened. The hinges creaked and the sound of wood splitting bit the dragon's ears. Anbari stared at the doorway. He turned his head back around the hallway and confirmed it was empty. There were no signs on the walls, the floor, or anywhere on Anbari from Slayne's attack. The area was devoid of life.

"Come this way, young dragon," echoed a voice from beyond the door.

The voice was familiar, but Anbari could not place it. It was just at the tip of his wings but still out of reach. He passed through the doorway and although dark, his eyes seemed to have incredible power to see. He was in a huge open chamber with many jewels and statues and an almost magical fountain of a snake of some kind coiled above a small pool. Beyond the fountain there was a peculiar wall of darkness that seemed to swallow his ability to see. Anbari reached his mind into the void but could feel nothing. He glanced around the room and then slowly approached the huge fountain.

A crash sounded behind him as the large wooden door he had passed though slammed shut and then magically vanished. The door was replaced by a magnificently carved wooden creature appearing to have a white feathered head and two large wings. He stared briefly at the new carving and then turned his attention back toward the fountain. The winged creature was fascinating, but he was more captivated by the creature on the fountain. He could not remember why this snake-like figure seemed so familiar. Slowly his mind began to form it into a different shape as if breaking a spell which protected its identity. As he stared longer, it became clear that it was not truly a snake. It was something much more primitive or simple. It appeared almost parasitic, like something one would find in a marsh. The widest part of its body was at its head while it gradually tapered down into a much thinner and pointed tail. It had two large eyes which stuck out on two tentacle-like projections above its toothless mouth. As the water from the fountain ran down its body, it gave the creature's skin a slimy appearance.

"Come closer, Anbari," issued a soft but ominous voice from within the void. Anbari lifted his head immediately, surprised by the speech but strangely not scared. The voice, like everything else he had experienced, was familiar, but he couldn't place from where. He dropped his wings to his side and chanted a few words. The void, which had been in front of him, now crept up and engulfed the entire room. However, as it did, Anbari learned that he could still see, as if the room was lit. It began as just shapes and outlines, but as his eyes adjusted, he could see with night sight that would make an elf jealous. He peered through the darkness and saw more of the same style of room with similar artwork as well. Along the far wall were several other magnificent wood carvings of tigons, canoks, dragons, and a strange painting of a human, similar to those they had met a short time ago, but this human had long black hair pulled back in a ponytail. He surveyed the entire wall and then stopped at a large pool that had a huge brown head sticking up from it. Two eyes rested high above it and blinked several times as the dragon approached. "Good," the creature said. "You have adapted well to your vision. You are accepting your gifts."

"My gifts?" Anbari questioned.

"Felt your power growing, I have. You are only beginning to understand what is inside you."

"What is inside me?" the dragon continued to question, his lack of understanding clear in his tone and words.

"Tell me, Anbari, do you know me?" the creature asked.

"You are Taiju," Anbari stated.

"But who is Taiju?" he returned.

"I do not know."

"What do you know, my son?" The creature lifted its body farther out of the pool.

"Hawthorne heard another dragon speak of one called Taiju. The one who spoke is a powerful dragon and believed Taiju was the most powerful creature on Troyf. A friend I met on our journey believed you could help us build a defense against some disturbed dragons who want to destroy life as we know on Troyf. Together we searched and ended up here."

"But who is Taiju?" he repeated.

Anbari held no fear. He was in an unknown place speaking to a creature the likes of which he had never seen before, and yet, he felt he was supposed to be here. He shook his head. "I don't understand the question."

"You were born more than one hundred years ago. You did not know your mother and father and you were not born in Draag. You fought your way into Draag and quickly began to move ahead of other dragons. You never were comfortable at Draag because you could feel the energy turning evil. You fear no dragon, but you worry that one called Bjork and one called Slayne are fostering the evil and if you don't stop it soon, nothing will."

"How do you know all that?" he asked, his voice soft and almost lost. "How did you even know my name?"

The creature lifted its body completely out of the pond and moved directly in front of the dragon. In a slow, deep tone, he answered, "Because I named you."

Anbari stared at him. Softly he whispered, "Father?"

***

Gunthen smiled. "So, dwarf, you seemed to enjoy Gnausanne last evening, particularly the ale. Do you intend to join us today?"

Lendzion was devoid of any humor. "If you are asking if I would be fine if we stayed one more night in this fair city, I absolutely would agree. However, my feeling is not driven by any dwarven ale, moreover, it is driven by what I am seeing at the far end of the lake. The speed of the water appears intense, to say the least."

Hoangis smiled and directed his comment toward the maneth. "My friend, you may be unaware but mining dwarves, like our friend here, are by no means fond of the water."

"Not fond of the water?" answered Lendzion. "If dwarves were meant to be on the water, Keabda would have given us…"

His words stopped and his voice became gargled. All eyes that had been looking toward the water turned back at the strange abrupt change in his speech. They turned in time to see the dwarf fall face-first into the sand, an arrow protruding from his back.

"Dive!" shouted Gunthen causing all to immediately fall to the ground while other arrows sailed toward the water. "Head to the tree line in the east. We can find protection there. Hoangis, provide whatever cover you can. I will carry the dwarf."

The elf was already releasing arrows in the direction of the bow fire and his keen eyesight locked in on some movement. He drew and fired and saw a creature fall dead on the adjacent side. As the others ran toward the trees with Gunthen bringing up the rear, the elf released two more arrows. Then he turned with amazing speed and entered the tree line as the returned arrows fell at his feet.

"Who were they?" asked the maneth.

"I couldn't tell," replied Tashro. "I felt no presence."

Hoangis was panting as he spoke. "I killed one. It was black, but to me it appeared to be a dwarf."

"More of the dark dwarves," stated Gunthen, who was kneeling above the dwarven king. "Hoangis, I am not gifted with healing. Can you help him?"

The elf knelt down next to the fallen king. He felt his chest and placed his hands above his mouth. Hoangis looked up sadly. "It is too late, my friends, for he has passed."

Their heads dropped as they stared at their fallen friend. Hoangis softly stated several words and removed a pouch from inside his armor. He sprinkled some dust across the body and like a song, it slowly vanished.

The maneth opened his eyes and let the silence engulf the three of them. Then he saw it. "They are the dark dwarves you spoke about, and they are coming."

"And there are a lot of them," Tashro stated.

"Where is our boat?" asked the elf, now standing beside his companions.

Gunthen pointed. "On the other side of that army."

Tashro turned. "Then we can't go that way. Follow me through the forest line. We will parallel the water to keep our bearings and then figure out our path down the river. If we do not find a way to use the water, we will add many days to our travel. Perhaps too many for us to find answers in time."

He was talking as they were moving and the three were breaking through the trees at an incredible pace. None were sure if the dwarves were looking for them in particular, or simply stealing their boat, but regardless, it would be too late for them to do anything about it. The boat was lost, and their only option was to flee.

THE DRAGON OPPRESSION

They ran without a break for most of the morning. Finally, as they came to a clearing that overlooked the water, Tashro stopped. "I do not feel any pursuit."

Gunthen was panting, but not as much as the elf. "How can you be sure? You said before you couldn't feel them."

"Because as we ran, I could feel their presence. Now, I can't."

Hoangis had paced around and then found a large rock he could rest on. "I have to rest. If they are still behind us, they are as tired as we are. I will be able to take them down with bow fire should they come."

"Relax, my friend. I agree with the canok. They no longer pursue. I believe they only wanted our boat." Gunthen took a seat on the ground in front of the elf while the canok moved to the edge of the trees.

The canok nodded toward a soft rumbling noise in the distance. "The rapids are right there. We have made it all the way to the mouth of the Draag River. If we continue on foot, we will enter Draag Forest. If we find a way to traverse the rapids, we could save time, but the travel would be much more dangerous, if even possible. The sound of the moving water is tremendous."

The elf nodded agreement. "Yes, my ears can hear much better than both of yours, and..."

Gunthen raised his hand to stop him. "To be honest, those ears just by their size should be able to hear if there are dragons at Draag Cavern, not just the roaring water."

Both Tashro and Gunthen smiled at the comment but the elf king was more displeased with the interruption than the shot at the size of his ears. However, he could not help but smile when he saw the maneth and canok's large grins. "It is good to see some smiles for a change," Hoangis stated, and then paused briefly as the other two nodded. "Now, if I could continue, the rapids do sound treacherous. However, we cannot spare the time. There are good vines here as well as wood. We need to build the best raft we can and use it on the river. We have to get to Draag."

To his surprise, there was no argument from either one. In fact, Gunthen stood and walked over to a nearby tree with a trunk as big around as the elf's waist. He leaned hard into the base and with one push, the tree came down. "One log," the maneth stated. "Tashro, clear the branches and I will bring down more. Hoangis, go find some strong vines. We will need a lot of them to hold up against the water."

Daylight was starting to fade when the three companions pushed their raft toward the water's edge. They looked at each other and the unasked question was clear: do they enter now or wait until morning? Not one of them hesitated and into the water the raft went. Gunthen had affixed a rudder and due to the speed of the water, they did not feel a sail was needed. The current grabbed them quickly and the maneth dug his rudder deep, guiding their boat to the mouth. The speed of the water was more than any of them had anticipated but they also knew there was no turning back.

"Port Gunthen," shouted Hoangis. "Dig in hard."

That was the only instruction the maneth heard until deep into the night, when they landed in a calm pool, soaked through their skin, but alive and together.

***

"Hello, my soon-to-be mother," stated Slayne.

Daphane lifted her eyes but could not move. The enchantment placed on her to accelerate her litter was having a detrimental effect on her body. She was struggling to hold onto life. Slayne had not anticipated this but it was of no concern; as long as she gave birth, the prophecy would be fulfilled. "Please, Slayne, remove this curse from me so I can carry them as normal. You will still have your young."

"Stop your begging, canok. It's a sign of weakness."

She squinted her eyes in pain. "I hurt, Slayne. Something is wrong. The babies are not well."

The black dragon instantly became concerned. "Do not let them die. You will carry them to birth."

The canok's eyes closed and she laid her head down.

"No!" exclaimed Slayne. He walked up to her and chanted some words. The canok seized upward with a gasping breath. "It is time, Daphane. It is time for you to take your place in our history and bear the young that will rule by my side."

She screamed in pain and then it began. The first birth was a stillborn creature that mostly resembled a dragon, but it was not a dragon. Slayne looked on in horror. Daphane looked down to her child and began to cry. "No, please, no," was all she could whisper.

The second birth was exactly the same as the first, stillborn and dragon-like. Again, the canok could greet her stillborn young with only tears.

Slayne leaned down and whispered, "You will bear me a son, or you will die."

It was not clear to the dragon if she had heard the comment or not. She screamed again in pain as the third birth occurred. A canok, red coat with a black diamond patch on its forebrow. The pup made a soft screech and Daphane quickly used her nose to push it closer to her.

"One lives. I have my son," stated Slayne.

Daphane shifted and the final pup was born. Another canok with a red coat but this one had a white diamond patch on its head. It too let out cry until it was pulled into his mom's belly for warmth and milk. "Two canoks live. This confirms that nobody will be able to stop us."

His elation was clear, and he turned and began to shake his head in excitement. With his attention drawn away, he did not hear the soft chant from the mother who lay on the ground barely holding onto life.

"What are you doing?" Slayne finally stated. "No!"

He reached down and grabbed the two pups in his talons and in one fatal breath, scorched Daphane's motionless body. The pup with a black diamond patch watched closely as her mother burned but the other pup was held to the side out of view. The wall of fire sent the ice floor into instant boil. The pups cried as they were swung from the dragon's piercing grip. "I did it," he said softly, also watching as the female body of the canok lay motionless in the pool. "Nobody can stop me now."

As he spoke, a wind began to churn and spin in the spot where Daphane's blackened body lay, then lifted her in the air. As the swirling movement spun around, her body disappeared, and in its place, a creature Slayne had never seen before appeared. In place of the canok now stood a creature with large brown and heavily scaled body. It stood on two legs with taloned feet, but it also had two other limbs which hung as arms from its side. It had a fat belly which probably pushed its total weight into the thousands of pounds. Its neck was equal to its tail in length, both incredibly long and well-stocked with heavily armored projections. Slayne knew one of its main attacks would be with the violent use of its tail, like a sword. One touch with one of its spikes could create a hemorrhage so deep, and true death would be instantaneous, even on a dragon.

Slayne stepped back in fear. "What are you?" he asked.

The creature opened one taloned hand and shot a ball of fire directly into the dragon. Slayne immediately chanted a few words in defense but the ball struck him completely unhindered. Slayne fell back in pain but quickly turned and released a magical ball directly back at the creature. The creature opened its arms and let the ball strike directly in the chest absorbing the magical burst into its body. Its eyes grew red and then softened as it grew stronger with the burst.

"What in all of Troyf?" Slayne was struggling to get back to his feet.

The creature took several steps closer to the dragon. In perfect ancient dragon speech, it said, "Tell Bjork the prophecy has changed. The canok will not be used for your plan. The one known as Daphane has summoned me to ensure it. The canok will be divided. They will not follow these two. They will not follow any. They will follow their own honor." The creature lifted its head in the air and screamed louder than any sound Slayne had ever heard. He buried his head in his belly trying to protect himself from the feeling that he was about to explode. The nearby ice on the walls of the cave cracked and the sides began to give way, and then the creature was silent.

Slayne climbed back to his feet. "What are you?" he asked again.

"Until one can defeat me, I will remain with the canok. Until then, the canok will forever be changed." The creature screamed again sending Slayne back into his cowering position. He still held the two pups in his grip and to his surprise, they seemed unaffected by the creature's roar. As quickly as before, the creature was silent. When Slayne looked up, it was gone. He pushed himself to his feet.

To himself he said, "I will have to tell Bjork about that creature, but it will be of little concern. It can stay with the canoks forever. We don't need the canoks, we just need…"—he lifted the two small canoks to his eye level—"you two." He stopped when he saw them. "What has happened to you?" he continued in a confused voice. In his talon he held the two pups, but both had lost their thick red color. One was as black as the night across its whole body with one exception. On its forebrow it had a white diamond patch. The other was as white as the icy ground outside the cave, but on its head was the same diamond patch in black. He stared at the two as he set them down. "I will call you Almok," he said to the black one. "And I will call you Kirven," he stated to the white. "I see the spell that accelerated your birth is continuing with your growth. This was unexpected, but very good. We will be ready sooner than I thought. It is time to head back to meet Bjork. It is time to fly."

He picked up both pups in one talon causing both to emit a growl-like sound making the black dragon smile. "Yes, my pups, be prepared to be angry." They disappeared into the clouds.

Chapter Eleven

"Are you my father?" Anbari asked again.

The creature laughed. "No, I am not your father, at least as you understand the word."

"What does that mean, as I understand the word?" he asked.

"It means that your mother and father brought you to me before you hatched. Powerfully strong they were. Others on Troyf looked to them as gods, rather than dragons. They could feel things, see things. They could see what was to be. They hid you from the others. They hid you with me."

Anbari still looked confused. "Why you? Are you the one I was seeking? Are you Taiju?"

The creature smiled. "Taiju I am, that much is certain. Why me? I cannot say?"

The dragon knelt down closer to him. "Please, tell me all that you know. I have no memory of my parents."

Taiju moved back toward the pool and slowly slid under its surface and then returned with his two raised eyes lifted high above his head. "You have no memory of your parents because the day they left you with me, was their last day alive. I don't know the circumstances surrounding their deaths, but they believed something was not right. They knew their offspring would suffer the same fate if they did not hide your existence. They came to the one place they believed no creature would ever search. They found me sitting on a wet log in the marsh. And they created all that you see here, me included. They have made me what all creatures dream to be—immortal." His voice trailed off and he whispered, "A dream, and a curse."

"What are you saying? They built this elaborate cave and gave you power?"

Taiju smiled. "Your words are simple, but essentially true." He ducked back under water and then returned. "They gave me their powers. They taught me how to pass them. It was so much for me to hold onto. They instructed me to return their powers to you. Upon your hatching, I passed that which I was to do onto you. With each day you live, those powers will grow, and mine will fade. I was told should you ever return, should you ever find me, I could pass them to you at once. In all this time, no creature has made it to my lair. I have seen others wander the cave, but eventually their lives fade. You have finally returned, and this burden on me may be lifted." He lifted himself back on the ledge of the pool. "Are you ready, Anbari? Are you ready to become all that you should be?"

Anbari shook his head in disbelief. "This is all too much. I can't…"

"Touch your wing to my head, my son. This is what your parents died for."

Anbari did not speak further. He reached his wing out and gently contacted the slimy skin of Taiju. It was as if a bolt of lightning had struck him. He was unable to break apart and his body shook in pain. He roared and fire shot across the room, though the burst was not in his control. Suddenly, the environment melted. Taiju, the cave, the pool—everything was gone. He was standing in a glade surrounded by trees. He had never been to this place before, but he held no fear. It was as if he was supposed to be here.

"Look at him, Archala, he looks so much like you."

The voice caused Anbari to swing his head immediately behind him. He froze on who had spoken.

"He does, but I see you in his eyes, Anthose," the other dragon said.

"Who are you?" Anbari asked, his voice now showing fear. It was not fear of what was about to happen, but fear of who he believed may be before him.

"You know who we are, son," the female voice said.

"We are your parents," stated the large male dragon. "I am Anthose, and your mother is Archala, if you prefer to use our names."

"We have never seen you before us as such. You are truly amazing." Archala was smiling larger than Anbari had ever seen a dragon smile.

Anbari started to speak and then stopped. He looked away as if verifying this was real. "But how can you…"

Anthose stepped forward. "We have very little time, and we must tell you that which we can. Please use this time to hear us."

Anbari stepped forward as if he was going to reach out to them.

"No, son, we cannot touch, or this space will be lost. We can't explain everything; just know that when your power was fully passed, this time was going to come."

His mother interrupted. "We are so proud of you. We never thought it would be so soon. We never thought you would seek out Taiju."

Anbari was clearly still confused but there was nothing he could say.

His father continued. "Before you were born, we sensed evil growing across the land. Dragons were by far the most powerful creatures, but others were beginning to evolve. None were as strong as your mother and I, and that is why others approached us."

Archala stepped closer and her voice was soft. "They wanted us to lead them in a takeover of the world. One dragon was behind the idea. His name was Bjork. His desire for power exceeded none other on Troyf. He was strong as well, probably equal to each of us alone, but he knew we were together. He needed others to defeat us."

Anbari nodded. "I know Bjork. He approached me as well, but he never mentioned either of you."

"Of course he didn't, son," Anthose answered. "Nobody knows you are our son."

"If they did, you would have been killed as a child," Archala interrupted. "Any son of ours would carry our combined power. That combined power would grow to exceed that of Bjork's."

Anthose nodded agreement. "Bjork probably approached you because he sensed your power even as a young dragon. He would be looking for any who would support him. There are two others we recognized with strong power. A red dragon named Draketon. Strong but reckless."

"But we never sensed evil intentions in Draketon. Just innocence," added Archala.

"And then there was Slayne. A black dragon," his father stated.

"Be weary of this dragon, my son," she added. "For he is confused and easily manipulated. He will become a vessel to destroy this land, we are sure of it."

Anbari nodded. "I know of Slayne as well. He has organized the dragons. It is why I have fled Draag."

His parents looked at each other and their eyes narrowed. "You have fled Draag?" Anthose asked.

"I have," replied Anbari. "I had a confrontation with Slayne. I was not prepared. I have a friend with me. She joined me. She helped me escape, and now searches for those who will support us against the other dragons who have been turned."

"No, son," Anthose stated. "If Slayne and Bjork have already turned the dragons, there is no support on Troyf strong enough to defeat them. You had to stop them before they turned the dragons."

Although Archala agreed with Anthose, she had centered on a different word in her son's response. "What friend? What female dragon now joins you?"

Both Anthose and Anbari were caught by her abrupt interruption and tone, the lack of distrust clearly carried within it. Anbari turned to face his mother. "Her name is Hawthorne. Don't you know her?"

They glanced at each other, and then back to their son. Archala's voice softened just a bit. "There was no dragon named Hawthorne when we were part of Draag. Be careful, my son. She cannot be whom she appears to be. We would know."

"There is only one other dragon that could help you," added Anthose, "but we fear she has passed, for she has been lost for over a dragon's lifetime. Her name was Carlascom. She was the most powerful dragon of her time."

"What happened to her?" Anbari asked.

"We don't know, son. She was our leader. She held balance in the world." Her voice trailed off then she added softly, "Then one day, she was gone."

Anbari paced around a bit and then turned back to them. "Hawthorne is good, I can feel it." He paused and watched his parents' faces fade in concern. "She is also strong with magic. She doesn't understand it yet, but it is there, beneath her reach right now. I can help her bring it out. Together, she and I can find the support we need to turn the dragons back."

"No, my son, you cannot," Anthose answered coldly. "If Bjork has already turned the dragons, you will not be able to defeat them nor will you have the strength. You would need more dragons before you would ever get them to listen. They will destroy you and any you bring to fight with you. The dragons are simply too strong."

"Then I need to find more dragons," Anbari answered.

They both smiled, but the depression at their failure to protect the world from Bjork was clear on their faces. "There are no other dragons, my son. Only every two hundred years when the eggs hat—"

Anthose stopped in mid-sentence and swung his head to Archala. She recognized what he was about to say and nodded in agreement.

"What?" Anbari asked, seeing the change in both of them.

"When the eggs hatch, my son, that is the key. You need to turn the young dragons to your side. You have to make them understand the balance of life on Troyf. That is the only way you will have the numbers you need."

"How can I do that? The eggs are deep within Draag, and Draag is controlled by the dragons who have sided with Bjork and Slayne."

Archala leaned in, the energy in her words driving her forward. "Draw them out. Let the dragons come to destroy the other races. When they do, go in and enchant the entire area where the eggs are resting. Protect them from the dragon's return. Then you must be present when they hatch. When they see you, they will follow."

"But how? I don't know…"

Anbari was cut off by his father. "Our time grows short, my son, but this is the only way. Find all the support you can from every race. They will need to be protected against the dragons, for they must take the brunt of the attack while you are at Draag."

Archala interrupted, "What about the canoks, Anthose? They could help at Draag. Their magic could move the eggs to another plane, much like their home today."

"Yes," replied Anthose excited. "Get the canoks to help you. They will resist, but without them, your magic will not hold to fully protect the eggs."

They looked down to their son who returned their stare showing a deep level of confusion. "I don't understand." He saw his parents begin to fade. "Wait, Mother? Father?"

"We love you, our son. We are so proud of you."

And they were gone.

Anbari opened his eyes laying on the ground in front of Taiju. The creature lifted his head from the water. "Special dragons, Anthose and Archala, don't you agree?"

"My mother and father?"

"Yes, dear boy, your mother and father." He paused and then narrowed on the dragon who sat still bewildered before him. "It is time for you to go. You have the power to leave now; make it so."

"Taiju," Anbari returned. "I have one more question."

The creature stared at him. "What is it, my son?"

"Earlier you stated, 'they instructed me to return their powers to the two of you,' but I am just one. What did that mean?"

Taiju smiled. "Smart are you. Smarter than even your parents believed possible." He paused and dipped his head under the water briefly before moving slightly out of the pool. His voice was soft but direct. "There is prophecy in motion. They have put it in order. It is beyond anything you could even believe and unable to be said. But you will know it when it arrives. I have passed you powers. In time, you will learn how to harness it. You will find a way to store this power in a staff, and when the time is right and you have found the vessel to wield it, you will pass it on. You will pass it to the one creature who may bring the races together." He paused and his voice turned deep and slow. "But if this prophecy is prevented and you are unable to pass this staff, then all life as we know it will cease to exist."

"What staff?" Anbari asked. "What power?"

"You will know both answers when the time is right," Taiju answered.

"Who is the vessel to carry out this plan?"

Taiju laughed and coughed slightly as he did so, demonstrating that his health was not where it should be, but also knowing nothing would ever bring him to that final breath. "That, my son, is the right question."

***

"Anbari?" stated Hawthorne, pushing lightly on his side. "Anbari," she repeated again, causing the large dragon to open one eye and stare at her. "Thank God," she added. "I could not wake you."

He lifted his head to find he was still lying in the small cell-like room in the hallway. "Has something happened?"

She nodded. "The hallway has changed. There is a new passage, but we still can't get through."

He climbed to his feet, a strange sensation taking place within him. He felt a surge of energy at his fingertips. He was not sure what it meant, but he was sure it was related to his visit with Taiju, his parents, or his dream, or whatever it was. He brought his mind back to his companion. "Changed? How?"

"There is a new doorway. We can see it, but there is a force blocking our passage."

He smiled and began to walk the direction she pointed. He knew what he had to do, or at least what he needed to accomplish. How to do it was another thing, but he was very sure this new passage would not be a problem. "Come on. It is time to go."

He approached the new passage and spoke a few words, not sure where they had originated from. Instantly the force field blocking the doorway subsided and all the eyes of his companions turned toward him, but none bit through him like daggers as much as Fehr's.

"What in all of..." he sputtered. "I have been in this mine for years, no many, many years, and in one night you discover a way out."

The elf ignored the bandicoot's comment. "What about Taiju?" Ku asked. "We still have to find Taiju."

"No, we don't," Anbari replied. "I met him last night."

"You what?" exclaimed Ku.

Hawthorne had a much softer tone, "How is that possible? We were all together?"

"I don't know," Anbari replied. "It was like a dream, but it was real. I think Taiju was expecting me." Anbari had just passed through the doorway and instantly returned to full size. He was waiting for his friends to do the same. He peered his head back in. "Are you guys coming?"

Fehr smiled. "Right behind you, big gu..." He was cut off as he plastered his face against the still invisible but very hard surface. "What the he—"

"Just kidding, Fehr, you may cross now," replied the dragon laughing.

Fehr gingerly reached his paw out this time and pulled it back as if it had been severely shocked. "Just kidding," he stated toward those behind him. He leaped through without a care. "That was not funny," he stated to Anbari, the bandicoot still rubbing his head. "And trust when I say I will return the favor." He paused, took a few steps as the others fell in behind them leaving the cavern, and then added, "But tell me about this dream. It sounds like an excellent story I should tell my family."

Anbari smiled. "There is not much to tell about Taiju, but I did meet my mother and father also." He stopped and looked at their blank faces. "We have much we can discuss, but for now, let's get out of this swamp. We are headed to the canok homeland."

Ku stood strong in defiance. "No, we are not. We are going to head across the North Sea and find those who can help. There are said to be ones with incredible power. They guard the passage between life and the afterlife, and they will want to prevent an extension of death across the land. But I needed to speak to Taiju about the weapons. We needed his help."

"I already know that which we need to do. I can create the weapons needed."

"How?" asked Hawthorne. "I thought you said you were limited to how you helped those humans with their weapons?"

"I did, at the time, say that," he responded. "But I have been made to see things much clearer. What was lost in my head is now taking shape. The same way I passed through that barrier, I can create what you need."

Ku remained where he was and refused to step forward. "I cannot return to the canok homeland." He paused. "I left there under questionable circumstances."

Anbari turned to directly face the elf. "What do you mean, questionable circumstances?"

"I mean Hoangis has fooled the canok queen into believing I was part of the evil. Daphane banished me from their homeland."

"All the more reason we must return. We must clear your name and place the target for our direction upon Hoangis." Anbari thought a moment and remembered they did not know what his parents had told him. "The canoks are key to this. We need them if we are going to defeat this band of dragons. We need them to help take Draag."

"Take Draag," exclaimed Ku. "Are you a fool? You cannot take Draag. Slayne has mobilized all the dragons by now. You are two dragons. What do you think you can do?"

"Yes," said a voice from behind. "What do you think you can do, Anbari?"

All eyes turned to greet the grimacing stare of a large red dragon. "Draketon, thank our gods you are all right."

"Gods have nothing to do with it, Anbari. I heard you say you intend to take over Draag. You know I cannot let you do that."

"Draketon, what are you talking about? You can't have fallen under the misguided direction of Slayne and Bjork. They want to destroy our world."

"No, Anbari, they do not. Our world is of dragons. Our world is based in Draag. I saw what you did to the dwarves. I know who is really behind the movement to assert dragon rule over all life. How many races do you have to destroy before you stop?"

"No, Draketon. The last thing I wish to do is destroy Draag. I wish to protect it, from Bjork and his mad ways." The red dragon stared at him, but his belief was unchanged. Anbari continued, "What were you sent here to do, Draketon?"

He smiled. "I was sent here to kill you, but something tells me you already knew that."

Ku moved toward the trees to get out of the way, and as the elf stepped away, Hawthorne stepped in closer to her dragon counterpart. Anbari noticed both movements but did not acknowledge them. He held his stare on his counterpart. "You cannot destroy me, Draketon, and I do not wish to destroy you. Therefore, we are at an interesting stalemate."

Draketon nodded. "Then what would you have us do? You know I cannot return without something to prove my task has been completed."

"You will have to, my friend," Anbari replied.

"No, I do not." The red dragon sucked in deep and let out a wall of flame that scorched everything in its path. The width of the fire eclipsed both dragons before him and almost reached the outskirts of the marshy area Ku had moved to. The elf stepped back even further and then took a moment to look around. He knew what he had to do.

Hawthorne cringed as the wall of flame reached her but then she instantly relaxed. She could see nothing but red and blue flame. The heat was tremendous, but she did not move. The fire breath ended and Draketon stared upon what he had done.

"How?" he asked. "I enchanted the flame to penetrate magic. How could you have stopped it?"

"Because my magic is stronger than yours will ever be." Anbari opened his mouth and sent the same wall of flame toward the red dragon. The dragon screamed in pain as the fire burned against his scales and then was quickly extinguished. "Now leave, Draketon. Decide where you wish your loyalties to lie. I am a friend to all dragons—dragons that wish to live in harmony in our world with all creatures."

"How could you have so easily passed through my defense? It doesn't make sense." The red dragon, still in pain, stepped back from Anbari as he stepped closer.

"Leave Draketon and tell Bjork I am coming for him and Slayne."

Draketon turned and took to the sky. He did not look back nor slow his speed. He remembered not long ago when he and Anbari had sparred and the two were equally strong. That was no longer the case. Anbari had grown stronger, and his warning to Bjork was real. He thought about his direction. He didn't want to deliver the message. He didn't want to go to Bjork, but he knew he had to. If he were to run, he was certain he would be found.

"Okay," stated Fehr. "Enough is enough. Where did you learn all that cool stuff? You have to teach me. If you agree, I will only use it for good. Simply pass it to me, and I will show you. What other reason would I have to—"

Hawthorne cut him off with her wing. "Anbari, are you okay? That was amazing. Do you agree, Ku?" She paused and turned her head to where he had moved. "Ku?"

"He is gone, Hawthorne," Anbari stated. "He used the opportunity to run. I don't know why. It possibly had something to do with returning to the canoks. We must find their homeland."

"How are we going to do that?" asked Hawthorne. "Only Ku knows where it is."

Anbari began to shake his head when Fehr answered, "I know where it is?"

The silver dragon smiled. "How would you know where the canok homeland is?" he questioned, clearly not holding any level of truth in the rat's words.

"I followed other canoks there. I follow everyone. It's pretty simple, actually. All—"

"Can you take us there?" interrupted Anbari.

Fehr frowned at the interruption but only for a moment before he realized it was his turn to speak again. "Sure can, big guy. It's easy. It is not even a difficult walk." Fehr was becoming quite pleased with the discussion and his part in it.

"We don't need to walk," answered Anbari, starting to kneel down. "Hop on, Fehr. If you find this place, you deserve the ride."

"Sounds like a plan, big guy. Head northwest, toward Elvinott."

And they were off, with Hawthorne bringing up the rear.

Anbari turned his head back toward the rat. "Wait, you know where Elvinott is also?"

***

"What do you think that is?" asked Tyne.

"I would call it a village, but just barely," replied Stoven. "But I sense a presence there. Someone we know."

"Who?" asked Tyne, tilting his head lower as if concentrating harder on the mass of creatures beyond the clearing in front of them. "I don't sense—"

"Maneths," interrupted Stoven. "Two of them." He stopped and pointed with his front leg. "There they are. I recognize one of them. It is Geoff."

"What do you think they are doing there?" asked his counterpart. "Do you think they are part of this?"

"It looks like they are showing them how to build better structures," replied Stoven staring across the field. "I think we should ask."

"You think we should just walk in and say hello to these creatures?"

Stoven smiled and took a step out of the tree line. "Yes, yes, I do."

As he exited the safety of the forest, one of the human guards saw the movement and shouted, "Time to hunt, boys! Come on and grab your arrows."

Geoff and Selbee turned their heads to see the commotion and followed their gaze. "No!" Geoff shouted. "These are friends."

Octavius heard his words and translated them to the others, but several had already bolted from the village into the glade with their weapons drawn. Selbee turned to Geoff. "Should we pursue?"

"Do you think the humans will be any issue for the canoks?" Geoff asked.

Selbee did not reply and just smiled. After a moment, he added, "I do think I would like to watch."

"Me too," Geoff replied. "Let's go."

They dropped their tools and ran toward the village edge. By the time they arrived, it was already over. The four humans were on the ground with their weapons broken and tossed aside. The two canoks were pacing back and forth in front of them explaining how things would go. The largest of the humans and the one who had first called to the others slowly stood and pointed toward the city.

Selbee smiled. "I guess the humans will be leading the canoks into the city."

"I guess so," Geoff answered. "We should meet them at the gate. I am sure they wonder what we are doing here."

Moments later, Stoven and Tyne reached the outskirts and were met not only by the maneth, but also several humans, including their leader, Octavius. "Greetings," stated the human king. "Our new friends, Geoff and Selbee, have informed us you are friends. Is this correct?"

The two red-coated canoks looked toward the two maneths and then back to Octavius. Stoven replied telepathically, *"We indeed are friends to all creatures on Troyf who are pure of heart. Is that you?"* The message was silent but was heard by all around in whatever their native language was. An amazing quality all canoks had. They could make those nearby hear or not hear any message in whatever language they chose without ever saying a word.

The king was taken by this method of conversation but with all the magical things happening, he accepted it without issue. In perfect human tongue, he answered, "We are friends to all on Troyf. We seek knowledge and guidance, which clearly with your advanced speech, you possess."

To both Geoff and Selbee's surprise, they understood the human speech. It was as if having the canoks connect to them telepathically at the same time as the maneth, brought that level of knowledge to them.

The king turned and glanced quickly to Geoff who took the lead in the conversation. "Stoven and Tyne, it is good to see you again, though we are surprised, equally as surprised as I am sure you are to see us."

"Indeed," replied Tyne. "Just what is the reason for your presence here?"

"We are seeking the Elven king as well as your queen. King McCard sent us to follow up on the only direction we knew. And you can see what we found." He motioned to the makeshift village behind him. "Can I ask what your reason for travel is?"

Geoff had motioned toward the city which included him turning and beginning to walk as he spoke. Stoven fell in beside him. "We seek only to find our queen. If we are able to help her, then we will, but above all, we want to find her."

Geoff understood and was about to speak when he saw the two canoks begin to act strangely. They looked at each other and Tyne's knees buckled. Stoven coughed and then roared as if a knife had been jammed into his side. Both canoks found themselves on the ground almost in full convulsions. Their bodies lunged side-to-side on the ground even rolling into each other several times.

"What is happening?" asked Selbee.

"I don't know," shouted Geoff, bending down to try to support the throbbing body of Stoven. When he touched the canok, it again roared and even snapped its teeth at the maneth. Dust was being kicked up at a violent rate. Geoff stood and moved away from the two canoks as it seemed almost dangerous to be next to them. Then, all motion stopped. The dust finally cleared and all those in the area stared at the two in disbelief.

"What in all the gods just happened?" asked Geoff.

Stoven lifted his head slowly and stared around, appearing as if he did not know where he was. "What happened?" he asked, staring at the maneth. "We were walking and talking and then everything just went blank."

Geoff did not answer at first. He stepped closer to the two. "Do you see yourself or your friend? That is what happened."

Stoven looked down to his legs and almost fell over. He then turned his eyes on his counterpart and stared in disbelief. Stoven was white as new fallen snow. Even his tongue, paws, and eyes were solid white. When he looked toward his friend, he saw the same thing, only his fur, tongue, eyes, and paws were completely black.

Tyne stirred slightly and then he too lifted his head, his teeth gritted tightly with drool falling to each side. His voice was raspy, almost devoid of life. "Finally, I see things clearly," he scowled, staring up and down his black fur. When the two canoks' eyes met, instantly they were in the air with a leap toward each other. The fight was intense as each abandoned any magic and used their primitive method of fighting against the other. Both canoks bled profusely and all those around had no idea what to do. Geoff tried to intervene and was caught between the two taking deep bites from both. Suddenly, Stoven was thrown clear for a moment and before Tyne could attack his fallen prey, Selbee laced his club across the black canok's face. Tyne was thrown several steps to the side, rolling and landing with a spin back on his feet. He stared at the group before him, turned, and darted back across the clearing away from the city.

"Do we follow?" asked Selbee, still with club drawn.

"No," replied Geoff, still pressing the inside of his arm against his side to slow the blue blood from flowing to the ground. "We don't know what happened, but there is someone here who can tell us."

All eyes fell to Stoven who still rested, panting on the ground. The canok did not stand. His front leg appeared severely injured, the fur that had been crisp and white previously now matted with wet, white and black blood. He lifted his head to the group. "I have no idea. I have never felt pain like I felt at that moment. It was as if my insides were set on fire and burned away and I was left with this metamorphosized body."

Geoff knelt down next to the canok. "Why did you attack Tyne?"

The minute our eyes met, I felt pure evil. It was as if I received everything that was good with canoks, and he received everything that was evil. At that moment, he only had one purpose: to kill."

"But what caused it?" asked Selbee.

Stoven shook his head. "I must assume this ties back to our queen. Her kidnapping changed the future of the canoks forever."

Octavius, who had been silent since this transformation and ensuing battle, stepped closer to Geoff and the canok. "I don't understand any of this, nor do I understand how I now know all of your words. I can understand things like never before, but what just took place, I can offer no support. I am not sure you should be in our city, but we have nobody else."

Stoven stepped closer to the human. "I am Stoven, friend to all on Troyf, and I have impressed all languages within you and those around. You will be able to communicate with all of us. As for allowing me in your village, I can assure you that you have nothing to fear. Now more than ever, I have but one goal—to find our queen and save our world. I must assume this division has occurred among all the canoks. My home is most likely in disarray. Only my queen can bring us back together."

Octavius understood the words, but still was hesitant. Geoff nodded to the canok and turned to the human leader. "I will vouch for Stoven. He was with all races for the feast that I told you about. He will be an ally to us all. Let's go to the city center and talk. We have to decide where our next steps will take us. I can tell you, I believe we must go to Draag."

Octavius looked to each of them and then smiled. "We have nothing to lose. You may all join us. Please come to our small city and let's talk. I don't know of this Draag, but we will join you if you feel it will save our world."

The group turned and slowly made their way back to the city. The commotion as they passed was great as all came out to look upon the new visitors, but an ominous feeling began to seduce those around. A fear of the future was written across every face.

***

"I can't believe we have traveled through the entire forest and run into only two bands of trolls," stated Gunthen.

"I can't believe you beheaded the last band with one swing of that club. How hard do you swing that thing?" Hoangis was shaking his head in disbelief as he spoke.

"Evidently hard enough to separate four heads in one swing, but who is counting?"

The elf acknowledged the comment, but truth be told, he held such a high value of life that even the death of trolls struck him hard. He had aided their passage, as all elves would, but he also knew that when they stumbled on the trolls, had Gunthen not acted so quickly, it could very easily have been one of his party lying dead. He recognized the state they were in. Evil had placed its footprint on their world, and they needed to do whatever they could to stop it.

Gunthen raised his hand. "I think we are here."

He pointed ahead and the other two moved in closer. Down a gradual hill the forest opened up into a small clearing. Just beyond that clearing was a cave. In front of that cave stood eight large dragons. "Well, what in all our gods' names are we supposed to do now?"

"We have traveled until our…" Tashro stopped in mid-sentence causing the others to look down to him.

"Tashro, are you all right?" asked Hoangis.

The canok's eyes rolled back into his head and his front legs buckled underneath him. He fell forward, face-planting on the ground. The canok rolled over and let out a yelp that instantly drew both Hoangis and Gunthen's attention back to the dragons. Fortunately, they were too far to hear. Hoangis moved closer to Tashro and placed his hand on his side trying to comfort or at least stabilize him. The canok throbbed in pain and then convulsed in rapid movements on the ground. Moments later, it happened, and everything stopped.

The canok lifted his head. "What happened?" he asked.

The two just stared at him, their eyes glossed over.

Tashro pushed himself up and returned the stare. "What?" He paused. "What just happened and why are you looking at me like that?"

Hoangis approached the canok and softly touched his fur. "You have been changed. As I touch you, I feel tragedy has engulfed the canoks. Something terrible has happened."

Tashro looked down to his leg and twisted his head to his back. His deep red coat had been replaced with a bright white fur across his entire body. The canok felt a weakness in his knees and fell backward. Neither Gunthen or Hoangis was in a position to catch him, and the canok found himself resting on the ground. "I feel something grave has happened. I feel the canok homeland is lost. The canoks are lost. We are divided. I hear screams of pain. I feel fear. A great tragedy has occurred."

The three remained in silence for some time. They didn't move and rarely acknowledged the dragons below them. The need to speak was replaced with a fear of the unknown. If not for the noise to the south, they may have remained as such the rest of the day.

"What was that?" asked Hoangis.

"I feel nothing," added the canok, "though I don't trust my senses right now."

"It sounded like someone or something is headed this way."

"Should we flee or face them?" asked the elf.

Gunthen motioned to the hill toward the cavern entrance. "Well, to flee sends us into the dragons. Therefore, I suggest we face whoever approaches."

Hoangis nodded. "Good call. I will head around the back. I can move without being heard. We will pin whoever it is between us, but I think we need to keep them alive. We need to learn how to get into these caverns. Whoever this is running freely through the Draag Forest should absolutely know every option to enter the caverns."

Gunthen nodded in agreement and the elf vanished.

Tashro leaped to his feet. "I will move into the trees. Should you be surrounded, I can provide an unexpected support."

"Agreed," replied the maneth. Gunthen drew his club and stared toward the tree line in the direction of the noise.

The sounds of movement continued, and they were growing louder. The maneth smiled to himself because he was certain it was not an elf or a maneth. It would have to be something with no intelligence to move through the forest as such. He assumed it was simply another group of trolls. He only hoped he would be able to handle them as easily as he had the last group. He could tell they were within sight if the tree cover was not so thick. The sounds of their movement on the forest floor was too great. He lifted his club higher and moved to stand against a large bush at ground level to prevent his early detection, when the group of trolls entered the small glade. His muscles tightened on the club, his grip firm and at the ready.

"Stop kicking me, you stupid dwarf," stated Bretton. "I don't care if I lost the bet; enough is enough."

Jermys smiled. "I will continue to kick you up until we..."

Gunthen grabbed the dwarf from behind placing his large paw across his mouth. Bretton immediately drew his hatchet and prepared to throw before stopping at the recognition of his maneth friend. "Gunthen," stated the small dwarf twin. "I can't believe we found you."

"I can't believe you are still alive making all that noise."

After Gunthen released the dwarf, Jermys and Bretton smiled broadly. "What are you doing here? You are lucky we did not kill you upon entering. What could one maneth do against both of us?"

"Well," stated Hoangis from behind, arrow knocked in his bow, "I am pretty sure you would not have done much to harm my friend here."

Tashro stepped out. "I concur with the elf."

Both dwarves swung their heads toward each of the new visitors. "Damn, Jermys, I told you we needed to bring more dwarves."

The dwarf twin nodded. "The good news is, we found who we were looking for." Their eyes locked at the same time on Tashro. Jermys continued, still holding his hatchet at the ready. "Wait, what happened to you? You are all white?"

The canok nodded. "It is a long story."

"And one for a later time," interrupted Gunthen. "What are you both doing here? You were supposed to return to Feldschlosschen and inform Krystof of our plans."

"We did," answered Jermys. "And when he learned that our king was on this mission alone, he immediately sent us to Gnausanne to meet with you. It did not take us long to learn that we missed you as the commotion left behind in the gnome city clearly spoke of your presence. We spent the night there, downed a few ales, and then headed this direction." His comments paused, he looked around, and then turned back to the maneth. "Where is our king, and what happened to Tashro?"

Instantly the group's elation at having new visitors ended and the pain of the current environment was thrust back upon them. Gunthen nodded for all to take a seat. He motioned to the dragons at the cavern entrance, so all knew to remain quiet. He then ran through all that had happened. Both dwarves' heads fell upon learning of their king's death. However, they seemed equally as concerned on the change in Tashro.

Jermys spoke softly, ensuring his voice would not alert the dragons below. "An attack on the canoks as such must be from an immense magical source. Who or what could be behind it?"

"It has to be the same evil growing across the land, and I still believe the source to be right below us, here in Draag." Gunthen pointed to the dragons at the cavern entrance below. "But I have no idea how to get there."

"Do you have any ideas?" Jermys asked Tashro. "I mean, the attack was on you."

The canok pressed his lips together tight before speaking. Then, telepathically to prevent all possible sound, he spoke to the group. *"The attack was not upon me personally. I feel the pain of all canoks. Our world has been divided."*

"What do you mean, divided?" asked Hoangis.

"I feel that some of the canoks have chosen, or more aptly been selected, along a different path than that of our heritage. I feel some canoks are now distanced and lost. I feel they will no longer follow the canok way."

"What do you mean?" asked Hoangis. "They will join with the dragons?"

Tashro did not speak but just shook his head affirmatively.

Silence again engulfed the small group for what seemed like a very long time. Gunthen spoke, "Jermys and Bretton, is there any chance you know the way into Draag Caverns? We need to determine what in all of Troyf is going on here and the only way we believe we can do that is to get inside."

Bretton smiled. "I have been here before."

All eyes swung to the twin dwarf, but none struck as harshly as his brother's. Jermys frowned. "When have you been here? You have never traveled as such without me, and I have never been here."

"I have, brother. Lendzion"—Hoangis cringed at the dwarf using the name of someone passed but did not speak to it— "and I both came here together. I was assigned with his guard and you remained in Feldschlosschen."

"I remember, but you did not go to Draag, you went to…" He paused as he suddenly understood. "That is why your trip took so much longer than it should have. We even sent out search parties."

"We could not let everyone know. It was too dangerous, and if it ended up not working, then the rest of Feldschlosschen would be spared."

"What not working?" asked Hoangis.

"The dwarves were fearful of the unknown; in this case, we were fearful of the dragons. Our king believed he could provide a deal with the dragons to protect our mines. When we left, he told me he had been successful."

Hoangis stared questioningly at the dwarf. "What deal? He never mentioned a deal to us."

Bretton lowered his head. "He would not say, but he was sure of its success."

"What dragon did he meet with?" Gunthen broke in, interrupting the conversation between Bretton and Hoangis.

"I don't know that either," answered Bretton. "I wasn't allowed in the large chamber where they spoke. I did see there were at least two dragons, and one was completely black."

"Slayne," stated Tashro.

The others turned to him. "How do you know a black dragon?" Hoangis now asked the canok. The tone he used was verging on distrust as each word said by his companions suggested they had more knowledge than they shared.

The canok shook his head. "I don't know of the dragon, or by that I mean I don't know the dragon personally. I simply know that my queen spoke to the very same black dragon. However, she did not return feeling that a deal was made. She felt concerned this dragon would be harmful to all life on Troyf. She didn't feel it would immediately touch the canok homeland but did believe it would eventually reach us as such."

"It appears it reached out and touched the canok homeland before she expected," Gunthen stated.

Tashro nodded at the truth behind the statement but did not like hearing it so directly. Hoangis moved closer to the group to ensure he could keep his voice low but still be heard. "So, the king of the dwarves had a separate deal with the dragons which he did not speak of to us. The queen of the canoks tried to reach a deal and was unsuccessful. The queen was taken, most likely to reconvince her for the deal, and the king pushed himself into our party. Should we assume now that his intentions were not just?"

Both Jermys and Bretton tightened their stance demonstrating immediate defiance to the statement. "I trust you are not implying our king was not just in his actions. I can say for certain that any decision he made would have been for the good of the world, not just the dwarves."

"But can you?" asked Hoangis.

"Can I what?" the dwarf returned.

"Can you actually say for certain?"

Nothing more was said on the subject but both Gunthen and Tashro could see the anger brewing in the twins' eyes. Gunthen used the opportunity to ask the critical question of the time. "We need a safe path into Draag. We cannot face the dragons directly because, worst case, we would lose, and best case, they would alert the other dragons, and"—he paused and smiled slightly as he repeated— "we would lose." He let the statement sit for a moment and then continued with the original subject. "So Bretton, you said you have been here before. Can you get us in?"

The dwarf was still clearly upset about the conversation involving their king's intentions, but the question snapped him from his momentary state of mind. "There is an entrance on the far side. With rope or vines, we can lower ourselves in. It is dangerous and if there is anyone in the area of the cavern when we enter, we will have no way to defend ourselves."

"What, like a hole?" asked Gunthen.

"No, more like a window to the sky. It is not guarded, but with the right plan, it would not be hard to enter."

"Can you lead us there?" the maneth asked.

"Can you trust me to lead you there?" the dwarf responded, the sarcasm clear in his voice and directed toward the elf king.

"Can we?" Hoangis asked, not a touch of sarcasm in his tone.

The dwarf did not answer and turned away in disgust. Gunthen swung his head to the elf. "Yes," the maneth stated clearly. "I am sure we can trust you completely." He glared at the elf and then back to the dwarves. "How far is it and when can we leave?"

"Half a day," he said without delay. "And we can leave when you are ready."

That was all the action needed to get the group to gather their belongings and head out. Bretton and Jermys took the lead, though it was Bretton who was clearly in charge of their direction. The two brothers remained close. The tension from the exchange was still present, but with the plan in place and the path taking them around the dragons, the mood gradually improved. But even with the small lift, no words were said between any of them.

***

"The canok homeland is straight ahead of us? Is that still where you want us to go, Fire-breathing Beast Master?" Fehr asked. The bandicoot, Hawthorne, and Anbari rested in a clearing from the hard flight they had been pushing through toward the canok homeland.

"What did you call me?" asked Anbari.

Fehr smiled. "Well, I don't really like your name. It doesn't instill fear in anyone. But if we called you Fire-Breathing Beast Master…now that means business."

"No, you will still call me Anbari. I would hate to leave you behind, bound to a tree in goblin-infested forests."

The rat grimaced. "You wouldn't do that Fire-Brea—" He stopped in mid-sentence when Anbari turned and glared his direction. "Okay, okay. How about if I call you FiBBaM instead, and only you and I know what it means?"

Anbari looked at him strangely. The rat saw the gaze. "FiBBaM. You know, Fire-Breathing Beast Master, but I added the *i* and the *a*."

Hawthorne smiled broadly. "Yes, Anbari, FiBBaM sounds like a great name."

"If I hear either of you call me that even one time, it will not go well for you."

There was no sarcasm in his tone this time. In fact, he was cold and dark, as if he could absolutely hold true to his statement should someone actually say something even in jest. Both his friends silenced their comments without question, but still smiled ever so slightly toward each other.

Fehr quietly asked, "So, where to now?" He gulped and even more softly stated, "Anbari. Do you want to continue to the canok homeland? You know, they may not allow you to enter."

The dragon looked toward both of them, and he saw they were still fighting to keep their smiles back. Ignoring their state, he asked, "What do you mean, not allow us to enter?"

Fehr immediately forgot about the name-calling and went straight to his story. "Well, when I watched others pass, they went between these large stones. Some passed through and vanished, and others just remained in the field. It was like a doorway that only let certain creatures in."

Anbari thought about this and considered why they even needed to go to the canoks. Maybe they simply should continue on the path they had described before Hoangis left. He shook his head. "I think we should skip the canok homeland. We may not even be able to enter and even if we are allowed in, they may not share the information we need. Therefore, we need to find the humans we passed and take the weapons back. Then we are going to take those weapons and head across the North Sea. I wish to find the guardians of the afterlife. I need their help."

The two looked at each other questioningly. Hawthorne answered, "The Realm of Darkness?" she asked. "May we inquire as to where this idea came from, and what should we do about Ku?"

Anbari lowered his head and spoke more softly, "It simply came to my mind. Whether placed there by Taiju or my parents or simply part of a dream, I can't answer, but I do know it is how it should be. Ku wants the weapons. The Realm of Darkness is where he wished to take them. I want to know why. And for that matter, Ku will most likely be trying to get there on his own. We need to get back together with him. I believe he fled in fear, not for what we were fighting for."

"But how will he be able to get there on his own? He can't get across the sea." Hawthorne was joining Anbari in leaning lower and speaking softer, as if they were protecting their plans from any others in the area, though nobody was around.

"Ku ran for a reason. I sensed something in him, but I can't place it. If we can find him and develop these weapons to help defend the dragons, then we can learn all the truths we need to know." Anbari turned to the rat. "Fehr, you may join us or go, it is your decision, but we leave at once."

"Oh, there is no chance I am missing this adventure. The Realm of Darkness. I don't even know what that is, but I can guarantee you, I am all in." He smiled and grabbed his pack without delay. "Do you want me to lead?"

Anbari stretched his wings. "Well, since you just said you did not know what it was, I think I will simply take the lead."

Fehr ran over to leap on his back and Anbari slapped him in the air with his wing. "You will ride with Hawthorne."

The rat coughed as he struck the ground sideways and rolled. "Yeah, sure, that is who I wanted to ride with anyway," he stated, though Anbari was already in the air.

Hawthorne walked over. "Want a lift, little guy?"

"I sure do," he replied smiling.

"Maybe as you ride, I can help you learn all the languages I know."

"How can you do that?" Fehr asked.

"Just place your paws on my neck and concentrate. I think I can allow you to grab it."

"Wow!" he stated slowly. "That would be incredible. I already speak great, but if I could learn more, the opportunities are endless."

"And the stories," she replied. "Imagine being able to tell a story to every creature on Troyf in their native language."

The rat almost fell off her back in flight just thinking about it.

***

Werner struck the ground in pain, as did Dantowin and two other canoks still waiting in their homeland for word from Tyne and Stoven. The young female, sister to the queen, writhed in pain. *"What is happening?"* she asked telepathically, though she was not sure anyone could receive her question.

Werner replied, but his voice was deeper and raspier. "I don't know," he replied, "but I feel such great pain within me, and also great power. Power like I have never felt before."

The canoks continued to roll on the ground and then everything became very still. They stood up and each of them stared at those around in complete confusion. Dantowin spoke to Werner and the canok next to him. "Your fur has changed. It is black."

"As has yours," returned Werner's still raspy voice. "But yours is white, along with Bascem's."

Dantowin swung her eyes to the canok next to her and then lowered her head to look at her legs. Werner was correct, they were both completely white, including their fur, paws, legs, and even their eyes and tongues. "What do we do?" asked the much smaller canok, her voice more timid than previously, as the fear of the unknown was written clearly across her face. She felt different emotions from those around her—graphic and aggressive tendencies as anger waiting to burst through.

Without even a pause, Werner replied, "I have never felt power such as this. We use it."

The black canok next to him nodded in agreement. "We are strong now. Strong with a different magic. I too can feel it. We use it for whatever we want."

Werner nodded, with drool actually dripping from his mouth. "Do you feel it, Dantowin? Do you feel the power?"

"Power?" she replied questionably. "I don't feel any..."

A bolt shot from Werner's eyes and knocked the smaller female back against the wall of the cave. "Then get out of our way. The canok are strong again, and we are going to show it to everyone. No creature will defend against us."

"What about the dragons? You can feel as I do. Dragons are here. Do you intend to fight dragons?" She was still carrying a tone of confusion and fear wrapped into one.

"I don't know what I intend to do," responded Werner's still raspy voice. "But I can feel them calling to me. Together we could become the two strongest races on all of Troyf. Perhaps the real enemy is before us right here."

Both Dantowin and Bascem stared hard at their longtime friend. "What are you saying?" asked Bascem.

"I am telling you to step aside, as my friend and I are leaving." He said a telepathic message to all canoks. *"Any that feel as we do, come with us and let's use this newfound power. Let's use it as it was always intended."* He turned back to Dantowin. "And it would not do well for you to try to stop us."

"We need to fix this," replied Dantowin. "We need to find my sister and fix this tragedy."

Werner smiled. "This is not a tragedy. I feel things I have never felt before. I will never give this back."

With that, the two black canoks pushed by the whites and found a group of other canoks outside their cave. "Come with me," shouted Werner. "For we have work to do."

Without hesitation, the other black canoks fell in behind and they were through the portal and gone.

Chapter Twelve

"What is our next move?" asked Octavius. He sat at a makeshift table set up in what could be called "city center" but was really just a large tent.

Geoff nodded. "I said it earlier. I believe we need to go to Draag. You have seen dragons. We know the evil is growing by what happened to the canoks. We have to take our best team and meet the others at Draag. They are probably in the forests now unless they met with issues." He turned and directed his next comment toward the canok. "Stoven, do you still feel evil is behind your change?"

The canok nodded. "Powerful evil, and it has affected my home. Tragedy has indeed struck."

Octavius stood and paced. "I don't know what to think, but more than that, I don't know what support my people can be."

Geoff stood and walked over to intercept him. "You have arms, don't you? You have shields and swords. We need your people to stand beside us. We need to go to Draag Caverns and destroy whatever source is giving them power. I know it is there. The dragons have risen from the caverns. They have tapped some power and are using it to spread that evil across the land."

There was a long silence that gripped the room. Although no question had been asked, those around were waiting for the human leader to answer. Octavius stared directly into the maneth's eyes. "I will have my people go with you. We are not strong, and we don't have many weapons, but we will bring our arms."

Geoff smiled as did the others. He turned back to the table. "Now, let's draw up…"

His voice was cut off from screams outside the tent. "*Dragons!*"

The word was said in the Dragon tongue. Although most did not speak it, they all knew that one word clearly, and the panic caused upon its issue created a stir in the area like none experienced before. The humans ran every direction trying to avoid the wall of fire they knew was about to strike. The two dragons drew near just as Geoff, Selbee, Stoven, and Octavius made their way outside.

"They are the same two I met before," stated Octavius.

"Then maybe they don't mean to attack," stated Selbee. "But I don't know if we want to wait to find out."

Geoff and Selbee both removed their maneth clubs, though neither would do much against a wall of fire. The two dragons were within range of covering the area with their wrath but still, nothing came. They drew very close, angled their wings, and landed directly in front of Geoff and his team.

Anbari's voice was deep and unrelenting. "I provided these humans weapons which were before their time. I need those weapons back."

Geoff stepped forward. "Who are you, dragon, and why do you worry about such a thing?"

Anbari lifted his head and shot a sheet of fire into the sky heating up the entire area and causing all around the village to continue to run for cover. All except the four standing strong before them. "Return the weapons to me, Geoff, or I will destroy this village and take them."

Geoff was completely taken by the use of his name. His mind retraced everything from his past and never could he place where this dragon could have learned his name. He was about to speak again but was cut off.

"I can feel everything about you, Geoff," interrupted Anbari. "I have powers you cannot even imagine. Now let's waste no more time with this. Where are my weapons?"

Hawthorne and Fehr did not speak. In fact, Fehr was almost completely unnoticed hidden on Hawthorne's back. Although Hawthorne didn't agree with the direction her counterpart had taken, feeling they would have been just as successful to come in and politely ask for the weapons, for whatever reason, Anbari thought differently and she was in no position to argue against it.

Geoff turned to the human leader. "Do you have the weapons the dragon speaks of?"

"We do," Octavius answered.

"Why don't you go fetch them and the dragon and I will talk a bit more?"

The human heard the direction and left without comment, dropping his sword directly at the dragon's feet as he left.

"You are making a wise choice, Geoff," Anbari answered.

"You know my name, but I do not know yours. What is your name?" Geoff asked.

"I am Anbari, and this is Hawthorne. That is all you need to know."

Geoff ignored the comment that was stated to simply shut down the conversation. "Anbari, I am confused. We are confident there are dragons behind much of the evil taking over the land. The canok with me is a perfect example. Their queen was kidnapped by one of yours and then their nation divided by some evil. Therefore, I need to know much more than you are stating; but for starters, are you part of this evil? Because if you are, I am wondering why you simply did not destroy this small village and take that which you want?"

This froze the large dragon. His eyes narrowed on Stoven, who returned the stare without flinching. Anbari stepped closer. "Where is Daphane?"

Geoff had done all the talking but this question was definitely directed to the white canok. "We do not know. Several moons ago a black dragon came into the maneth camp and took her. It was only this day when the transformation of my race occurred. I believe my entire homeland has been divided. Some of us are white, and some are black. Those that turned dark seem to have different emotions driving their actions to hatred and rule, but I cannot be sure. It is just what I have felt."

Anbari turned back to Hawthorne with fear growing across his face, and then back to Stoven. "I have recently learned to trust feelings from within more than what my own eyes tell me. Stoven, I feel your questions within you regarding my presence. Push that aside for now and let me know one thing and one thing only: Do you believe those that turned dark have a new level of power and their intent is to use that power against other races on Troyf?"

The question was odd to Geoff but maybe it was something Stoven carried within him that the dragon had sensed. Without hesitation, Stoven answered, "I do. I felt it in my counterpart Tyne before he fled. There is a force working beneath them. I believe some will be able to fight against it, but most will be seduced by the lure of power, a drive never before present in a canok."

There was silence as Anbari leaned back and took in all that was said. Geoff used the opportunity. "You did not answer my previous question. Are you part of this evil?"

Anbari's voice softened. "No, son, I am not."

Geoff immediately felt a calmness come over him. "Then you need to join us in our quest for Draag. I believe we need to destroy the caverns to destroy the dragons. There is something there giving them power."

Anbari lifted his head in the air and thought for a moment. He could see the determination in the maneth's eyes. "How do you know this? How do you know there is something in Draag that the dragons are using for power?"

Geoff shook his head. "The truth is, I don't. I simply believe that if we destroy the dragons' homeland, the same way something penetrated the canoks' homeland, then the dragons will be vulnerable, just like the canoks now."

Anbari smiled. "Your insight serves you well, Geoff. You will be a great leader in this world someday. I can feel it."

The large maneth did not know what to do with that comment, so he nodded but didn't speak. Anbari continued, "There are two things which you must do at Draag."

This was not at all what Geoff expected to hear. He expected to hear that he was wrong. That going to Draag was a simple death sentence as the area could not be penetrated. Instead, not only was he to lead a team there, he had two areas to target. "Then I am right. Their power is drawn from there?"

Anbari shook his head providing the message for Geoff to simply remain quiet. All would be told in time. "The main dragons behind this evil no longer require any power from Draag. However, many others do. You must do two things. Find Sabast. He is a dragon I am certain will help you. He, like me, does not require Draag to wield power. However, unlike me, he does not wish to be involved. He will accept whatever fate is passed his way. You must get him involved when you are there."

Geoff nodded understanding. "And the second thing?"

THE DRAGON OPPRESSION

"You cannot destroy Draag. Hidden deep within its caverns are the eggs of the next generation. For us to win any war against the dragons, we need the support of the young. If they hatch and turn to the side of evil, nobody will be able to stop them."

The maneth still held his club and pointed it toward the dragon. "Why would I not just destroy the eggs and thus end the risk?"

"Because I will not let you do that." He paused and looked toward Hawthorne. "To do so would end the race of dragons. We must turn the young away from the evil."

"How are we going to turn the dragon young to not follow their own kind?"

"We must find a creature that will unite all races. They must build the trust of the dragon young as well as the trust of the canok, the maneth, the elves, dwarves, and humans. One powerful soul to bring them all into balance."

Geoff understood the reference but held no belief this could occur. "You speak of things well beyond our reach. There is nobody to stand up to the dragons. Not even the two of you."

Anbari smiled. "You are correct, there is no one person today that can do that, but didn't you say you plan to lead your party to Draag? By doing that, you *are* standing up to the dragon evil. We need all races to join that effort and find a way to keep that evil at bay until the young are born. To do that, you must seek out Sabast. You must find the Revel Rock deep within Draag Caverns and destroy it. If you can do that, we will have two hundred years to find a way to bring the dragon young back in line with all of Troyf and end the path of Slayne and Bjork in one final sweep."

Geoff looked at him strangely. "Revel Rock? Slayne and Bjork. What are you talking about?" Hawthorne ignored Geoff's question and spoke directly to Anbari, her tone very clearly concerned. "No, Anbari! If they destroy the stone, then all live dragons will lose their powers, you included."

The silver dragon nodded. "No, the dragons who have found that power through the source will indeed be set back, but I will not, nor will you, or Slayne, or Bjork." He paused and added, "And probably many I don't even feel at this time. Our power comes from around us. It builds within us, present from birth, not gained through an attachment." He turned back to Geoff.

"Destroy the rock, Geoff. Failure to do so will end your world as you know it."

Geoff stared at Hawthorne and then back to Anbari. "So you want me to lead a team to Draag, enter the dragon-infested caverns, locate a friendly dragon who may or may not help us, and then destroy a stone that carries so much energy within it, that all dragons are able to draw power from it?"

Anbari nodded. "A bit oversimplified, but essentially accurate."

"Just how in the he—"

Octavius interrupted Geoff's comment and returned, dumping three other weapons at the dragon's feet. "A hatchet, a bow, and a hammer all rested with the sword." He took a breath and then added, "They were our best weapons, but we believe we have discovered a way to build more. Several of my people have already begun fashioning them. We will have many prepared for when we depart. Take these back and do with them what you wish."

Anbari lowered his head in front of the human who did not cower but stood strong before the large dragon. "I sense you wish to have power. You wish for more weapons and magical powers at your fingertips. You must lose that desire, for it will be carried in your offspring."

Octavius was still breathing deeply. "I do wish for power, but only to lift my village to where it may defend itself against the likes of all enemies. If dragons are taking over this land, then I wish to be stronger than a dragon. I wish to be lord over a dragon, and if I can instill that desire in my son, then I will do just that."

None in the area liked the words spoken. They were very distant from how they had been previously. Something about the presence of Anbari in his village was causing this defiance. Geoff recognized Anbari was not their enemy. What was the human seeing, or feeling? What was driving Octavius's position and tone? Geoff knew he would have to keep a close eye on the human, and his trust had just taken a large step backward.

Anbari stated a few words and the weapons disappeared from the ground and appeared on his back in a wrap. The dragon turned to Hawthorne. "Let's go, we have a long flight ahead of us across the sea." He turned back toward Geoff. "The Revel Rock. Find it and destroy it. Sabast can show you the way."

The two dragons lifted off and within moments were out of sight.

"Do you believe that dragon?" asked Octavius rhetorically. "Taking our weapons and going on about some rock. He was using us."

Geoff turned to face the human. "Yes, I do believe him, and my trust with you is lessened."

"What does that mean?" replied Octavius, the tone of his voice depicting a rising level of anger.

"It means that if a dragon is here, speaking to us, not covering us in a sheet of flame, then they do not intend to destroy us. If they do not destroy us, then you listen to what they tell you and you act on it. There may only be two dragons on all of Troyf that currently think that way. Those dragons do not wish to rule, but in your conversation, you stated you did, and that is why I now question your direction."

"You misunderstood my comments. I simply want all to be equal. No creature should have the power to wipe out another creature."

Geoff nodded but ended the conversation when more yells were sounded from the camp exterior. "More creatures flying. It looks like two together," hollered a human voice.

All heads in their group turned to the direction of the voice. "No!" shouted Geoff upon seeing them. "They are friends."

The two maneths ran toward the approaching pair with Octavius and Stoven in tow. When they reached the human, Geoff grabbed his arm and pulled down his makeshift bow to prevent the guard from firing. "They are with us, friend," Geoff said.

Octavius and Stoven arrived shortly thereafter but Selbee and Geoff had already stepped out to greet their visitors. Selbee spoke first, "Madeiris, so good to see you. And Tantis, the same. I can't believe you carried your prince all the way from Elvinott. I pray all is well with your village."

"It is," replied Madeiris, locking wrists with Geoff as they met. They were both large and muscular and the site when they gripped hands was truly powerful. "Elvinott is well protected but we feared that sitting and not helping was not what our land needed. Tantis and I decided to fly the last known direction of the Queen of the Canoks and determine if we could help. I am pleased and surprised to see this group here, and I am not even sure where here is…"—he paused and turned to Octavius— "or who created it."

Geoff broke hands with the elf, had the same exchange with Tantis, and then stepped back opening his arm to the human leader, still speaking in the ancient dragon language they all could understand. "This is Octavius. He is the current leader of the humans who are building a city right here on the water. They have much work to do but still agreed to help us on our trek to Draag."

The elf prince nodded. "Very good to meet you, Octavius. I am Prince Madeiris of Elvinott and with me is the strongest flyer of all the elves, Tantisolandus Arnolin." He turned hard back to Geoff. "But what do you mean, trek to Draag?"

Tantis reached out his hand to grip the humans as he had Geoff, but Octavius appeared uncomfortable and confused, and the meaningful exchange was reduced. The elf broke the silence. "Please, call me Tantis, and don't read too much into the words of the prince. I am just a flyer, nothing special." He paused again with his long, pointed ears twitching in the soft breeze. "But my gut tells me you are not used to seeing elves, much less elves that can fly."

Octavius seemed to break from his momentary stupor. He smiled. "There is so much I have seen today that I don't understand or even want to believe, so an elf that flies really is just one of many."

The comment seemed to lighten the mood, and the previous exchange between Geoff and Octavius fell to the back. Madeiris, however, would not allow his last question to fade. "You didn't answer me. What do you intend to do at Draag?"

Geoff turned from the human leader to the elves. "That is an important question, but first tell me again, why are you here?"

Geoff had turned and started walking back toward the village center as he had asked, so the others fell in behind. Madeiris let his previous question remain unanswered and replied to his friend as they walked. "Elvinott is secure. I organized a meeting of the elders in my father's absence to discuss our best action. We decided Tantis and I would scout toward the North Sea and determine what the situation was. If we were to recover the canok queen in the process, even better."

The maneth understood and his lips were pressed together as he shook his head. "We have had many things happen since arriving," Geoff began.

"Things you may have trouble believing, but I can tell you this, when you learn why we have decided to do what we are going to do, you may think twice about being here."

"We are here to help," replied Madeiris. "You tell us what you need, and the elves will be there. We have several other elves on their way behind us."

They reached the center tent, and all went inside. The other humans in the area were still in disarray, but when they saw the elves, they stopped and watched. They were tall with tan and green skin and long pointed ears. The wings on the back of Tantis caused many to point and whisper. Both elves smiled at the actions, but neither commented. When the group made it into the room, Selbee turned to the two elves. "I tend to agree with Tantis. It seems those here haven't seen many elves before."

Tantis nodded. "Especially ones with wings," he added.

They all smiled but the tension of the times drove a more somber direction. Geoff relayed the entire saga to the current point then Madeiris took the floor. "Well, it is clear that the elves will support your direction. I cannot get a full army to join you unless you wait, and I do not think you wish to do that, but the elves could prove to be a strong calvary."

Geoff nodded. "That might be the right play. We need a strong army." He turned to Octavius. "Nothing personal, but the humans are not prepared for this."

The human leader nodded. "I admit to no level of expertise. We are young, new to fighting. We will stand strong by your sides, but we will not be the force that turns the table."

The others accepted the description of the humans' abilities as they all had been thinking the same thing. Tantis again took the lead. "I will join you now. My flight can be a benefit as well as my eyesight and ability with a bow. We have a handful of others coming by foot, and they can walk with the humans."

Madeiris was about to protest but then held quiet. Geoff reached over and slapped Tantis on the back. "We do need you, and I thank you."

Tantis nodded. "Madeiris, while your father is absent, you are the acting king. You go back to Elvinott and organize an army of flyers and ground elves. Send them to Draag. Send them as fast as you can. They will only be a few moons behind us. Our king and his small party are most likely already there.

There are two dragons working with us. We have a third to find. We have a plan, and now we need to make it happen."

Geoff roared in support. "We will find the Revel Rock and take down the dragon's power." He turned to Octavius. "When can your troops be ready?"

"You give the word, and we will be with you."

***

Bjork took several steps cracking ice under his talons and drawing closer to his apprentice. His voice was as cold as the air surrounding him. "So, you were successful in our plan with the canok queen. I was not sure you would be."

"You have given me direction, and I told you I would not fade from it." Slayne proudly laid the two pup canoks on the ice floor below him. "Here are the ones who will stand by our side. My two sons will bring the power of the dragon and the canok together."

"What is this?" stated Bjork, staring at the white and black pups before him. "These are not canoks. They have been enchanted."

"No, my master," replied Slayne, his voice carrying a level of defensiveness. "Never before have a dragon with my power and a canok with the power of the queen combined. There were two others stillborn who could not handle the combined life of two races. This is the definition of pure power."

"You are a fool. Daphane enchanted this birth and possibly the chance for all canoks to follow. I felt something. I did not know what it was until now. She is powerful, and your ignorance has cost us."

"She was powerful," Slayne returned. "She is dead now."

Bjork swung his head back toward the black dragon. "Are you sure? You killed her?"

"I did, my master."

"Then perhaps you are not as useless as I believed. We must determine the status of the canoks. We need them on our side if we are to be successful. Leave these pups with me. I will train them."

Slayne turned hard on the larger dragon before him. "No, Bjork. I will train them. I am their father. They will respond to me."

Bjork narrowed his eyes on the black dragon. "The pups will be here when you return. You have two critical things which must be done if our plan will fall into place."

Instantly Slayne's interest piqued. "What do you need me to do?" His voice lifted at the direction.

Bjork lowered his eyes. "If my feelings are true, the canoks are divided. If they are split, we need to bring them together under our rule. The canoks have the power to end this before it begins."

"Understood, my master. And what is the second thing?" asked Slayne.

"I believe Draketon has betrayed me. Find him and kill him."

Instantly Slayne was completely caught by the comment. "Draketon? He is with us, is he not?"

"He was with us, but I gave him direction which he ignored. He was to kill Anbari but did not engage. Had he fought and lost, I would have spared him, but he is of no use to me now." Bjork lowered his head to Slayne. "Draketon was to take your place by my side. He failed, and this is your place to hold and rule. You decide if you accept."

"I will kill Draketon, my master. Where can I find him?"

"You can find me right here," stated the red dragon from behind. "If you wish to kill me, then you can try right now, Slayne, but we both know you do not have the power. I am here to explain my actions, not defend them. I have information that will prove useful."

Slayne turned and immediately shot a ball of fire toward the red dragon. Draketon easily defended against it. "Stop embarrassing yourself, Slayne. It is not becoming."

Bjork smiled. "You are the one who failed me, Draketon. Coming here only extends that failure. If Slayne will not destroy you, I will. Slayne will stand beside me."

"Do you wish to know my information? It involves Taiju, but if you wish to kill me, then do it, if you can."

Slayne stepped close to him. "We will kill you—"

He was cut off by Bjork. "Quiet, Slayne, I will hear what Draketon has to say."

The black dragon swung his head back toward his master. Although he didn't know of one called Taiju, he especially didn't like the sudden change in Bjork when the name was said. Slayne's voice was strong but carried a slight drop in confidence. "We don't care about Taiju. We only want to know why you failed to kill Anbari. What more is there to say?"

Draketon shook his head. "You don't even know who Taiju is, do you, Slayne?"

The black dragon looked toward Draketon then toward Bjork.

"I thought as much," stated the red dragon. "Stop speaking and let the dragons who know what is happening in this world speak. You are nothing but a puppet. Stop doing anything before I cut your strings."

Slayne roared in anger. "You have nothing on me, Draketon. I did not fail my master, you did. Anbari is not dead. He is alive and on his course. I brought the canoks to Bjork's fingertips. You did nothing."

His words were hard and cold, and did hit the mark, with both Draketon and Bjork. Draketon cowered just a bit before returning to stand tall. "You don't even know what—"

"No more words, Draketon," interrupted Bjork. "Slayne may be young and stupid, but he does not lie. I told you to take care of Anbari, and you did not do as I asked. I can feel he now travels toward us. I can feel him across the North Sea. I give you this moment and this moment only to explain."

I found Anbari, and I found your two spies with him," replied Draketon. "I didn't wish to put your spies in a situation where they would have to give up their true direction to defend against me, and I could not beat all three of them."

Instantly Bjork opened his eyes wide and peered toward the red dragon. "What do mean, spies? Who were the three?"

"I know the elf king is with us and has been for many moons. I have seen him in Draag with you. And Hawthorne I have seen with Slayne. Somehow they have joined Anbari and infiltrated his trust."

Bjork smiled. "You are correct, Ku is my puppet. He will gather that which I need and then he will be killed, before he knows what he has done." His voice lowered and scratched like sand across a wound. "But Hawthorne,"—he turned to Slayne— "she is no longer with you. She has stayed with Anbari. Your failures, Slayne, continue to mount. Anbari has turned Hawthorne. Now his position has doubled."

Draketon continued, "I could not kill Anbari, for it would have meant to take on both of them, and they are strong. In fact,"—he turned to show his other side— "Anbari himself has grown stronger. He was able to block my attack and easily break through my defenses. These burns show I did engage the group, but quickly I knew I would be outmatched."

"So, you fled like a…"

Draketon sent a ball of fire into Slayne's unprotected face causing the black dragon to scream in pain, and then the fire extinguished. "Shut your mouth, Slayne, and pray I don't decide to take a more aggressive move against you."

Slayne recovered quickly and was about to return the attack when two balls exploded beneath each of their feet. Bjork shouted, "Stop it now! Save that energy for when it is needed."

The tone clearly showed there was more coming. Draketon did not wait. "You imply that you have a plan."

The large blue dragon smiled. "That fool Anbari is coming to us. He is seeking out the guardians of passage at the Realm of Darkness. It is appropriate that he dies in the place where those of evil heart will remain for eternity. Go there and kill him and take that which he seeks." He looked toward Slayne and Draketon. "Both of you."

"What about Hawthorne?" asked Slayne.

He thought a minute, and then scowled in a low tone. "Bring her to me, and if she refuses, kill her too."

The two looked at each other. Neither wanted to face Anbari. In fact, both knew that to face him would most likely mean their death. Neither liked the other very well, but for this direction, they both knew they needed each other. They looked toward each other and then back to Bjork. "We will go now," Draketon stated, lifting into the air just after finishing.

Slayne nodded and took off in his wake. He quickly caught up to the large red dragon. "You are just glad to be alive. You would have taken any direction that had you fly out on your own strength."

Draketon smiled slightly but did not answer; he knew Slayne was right. He was looking for any opening to leave.

***

Bjork closed his eyes and sat with the two canok pups in his icy lair. He felt the world. He could feel those closing in on Draag and smiled. He could feel Ku's presence drawing closer and knew he had to determine what best to do with him. And he could feel the growing village of humans, a new concern he had never experienced previously. He would need to wipe out their city as well as the elves and maneth, just like he had the canoks. He had already begun to split the dwarves. Much like the canoks, he believed they would destroy themselves as the two factions fought for power. He leaned back and smiled with balls of fire dripping from his lips. "It is all coming together," he stated to himself, and closed his eyes.

Chapter Thirteen

"What do you see?" asked Jermys.

"I see a very long fall that will kill us all," replied Hoangis. "I have never before wished to be a flyer, but it would absolutely come in handy right now."

The others nodded. "This is some secret entrance, brother," stated Jermys to Bretton, slapping his brother on the back. "Didn't you have a plan for getting us in?"

The other twin frowned at his older brother. "You said you wanted a way in. Here you go."

Gunthen nodded. "Don't worry, we will not have an issue obtaining entry. As we walked, I saw several trees with vines. Let's go back and collect them and we will lower each other down. I don't like standing out in the open like this anyway. Let's prepare the ropes and come back here once light has fallen."

They all agreed and moved into the woods without further comment.

Once the night had crept into the woods, the group of five moved out onto the open clearing on the hilltop. They found the opening and as Gunthen tied it off and then let it fall, they heard the far end of the makeshift rope strike the ground. "Good," stated the maneth. "It reached." He turned to the group and continued in a whisper, "I will remain here to provide extra support to the rope. You go down one at a time and then I will follow. We will have to leave the rope tied down. It could warn others of our presence, but we will have no way to remove it unless one of us stays behind."

"I cannot traverse such a direction," added Tashro. "I will remain. You may need my assistance should you exit quickly via this method. My only request is, if you leave the caverns by another method, you must return to let me know."

Gunthen was against separating and it was clear on his face. "We are not going to separate, Tashro. I will carry you down."

"Nonsense," the canok replied, this time more stern. "You said yourself, leaving the rope behind could alert those in the caverns to our presence. If I stay, then I will be able to pull it up after you are down. And as for you carrying me, I question whether the rope will hold your weight, much less you and me." He turned to the group not allowing the maneth to speak. "Go now, all of you. Find the information to bring back to our friends and allies. We must find the answer to save our world. The answer is in there, and it is up to you to discover it."

His tone and statement left nothing to be interpreted and none, included Gunthen, could argue with the logic. The maneth turned to the others. "You heard the canok, let's begin."

Hoangis automatically took the lead. "I will go first and rather than climb down the rope, I will tie it around me and Gunthen, you lower me down. It will allow me to use my bow as I descend if there is any trouble beneath us. Once down, I can secure the area as the rest of you descend."

Gunthen agreed and pulled the vine up, allowing the elf to tie it around his waist and shoulders in a harness. The maneth gripped the vine tightly and then the elf leaped into the opening causing the maneth's muscles to bulge and tighten. Slowly the elf was lowered into the hole.

"*I know what you are thinking*," stated Tashro telepathically to the maneth. "*You could just as easily lower me into this hole, but you now agree having one stay behind does solve some problems. I will be fine, my friend. Just do what you need to do and find what will help us..*"

Gunthen swung his head to the maneth who simply stared at him in return. Without speaking he continued lowering the elf until the weight dissipated and the elf was on the ground. Hoangis untied himself and looked around the room. It was a dome-shaped room with completely smooth walls. There was no place to tie the vine to give it a steady base so he simply gripped it tight. He felt it move in such a way he was certain another of his companions was starting down. He waved, though with the darkness, he was not sure he could be seen. Moments later, he saw the first of the twins sliding down the vine and soon thereafter, his brother was down as well. Gunthen, not nearly as smooth and effortlessly as the twins, bounded down and landed with a thud on the ground. The others smiled but their smiles quickly vanished when they saw the vine start to grow tight as it was pulled from above. Hoangis had grabbed it again after Gunthen had crashed down but now released it, and quickly it disappeared through the window. They looked at each other and for the first time realized they were inside Draag Caverns, the legendary home of the dragons, and none had any idea where to go or how to get out.

Looking up toward the hole they could see two eyes reflecting down. "*Go now,*" the canok said telepathically to all of them. "*When you need me, just concentrate on me and I will feel your presence to return. But you will have to be within this room, for it is where I have made the connection.*"

Without a word, Gunthen turned and looked both directions. "There are two exits. Does anyone have a preference?"

Jermys pointed to one doorway and simultaneously, Bretton pointed to the other. "Of course," replied Gunthen. The maneth turned to the elf. "Do you have a thought?"

Hoangis nodded. "If my orientation is correct, left will take us deeper into the caverns and right will lead us back to the entrance we left previously with the dragons guarding it. My belief is we should go deeper."

The maneth looked to both dwarves who appeared as if they were going to fight each other to win the decision. They locked eyes, each with a hand on the hatchet. "We go left, dwarves," he stated. "And I thought you guys inherently were gifted with direction in mines." He was trying to aggravate them even more, for a purpose he wasn't sure, but he liked it.

Hoangis caught the comment and added, "Yes, you would have thought if navigating mines was all you did in life, the two experts would agree."

The dwarves heard the comments and broke from their momentary lockdown between each other. "Just a minute," began Jermys. "We absolutely would agree on direction had either of you been clear on the goal. It was my intention to go deeper into the caverns and I am sure my brother was simply trying to take us to an area we knew to help each of you orient yourselves better."

"Of course I was," replied Bretton. "I can't believe you thought we disagreed." He laughed. "You are both so naïve."

Gunthen and Hoangis smiled at each other and watched as the two dwarves began to quietly argue, with Jermys kicking Bretton in the butt as they walked causing the twin to push immediately back in return. Hoangis and Gunthen smiled but did not speak further. As they began to walk out of the room, Gunthen felt something under his feet.

"What is that?" he stated in a loud and surprised voice.

Instantly all other talk ceased, and the others looked down to the maneth who was tapping his toes on the ground.

"What do you mean?" asked Bretton. "I don't see anything."

"It is not what you see," stated the elf, answering for Gunthen. "It is what you hear."

"What do you hear?" asked Jermys, standing next to his brother but not knowing why the maneth had continued to tap.

Gunthen pointed. "Do you hear the difference between this,"—he tapped in one area— "and this?" He tapped in an area adjacent to the first.

"Not really," responded Jermys. "Should I?"

"It has an echo," answered Hoangis. "It's hollow underneath."

"What does that mean?" asked Jermys.

"It means we are going to dig because I believe there is a door and third option for travel."

Jermys and Bretton looked at each other and shrugged. "Move aside," stated Jermys, pulling out his axe as he did so. "We'll have this cleared in no time."

The maneth and elf watched with wonder as the two dwarves cut through the hardened soil. It took only a few moments before the large, wooden door sat fully exposed. Bretton studied his hatchet and smiled. "Not one cut. Claudos protected my blade. How about you, brother?"

Jermys lifted his hatchet in front of him. "Same, brother. Our swing was true."

The two nodded, pleased with their work. Gunthen looked at the door and then back to the twins. "Claudos?"

"Claude was the leader of the dwarves long before any of us were born. He gave his life to the betterment of the dwarves. It is because of Claude that we have found our lives in the mines. He created our first tools. He built Feldschlosschen and Antaag."

Hoangis immediately reacted when the dwarf referenced Claude. Elves believed it was wrong to use the names of those passed. He did not respond, however, when Gunthen broke in. "You said he gave his life. What happened?"

The twins looked at each other, lowered their heads as if in prayer, and then lifted their eyes back to the maneth. "Nobody knows for sure, but legend holds that he made a deal with the dragons. It is that which we believe our king also did. We believe the dragons betrayed and murdered Claude, but all we know for sure is he never returned."

The discussion ended when noise was heard coming from the hallway opposite the direction they were originally going. "What is that?" asked Hoangis.

"You can hear better than me, what do you think?" followed Gunthen.

"Four, maybe five, with another much larger further behind."

"Are they coming this way?" asked Jermys, turning toward the hallway entrance with hatchet drawn.

"They are, and fast," replied Hoangis.

"Come on," stated the maneth. "We don't have time to investigate this. Let them see that we have discovered the secret tunnel. It will still be here when we return. Our first priority is to stay safe."

The others agreed and they all turned and headed toward the room exit opposite where the sound was coming. Jermys and Bretton took the rear with Gunthen ensuring there was nothing of concern in their path. They ran hard for some time before Hoangis stated between breaths, "I no longer hear any pursuit. I think we can stop for a moment."

The group stopped and remained completely silent. There was nothing. No sounds of pursuit, no sounds at all. Gunthen looked around the room as the elf took several steps back in the direction they had come, his ears twitching and turning to capture any signal from behind them. "I am confident the pursuit has stopped, at least for now."

"Look over here," stated Gunthen. "I think I can move these large rocks and behind them appears to be a small cave. We would have some protection and could stay here. It was night when we arrived. We could use the sleep."

"No!" stated the elf firmly. "We need to find out what is going on here. That room has something to do with it, I am sure of it. We must go back. Whoever was behind us has passed or returned. If they haven't, we can meet them on our terms, not theirs."

Gunthen was against it but after hearing the full description, he believed the argument was sound. "Jermys, Bretton, what do you think?"

"I think I am not a bit tired right now. I like the idea of us being the surprise visitor. I say we follow the elf's lead and head back. Maybe we even capture one alive and get all the answers we need."

The maneth nodded. "Let's do it. I will take the lead, twins stay back, and Your Majesty, keep your arrow ready, please. We may not have much time to react."

"Understood," answered Hoangis. "Don't worry about me. You are the one leading. You will take the first attack."

"We will be ready both directions," stated Jermys. "Don't worry about anything coming up our backside."

Gunthen nodded understanding and began walking. The trip back took significantly longer. The maneth was actually surprised at the amount of territory they had covered. However, when they approached the room they had entered originally with the hidden trapdoor in its center, instantly their concerns increased.

"What do you make of that, elf?" asked Gunthen.

"I don't know," Hoangis replied. "I hear nothing coming from the room, but the newfound light emanating from it does create a high level of concern."

Gunthen held his hand up for the others to stop, and he slowly crept forward. Hoangis saw the motion but he, like all elves, carried the ability to walk without making any sound. He ignored the maneth's guidance and continued directly behind him. Gunthen jumped when he felt his presence. The maneth rolled his eyes but continued to the doorway. He knelt down and peered his head slightly around the corner of the wall into the room. His eyes locked on one thing immediately.

Standing in the room now rested a free-standing, large, amazingly brilliant and clear, mirror. It was round, with a very ornate carved design in the wood surrounding it. It was on a stand giving the impression it could swivel vertically. Perhaps the most amazing thing about it was the mirror somehow generated light. There was no other light in the room. No torches on the walls or any other source, yet all could be seen. The other thing, which was immediately clear, was that the trapdoor they had just found was now completely absent, and the dirt floor in its place appeared to be polished granite, similar to the surrounding walls.

"So, where are those who were following us?" asked Hoangis, peering through the empty mirror room.

Gunthen slowly took a few steps inside the doorway. "I don't know, but more importantly, where did that mirror come from, what is its purpose, and where did the trapdoor go?"

The others all looked to where the secret doorway had been. Hoangis followed behind the maneth's steps. "There is magic behind this. There is no other explanation."

"We all know the dragons possess magic and creating new floors and hiding trapdoors is not out of their realm of possibilities." The maneth had walked in and was standing directly over the spot where the secret door had been. "Covering a door is one thing, but they can't change the fact that we know it was there."

"And this mirror is exquisite. The reflection is like none I have seen before." The elf was standing directly in front of it, his eyes almost staring through it. He turned back to the maneth who was now flanked by both dwarves who were inspecting the floor for potential break points. The elf smiled. "There is no point to try to break through the floor. Only magic will expose the doorway now. It would be protected against a physical attack."

"Then what would you have us do?" asked Bretton, his tone clearly displaying his negative feelings toward that comment.

The elf began, his voice softer in response to the dwarf's. "We came here to determine what was happening and if the dragons were behind it. We have seen dragons; we have seen magic. We need to find more. We need to choose our direction and go. The fact that these changes were put in place tell me they know we are here. The fact that we have not been attacked or at least chased begs the question as to why. We are but four. If dragons really do have a force honed to take over our world, where are they?"

Gunthen nodded. "We could not fend off even one dragon for long, if at all. Why wouldn't they simply eliminate us if they know we are here?"

Jermys now spoke, "It means they either don't know we are here, which based on this room I don't believe; they can't right now for some reason; or they are about to."

Hoangis stepped closer to the other three. "There is one more option." He paused and the others looked toward him with anticipation. "They are wanting us to do something here and are watching us or pushing us one direction or the other."

"Like bandicoots in a maze," stated Jermys. "I hate those creatures, but I hate more being one of them."

The room grew deathly quiet. Gunthen looked down both caverns and then pointed. "Let's head back where we came from. I do believe this direction will take us further into the caverns and the other way would take us back to the forests. I believe there is a series of caverns or at least a room beneath this room. If we would not last long against even one dragon, I question what we thought we could accomplish here. The fact we have made it this far is a miracle. I think we head down this cavern far enough to determine whether there is something worth continuing for. If not, we come back to this room, connect with Tashro, and get out. We need to bring an army of our races to have any chance of defending against dragons. We need help."

All understood his words and although they didn't all want to agree with him, they knew he was right. Hoangis replied, "Our mission here was wise, so don't downplay the direction. We are outnumbered, that much is certain, but if we are smart, we can find a secret here. If we can get that secret into the hands of our combined forces, they can exploit it. Nobody felt we were coming here to win. The goal was for at least one of us to find our way out of here and pass what we learn onto the others. We have already lost one, and there will be more bloodshed before this is done. Today is but one step for us to take to ensure our lives and our races will survive."

Gunthen shook his head and started walking with the others falling in behind. Hoangis stayed near the front and the two dwarves, as before, brought up the rear. Nobody spoke, and as they left the well-lit mirror room, the darkness of Draag Caverns seduced their party with each step they took into its belly.

Chapter Fourteen

"The two dragons stepped slowly from behind the trees to stand in front of a large, icy lake. Tears began to drip from Hawthorne's eyes. "This place is so cold."

"I am sure you are not speaking about the ice and snow. The death gripping me is almost beyond that which I can carry." Anbari stopped and turned to the large green dragon next to him. "Fehr, are you well?"

"What is this place, Anbari?" the small rodent asked. "It draws me into it, as if it wants me to join but cannot accept me."

"Yes," added Hawthorne. "It wants everyone but only accepts a certain few."

"Look below the ice," stated Anbari. "What is that?" He paused and then his tone changed significantly. "No, wait, don't look. Look away!"

"Oh no," replied Hawthorne staring downward. "Are those living creatures, trapped below the ice?"

Anbari lowered his head. "Not living." His voice was soft and faded away as he spoke. "They are those who were not accepted. They are trapped there to forever live out their deaths."

Fehr looked away. "So, we can't help them?"

Anbari continued to turn from the sight. "No, my son. To do so would possibly trap us with them. We need to go."

The three slowly moved toward a path that continued along the side of the lake's frozen edge. "Don't look down, my friends," stated Anbari. "Keep your eyes forward. We need to reach the guardians."

Slayne watched the two dragons walk toward a cave at the far side. Draketon followed his eyes. "Do you wish to attack now?"

The black dragon's voice lacked confidence and he stuttered as he started, "I-I-I...don't think so. Let's watch and see what happens. Let's see what these guardians do with them."

"You are scared," replied Draketon. "You don't want to be here any more than I do."

Slayne turned toward the red dragon. "Watch your tongue, Draketon. You are already in poor standing with Bjork. Don't bring me down to stand beside you."

"Stand beside me?" he questioned. "Stand beside me. I am here because I am not sure of the right decision. I am keeping my mind and eyes open. I guarantee you I will end up on the right side, it is just not clear to me what that side is right now."

"You are a fool, Draketon. Trust that I will tell Bjork about your lack of faith in our future."

"Are you threatening me, Slayne?" Draketon's voice was hard as he turned and narrowed his stare on the dragon beside him.

"No, my friend. I am saying if you are so proud of your feelings, then I will share them with Bjork. He is our master. If he decides he does not wish to..." The two dragons turned quickly when they heard a stick crack behind them. Draketon prepared to release a wall of flame but found himself thrown back and pinned against a tree, but not by physical touch. A magical force had him in its grip.

"Don't believe for a moment that you can attack me," stated a female voice. "Who are you? Who is Bjork?"

Slayne had not initiated any attack and was left staring at the large female dragon. She was blue and green and her colors were very ominous. Slayne paced sideways to create some distance between him and Draketon. "Who are you?" the black dragon asked.

She smiled through her jagged teeth causing balls of wet fire to drip from her mouth. "Do you really believe I need to answer your questions? Now tell me, who are you? Why are you watching the two dragons below, and what is their intention at the Realm? And don't forget my previous question; who is Bjork?"

Slayne took a step closer but did steal a glance toward his counterpart. Draketon was still pinned with invisible hands against a tree and though fighting to free himself, was having no success. "Perhaps a better response is, kill the red dragon and take your place at my side. Then I will take you to Bjork. You are exactly what we came for."

The response caught the new dragon by surprise. "You would have me kill your friend and join you. What is in it for me?"

"Whatever has brought you to the Realm of Darkness means your power exceeds that of my counterparts. You have easily controlled him and brought him to a level of complete incapacity. You are a perfect partner for us."

The dragon took a step closer and her tone was slow and deep. "Why would I join you?"

"How does ruling over the world sound?"

She smiled and nodded. "This Bjork wishes to return the dragons to the ways of the past."

"Bjork wishes to ensure the dragons will never serve." Slayne was growing in confidence and his eagerness to move forward was clear. "Yes, the three of us together can do exactly what you say."

She nodded. "I am the only creature to ever escape the permanent swim of death beneath the surface of the ice lake. I have sworn I would never allow these tragedies to continue. If Bjork will support this direction, then I will stand with him."

"Then kill the red and let's go meet with him."

She turned to Draketon and narrowed her eyes. "I would tell you I am sorry, but I am not. If you are what stands between me and revenge on the guardians, then I will kill you without a second thought." A ball of fire larger than Draketon's entire body engulfed him in flames. Slayne nodded and the two dragons opened their wings and lifted into the air.

The black dragon turned to his new counterpart. "What should I call you?"

"My name is too difficult for you to say, so simply call me Suzanne."

***

Anbari entered the cave and his eyes panned the entire room. It was a circular rock opening with no apparent exit. Hawthorne stood next to him with Fehr on her back. "What do we do now?" she asked.

"I don't know. For now we—"

He stopped in mid-sentence when a form appeared before them. There was clearly a presence, but the form was partially transparent. It appeared as a dragon but was not any dragon Anbari had ever seen before.

The apparition spoke with a deep, slow voice in perfect Dragon tongue. "I have taken a form which will be most comfortable to you. Why have you entered the Realm, Anbari of Draag?"

"We wished to meet with the guardians to discuss some evil in the world and a path to prevent its spread. I don't wish the future of all dragons to be forced to reside within the ice lake. I wish to save my race from a fate which they don't deserve."

"How may one dragon do such a thing and why do you believe the guardians can, or even would, assist?"

Anbari took a breath as he thought about his response. "Because I believe the guardians' main goal is to prevent those from becoming trapped here for an eternity. I believe there is a rift in the world that will allow a balance. I have felt it since I began to learn more about my powers. I wish to provide a path for that power, and I believe these weapons are part of it." He laid down the weapons he had created from the crude wooden weapons the humans had carried upon their first meeting. "Something told me to fashion these weapons and bring them to you."

The form before them followed the weapons to the ground as Anbari set them down. Suddenly, the form vanished, as did the weapons. The three looked at each other and then, as quickly as the apparition and the weapons, Anbari vanished as well, leaving Hawthorne and Fehr alone in the cave.

"Well," stated Fehr lightheartedly. "I guess that means we wait. I wonder if there is anything loose in here that I could take…"

"Stop, Fehr. Do not steal anything from this cave." Hawthorne glared at the small pest.

He raised his two front paws. "Okay, okay, but I am still going to tell people I tried, and this is going to be one great story to tell."

Moments later there was a flash and Anbari returned. The dragon coughed slightly causing the other two to jump. Hawthorne ran to him. "Anbari, what happened. Are you okay?"

He nodded. "Sorry I was gone so long. The knowledge they gave me was tremendous." He laid down three weapons. They glistened and shined.

The female dragon smiled. "You were only gone for a moment, and what are those weapons?"

"These three weapons are connected. They will bring tremendous power to those who wield them. It will be a power that will have to be mastered and understood, but if they are used together, they will be able to defeat anything. Those who hold these weapons can bring balance to the world. We must take these weapons and give them to those of honor who can keep them until they are called for."

Fehr looked on amazed at the incredible craftsmanship, but quickly he realized a flaw in the discussion. "You left with four weapons, I only see three: a bow, a hatchet, and a scimitar."

"The fourth weapon—a hammer—is hidden with my possession. The guardians believe it to be theirs. I have promised its return but I fear they believe I am stealing it. I simply am not ready to allow anyone I don't know and trust to be in possession of the items that can prevent this evil movement. Therefore, they have to take my word. I can't allow any of the weapons into the hands of those who wish to misuse them. It will provide power to those individuals, but it will also limit the power of all of them used together. I believe the bow must remain with the elves of Elvinott. I was told to find Claude for the hatchet, but I don't know where or how to do that. If I cannot locate the dwarf, I will find another option." He turned to his dragon counterpart. "And the scimitar is to remain with you, Hawthorne."

Hawthorne looked on in disbelief. "With me...but why me?"

"The guardians stated that you hold the key." He lifted the scimitar to her, saying a few words. The sword disappeared and she felt a change under her scales. "You are one with honor."

She looked on in disbelief, but her tone changed as she felt the magical weapon within her being. "So, we do have a path to bring balance. We do have a way to win." She paused and leaned in against Anbari's neck causing a soothing between them both as they made contact. "Is there anything more?"

Anbari nodded. "There is one thing more. There is a ring. It is a ring of the weapons. It will harness the power of the weapons until they are matched to their final home. We are to hide the weapons as I have said. The ring, however, I must give to one who is chosen to bring balance to our new world."

The green dragon appeared amazed. "Who is that? How are you going to know who this creature is?"

Anbari smiled. "The guardians wouldn't tell me, but I already know. I know who is to bring balance."

She smiled broadly. "Who, Anbari? Who shall wear the ring?"

He knelt down closer. "The one who led us here. The one who led us to Taiju. The one who has been fighting this battle before a battle even existed."

She looked on questionably. "Who is that?"

He lifted his head to both of them. "Ku."

Chapter Fifteen

Geoff pointed. "We should pass through the Dry Sea. It will include dangerous temperatures, but it will reduce our travel in half. We should travel at night when the heat is not as great and find shelter during the day. Do you agree?"

Next to him were Octavius, Tantis, Stoven, and Selbee. Behind them were nearly one hundred humans and a handful of elves. Octavius nodded. "We will follow your lead. We don't know of this Dry Sea or Draag. We are here for support but need your guidance."

Tantis and Stoven nodded but didn't respond further. Nobody was going to assume an additional leadership role. In fact, each was grateful for Geoff's position. He was a young maneth, but confident. Stoven more than any of the others recognized how important confidence would be for this journey. Tantis made a quick gesture to the maneth, pointing to the air. Geoff nodded positively in response and quickly he opened his wings and lifted himself up. Moments later he was out of sight ahead of them.

"Amazing," stated the human leader. "I can't imagine having the gift of flight."

They all understood. It was truly incredible to see. "We should hit the edge of the Dry Sea by midday. We will make camp on its outskirts, get some rest, and then travel through the night. We could reach the edge of Draag Forest within two days. Then the trek will become much more dangerous."

The last comment caught the human's attention. "More dangerous? How so?"

"Well, none of us are experts on these forests. On the Dry Sea, we will not be ambushed. We will be able to see for a great distance, even during the night. We also will have Tantis available to scout and prepare us. In Draag, we don't know what to expect. I have explored there only once. I do know that the forest is thick, perhaps the thickest on all of Troyf. It means Tantis can't help us there, and an ambush will not only be easy, but probable. It will also be impossible for us to pass through quietly. We have a hundred men who are not used to walking and fighting like elves. They need to learn, and they need to learn quick."

The human leader understood. The sounds of the men behind were loud. There was much talking, even hollers at times. Octavius used the opportunity to slip to the back and offer some instruction to the men. He knew he wouldn't be able to teach them to walk with the skill of an elf, but he could at least end the talking. To Geoff's surprise, in moments, it was close to silent.

"Nice work," the maneth said when the human returned.

"We will see how long it lasts," Octavius replied, the lack of confidence clear in his voice.

They reached the edge of the desert, and Geoff gave the signal to set up camp. As he had stated, there was no reason to spend any daylight walking across the sandy base of the Dry Sea. But at night, the temperature dropped significantly, and travel would be easier. There were other dangers during this time, but in their numbers, the few animals out looking for prey would not engage a party of over a hundred. He was certain of that.

Tantis returned and gave the all-clear for the area ahead. Geoff arranged for different shifts of guards, and in very little time, their camp was set. They had half a day until the sun went down so they would use the time to sleep. As Geoff lay in his tent, however, sleep wouldn't come. His mind was filled with the plan, or lack thereof. They were headed to Draag. They were hoping to meet up with a very small party that had already braved the trip. However, what if they didn't connect? What was the plan then? How would a hundred untrained and weak human warriors fight a dragon? Geoff already knew the answer as he was closing his eyes. They were going to die.

Hawthorne, Fehr, and Anbari left the cave and began their slow walk across the ridge along the ice lake. Faces appeared under the ice, pressed hard against it with fear and pain in their hollow eyes. Though no sound was heard, they appeared to be screaming. Fehr could not help but look.

Hawthorne noticed his stare. "Don't look, my son. The pain and suffering beneath that ice is like nothing any creature should experience. Just seeing the devalued life might bring an elf to their knees. Their love for life would not be able to accept this place."

Fehr leaned forward. "Do you mean those that do not gain passage?"

Hawthorne nodded and kept her voice low in response, "I believe so. If they lived an impure life or were not accepted by their god, they would be pulled down here for eternity. Nobody has ever escaped from this fate…"— she paused, then added— "at least that I know of."

"What was that?" broke in Anbari, hearing something around the crest of the ice ring. "Up in the trees. I heard something."

"There appears to be a faint fire burning too," added Fehr.

"You both wait here, and I will check it out." Anbari began to walk away and then noticed Hawthorne was right on his heals. He turned to the female dragon. "What are you doing?"

"Fehr and I talked and agreed the meeting with the guardians must have affected your mind. We both thought you told us to wait, but we knew we must have misheard you because you would never suggest such a thing."

Anbari shook his head but wasn't going to argue. "Stay behind me."

They slowly walked up the hill, and as they came close to the source of the faint noise and fire, Anbari immediately knew what it was.

"Draketon, are you okay?" shouted Anbari.

The red dragon did not move, and the burns across its body were significant. Anbari checked for life and nodded to the others. "He is alive, but just barely. We need to make him comfortable. Hawthorne, do you have any ideas?"

"I'm afraid not. The burns are across nearly his entire body. It is…"

As she spoke, the scimitar under her armor skin began to hum. All three of them heard it but none knew what to do. Anbari walked over and Hawthorne lifted her wing toward him so he could see the sword. He took it out and the humming grew louder. He carried the sword over to the fallen dragon and placed it across the dragon's chest. The humming grew in intensity causing Fehr to cover his ears and Hawthorne to turn lower and shake her head as if trying to protect herself. Anbari did not flinch and leaned forward, slowly resting the sword on the dragon's belly. The noise grew so loud even Anbari wanted to look away, but he refused. He turned his eyes toward his friends and instantly felt fear when he saw Fehr fall unconscious. Then, as quickly as it had started, it ceased.

The two dragons slowly lifted their heads. The red dragon's scaley skin had sunk into his body. The burns had been so severe that areas of bone had been exposed. However, as the two dragons looked upon their counterpart now, all signs had vanished. The dragon was still motionless, but they could now see clear breathing. The scimitar rested on Draketon's chest, but sound no longer emitted from it. Anbari recovered the sword just as Draketon's eyes opened.

The red dragon's eyes were filled with fear and then calmed. "Anbari, have we both passed?"

"We have not," he answered, his voice soft but still questioning. "What do you remember?"

Draketon quickly looked around the area. He saw Anbari before him, and Hawthorne to the side. She had moved to tend to Fehr who was breathing, but not awake. "Where am I?" the red dragon asked.

Again, Anbari held his eyes on him. "What do you remember? How did you end up at the Realm of Darkness?"

"The Realm?" he stated softly. "Slayne and…" His words stopped, and he looked up to the dragon before him. "We were sent to kill you." He turned to Hawthorne. "And you as well, if you refused to join us."

"Who sent you?" Anbari asked immediately. "And who is the *we* who was sent with you?"

"Slayne was with me," he replied. "And Bjork sent us. He had already sent me to kill you before, at the Gar Swamp, but I chose to leave. Then, when he learned you were free, he sent us both to destroy you." The dragon stood. "But how do I live? The flames were so strong. The magic preventing me from defending it was too great. I felt my wings burn from my body."

Hawthorne lifted Fehr onto her back and walked over to stand beside her counterpart. "But if you were sent together to kill us, where is Slayne now and why did he turn on you? Was that the plan all the time, to destroy you?"

Draketon now stood completely and stretched his wings, looking at them in disbelief. "No, Slayne and I do not agree, and I am still not sure of the right direction, but we were going to do as instructed. It was when the female dragon surprised us that all changed. I saw it in Slayne's eyes. He was seduced immediately with her power, and her power was great. I felt evil in her. She said she was the only creature to have ever escaped from the ice lake and has returned from the afterlife to seek revenge on this world. I believe that to be true."

"What was her name?" Anbari asked.

"She said it was Suzanne, but I can't be sure. By that time, I was already lost. She never needed me, and Slayne saw an opportunity to bring incredible strength to Bjork. Killing you was no longer a priority, which to Slayne meant neither was I."

"Where did they go?" asked Anbari.

"Back to Bjork, I think, but I can't be certain of anything. I tried to defend it, but it was as if she controlled my mind. I could do nothing but take it." He paused and then turned to both dragons before him. "How did you save me? My burns were too great. No magic could have brought me back."

Anbari nodded. "Safe to say there is magic out there that can, but it is not something we are going to share." He turned to Hawthorne to ensure she understood. "Draketon, you meant to kill us. You took direction from a dragon who wishes to rule our world and will destroy any race that opposes him. I have but one question for you. Are you my friend or enemy?"

The comment sat in the air for moments. Fehr had started to stir but both Anbari and Hawthorne held their stare on the red dragon.

The bandicoot lifted his head and blinked his eyes. "What in all of Troyf was the sound? It nearly burned my ears off." He turned his head to follow Hawthorne's stare. "Holy dead goblins, how did that burnt meat get back to normal?" When he heard nobody laugh at his comment, he bounced his eyes across each of them. "Okay, what did I miss?"

Hawthorne smiled slightly at the small rat. "Nothing too big, Fehr. Anbari saved this dragon's life, this dragon who was sent here with another dragon to kill us. Now Anbari has asked this dragon if he is our friend or enemy, and the dragon does not wish to answer."

Fehr turned to the red dragon. "Well, Big Red, if I were you, I would think long and hard about who tried to kill you and who saved you. Seems the answer would then be pretty easy."

Anbari nodded. "You would think so." He turned to Draketon. "You know, bandicoots have a way with words. What is your answer, Draketon?"

The red dragon paced in a side-to-side motion as he looked at those before him. He did not seem to be struggling with his answer; he was struggling with how he would tell them. "I have never had loyalty to Slayne or Bjork. However, I don't feel your direction is the way. Slayne showed me the vision of you using your powers to split the dwarves. How can I follow that? I have seen what the other creatures in this world think of dragons. Most wish to destroy us. Most see us as creatures who will destroy their villages with fire and wind. We cannot live in harmony, that much is certain. So, when you ask the question, am I your friend or enemy, my answer is complicated. I will never again do any harm to you, but I can't stand by your side either."

"I respect that answer," stated Anbari, "but I will tell you I have never harmed any race on Troyf, much less split the dwarves with magic. Slayne lied to you, the same way he has lied to every dragon."

Fehr didn't give Draketon a chance to answer. "You respect his position?" asked Fehr. "You just saved his…"

Anbari lifted his wing to the rat causing him to silence. "I can respect that, but I then must ask, will you go back and stand by Bjork, Slayne, and this Suzanne?"

Draketon smiled. "To them I am dead, and I would like to stay that way. Instead, I believe I will travel to the South Sea. There are islands where I can find peace. Should you build this world you believe is possible, come find me and I will join you."

"Fair enough," replied Anbari. He turned to Hawthorne and Fehr. "Come on, we have work to do."

"Anbari?" said Draketon, his voice now soft and caring.

The silver dragon turned and looked back to him. "Yes, Draketon?"

"Thank you. I don't understand what or how you did what you did, but you have given me a new direction and a second chance. One I can be proud of."

"You have great power within you, Draketon. I have felt your power to be one of the strongest. Slayne and Bjork have felt that power as well. Slayne was threatened. Bjork was not. Use your power for good, my friend, and you will find true peace."

He nodded understanding. As the two dragons with Fehr on Hawthorne's back walked away, Draketon added, "If you wish to find Bjork, he lives in the ice mountains on the far side of Cindif. He will do whatever it takes to destroy you. He feels you are the only thing that stands between him and his rule."

Anbari did not answer but simply took to the air, with Hawthorne and Fehr in his wake.

Hawthorne caught his side and asked, "Where are we going?"

"I am taking these weapons to where they need to be kept safe. I wish the hammer to go to the dwarven mines outside Icly. They are abandoned. I will protect it from Slayne and Bjork. Only a maneth will be able to grab it. The hatchet I will give to Claude if I can locate him. If I can't, I have another idea. The bow I will give to elves in Elvinott. They will hide it within their enchanted forest. The scimitar will remain with you."

"And the ring that ties them all together?" she asked.

"I will keep the ring, Anbari," answered Fehr. "I will protect it."

Anbari smiled. "Thank you, Fehr, but there is someone who has been fighting this battle from the beginning. He should be the governor of the ring. From this point forward, it will be called the Ring of Ku."

"Are you sure?" asked Hawthorne. "His departure just does not sit well with me."

"Do not judge in these times. He is pure of heart. I could feel it with the guardians. He is the right choice."

"So, where are we going to find Ku?" she asked.

"I believe he is still trying to find passage to the Realm of Darkness. I believe we will find him with the humans by the North Sea."

***

"You better be here to tell me he is dead, and bringing another dragon with you to expose my lair is most likely going to bring about your death as well."

Slayne took a step back at the abrupt and harsh greeting. "Don't react too quickly, my master. I bring you something better than Anbari. I bring you a dragon stronger than Anbari."

Bjork moved closer. "It is true that I feel power within you that I have not felt in others."

He could not finish his next statement as a ball of fire shot from Suzanne directly toward the blue dragon. Bjork easily stopped the ball in flight, spun it several times, and then returned it toward the female with tremendous force. Suzanne enchanted a magical barrier that absorbed the ball causing it to vanish. Both dragons looked toward the other in disbelief.

"I have never seen another dragon stop my fire," stated Suzanne, her voice intrigued but also with a nervousness about it.

"There has been only one dragon who has ever stopped my attack as you just did, and that dragon I want dead." Bjork stepped closer. "I don't know what you are after, but if you join me in this endeavor, I will ensure your power is never challenged."

"My story is simple. I wish to destroy every creature in this world who sentenced me to the death I have been suffering for longer than I can describe. I have been given a second chance to avenge those who put me under the ice. My power was too strong to keep me hidden, my abilities too great. I do not know this Anbari, but if he represents all that is in this world, then I will join you when you destroy him."

Slayne smiled and felt the power growing in the room, but it was Bjork who spoke, "Come now," he said to her. "We must talk and learn each other's strengths. Together we will be unstoppable."

"What would you have me do now?" Slayne asked.

Bjork swung his head back toward the black dragon in disgust. "Leave us. We will call for you when needed. Your blundering has already drawn this plan out much too long. There is an imminent threat to Draag, but it also means those attacking have left their homelands exposed."

"A threat? Do you wish me to go to Draag to protect it?" Slayne asked.

Bjork looked at Suzanne and the smaller female dragon answered, "No, I believe he said there are forces attacking Draag. It may or may not be protected, but while they do this, the homelands of these forces are relatively unprotected. Destroy the homelands, you fool. Gather some dragons and don't give these forces a home to come back to." She turned to Bjork. "Do you agree?"

Bjork smiled. "You see, Slayne, that is why I had to consider Draketon. That is why I had to continue to look for my champion. Because you are a fool. What happened to Draketon, or did he tire of you as well?"

"If you are referring to the red dragon," interjected Suzanne, "I killed him. I sensed distrust in him. He would have turned on me, so I didn't give him the chance."

Bjork smiled. "Good. Good. Just the kind of determination and decisiveness I want to hear." He turned to Slayne. "Now go, you fool. See if you can do anything right. Gather some dragons and destroy the maneth and the elves' homelands. I also feel some power growing by the North Sea. Whatever it is, stop it before it starts. But do not harm the dark dwarves. They may turn out to be my greatest work, next to these two." He reached down and patted the two small canoks that walked directly behind him. "These two are going to change our world."

"Your greatest work?" Slayne questioned in return. "They are my…"

Bjork swung his head toward him with fire burned in his eyes. "Do you have something to say to me, Slayne? I trust you will use your words carefully."

Slayne cowered slightly. "No-no," he stuttered. "I will gather some dragons from Draag and destroy the homelands."

Bjork shook his head. "I have already alerted the dragons at Draag ahead of your arrival. They are setting a trap for the fool party. Plus, I have dispatched three dragons on my own to gather any who escape. Draag will be well protected."

Slayne smiled. "Then there is nothing to stop us."

Bjork returned with a glare. "Us?" he questioned. "Slayne, get out of our sight. Suzanne and I have much to discuss and you are not my concern. Try to finish what I tell you this time."

The black dragon understood the comment and did not respond. He simply lifted the two canoks onto his back and opened his wings into flight. Bjork motioned to Suzanne to join him back in his cave.

***

Hoangis pointed. "We have been wandering for some time. Now the tunnel splits in two. I know we said we needed to stay together, but at this pace, we need to cover more ground."

Gunthen replied., "No, it is too dangerous to split up. We have to stay together."

"I agree with the elf," replied Jermys. "We all knew the risks when we agreed to come here. Our safety is not the priority. We have to determine what is occurring with the dragons. The fact we have traveled so long and not seen even one dragon should itself be a concern. Where are they? The second someone steps foot in a Feldschlosschen mine, the dwarves know it. The dragons have to know we are here."

"That is it," replied Hoangis. "They do not need to attack us because they are so well hidden in these caverns they know we will never find them. We have to split up. We have to cover as much of the area as we can with the hope that one of us can break this secret code the dragons are hiding behind."

Gunthen was about to protest again but held his tongue after seeing the confirmatory nods on his companions' faces. "Very well, but nobody goes alone. Hoangis and I will take the tunnel on the right, and Bretton, you and Jermys take the one on the left."

"Pardon me for saying so, Gunthen," started Bretton, "but should Jermys and I split up? We are more comfortable in mines than either of you so it may prove beneficial."

"I considered that, but I think you will do better together. You have to figure this out, and I want both your minds working together. However, let's do this. It is probably two hours till nightfall. Let's walk for two hours total. After one hour, turn back and let's return here and regroup. That way we can explore but still stay together."

"So basically, walk for one hour and then turn back?" stated Jermys, shaking his head in the process. "Doesn't that seem like a waste of time? We don't have the time to double our steps. We need to search and find what is going on. I still go back to what I said before; we did not come here to hang out together. We came here to find proof of what is happening in our world and determine a way to stop it. If we do what you say, we will waste two hours walking back and forth. No…" He stood next to Bretton. "I will agree to walk with my brother, but we will continue until we find something. If we do, we will head back to the mirror room to escape and get word back, or we will find another way out and do the same thing. But I suggest when we split up this time, that it be the last time the four of us see each other in Draag. The next time we meet will be back in our cities taking the next step against whatever evil is spreading across Troyf."

It was clear that Gunthen did not agree with this at all. "There is no chance I can allow..."

Hoangis placed his hand on his shoulder causing the maneth leader to stop speaking and turn to the elf. "Our friend who started this journey with us has already passed. Jermys is correct, we all knew that death was a potential outcome of our trek. We have but one goal, and that goal is to find the secrets hidden within these twisting and, I fear, magically protected caverns. We have spent a great deal of time searching with little success. We don't know what has happened in our world during our absence. We need action. We will double our search by following Jermys' lead and his bravery should be an example for us all. We must go forward as he suggests."

The others nodded in agreement and all eyes fell to the maneth. He struggled with a response at first and then while pressing his lips together, nodded in agreement. "Okay," Gunthen stated, "but I still say we should regroup at some point. Let's plan on the maneth camp in no fewer than ten moons. If not you, then send a representative."

"Agreed," the others stated at the same time.

They reached their hands in and pressed their knuckles together in a powerful show of unison. "Stay safe," Gunthen stated as they broke. "Please stay safe."

***

"My king," stated the human cadet. "One of our team was found dead this morning with no apparent reason."

The eyes of Octavius, Geoff, and Tantis all turned in fear to the human who had entered their tent just off the Dry Sea of Nakton. Octavius answered, "Show me."

The human led the group to the body on the ground. His face was pale and body cold. They looked down to him, felt his face, and the human king looked to the others. "Do you know what could have done this?"

Tantis pointed to the dead man's arm. "Is that a hole in his forearm? That small break with the spot of dried blood and other mass expelled from it?"

Octavius was still standing over the body and looked closer to where Tantis had directed. "Yes, what is it?"

"Boreworm," he replied. "Nothing catching, and nothing to fear. It finds living creatures usually while they sleep, and tunnels through their body destroying everything in its path. There is a cure if caught early, but also very rarely successful. You have to get the worm out of the body. It secretes a toxin that incapacitates. Once it reaches the heart, there is no recovery. For your soldier, we are too late."

The human king lowered his head and then motioned to the soldier that had led them over. "Wake all the troops. Make certain they are well. Check for any breaks in the skin. Let's not lose any more men before arriving at our target."

The man left without further comment. Octavius turned to the others. "One man lost will not change our direction, but are there other such things we need to be concerned about?"

Tantis shook his head. "There is danger all across the land, but our focus is Draag. That is where we will face the biggest threat." He paused and then spoke mainly to Octavius. "Pull your men together. We will have a warrior's funeral. I have a special dust which will help his transition to the next journey."

Octavius placed his hand on his deceased soldier's chest and bowed his head. He rose and began to gather his troops in a circle. Tantis stepped forward, said several words, removed a pouch and spread a light dust across the body. A cool breeze blew by their faces in a swirling motion and then the body vanished with a soft light.

After a long silence, Octavius raised his eyes to the other leaders. "Come now, time is of the essence. Let's gather our troops and head across the Dry Sea. We must reach Draag."

Geoff was pleased to hear the words. His time with the human had been short, and there did seem to be some struggles for power within him, but maybe he was just trying to grow and protect his very young kingdom. The maneth roared signaling to all that it was time to pack up and move across the desert. The daylight was fading which meant travel would be possible. He only hoped they could make it far enough to find shelter on the other side. If they were trapped on the Dry Sea by midday, they may lose half their troops, and those that did survive would be of little use. They had to make good time. Geoff, as well as the others, knew it.

THE DRAGON OPPRESSION

Tantis took to the air, and the mass of humans, with a handful of elves, maneth, and a single canok, followed behind. To Geoff's pleasure, they made excellent time and even before the first sign of the morning sun, they could see a tree line in the distance marking the edge of the forests. They had not run into resistance, which made the maneth believe they would be able to arrive unexpected. He was standing next to Tantis who had just landed when he heard the cry.

"What is that?" shouted a human voice from the rear. "Something approaches in the sky."

There was a shudder through the ranks, but no more words were said. Geoff and Tantis stared at the dots. "Please tell me, those are just elves, correct?" asked Geoff.

"No," replied Tantis staring hard, his Elven sight straining to make out what was in the rear. "They are too large."

The minute he offered the description, both knew the answer. Geoff put his paws to his mouth and shouted, "Everyone, to the trees, as fast as you can run! Drop your provisions if you need to but keep your weapons. You have to make the tree line."

Instantly the troops broke into a full run. Although the elves with them were faster, the humans kept up fairly well. Geoff and Tantis remained until all creatures had passed and then they followed. Geoff had his maneth club pulled to his side and Tantis had his bow ready.

The elf spoke as he ran. "I am going to stop and take flight. I will slow them down, even if only to give the troops a moment longer."

"Do not, Tantis. You are no match for three dragons. They will wipe you out without slowing down."

Tantis looked back as Geoff answered, "We are not going to make it."

They both stopped as the others continued at a full sprint forward. They looked at each other, locked wrists in a tight handshake, then turned to face the oncoming dragons. Geoff raised his club and Tantis prepared to release bow fire.

"Let's see what steps they take before we fire," stated Geoff.

Tantis nodded. "If we wait and they choose to roll a wall of fire across us, then we will never fire."

Geoff nodded in return. "If we fire and they don't intend to roll a wall of fire across us, then they will wipe us out. We cannot beat them, not today anyway. We are not prepared."

The elf understood the reasoning, but a question immediately came to him. "Then why are we going to Draag? There will be many more than three dragons waiting for us."

"Hoping that others are doing the same," the maneth replied as the dragons reached the outskirts of Tantis's bow range.

"Are you sure, my friend? I need to fire now if I am going to."

Geoff did not answer the question but responded a different direction. "Lower your weapon and do what I do." He began waving as if to call them in.

Tantis looked at the maneth questioningly but did the same nonetheless. He whispered, "If we get out of this alive, I will owe you more than I have to give."

Geoff whispered in return, "If we get out of this alive, you need to give me some new armor because I think I just soiled this set."

The elf could not help but smile as the three dragons, though adjusting their flight to remain protected, landed in front of them. A large blue dragon spoke, "Why do you call us down, and who are you?"

Geoff took a step forward, trying to show no fear. "We are bringing some troops to Draag to help defend the dragons. We have been sent to assist."

The three dragons looked at him, but again the blue spoke, "What are you?"

"I am a maneth and he is an elf. We have left our races behind and brought others who feel as we do, that we cannot defeat the dragon way."

The blue smiled. "We are to destroy the maneth and elf homeland. We must first gather more dragons. Did Bjork summon you?"

Geoff had no idea who Bjork was, but he was not going to let that stop him. "Yes, Bjork told us to head to Draag."

The three dragons smiled. "Very good. We understand there is a small force there trying to infiltrate our boundaries. You may be able to find them first. Continue to Draag and kill any who don't feel as you do. We must stop any chance of survival of any races that wish to stop us."

"Yes," replied Geoff in a tone to show strong support. "We must." He turned to Tantis who nodded in agreement, but the elf's expression showed that he was clearly uncomfortable with the conversation. Geoff continued, "When will you be descending on the maneth camp and elf city? We may have others who can join you on this trek."

The blue smiled. "No, it is my understanding the maneth and elf camps will be no issue. The three of us are headed to the maneth camp, and we are going to gather others to head to Elvinott. Bjork has stated that there will be little resistance."

"Very well," stated Geoff. "We will move on to Draag and find the intruders, then wait to hear about your successes."

"Excellent," returned the blue to the nods of the other two. They opened their wings and departed without another word.

Tantis reached up to Geoff's shoulder and turned the large maneth to face him. "What are we going to do, Geoff? Even if we are successful and find what we seek in Draag, we will have no homes to return to."

"Will the enchantment of Elvinott protect it?" Geoff asked.

"I have no idea. I doubt Hoangis has any idea. It is strong, but it has never been tested. If the dragons have grown strong with magic, why would I believe they have not exceeded that of the elves?"

The maneth turned to see the black dots in the sky slowly getting smaller over the wooded trees ahead of him. "They will wipe out the maneth camp. It has no defense as such. I have to go back."

"But these troops need a leader. They cannot be left to follow Octavius. He has—"

Geoff cut the elf off. "Tantis, I know what I am about to ask you is great, but I need you to trust me. The maneth camp can't defend against dragons. That much is certain. I will run directly to the camp. We will evacuate to Elvinott and the maneth will help protect your home. I will get word to them and help them prepare." He looked into the young elf's eyes. "You need to lead these troops in. You need to find the Revel Rock and destroy it."

"These troops follow you. My flight will gain much time. I can fly to your camp and bring the maneth to Elvinott. You need to stay."

Geoff shook his head. "I don't deny that you could most likely save some time, but the maneth are proud of their heritage and their lives. There is a chance they would follow you, but there is a greater chance they will stay firm and defend our home. I know I can convince them to move."

They stared at each other without talking for several moments. Finally, Tantis nodded. "Very well, but go in haste. You don't have time to spare and both our homes must be protected."

Geoff did not speak again. He placed his arm on his friend's shoulder and then took off at an amazing pace back across the Dry Sea of Nakton, though a slightly different direction than where they had come from. Tantis lifted himself in the air and flew into the trees to gather the troops and explain what had occurred.

***

Bretton stared at his twin as they both looked perplexed at the shiny mirror before them. "How did we end up back here? You were leading several hours ago. You must have turned us around."

Jermys returned the stare with fire burnt into his eyes. "No, I never turned. I followed the mine completely through. We never had a split. It must have been you who caused us to turn around. You have never been able to lead us as well as…"

Bretton drew his weapon. "To the end?"

Jermys joined his brother and lifted his axe. "To the end!"

Both twins released their hatchets without any further words. The strike was pure for both of them, and a large chunk of the wall broke free in two spots and landed on the floor of the open room. They both quickly went over to inspect their pieces. Bretton shook his head. "Yours is bigger."

"Nope," replied Jermys, "yours is definitely bigger. Look at the diameter."

"Maybe, but yours definitely has more weight. Who aims for the most dense area with the iron ferrite composition?"

They looked at each other, nodded, and let the matter drop. "Let's call this one a tie. Neither of us caused the turnaround. Something about this cavern brought us back here." Jermys had walked to the far entrance as he spoke while Bretton approached the mirror.

"This glass is exquisite," he stated as he stared at his reflection. He lightly touched the mirror. "I can't even put a streak on it."

He turned around as he felt something had changed. "Jermys!" he shouted. "Jermys, where are you?"

Jermys turned back to the mirror to discuss what their next step should be. He froze when he saw it. His twin was gone. "Bretton?" he stated softly, removing his hatchet again. "Bretton, he stated louder, his voice echoing off the walls of the empty room. Then he heard it. Footsteps coming fast, but not dwarven. They were too loud and too large.

Jermys darted out the opposite doorway but stopped when he was clear of sight. He heard the noise behind him continue to grow louder but he knew he had to find out who or what it was because the coincidence was too close. It must have something to do with Bretton's disappearance. His eyes grew wide when he saw the first large blue dragon burst through the far opening and enter the room followed by two others.

"We are here," the blue roared. The dragon opened its mouth sending a wall of fire into the corridor, causing Jermys to dive further to the side as the heat rolled passed him.

Jermys recovered quickly, ready for the dragons to follow his trail, or scent, or use whatever method to determine he and his brother were there. However, no dragons came, and the previous noise had completely subsided. He slowly peered back into the mirror room and it was empty.

***

"What do you want to do now?" asked Hoangis.

Gunthen shrugged. "I don't know. I suppose we have to split up. I said before that everyone should stay together, but we are finding nothing. We don't know anything more now than when we left my camp."

Hoangis pointed. "I will go this way. The cavern appears as if it goes further down. You take the other way."

The maneth was about to protest, but as he thought about it, neither knew what was in either direction so it really made no difference. "Very well. May your god be with you, Hoangis."

"We must still plan on meeting the others as soon as one of us finds anything, and then escape. The word must get out."

Gunthen nodded. "I understand. Stay safe, my friend. We shall meet again."

Hoangis nodded and then darted down the opposite cavern.

Chapter Sixteen

"Slayne, you sent us here to gather more dragons. Why are *you* here?" the blue dragon asked.

"Because we have evaluated our plan and realized that we do not only wish to weaken the other races, we wish to destroy them. I want all the dragons who follow me to join us."

The blue dragon smiled, and fire dripped from between its teeth. "This move is aggressive. Is Bjork sure it is the correct direction? We know there is a crowd within Draag's walls now. We passed a small group coming to help defend our caverns, but others have been seen in their wake, probably coming to destroy those that deserted their lands. Should we leave the caverns unprotected?"

"What do you mean you passed a group coming to help defend? Are you saying some of the maneths and elves wish to follow the dragon way?"

The blue nodded. "Yes, it appears they believe they cannot defeat us and rather than defend their lands, they will join and serve under our rule."

Slayne smiled broadly. "This is even better than I thought. Now we must destroy all that is left in their lands. No living creature shall remain. Gather all the dragons." He stopped when he saw the blue dragon's expression. "What is it?" he asked.

"Just a clarification among those we saw. There was one that called itself an elf and one that called itself a maneth. We spoke to them. But when we approached, we were able to see a larger number ahead that were different. They were neither maneth nor elf."

Slayne continued to nod. "These must be the ones who are building a settlement on the North Sea. We shall crush them now, before they can be established. They will learn who truly rules this world."

"But still, what about protecting Draag? Can we really leave it alone?"

Slayne was breathing fire through his excitement. "The group you saw will defend the site, and if they don't, nobody can find the secret passage to our hidden caverns and the Revel Rock. The dragons that gain power from it will remain strong. I, like Bjork, do not draw power from the stone. I will remain here to ensure all is protected. Now go, gather all the dragons. Go first to the elves, as they will require the most strength. Send only a few to the maneth camp. They are unprotected and surprise will be on your side. Then go to the North Sea. Whatever is there, level it."

"What about the dwarves?" asked the blue.

Slayne did not hesitate with his answer. "They, like the canoks, have been divided. Let's allow that division to take hold and see what transpires. Perhaps the situation will solve itself."

"Very well, Slayne," replied the blue. "We shall leave at once."

The blue left with its two counterparts following in its wake. Slayne moved over and stood next to a pedestal in the center of the room. On the pedestal sat a large blue stone that hummed slightly as it rested. He said a few words and although the humming continued, the stone vanished.

"No, even if this small force makes it here, they will not know where to look," the black dragon said to himself.

"What do you mean, Slayne," stated a deep voice from the side.

The black dragon swung his head around ready to attack then softened his stare when he saw who had spoken. "Sabast, your place here has ended. When Anbari left, so did everything the two of you have stood for. You are too old now to take a position against me. At one time you were the most powerful dragon on Troyf. Now you are a fraction of that. Go now, as I do not wish to destroy you."

The green dragon narrowed his stare on his counterpart. "Slayne, there is much more at work here than you will ever know. I am no threat to you, but there is a threat among your own. You have done so much to create a loyal following that you don't understand all. If you wish to kill me, then do so. If not, I am going to live the rest of my days behind the falls. There is nothing left for me here."

Slayne took one step closer. "I could kill you, you know. I could do it right now."

Sabast was much larger than the younger Slayne and the green dragon took two steps to be closer. "Slayne, you can't even keep your precious Rock hidden."

His eyes swung back to where he had enchanted a spell that caused the Revel Rock to vanish from sight. However, once again, it reappeared, the steady hum and blue hue bringing both sound and light to the room. Slayne again enchanted a spell but nothing changed. He turned back to Sabast. "Change it back, Sabast. Change it back now."

"Or what, you fool dragon? You will kill me?" The green dragon smiled under his breath. "You naïve child. Do you think I don't know when death will find me? Go now, for I can no more change it back than you can. It is not reversable. The stone will be seen by any who enter."

"Those intruders you felt had no chance of finding the secret passage have already had one pass through. More will be coming, but one, in particular that you should fear."

Slayne's anger was growing and just as he was about to bring all his power against the larger green, he stopped on those final words. "Who? Who should I fear?"

Sabast smiled. "Still looking for someone to give you all the answers?" questioned Sabast. The green dragon turned to walk out leaving Slayne staring hard.

"Say who it is, Sabast, or so help me I will destroy all that you care about in this world."

He stopped and turned back to him. "Everything I care about is gone, Slayne. There is nothing more you can take from me."

"Who is it, Sabast?" he stated again, this time in a strong tone that foreshadowed an attack was coming.

The green dragon narrowed his stare. "The vision is not clear. Perhaps one from the new North Sea settlement. Perhaps an elf or a dragon. I can't be sure, but I do know the threat is real. Maybe not today. Maybe not for hundreds of years, but one will be coming."

Slayne roared and shot a burst across the back of the older dragon as he turned away again. The attack struck his scales and although Sabast did feel sharp pain at the point of impact, none showed in his response. "You are so young, Slayne. Can't you foresee your own death?"

The black dragon froze on that comment, and Sabast disappeared out of the corridor. Sabast had headed the direction of the pool away from the mirror room and cavern exit. There was no way out from there, so Slayne knew he could return to deal with Sabast and get the answers he wanted. Just as he was about to leave, he heard voices approaching. He ducked into the shadows and waited.

***

"Where in all of Troyf am I?" stated Bretton to himself. "These caverns are all wrong. Every time I expect I know where I am, my direction is reversed. I have returned to the same room three times and have no idea why."

The dwarf had been talking to himself for nearly a day. His twin had vanished and the mines had changed. He had found several rooms but came across no living creatures. But most concerning to him, no matter what direction he went, he ended up back at the mirror room. The fact he was truly lost created so much anxiety in the dwarf he knew he had very little chance of escape. He knew his only answer was to continue walking, and so he did.

***

"Tantis," stated Selbee. "What do you want to do?"

The elf looked down upon the cavern opening watching the twelve dragons move and react as if preparing for battle. "I don't know. Right now, keep the troops well back, out of sight, and quiet. We have no chance against that many dragons. We need a diversion of an extreme proportion, but we need it to not take all of our troops." He paused and his voice softened. "And we need those who create the diversion to have an opportunity to escape."

"Aye," Selbee replied. "I can make a commotion that will bring many, but possibly not all."

Tantis stared at the maneth and he knew who Selbee was. He was a Dimat, not one built for battle. Selbee may be able to draw the dragons away, but for him, it would be his last stand. As they stared into each other's eyes, they both knew that would be the result. Tantis placed his hand on his counterpart's shoulder. "I can't let you do that, Selbee. We will find another way."

"There is no other way," he said, his voice strong but still a whisper. "Nobody else with us has my size or speed. I know you think of me as a Dimat, one who seeks negotiation over battle, but there is no negotiating today. There is no negotiating with dragons. You can see it as well as I. They are preparing for battle. They know we are coming. The three we met recognized Geoff's trickery and have prepared them. I can make enough of a disturbance to appear to be an army moving. Even if they all don't leave, their attention will be drawn. It is your only chance."

"As much as I can't condone a creature giving its life, Selbee is right," stated Stoven. I will go with him. I will protect him from detection with what magic I have here, though something here is limiting my power. I can feel it."

Tantis began to speak but was cut off by Selbee. "Out of the question. You may protect me for a short while, but you will only delay the inevitable. This one must be left to my hands. You will be needed inside the caverns. We all agree with that."

Tantis nodded. "Thank you, Stoven, but Selbee is correct. Although I have the same feelings, it is the only way."

The maneth, Stoven, and Tantis stared at each other and each knew the answer. Selbee pressed his lips together and then spoke as he nodded. "I will prepare my things. Get the troops ready, for your opportunity will be small. You will need to act immediately for this to work, and a second chance will most likely not come your way."

It was a short time later as nightfall began to engulf the forest, and Selbee locked hands with Tantis. The elf reached his second hand around his shoulder. "Be safe, my friend. If we are successful inside Draag, we will come to find you. Find a hole you can dive into."

Selbee reached his hand across. "You be safe as well. I don't know which is worse, my taking on as many dragons as I can by myself, or you fighting with this group of humans who struggle to hold a sword, much less swing one."

Stoven had walked closer and heard the last comment. "I give you better odds, Selbee."

The two broke and all smiled at the white canok before them. "Are the humans ready?" Selbee asked.

Stoven nodded. "I believe I have communicated the same message to all of them. They have moved up and will attack on Tantis's signal."

"Then I guess this is it," he stated. He nodded back to Tantis. "May Shriak be with you this day, Tantis."

The elf smiled and bowed as Selbee turned and moved through the trees away from them. His movement was silent rivaling any elf, but shortly thereafter, sounds that matched dozens of men roaring through the trees began to echo through the area. Tantis swung his head down to the dragons who instantly had gone into a stir. About half appeared to be ready for flight to investigate when three new dragons emerged from the cavern. They seemed to be led by a blue.

Tantis whispered, "That looks like the same blue dragon Geoff and I met on the Dry Sea." He listened as best he could but could not make out the words the dragon was saying.

"What's going on?" asked the blue.

"We don't know, Graven," replied a brown dragon close to him. "A loud noise in the trees. Sounds like a large army. I was about to send several dragons to investigate."

"No," replied the blue. "Send two. That will leave thirteen of us here." He began speaking louder allowing all in the area, as well as Tantis, to hear. "Two of you go see to this disturbance. Eliminate whatever it is. If it claims to be friendly, determine its truth. If you have any doubt, eliminate it. The rest of you have been selected to lead the greatest attack in the history of our world. We are going to eliminate all opposition to the new dragon way. There are three races we must eliminate. I am going to lead another twenty dragons that will attack the elves. They are the strongest with magic and will need more force to break through. There is some new settlement near the North Sea. You nine go there and destroy anything you see." He motioned to nine dragons on his left. "We do not know how strong they are so be prepared for anything. And the remaining four..." He now looked to the brown dragon who had spoken and the remaining dragons around him. "Go and find the maneth homeland and kill all of them. They will provide little resistance as they fight with their clubs. Burn them and their clubs to ashes."

Tantis pressed his lips together fighting to remain in control. It was clear Stoven had not heard the words. He did not know whether it was better to tell him or not.

Then the blue dragon called Graven continued, "And one more thing. There are two races of canoks and dwarves now. If you see any white canoks, kill them on sight unless it is a white canok with a black diamond patch on its forebrow. The same goes for the dwarves. Slayne has created a race of dark dwarves. They are much darker in color and they will fight for us. But he was unable to reach the Feldschlosschen dwarves. He believes the dark brothers will destroy Feldschlosschen on their own, but if you see a mining dwarf, they should suffer the same fate as the white canoks. Destroy them all."

Tantis looked down toward his all-white companion. "They are going to attack Elvinott, the maneth camp, and the humans. They are also going to seek out and destroy the mining dwarves and white canoks." He paused and knelt down to whisper to the canok, "The time is now. They are starting the war."

Stoven growled slightly as he heard the words. As he did so, the dragons took off in flight every direction. They saw two that flew toward the woods in the wake of their friend and the others lifted in the air in multiple directions.

Stoven lifted his paw forward. "We go now, or we don't go at all. More dragons will come to reinforce this entrance. They would never leave it completely unprotected."

Tantis gave the signal. The canok had prepared the human troops to move swiftly. When the elf heard the rumbling of the humans, he just shook his head. "I can't believe this is who I was chosen to lead," he said to the canok.

Stoven just smiled. "It doesn't matter now. This is who we have, and we must move without delay." Tantis heard the urgency in his voice and opened his wings into flight. He quickly moved to the front. He had his bow at the ready but to his surprise, there were no dragons left. He heard a roar from the forest in the direction of Selbee and bowed his head. Within moments, the entire battalion was inside the cavern entrance.

***

"What are you doing here, maneth?" stated the tan dragon standing above him. Blue blood was seeping from Selbee's face where its talon had torn his helmet free and cut from his eye nearly down to his chin. Selbee was lying on his back and struggling to stand. His club had been thrown clear, and he swung his head to determine if it was within his reach. The dragon followed his eyes and continued his thought. "Go ahead, reach for the club. See if you can get it." Just as the words came out the dragon shot a wall of fire to where the club laid sending the nearby trees and the wooden weapon he had carried into flames. Selbee's eyes fell.

"I ask you again, maneth, and this will be the last time. Why are you in our forests?"

"I am here to destroy Draag. I have come on my own to find whatever gives dragons their power and was going to use my club to destroy the source of that power."

The two dragons could not control their laughter. "You are a fool."

Selbee turned his expression into one of determination. "You are correct," he responded, causing both dragons to stop laughing and stare down to him. "I was a fool. I see now there is no way our feeble forces could mount any defense against such a superior race. You are too strong and too great in numbers. The only option for the maneth is to join the dragons."

"I do not believe you, maneth," replied the tan dragon. "You would say anything to save your life. And as we both stand here before you, let me say that nothing will do that now."

The dragon arched his head back and was about to expel a wall of fire that would mark Selbee's last breath when a new voice spoke from behind them. "Imagine if you were to bring a maneth to Slayne who would join him. Even if we are successful and destroy their homeland, some will live. Who could infiltrate the remaining maneths and turn them to Slayne's side? Think what that would mean for you, the one to bring about another race under dragon rule."

"Draketon," stated the tan as it turned to face who had spoken. "What are you doing here?"

"I was on my way to the South Sea and thought to myself, why don't I want to be at the dragon homeland on this glorious day?"

The tan dragon nodded. "I agree. This day will be remembered forever."

"And you, maneth," continued Draketon, "imagine the power you would have as ruler over the maneth. I am sure Slayne would make it so, should you help him."

Selbee's eyes widened as did the tan's. The dragon turned toward the fallen maneth and saw the change in his eyes. "This is your one chance, maneth. Do you wish to go before Slayne? He will not show any mercy should you cross him."

Selbee pushed himself up. His voice was strong considering the position he was in. Blood still flowed from the wound on his face. He coughed slightly and used his front paw to wipe his cheek clean. "I know I can move up the maneth ladder and influence their direction. With support from Slayne, and some assistance in clearing the throne, I can assert myself as king of the maneths. Should that happen, I will have the maneth follow the law of the dragons."

Draketon looked on and was impressed by the performance. Even he felt the maneth was speaking the truth. The tan dragon nodded. "Then what is your name, maneth?"

He took a small step toward the tan dragon. "I am Selbee."

"Well then, Selbee, come with me. I will take you to Slayne and he can decide your fate."

The tan began to open his wings but Draketon stepped closer preventing the action from occurring and stopping all flight. "Where are the dragons who should stand guard outside the caverns?"

"Slayne has sent several groups to the races that must be destroyed. The maneth camp has the fewest, then the elves and the North Sea. We will destroy them all."

The red dragon frowned. "What will be left? Does Slayne want to rule no one?"

The tan dragon now shared the thought. "We should stop the attack on the maneth. They are of no concern to us physically, but now that we have an inside track to rule, we should allow the action to happen and build an even stronger force to follow our leader."

Draketon nodded agreement before he added, "You two go and stop the dragon attack on the maneth homeland, and I will take Selbee before Slayne."

The tan turned to face him directly. "There is no way that is going to happen. You just want to take credit for the capture. You stop the attack, and we will take the maneth to Slayne. If you don't get there in time, so be it."

Draketon's plan to keep the maneth alive was solid, but he could see in the tan dragon's eyes that there was no way he would change his mind. Draketon was also not in a position to fight two dragons. He quickly realized the maneth would be on his own, but if he could respond the way he just did, perhaps he could convince Slayne he would fight for him. Draketon recognized the pause was too long and quickly responded, "Very well. I will stop the attack and you take the maneth. I will go at once." He leaned in close to Selbee and whispered, "Talk like you just did and you may make it out of Draag alive."

The tan dragon leaned his head down in front of Selbee's face. "Don't disappoint me, maneth, or I shall take enjoyment in your death. It will be slow and full of tremendous pain." He laughed as did the other dragon still standing next to him. With fire dripping between his teeth, he motioned the maneth forward. He nudged him in the back to improve his pace and then with his teeth, grabbed his mane in frustration and lifted him into the air. Selbee roared in pain, but the dragon did not relent. To Selbee's surprise, they did not fly to the cavern opening. Instead they flew to an area deeper within the forest, to where the hills turned into taller mountains. The dragon landed where an opening appeared on the surface.

"We will enter here. Do not..."

The tan's voice was cut off as a magical beam struck him in the back. He turned to see a white canok standing before him. "Let the maneth go," stated Tashro.

The dragon laughed. "Do you really think you can defeat two dragons?" replied the tan.

Selbee was released when the dragon spoke and landed on the ground. Tashro glanced to the maneth to verify he was all right. Then he brought his attention back to the dragons. "No, but my friends and I believe we can at least try." As he spoke, twenty more all-white canoks appeared from the trees behind.

The laughter from the dragons ceased immediately. "Interesting. I heard about your divided nation, but even twenty canoks are no match for us." The other dragon took his place by the tan's side. "I have but one question for you," the dragon continued.

"What is that?" replied Tashro.

"Do you wish to die by fire or the piercing of my teeth through your flesh, because to me, it doesn't matter."

Tashro and the other canoks closed their eyes and began to incant some spell between them, though the dragons heard no words. Without warning, the dragon next to the tan fell down as if being strangled. It writhed in pain and then was suddenly silenced. "Are you sure you wish to fight us, dragon?" asked Tashro.

He laughed. "My counterpart was weak. Your mind control won't work on me." He opened up his mouth and laid a wall of fire across the glade. Several canoks fell to the ground, their fur slightly burnt, but they quickly recovered and then all stood as they had before. The tan dragon took a step back in fear.

"You see, dragon, we are vulnerable when we are alone, but together our powers expand exponentially. You can't defeat us. Now release the maneth or we will kill you just like we killed your counterpart."

"Or perhaps you will die instead," echoed a raspy voice from behind them.

Tashro turned to see a wall of black canoks, all clearly linked together just as the whites had been previously. Instantly the canoks attacked in battle. Magic was of no use so they went for each of the other's bodies, biting with all the force they could muster. The tan dragon saw the confusion and grabbed Selbee in his mouth and disappeared through the sky window of the mirror room. They could hear the fighting until their feet struck the floor.

"Now, maneth, prove to me you are worth the risk." The dragon walked over to the mirror and pulled the disoriented maneth with him. He kept his wing in contact with the maneth and then touched the mirror lightly. Instantly they vanished from the mirror room to appear in the exact same room an immense distance below the first one but reversed in layout.

Selbee looked up toward the dragon's amused face. All sound was gone. No more fighting or battle could be heard. The mirror still stood in the room, but the skylight was beyond sight. "What just happened?" the maneth asked.

"In due time, maneth, and only if Slayne dictates as such."

The tan dragon moved away from the mirror and began walking down one of the two corridors exiting the room. He looked back to Selbee. "Are you coming? There is no turning back now."

The maneth looked around the room one more time and then disappeared behind the dragon.

***

Several maneths shouted as they heard the noise of someone approaching. "Geoff, you return," hollered one when he broke through the trees.

He hurried toward the group. "Where is the king? Where is McCard?"

When the large group of maneths heard Geoff's tone and saw his face, they quickly realized all pleasantries of his arrival would be short-lived, and Alhize, the first maneth he reached who sat midway up the Dimat Line, pointed to the king's tent. "There, my friend. The king is in his chambers."

Geoff issued no other comments and turned and headed directly to where Alhize had pointed. He arrived at the tent just as the flap opened and McCard emerged. Geoff's surprise at seeing him was eclipsed by the surprise in return. "Geoff? I heard the commotion. What brings you here in such haste?"

Geoff was breathing hard and in between breaths, he answered. "My King, I have grave news which I must tell you, for the maneth have to act immediately."

McCard lifted his arm to him. "Come in, my son, let's talk in my chambers where we will not be disturbed."

The two maneth entered the tent where Geoff then immediately presented everything that had happened. As he told the king about the pending attack from the dragons, his eyes sank. "Then we have our answer," replied the king. "The dragons are behind the evil, and they are bringing that evil to our doorstep."

"What can we do, my King? Do you wish me to prepare our troops to defend our home? We can build a strong line to defend when they arrive. They won't be expecting us to be pre—"

Geoff was cut off by the king's raised hand. "No, my young soldier. I have seen the dragons of the past fight. I have seen their destruction. Against one dragon, we may have a chance, but against many, we would be lost." His voice trailed off as Geoff saw he was clearly deep in thought. "Perhaps our Feast of All was the right answer. Perhaps bringing our friends together in a place of solitude would provide what we all need to survive."

Geoff tilted his head as he did not follow the comment, but he also did not interrupt. There was a slight appearance of an idea coming to fruition in the king's eyes and the worn-out battle maneth was not going to interrupt him. The king lifted his head and stared directly into his eyes. "Prepare the camp. We are going to move, but do not remove our tents, and provide me a list of your best choice for a battalion to be left behind."

"Left behind?" Geoff questioned. "A battalion? Wouldn't Gunthen be a better option to choose a team?"

The king placed his arm on Geoff's shoulder. "No, Geoff, Gunthen is not here. You have fought hard to gain this information and probably save the lives of our entire race. This is your job now. Find thirty of the best maneths you wish to stand beside you and bring them to me. I will speak to each of them, for what I am going to ask must come from the highest order." He removed his hand and smiled. "Now go, son, time is critical."

Geoff exited without further comment. McCard sat down on the ground cross-legged and lowered his head in meditation and prayer.

***

Geoff returned with thirty of the most heavily armored maneth ever assembled. He had told them each to be prepared for the hardest battle of their lives. When he said that the orders came directly from the king, many of them added dress gear they had never worn before. They stood in a line outside McCard's tent when Geoff saluted the king as he pushed open his tent to stand before them. The king returned the salute to Geoff and then one-by-one walked down the line taking the maneths' paws in his and exchanging some words of praise. He then turned to address the entire line at once which had become surrounded by nearly the entire camp as word had spread of the commotion.

Geoff brought over a large stone and dropped it in front of the king's feet to give him something to stand upon. In a strong and loud voice, the king began speaking so all could hear. "To all the maneth of this camp and our home, but especially to the thirty brave maneth who stand directly before me as proud representatives to defend our lives. As king of our great land, I must be the one to bring you grave news. Today I learned from Geoff that an army of dragons has been formed and through his great work, their plan has been revealed." The area went silent as they waited to hear their king's next words. "The news I have, however, will forever shape the maneth homeland as well as all the races on Troyf. This dragon army is sending detachments to each of the races we call friends. The detachments are not being sent to issue laws or rules on following the dragon way. They are being sent to wipe those races from existence."

There was a spattering of talk and comments as his words were passed between brothers, families, and every maneth before him. Several held hands, lowered their heads, or knelt down. Even prayers were heard softly among the group and a few had tears fall lightly across their cheeks.

"What are we to do?" echoed an elderly voice from the back. "We aren't prepared to fight dragons."

The king gently lowered his eyes feeling the pain and fear of those before him. His voice remained strong, and he spoke mainly to those thirty who stood directly in front of him. "You are right, we are not prepared to fight the dragons, but we also cannot simply flee. They will chase us down until none of us remain. I also fear for the other races. Only together can we survive." He paused as the words were coming difficult to him. "We will leave a small group of thirty maneth to be led by Geoff. They will remain here until the dragons arrive. They will provide such a strong defense against the dragons that the dragons will believe the village remains in full. Their fight will be tremendous and by the will of the gods, they will find their escape."

The group in front stood strong, but as Geoff looked down the line, he could see the fear growing in their eyes. Another voice from the crowd of maneth hollered, "But where will the rest of us go? Why will not all remain to fight?"

The king raised his hands. "My friends, please understand, I have seen dragons. I have seen the destruction they bring. The maneth are strong with the forest and the trees. We are one with the animals, but we can't defend against a dragon attack. The rest of us will go to Elvinott. We will fight beside the elves and save their land. It is protected with magic, and the elves are skilled with bows. From Elvinott, the maneth can provide support that may help save both races."

One of the maneth in the front line stepped forward. "But, Your Majesty, if you state that the maneth can't defeat the dragons, what is it you wish us to do?"

The king again lowered his eyes, but it was Geoff who moved to stand beside his king to answer. "You will follow the lead of Alhize of the Dimat Line and myself of the Batt Line. We will create two fronts of fifteen maneth each. We will prepare as much defense as we can. We will create chaos in the woods. We need the dragons to believe they have captured our village unprepared. Return what attack we can, but the goal is not to bring down any dragons. We then flee to the forest the opposite direction of Elvinott. We need them to believe they have destroyed the camp, and if they pursue, it must be away from the elves."

The thirty maneth on the line began to shake their heads. They understood the plan. It was simple misdirection. They were going to buy time for the other maneth to get to Elvinott. The maneth who had asked the question replied, "We will not let you down, my King."

The other maneth roared and the power growing among them was great. McCard smiled. "I know you won't, my friends. Now, time is short, and we must move quickly. All maneth, gather only your necessities. Gather any weapons you have. We will leave before the sun moves. It is time we head to Elvinott, for it is our only chance."

***

"Dragons!" shouted a voice pointing to the sky causing others in the area to run for cover.

"Man the harpoons," another voice shouted.

Anbari closed his eyes while he angled his wings downward. He spoke with telepathy to those on the ground. *"We are returning as friends. We need your help."*

The message was sent to all within sight. Instantly the commotion in the village center ceased and word was spread. Anbari and Hawthorne landed softly on the ground with Fehr happily sleeping on the large female dragon's back.

Anbari nodded to those that greeted them. "Who is in charge?" he asked.

A tall human stepped forward. "With Octavius on his mission, he left me to lead the village. I am Deklan Sherblade."

Anbari lowered his head to Deklan. "I am looking for an elf. He would have been traveling alone."

Deklan raised his hand. "If he went by the name of Ku, he was here and left."

Instantly both Anbari and Hawthorne grew excited. "What was his direction?"

The human continued. "He originally was seeking transport across the North Sea. However, when he learned about the force heading to the dragon homeland, his new direction was in their wake. He was many days behind them, but traveling alone he would have made better time."

Anbari leaned in closer to Hawthorne and whispered, "I told you his intentions were good. He is heading to join the battle against the dragons. We have to get him the ring. Its powers would be of great aid in his battle."

Hawthorne did not respond but her expression clearly showed she agreed. "What is it you need from this elf?" the human asked.

Anbari turned back to the small group. "Guard your land well, my friends. Prepare for an attack. I am not sure when or by what method, but I can feel the tension growing. We must find this elf as he is the key to keep balance between all races on Troyf."

The humans did not understand everything, but they did clearly hear one statement: *Prepare for an attack.* Deklan lifted his sword to the two dragons. "Go find the elf. We will prepare for any attack brought upon us. We have fashioned many weapons and will continue in haste to make more. If this elf is the key to our success, then please go now and find him."

Anbari nodded and without another word opened his wings, kicking up a wall of dust from the ground as he and Hawthorne lifted in the air. When they were well out of earshot, Hawthorne stated softly, "They have no chance against a dragon attack, do they, Anbari?"

The larger dragon pressed his lips together. "No. They will be wiped clean before they even know what hit them." She stopped in flight and hovered in the air causing Anbari to do the same. "What is it?" Anbari asked.

Hawthorne glanced down toward the village now just a small spot on the horizon. "If we are truly fighting for what you claim, fighting for all life on Troyf, how can we leave this village to be destroyed? Maybe their growth and development also brings balance to our world. Maybe one of these humans is part of the puzzle as well."

Anbari laughed slightly at the comment. "I sense nothing of significance from this race. Their presence is, and will always be, a nonfactor. However, I can't argue with your words. Either we are fighting for all life or we are not. What are you saying we should do?"

"I will remain. I can create some barriers for the village, and I will see the dragons coming before they arrive. I can help them fight."

"Hawthorne," Anbari stated softly. "I can feel the power within the dragons now. They have learned to tap into the stone and they no longer are simply powerful creatures of flight and fire. They are strong with magic. If they send many, you will not be able to defend against them. Your life would most likely end."

"I know," she replied, "but if I leave them alone, I may be alive, but unable to live."

He understood her meaning. He nodded to her and while hovering there together, they reached their necks out to wrap around each other. She turned and headed back toward the small dot just shy of the North Sea. Anbari turned and cut a narrow path through the cool wind toward Draag.

***

"Tantis, I hear footsteps up ahead," stated one of the humans.

The elf looked down to Stoven who shook his head. "I sense nothing. It could be protected by magic, or it could just be these caverns blocking some of my abilities."

Tantis understood and motioned to the soldier who had just reported the information to move the rest of the troops back as quietly as he could. He knelt down next to the canok. "Come with me. Let's you and I investigate this. If it is an ambush or something we cannot handle, I will stay, and you retreat to get the troops back down to where the cavern splits. It will be your only chance."

Stoven didn't like the plan, but he didn't have a better one. No position was safe, so he had no argument. He lowered his body just above the surface and began creeping forward, the elf moving to the far wall to give some protection as well. They peered around a corner and their eyes took in a large open room. There was some light coming in from a skylight up above but other than a large freestanding mirror near a far wall, the room was empty. Tantis saw one other exit on the opposite side. The footsteps were drawing louder, and the elf believed they were about to enter from the other side.

***

"I don't believe it," stated Hoangis.

"I don't either," replied Gunthen. "First we come back together when two caverns combine and now we have doubled back into the mirror room where we started. We are not going to find…"

His comment stopped when Hoangis raised his hand. "I hear something?"

"What?" whispered the maneth.

"Breathing," he replied.

They ducked behind the cavern opening and waited. Gunthen continued to whisper, "Do you think it is dragons?"

"No," the elf king replied. "It is someone in hiding just beyond the other side of the room. They wait to attack. Their breathing is rapid as if nervous."

"What do you think we should do? Retreat?" asked Gunthen, his voice showing he was typically not comfortable with the word.

The two looked at each other and then the elf replied, "What good would that do us? We have wandered these caverns for days and found nothing. We have split with the others and even separated ourselves only to find our way back here. We have been waiting to find someone else. Why don't we just go greet them?"

The maneth nodded. "Then let's walk out, greet this enemy, and find some answers."

Hoangis held up his hand. "No, we have to think about our goal. Only one of us should go. The other should prepare to either aid in surprise or leave to continue the mission."

"Very well," replied Gunthen. "I will go."

"You and I both know that makes no sense," returned the elf. "You are much stronger and more apt to survive in further confrontations. If this is but one or two goblins, dwarves, or black canoks, I would still have a chance to work my way out of it. However, if it is an all-out assault, we cannot both go down. Wait here and I will go."

The elf did not remain for further discussion and walked out into the mirror room. His steps were slow and guarded, but once he had broken the barrier of the entrance, he knew he was exposed. He did not stare at the mirror but remained focused on the far side. He froze when in the darkness he saw two sets of eyes.

"Hoangis," stated Tantis from the doorway, stepping out so he could be seen. "You are alive?"

The elf king's shoulders dropped, and he ran several steps to his longtime friend. The two embraced and Gunthen and Stoven stepped out with them. The meeting was one which none had expected. The feelings were so high that it seemed they had just won an important step in the war, although deep inside they knew nothing had changed. Then, one-by-one the humans emerged behind the group.

Hoangis's eyes grew wide, as did Gunthen's, when they saw the number of soldiers the two had brought. It was the maneth who first spoke to Tantis. "How do you have all these to support us. Where are they from?"

Tantis smiled. "We have much to discuss. These are humans from a land by the North Sea. They have joined us to help defend our world. However, time is of the essence. There are attacks in place on Elvinott, the maneth camp, and the humans' homeland." He paused as his voice softened. "Dragon attacks."

Both Gunthen and Hoangis cringed with the elf king having to take a knee. The maneth continued his questions. "Where is Geoff? Was he not with you?"

Tantis removed his bow and knelt down beside his king, but kept his eyes lifted to Gunthen. "Geoff was with us. We went to the North Sea and upon building this force and making our way to Draag, we crossed a dragon who believed us to be dragon forces. He learned of the plan and immediately went to the maneth homeland to warn them and then on to Elvinott. I have no way of knowing if he got there in time."

Just then Stoven stepped through the opening and Hoangis's eyes fell to him. "Stoven, what has happened to the canoks? We saw the same thing with Tashro."

The four-legged creature slowly walked up to the elf who remained kneeling so they were at approximately the same height. "I can't say. One moment we were together and strong, and the next we were two. Next to me was my longtime friend, and then nothing but fear and hatred was carried within him. His heart had turned to pure evil and the canok way was no longer his way. Those canoks which have black fur will destroy us, I am sure of it."

Hoangis reached out and stroked his fur. "I felt something in my heart. I didn't know what it was. I had hoped it was limited to only a few."

Stoven shook his head. "No, the canok homeland is no longer as it was. The black canoks have fled to the trees. I must assume they are regrouping. Should they join the dragon armies, they will be very difficult to defeat."

All conversations stopped as the mirror suddenly began to hum and then change followed by two canoks appearing as if entering through a door.

Chapter Seventeen

Bretton stepped through a new doorway and knew right away this was a room he had not been in before. He had been walking for days and although he was certain he had backtracked several times, he was in a new section of the caverns. There was a hallway that headed west. In that direction he heard what he believed was running water, like a stream. However, to the north he heard voices, although faint. He did fear who or what he may encounter, but knew if something did not change, their mission would fail. He thought about his brother and wondered where he was and if he was all right.

He crossed into the room and there he saw it. Sitting on top of a pedestal with a blue hue around it was a diamond-shaped stone that hummed softly. He removed his hatchet and began walking toward it. His eyes shot across the room. Much of the room was clouded in darkness but he saw no movement. If another creature was there, they would have said something because he would have been easy to see. He continued toward the stone and when he stood directly in front of it, he lifted his hatchet and swung.

A deep bellowing laugh echoed off the walls. Bretton had dropped his hatchet as upon contact, the blue shell seemed to harden instantly and returned a force to the small dwarf that he could not withstand. His hatchet rested several feet from him. When he looked up, the black eyes of a large black dragon were staring down upon him. "What are you doing here, dwarf?"

Bretton quickly pushed himself up but had no chance to recover his hatchet. "I am here to destroy this Rock, and I will do that."

Again, Slayne laughed. "And how do you intend to do that? I could kill you now with one breath."

"Then kill me, dragon, because I will die before I fail in my goal. I am lucky I found the Revel Rock first."

Slayne stopped his laughter and stared hard at the dwarf. "So, you know about the Revel Rock? You know it provides power to many of my dragons? How do you know this?"

Bretton was slowly moving closer to his hatchet. "I don't have to tell you a thing."

Slayne said a few words and the dwarf was thrown against a wall with magical hands holding him there. "Almok. Kirven. This dwarf feels something for his brother. He is in the cavern somewhere. Find him and kill him."

The two canoks stepped out from the shadows, and the black canok, Almok, was drooling as Slayne spoke. The white canok, Kirven, seemed hesitant on the direction, but did not offer resistance. They both turned and ran out of the room. Slayne turned back to where Bretton was pinned. "Do you want your brother to live or die?"

The question caused instant hesitation in the dwarf. He stuttered. "I-I-I want to…"

"Stop your hesitation. You have only moments to decide. My two canoks will kill him without question. If you wish him to live, you have one option. Your pathetic attempt to destroy the Revel Rock was useless. You can no sooner destroy the Rock than stop my dragons. You have one option to save your life and your brothers."

Bretton stared at the dragon not knowing what to say. He glanced back toward the Revel Rock still resting on the pedestal. It was undisturbed by his swing. Bretton opened and shut his hand that had held the hatchet. The pain in his fingers from the impact was intense, but there was clearly no damage to the shell around the Rock. "What are you going to do to my brother?"

Slayne smiled. "That is easy. I am going to kill him."

"Don't kill my brother," stated Bretton.

Again, he laughed, this time Slayne sent a wall of fire toward the elf that dissipated just before it struck the dwarf, but the heat still turned his face red.

"You don't tell me what I can or can't do. What can you offer me to *not* kill your brother?"

There was a long pause as Bretton thought about the question. Sweat started to roll down his cheeks. He started to answer but remained quiet.

"Very well, dwarf. You will never see your brother again." Slayne closed his eyes and appeared to be in conversation with someone which Bretton assumed were the two canoks who had just left.

"Stop!" interrupted Bretton. "What do you want from me?"

Slayne smiled. "Nothing much, just your loyalty when I need it."

The dwarf looked questionably at the dragon. "What do you mean, loyalty?"

"I mean that when I ask, you will join me and my two canoks and do whatever I ask."

Again there was a long pause. The dwarf looked down to the ground and then back to the dragon. "I will do whatever you ask when you ask, with one exception. I will not bring harm to my brother or any dwarf. If you ask me to do that, I will cancel our agreement."

Slayne leaned back and then moved his head down directly in front of the dwarf. Bretton could feel his hot breath across his face, but he did not move back. Slayne smiled. "Done. When I ask you to join me, you will. It does not matter where you are or if it makes sense to you or not. You join me or you and every dwarf I find will die, starting with your brother. Do you understand?"

Bretton nodded. "I do understand, and my word is good. I will honor our agreement. Do not kill my brother."

Slayne closed his eyes. "*Almok. Kirven. If you find the dwarf, leave him be. Don't harm him. Kill anyone who is with him.*"

The dragon stared down to the dwarf. "It is done. Now leave me. Don't speak to anyone about our agreement, or it is voided, and I will kill every dwarf. I have already split the dwarves and created an army of dark brothers that will consume all your time. You have little chance of living as it is, but if you do, you will honor me. Don't forget it."

Bretton looked toward the dragon in shame. "I will honor you. My word is given."

Slayne paid the comment no mind. "Leave me, for there are others coming and I need to understand what direction I will take with them. Know that by leaving here alive, you have done something no other creature has ever done."

Bretton hurried out of the room gathering his hatchet as he moved. He felt confused on the exchange, but saving his brother was something he felt justified his decision. He would honor his decision but hoped he would never be asked to. He walked out of the room and he too heard noise coming from the same path he had previously used. He heard water and opted to move toward that sound and avoid further confrontations.

***

"Quick," stated Stoven. "Get back into the cavern."

The group quickly moved into the cave from the direction the human army had arrived. Gunthen ducked into the other side where he and Hoangis had entered with the elf following the larger group.

Appearing out of the mirror as if materializing out of the air were two canoks—one black and one white—and both with a diamond patch on their forehead. They immediately took some steps and then the white canok stopped and looked toward the far cave.

Almok stopped as well and asked, "What is it, Kirven?"

"I sense something. I feel like…"

"Feel like what?" asked Gunthen stepping out from the other doorway.

"What is he doing?" whispered Octavius.

Tantis leaned down next to the human. "Keep quiet. He is giving us time to leave. Stoven, what do you think?"

The white canok spoke using telepathy. *"I think they can sense me. We need to retreat at once."*

"No," stated Tantis. "We have numbers, and we have to act. We did not come all this way to run."

Stoven continued, *"They are strong. Much stronger than me. I don't know them, but they are not all canok. They are more. I can sense them the same way they can sense me. If they escape, they will alert all of Draag and our plight will be lost."*

Tantis stared back at the three in the opening before them. "We will wait, but we will not run." He turned to Octavius. "Get your men ready."

"Ah, a maneth," issued a raspy voice from the black canok.

"Not just any maneth, but the leader of the Batt Line. I am here to determine what evil is growing across the land, and I believe you can answer that for me."

Almok smiled. "The evil growing across the land?" He paced in front of Gunthen who stood stoic with his club lifted. "We are the evil growing across the land." He narrowed his eyes on the maneth and suddenly Gunthen's body was thrown to the ground, his club dropped, and both paws gripped his chest.

Kirven stepped forward. "We could kill you right now. If you wish to live, tell us what the plans are for the races attacking Draag. Tell us now."

"I will tell you nothing. You are not even real canoks. You don't look like canoks and you don't act like canoks. Canoks are friends to those in the world. You have teamed up with dragons. Don't pretend you haven't. If Daphane was here, she would correct your lost direction."

The use of Daphane's name struck both canoks, but it struck Kirven deeper. He took another step forward. "I know that name, but I can't place it."

Almok interrupted the conversation, his voice still deep and unforgiving. "Don't worry about names from the past. The new canok are about the future, as are the dragons. We are one and we will not be stopped, and we don't ever have to worry about Daphane again."

The comment ended the conversation. Gunthen turned his attention back to Almok. "Then let me go and I will help spread your message to all. You are an unstoppable force. All races must fall in line to your rule or be destroyed. I recognize that now."

Almok opened his eyes for just a moment, then narrowed them on the maneth before him. He smiled. "You almost had me believing you, you fool maneth."

"It was worth a try," Gunthen replied, grabbing his club and swinging as hard as he could toward Almok's outstretched nose. The club stopped just before contact and Gunthen's arm began to shake and then his weapon fell and rolled harmlessly to the side. For the first time, fear grew across his face and in his eyes.

"You fool," stated Almok. "There are many ways to die, and you just chose…"

All eyes turned as a wall of humans, an elf, and one white canok broke into the area with weapons drawn. Almok turned toward the group clearly surprised by the sudden movement. "What?" he questioned. He turned back to the maneth, spoke a few words, and then swung his head back toward Kirven; both recognized the situation. "Run," he stated.

Both canoks dove into the mirror and vanished with arrows from the elf striking the glass in their wake. "Do we follow?" asked Stoven.

Tantis nodded. "It is the passage we were looking for. We absolutely follow. We need to…" He stopped when he saw Octavius on top of Gunthen applying pressure to his chest. "What is it, Octavius?"

"He doesn't breathe. His eyes have fallen back."

Tantis and Stoven went to his side, and they too saw what the human had stated. Tantis pulled Octavius up from beside the maneth. Softly he said, "He died for us. Let his body pass and make his death worth something."

They all bowed their heads and stood in silence for an unknown time. The human shook his head in disbelief as Tantis removed a pouch and sprinkled dust across the maneth's body. A soft glow grew across Gunthen's final resting spot and then the body faded into oblivion, leaving a peace among the group impossible to have anticipated in these trying times.

The silence in the room was deafening considering the large number of human troops in the area. Tantis brought the group back to the present. "Now, let's check out this mirror," he stated. "We must follow the canoks and see what evil is hiding behind this magical doorway."

Stoven walked up and inspected it closely. "I feel it is a barrier, enchanted somehow to appear as one thing but is actually something completely different. If not for seeing it, I would never have felt it as such. Its secrets are hidden deep within."

"How do we access it?" asked Tantis.

The canok reached its front paw out and lightly touched the glass. Instantly Stoven was in the same mirror room but now he was completely alone. Within moments, the elf was standing next to him. "Come on," Stoven stated. "Bring the others through. The two canoks went this way." He pointed down one of the corridors. "I can feel them."

***

Kirven and Almok raced down the corridor heading back toward Slayne and the Revel Rock Chamber. Kirven motioned to the black canok to stop. "Who is Daphane?"

Almok stared at his twin brother. "You don't remember?"

Kirven looked puzzled by the response. "I don't."

The black canok smiled. "Then it is probably best you keep it that way."

Kirven looked back toward the path they came from. "They are coming through. We will finish this conversation later."

"Yes," answered Almok. "For now, we must warn Slayne to protect the Revel Rock."

"Kirven, my name is Stoven. I learned your name in your conversation previously. We are part of the divided canoks, but still hold our true heritage. The truth is within you. I will not fight you. Stop and listen to me. Your mind is clouded."

The white canok slowed his run next to his black twin brother. "What is it, Kirven?" asked Almok, slowing to stay next to him.

Kirven seemed to be in deep thought. "You go ahead. I will stay and create a diversion and slow them. I will be behind you shortly and join you outside the caverns."

Almok hesitated a moment, but his desire to pass the info on to Slayne exceeded his concern over the reasons for Kirven's decision. "Very well. Do not get injured, brother. We have our strength together."

The black canok continued without delay and Kirven stopped. *"I am here, come alone."*

***

"Where are you taking me?" asked Selbee.

"I already told you where we are going and who we are going to meet. You will have one chance to convince him that you can help us. Otherwise, you will die."

Selbee ignored the attempt by the dragon to place fear in him. He had been consumed by this question since it first arose. He did not wish to die, but he didn't want to betray the maneth either. However, he knew nobody would defeat the dragons. That was clear. The only chance he had was to make this deal to protect the maneth against extinction. With each moment that passed, he knew this was the right decision. "Don't worry, dragon, I will assist you with your plans. I am wise enough to recognize it is the only way we will survive."

They walked into a large room and immediately Selbee saw a rock resting on a pedestal with a blue hue around it. Next to the pedestal and the rock was a large black dragon. Slayne stepped forward. "What are you doing here, Raistan? And why have you brought a maneth?"

"This maneth has offered to be an ally to lead the maneth under our rule. He requests assistance to remove the king and put him in his place."

Slayne moved closer to the maneth so the heat from his breath moved his mane as he spoke. "What is your name, maneth?"

His voice did not quiver. "Selbee. I am midway through the Dimat Line."

"I don't care about your trivial hierarchy," replied Slayne. "What happened to your face, Selbee?" He said the name with a touch of laughter beneath his speech, actually making fun of the maneth's injury.

"I wounded the maneth when we found him. I was going to kill him," interrupted the tan dragon.

Slayne turned his eyes to the other dragon and then back to Selbee. "So, did you offer your service in exchange for your life, and once you escape from here, will you no longer hold up your end of the bargain?"

"Do you think me a fool?" replied Selbee. "The dragons can destroy every living maneth with little effort. We are not one with magic or any other means of defense. I can see what the future holds. If I wish to have the maneth survive, as a lead diplomat for our kind, I must negotiate a plan."

Slayne leaned back and smiled. "I don't believe you, maneth, but time will tell if you earn my trust. For me, it is worth the risk, because there is no risk.

The minute you betray my trust, I will kill every maneth in this land. Do you understand me?"

"I do," he replied.

Just then Almok burst through the entryway. "Slayne, there is trouble in the caverns?" He stared at the maneth and issued an instant enchantment sending Selbee to his knees in pain.

"Almok, release him," stated Slayne.

"But I just killed one of them in the mirror room. They were part of a large force coming this way."

Slayne looked down to Selbee. "What is he talking about?"

"I don't know about any maneth with them, but there is a large human force led by an elf and canok. They are seeking the Revel Rock."

"How do they know about the Revel Rock?" Slayne asked.

Selbee pushed himself up, not taking his eyes from the black canok that returned the stare. "A dragon named Anbari. He told them to destroy it."

"Get up, maneth." He turned to Almok. "We have a back way out. Where is Kirven?"

"He is waiting to slow their progress. He will meet us outside the caverns."

"No, we will not leave him. Go find him and bring him to us. You should not have separated."

Almok heard the tone in the dragon's voice and immediately left through the doorway.

Slayne stared down at Selbee who stood without fear. "If you are going to lead the maneth, you have to get back to their homeland, or whatever is left of it."

Selbee nodded. "I am already injured. Strike me more. Leave me for dead. If they are truly coming, they will save me."

Slayne smiled. Without another word, he lifted his talon and the maneth was unconscious on the ground.

Raistan smiled. "You should have let me do that."

Almok and Kirven broke through the doorway. Almok's raspy voice broke the silence. "Kirven stalled them by redirecting them to a new passageway."

"It will only buy us a few additional moments before they realize. There is a canok with them that can sense our presence," Kirven added.

"What happened to the maneth?" asked Almok.

"What was needed to be done," answered Slayne. "Let's go. I have created a new magical passageway only we will be able to use."

They started to leave and Almok asked, "Shouldn't we take the Revel Rock?"

Slayne shook his head. "It draws its power from this place. It can never leave, but I have protected it with a magical barrier. They will not be able to touch it, much less destroy it." He smiled and added, "But they may die trying."

Almok smiled as well. The two dragons and two canoks hurried through the opening in the stone wall that vanished as they passed.

Moments later, Tantis burst into the pedestal room with Octavius and Stoven in his wake. Their eyes scanned the area quickly and immediately the canok and human ran toward Selbee who laid motionless on the ground.

"He is alive," stated the elf.

The canok did not take notice as his focus was on the glowing stone in the center of the room.

Octavius adjusted the maneth as best he could to lay him flat from the balled-up pile he had landed on. The maneth groaned but didn't resume consciousness. When Tantis did not hear a response from Stoven, he turned to where the canok had been and saw he had moved directly in front of the stone pedestal.

The elf rose and walked over to him. "Is that it? Is that the Revel Rock?"

Stoven refused to move his eyes from the rock. His voice was low and carried a lost tone. "I don't know, but I can tell you there is great power in it. Power I have never felt before. I have no idea where or how it came to be."

The elf pulled his bow and drew an arrow toward it. "These arrows will penetrate stone. Do you think I should try?"

This time Stoven did look up to the elf and saw what he was planning. "I do. I can't say what will happen, but this is what we came for."

He released the arrow, and light brighter than the surface of their sun exploded in the room. The elf and canok were thrown hard against the wall behind them. The entire human force that had made its way into the room was sent equally to the ground. A sound so loud it brought several to the point of unconsciousness penetrated each of their ears. Then, all was silent.

"What in all of Troyf was that?" asked Selbee, pushing himself up.

"Selbee, are you well?" stated Octavius.

He was out of breath and clearly not as well as the previous statement implied, but he still forced himself up. "I am alive, put it that way." He staggered on his feet but then stabilized. "What was that explosion?"

Stoven stared questionably toward the maneth. "How did you get here, Selbee?" he asked, ignoring the maneth's question.

His attention was drawn to the canok. He stuttered. "I-I- I... can't remember. I was in the forest. Dragons were all around me, and then I just woke up here."

Stoven looked at him but was cut off from further comment by the elf. "We are just glad you are back. Do you have your club? My arrow did nothing but set off some magical protection. Maybe your club can break through?"

"No," stated Stoven, answering for the maneth. "It would most likely rip his arm off upon contact. I sense great power protecting it. There must be a magical answer."

"Can't you do something then?" asked Tantis.

"The magic is far too great for me," replied Stoven.

Selbee, sensing the lack of trust from the white canok, gathered his strength and ran toward the pedestal. He had no club as it was destroyed outside the caverns, but it was clear he intended to crash directly into the stone with his body. "I must try," he stated as he ran.

"No!" replied Tantis, but he was too far to stop the maneth.

Light and sound again exploded from the impact. All were thrown back and the maneth was sent flailing wildly. He struck the wall with such force to create a crack from the floor halfway up through solid granite. His body fell limp in a pile once again.

Tantis pushed himself from the ground. "Is everyone all right?" he asked, spit dropping from his mouth through sheer exhaustion. He saw the human leader standing now looking around as well. "Octavius, see to Selbee. Stoven, come into the hallway with me."

The canok followed behind the elf, and Octavius, as well as several other humans, went to lend aid to Selbee. When Tantis cleared the room and added some distance between the two of them and the human army, he knelt down to the canok and whispered, "There is no way we can destroy the Rock, is there?"

The white canok shook his head. "There is not. We don't have the power. To be honest, I don't know who on Troyf would have the power. Maybe all the canoks together, or some with great power." He paused and sighed. "I don't know."

The elf did not change his tone. "Why did you walk on ahead earlier? You said you felt something. "I believe it was more than that. What was it?"

Stoven paced in a small circle and then stopped with his face directly in front of the elf. "I spoke to the white canok with the black diamond patch. His name is Kirven. I felt something in him compared to the black next to him. It was not necessarily goodness, but an openness to learn the truth."

"Since you are still alive, you must have been correct?" Tantis asked.

"I don't know," the canok continued. "He did wait for me, and he had no intention to attack. He kept asking about his origin. He didn't know where he was from. I told him he was on the wrong side of this fight, that he was being used by the dragons for his strength and power. He denied it. He feels strong loyalty to Slayne and the black canok, known as Almok. I believe he has the same mind as all the white canoks. I believe his heredity is to maintain the old way of the canoks, but he has never been shown what that is. He is young, but his maturity was accelerated somehow. He follows the black dragon now, but if something could make him see the truth, I believe he could be turned. If that happened, his strength and knowledge would be a tremendous asset to us. I believe he could destroy the barrier around the Rock."

Tantis nodded. "Thank you for your honesty. Let's hope he does turn, but for now, what options do we have?"

Stoven straightened his ears at a noise from the opposite direction. "Someone is coming from the other direction." Tantis heeded the warning and began leading the way back toward the pedestal room. As they moved, Stoven added, "But to answer your question, our primary mission has been successful. We determined who for sure is behind the evil and we located the Revel Rock. Perhaps regrouping with the others will allow the answer to destroying it. But my fear is, depending on how long that could take, we may not have others to regroup with."

As Tantis headed back toward the pedestal room trying to stay ahead of whoever was approaching, he whispered to the canok, "We are too close. Our villages are already facing destruction. We have to solve this riddle now."

"It is not a riddle, my friend. It is something much more real. The dragons have begun to learn a magic we cannot touch. It exceeds even our conception. Forget their strength in body, flight, and fire. If they can bend the laws of the world around us as well, we have no chance. I agree, we can't leave without destroying it, but I am also telling you we have no chance of destroying it."

There was no chance to hide the large band of humans, so the elf motioned everyone to be prepared to attack. The tension was at its highest. Tantis stood with an arrow knocked and ready to release. Then suddenly, a small, bearded dwarf turned the corner without slowing his step or checking for what might lay ahead.

"Don't shoot," stated Bretton. "It is me."

All relaxed and the dwarf dropped his arms with a smile. "I finally found my way through this maze, but reached a dead end down that hall. I was coming back because I heard what I thought was Elven speech."

Tantis walked up to the dwarf and gave him a powerful hug. "Good to see you, my friend. Any chance you have something that can break through that?" He pointed to the pedestal holding the glowing rock.

"I sure as hell can try," he stated, removing his hatchet.

"Not this time," replied the elf. "It needs to be something filled with magic. Direct contact nearly destroyed everything in this room last time." That comment reminded the elf about Selbee. He turned his head to see the maneth awake, but clearly still groggy. "You okay, Selbee?"

"I am," he replied through broken breaths. "Just give me a moment or two."

Tantis did not wait for further comments. "I say this with a heavy heart to all humans, and Stoven, Selbee, and Bretton, who have stood…"

"And Jermys," stated the dwarf approaching from the tunnel.

Bretton ran over and greeted his twin. "Jermys, you are alive? Thank the gods, you are alive."

Jermys smiled and tossed his axe in the air catching it in his other hand. "You bet your dwarven butt I am, brother. And you guys are making so much noise I am sure everyone in the caverns knows you are here."

Tantis smiled at the dwarf. "My friend, we will have to hear your story later, and we will heed your words on doing a better job concealing our presence." He turned back to the group that were whispering among themselves on the return of both dwarves. He continued in a softer voice, but still loud enough for all to hear, "We cannot defeat this magical barrier now. We must leave to get help. We have found the source of the dragon's power. We must now find someone who can help us destroy it. Time is critical, for our homes are facing a dragon battle the likes of which they have never seen. We must hurry. We will return to the mirror room and escape through the sky window. Everyone, gather your things and let's go at once."

There was no delay. In fact, the troops seemed eager to leave this place. Bretton, Stoven, and Tantis led the way with Selbee and Octavius bringing up the rear. The maneth, though up and walking on his own, clearly showed his fatigue. The cut along his face showed clearly with dried blue blood and his physical state was also greatly diminished. But you would not have seen it in his walk.

As they approached the mirror room, Selbee turned to the human. "Where is Gunthen? I thought he was with you. Did he leave ahead of us to go get help?"

Octavius lowered his eyes. "I am sorry, but Gunthen lost his life in a battle with the canoks. He defended us bravely, but his injuries were too great."

Selbee lowered his eyes in sadness while Octavius placed his arm on the maneth's shoulder. *Good,* Selbee thought to himself. *One leader is already gone. Everyone moves up. I need to figure out what to do about McCard. That is the key.* He turned to the human. "I am sure he fought bravely and made the maneths proud. He was one of the greatest maneths in our race. He will be deeply missed."

The human nodded. "He was a great leader who defended us with his life. Now, let's not have his death be in vain." Octavius turned to the elf who had moved beside them when he heard Selbee ask about Gunthen. "How do we win this one, Tantis? What can we do?"

The elf stood tall. "Now is not the time. We need to find someone with the magical strength to defeat the barrier around the Rock. But we need to find it fast. I only hope Anbari is near. I believe he is the only one who can help us now."

They touched the mirror and immediately found themselves in the identical room. Tantis knelt down to Stoven. I will fly up and gather Tashro and any others. We will drop the ropes and bring everyone up. It will take some time. Can you focus your senses around us? We will be vulnerable when this move is happening."

Stoven nodded as Tantis lifted himself in the air. He broke the plain of the opening and almost buckled over in pain. Before him rested the beaten and bloodied bodies of dozens of canoks, both black and white. His eyes moved across the massacre until he saw Tashro. He walked up to his friend and stroked his head. The canok laid with three black canoks next to him. It appeared he had been cornered and took all three down before another force overcame him. The fight in the area was brutal and having this amount of death surrounding Tantis brought him to his knees. Tears streamed down his cheeks, but he knew he must continue. Then he heard the leaves crack behind him and knew he was not alone.

***

"Wait," stated Kirven. "We need to speak."

"Nonsense, my son. It is time to return to Bjork's ice cave. We must wait there for our attacks to subside. Then we can finish our movement. We are days away from owning the world."

Almok heard the tone in his twin's voice and recognized the defiance. The black canok moved slowly toward his brother. "What is it, Kirven? If you have something to say, then trust we will listen. We are strong together."

Kirven stood tall and did not relent. The strength in his magic had developed quickly. He had command of his powers, and though still not fully developed, he carried much confidence. He believed he was stronger than his brother, but Slayne greatly exceeded his level, that much was certain. He could not let this turn into a fight, for he would lose, but he also knew the black dragon needed him. All Kirven wanted was one answer. How to get it was the question.

"What happened to my mother?" Kirven asked.

Slayne stopped and turned back toward the canok. Almok, who was already staring at his brother, moved several steps closer to the black dragon.

"Why do you continue to ask about your mother? She is gone. Your destiny is with me, your father, and your brother. It has always been that way. We are your only remaining family."

"I don't think so," replied Kirven. "I think you need me to fulfill your destiny, but I believe that my destiny lies along a different path."

Slayne stepped forward, and fireballs dripped from his lips as he spoke. "You can't have one without the other. It is the destiny of our world to be ruled by dragons. The way it used to be. The way it always should be. Your very existence is proof of that. The canoks were a race of one. Now, to fulfill this destiny, your mother split the race in two. She placed you and your brother by my side to ensure this. Do not question your mother's dying wish."

"My mother's dying wish?" repeated Kirven. "If it was my mother's dying wish, then why did she split us? Why are we not following her lead?"

Almok now stepped forward. "Kirven, you are my brother, but also my closest friend. You are part of me. What brings these questions? There is nothing I, or our father, would ever do that would bring harm to you. We are all one, and we need each other."

Kirven stepped back keeping a safe distance between the three of them. The tan dragon moved beside Slayne so the force in front of the white canok was significant. "What happened to our mother?" Kirven repeated.

Slayne lowered his head. "Your mother is dead, Kirven, and we don't have the time to debate this. You have only this moment to choose if you want this family, but know one thing—we want you."

"You don't want me," he replied. "I can feel your thoughts. You want my power next to you. Individually we are strong. Together we are undefeatable. I believe you killed my mother. I cannot stand with you."

"You can and will," replied Slayne. "Or you will die where you stand."

"You need me. You can feel it the same way I can. Without me, your plan will not succeed."

"Don't push us, brother. We will destroy you. You know we are stronger than any on Troyf, with or without you." Almok took several steps away from Slayne spreading out their offense. Kirven's head moved back and forth between the two. Almok continued, "Don't make me take arms against you. We are one."

"Did you know Slayne killed our mother?" Kirven asked, his question directed toward his twin.

Almok looked toward Slayne and then back to his brother, but the black canok did not answer. Slayne saw the hesitation and lowered his head to stare closer into Kirven's eyes. "Did your brother know that *I* killed your mother?" Slayne repeated, his stare turning into a small smile. The dragon paused, and his smile grew allowing even more molten drool to strike the ground beneath him. "What if I told you your brother killed her."

Kirven was about to reply but Slayne cut him off. "Don't speak. I sense where your mind is. So, I will offer you two options. We want…" He now paused and then chose his words more carefully. "We need you by our side. We are stronger with you than without you, but our plans will occur either way. I can feel one trait in you that I will trust, and that is honor."

Almok swung his head to Slayne. "What do you mean by that? You can't trust his word."

Slayne glared at the black canok, and although he did not speak, the message was clear. The dragon continued, "Kirven, I can feel everything within you requires that you will honor your word. That means I want you to stand by me and your brother and honor our direction. If you give me your loyalty, I will give you an opportunity to not stand by us."

"What do you mean, give me an opportunity to not stand by you?" Kirven asked.

Slayne stepped back and locked his eye on him. "I mean, I can't trust you right now. I am giving you a chance to defeat me, but if you fail, then you must swear your allegiance to me and our direction."

"I cannot defeat you…" Kirven began and was immediately cut off by his brother.

Almok broke in, "Join us now and let's move past this."

Kirven now stood taller and stepped forward. "I can't defeat you, but I will find the one who can. When the eggs hatch, it will be too late. If you turn the eggs to your way, then nothing on this land will stop you. Give me time to find the one who can fulfill what my mother"—he turned to Almok—"what *our* mother, wanted. If I fail, then I will join you without question."

Almok laughed. "The eggs will not hatch for 200 years. The dragon way will be in place in only a few moons."

"Then you have nothing to lose," replied Kirven.

Slayne smiled. "Kirven, you are just like your father, cunning to the end." He paused, paced to the side, and then turned back toward him. "There is one stipulation I must add."

"What?" replied Kirven.

"If we end this now, with the Revel Rock protected, and the races bow to our rule, you join us immediately. When the eggs hatch in 200 years they hatch to a world where dragons rule the land and all races respect that rule, including the canoks."

Kirven started to answer but was cut off. "And one more requirement," continued Slayne. "When this happens, you will do everything in your ability to convince the canoks to follow us. White and black. You will be the one who brings us all together."

Kirven stared at the black dragon and then to his brother. "You will not survive this, brother. You know this."

"Stop it, brother," replied Almok. "If you could defeat us, you would do so right now. We will not need to wait 200 years for the eggs to hatch. In days our world will be ruled by dragons and you will stand beside us."

"You and Slayne killed our mother, Almok. For that I will never stand beside you."

Slayne smiled. "You will, my son. You will."

Chapter Eighteen

"Anbari?" a voice said through telepathy. *"You have to slow down. You have been traveling without rest for days."*

He recognized the voice and although he should have been completely taken by the communication, he was so tired he continued as if the words were expected. *"I can't afford to wait. I sense great disturbances in the land. Bjork has organized the dragons to fight. They are moving to attack."*

"I too know that to be the case, but what can you do? You are a dragon. You can't destroy the Revel Rock. You know that. Bjork and Slayne know that. No dragon can destroy it. That is what makes its protective barrier so great. Only one with dragon blood has the power to destroy it, but the magic is such that no dragon can use its powers against it at Draag."

Anbari did not slow his flight as he replied, *"I know, that is why I gave the direction to the humans. They need to find a physical way to destroy it. It is the perfect enchantment, the only ones with the power to defeat it are prevented from using that power."*

Anbari slowed his flight. *"You have to run, my son. I am sorry to say it, but you can't win. You need to find a place so remote you will never be found. You can live to fight another day. Please stop and listen to me."*

The pleading tone of the voice caused the larger dragon to stop. He turned and faced back almost expecting to see his mother there. *"Mother, I can't give up. I can't let our world be taken over. I can't live and let thousands of others die."*

The space around him began to change and the faint outline of his mother appeared before him. "What is our other answer then?" she said through tears. "You can't fight the dragons."

"My only hope is this ring. It has powers I don't understand. I hope whoever wears it can destroy the rock and defeat the dragons. I hope that is Ku."

"Very well, my son," she replied. "Your father and I are preparing a retreat across the South Sea for you and any who follow. If you need it, you will find safety there. In the center you will find a storm; travel through the storm and your protection will be found. Use it when you need it, Anbari, and please know, this may be a fight you cannot win. If you need to run, then run."

Her form disappeared with her last word. "I will, Mother," he stated to himself before turning and adjusting his course straight toward Draag.

Anbari was truly feeling the pain in his wings when he reached the far side of the Dry Sea and a wall of trees marking the edge of Draag Forest. He landed at the edge, slowly stretched out his wings, and relaxed them on his back. With deliberate steps forward, he entered the trees looking for any signs of Elven tracks. Upon finding nothing, he lifted back into the air, above the trees, and flew at the hardest speed he could muster toward the caverns.

***

"Tantis, is that you?" questioned a voice from behind him.

The elf turned around with bow drawn and then quickly lowered it and stared in disbelief at who was before him. "Ku, Your Majesty." He knelt down on one knee. "You are alive."

Ku motioned for him to stand. "What are you doing here and what has happened?"

"A tragedy for certain. There is so much evil in our world right now. I don't know where to begin, but seeing you here before me makes me believe things may still turn."

The elf king was not sure how to play this, so he continued as if the truth about his past was still not known. "There is much death here," Ku stated. "We must prepare those passed."

Tantis understood and immediately removed his pouch. As he turned and began to pass over the bodies, Ku removed his knife and fell in behind the flyer elf. Just as he did, both elves turned when a hard wind from an unnatural source beat down upon them. Then, a large dragon landed in the same clearing. Ku quickly placed his dagger back under his armor.

"Anbari, you have returned," the elf king stated.

"Greetings, Ku, I have been looking for you."

The elf nodded and pulled his bow from his shoulder. "I am sure you have. I assume you—"

Anbari cut him off. "You did well to flee the Gar Swamp. Your perseverance to find your way here is impressive. I am very glad I found you because Hawthorne and I were able to meet with the guardians, and I have the weapons we need to be successful against the dragons. I believe you are the key to saving our world. I believe you can master the power I provide and end this spread of tyranny."

Tantis smiled. "Are you certain? I have an army in the caverns below the window. They can take you to the secret room with the Revel Rock. If Ku can destroy it, then we can prevent further attacks on our homelands."

"What attacks?" asked Anbari.

"Slayne has sent dragons to our villages. I am sure they are already there. The elves, humans, and maneth are, or will be, facing an onslaught of dragon magic and fire, but if we destroy the Revel Rock, perhaps that will at least even the playing field."

Anbari thought about this and then stepped closer to Ku. "Ku and I will not require the army. Pull them out of the caverns and prepare this area of devastation by way of the elves. It is painful to lay eyes upon, but if we are not successful, these results will be carried to all nations. You must then return to your homelands. My counterpart, Hawthorne, waits in support in the human city on the North Sea. She will provide the necessary defense much like the enchantment around Elvinott. Both will buy us time, but if we are not successful, the end results will be the same." He stopped and spoke mainly to Ku. "Come with me, my friend. We have much to discuss and plan. We must move quickly or more will die."

Ku was not sure what to make of this. He had believed Anbari would be hunting him down after leaving him at the Gar Swamp to die. Instead, the dragon seemed to believe Ku was not only on his side, but a key to the future to defeat the dragons. He hoped that did not change. If what Anbari said was true, it would provide him the opportunity gain tremendous power, and in turn kill Anbari and take a major step forward in the ranks under Bjork. He smiled back to the dragon as he thought about where this may take him. "Of course, Anbari. Tell me what you need me to do, and I will do whatever I can to master whatever magic weapons you hold."

Anbari nodded and began walking into the trees. "Come, we must discuss this alone."

It took a while, but once Tantis had fashioned some vines and lifted several up by flight to help the others, the humans had been rescued out of the caverns and now stood in the glade between the mirror room sky window and the trees. Tantis had aided passage to the bodies and there was much commotion wondering what their next steps would be. Rumors had already been passed about the large dragon working with them and the return of the elf king who was going to gain the power needed to destroy the Revel Rock. The mood had grown even festive. It was amazing that deep in the most dangerous part of Troyf this level of excitement could be present. Tantis stood next to Stoven when he quieted the crowd.

"My friends, please know this battle is far from over. I don't know the plan, but I believe we should return to our homes to help defend any attacks upon them. I only pray we still have homes to return to. Our friend Anbari, the most powerful dragon in our land, is going to help my king gain the power needed to destroy the Revel Rock. When that happens, the dragons will be vulnerable. We have to focus our attacks at that time. You must be ready. We have to move at once to our lands. I believe the maneth have already fled to Elvinott so I will find them there. The humans must return to the North Sea. There is a dragon at the North Sea, a friend of Anbari's. She will help defend the city until the Rock can be destroyed. We must go at once. Send your men back to the North Sea. Defend yourselves and be ready for anything. This is our most critical time."

The humans raised their weapons and shouted, then quickly began disbanding into groups to head back through the Draag Forest. Hoangis and Stoven stared on in disbelief.

***

"What is it you have for me, Anbari?" asked the elf, trying not to show much eagerness.

His voice was deep and tone as serious as he had ever spoken. "The guardians fashioned four weapons which I will distribute across our land to be used when the time is right. They will have great power when the chosen ones are identified to wield them. However, the object that harnesses the power together is this ring." He opened his talon to reveal the ordinary looking ring resting inside his grip. "It carries with it an old magic lost for thousands of years on our land. It will be difficult to master, but whoever is able to master this power will be the most powerful creature on Troyf."

Ku fought hard to control his excitement. He pressed his lips together to prevent his desire to obtain this power from showing through. He kept his voice low and calm. "So, there are weapons and a ring. I too believe it is my destiny to wear this ring, but why would you not also entrust me with the weapons?"

"No creature will be able to control them all. I don't believe there are many in our world that have the ability to wear the ring and master its powers, but I believe you do hold that power. Take the ring, Ku of the Elves, and show me that you are the chosen one."

The elf reached out his hand and gently removed the ring from the dragon's talon. He did not feel any power at first. He stared at Anbari who nodded to the elf. Slowly, he slid the ring down his finger. As the ring nestled in place, the elf's eyes grew wide. He lifted his hand in the air to inspect the ring on his finger, and then the pain struck. He doubled over gripping his belly with both hands. He screamed and then was silent. His large green eyes teared as if acid had been thrown in them and then closed tight. The ring began to emit a light of such proportion Anbari had to look away as he feared he would lose all sight. He felt his retina burn. Ku stumbled several steps forward and then fell to the ground with his face buried in the soft dirt. He rolled around in pain and then all activity stopped. He remained motionless on the forest floor when Anbari opened his eyes, one at a time, to see what had transpired.

"Ku," the dragon stated. "Are you all right?" Anbari moved beside him and shook the elf. He looked to the elf's hand and saw the ring still in place. "Ku, can you hear me?"

The elf opened one eye and tried to focus on the dragon. "Anbari, is that you?" His voice was choppy and soft.

"Yes, Ku, it is me. You have placed the ring on your finger. How do you feel? Can you control it?"

"If it truly is you, then take two steps back before I reduce you to dust." The elf's voice was much stronger now, and the tone defiant.

Anbari tilted his head. "What do you mean? Why would you…"

"Do not address me again other than by calling me Master. Give me the weapons of the ring and remove yourself from my sight or I will kill you. If you refuse me the weapons, I will kill you and take them. I don't have time for talk. This is your only chance. Do it or die."

"Ku, you have not mastered the ring. You have only begun to recognize its powers. You cannot defeat me. You are the chosen one. You are…"

Ku flashed a sinister smile. "You are right, I am the chosen one. Chosen by Bjork to rid the world of any force that intends to stop the dragon rule. I will destroy you and return to Elvinott to lead whatever elves are left to follow the rule of the dragons. They will be beaten down and will gladly follow the dragon rule, especially if their king is telling them to. Bjork has thought of every alternative action. You have no chance. Now step back or I will kill you. This is your last warning."

Anbari lowed his head and issued a bolt of energy the strength of which would have brought any dragon to its knees. Ku lifted his hand bearing the ring to the bolt and absorbed it as simply as brushing away a fallen leaf from his path. Anbari was now stepping back.

"You see, you fool. You can't defeat me. You can't even stop me from doing this." He shot a bolt of lightning toward the dragon which sent him crashing backward. Anbari's defense did nothing and the pain from the contact was immense.

Anbari quickly got back to his feet only to see the elf stepping forward. Another bolt shot outward and struck Anbari across the face. His head rocked and it almost struck his back before flipping to center. Another bolt shot toward the dragon and he closed his eyes and focused a different direction.

The bolt absorbed easily into his hand. Ku looked on astonished. Anbari now took a step toward Ku who sent another bolt toward the dragon. Each was received the same as the last and absorbed into his talons. He spun the energy round and round like a ball in front of him.

Ku's eyes grew wide and the elf took two steps backward. "How did you do that? You can't defeat the power of the ring."

Anbari smiled. "You already said it yourself, when you said to give you the weapons of the ring. The weapons and the ring have a symbiotic relationship. Neither may be used against the other. I carry several of the weapons, therefore, you cannot defeat me. I just needed to bring the weapon's powers up to receive your attack."

Ku took this in and stopped moving. He smiled broadly. "You are truly a fool, Anbari, as Bjork has said. You just told me the one thing I needed to know. If I can't defeat you, then you also can't defeat me. You are unable to use the weapon's powers against the ring." He now stepped forward and stood directly in front of the large, silver dragon. "We have a stalemate, and therefore my last comment stands. Get out of my sight."

Anbari lowered his head, giving the impression that Ku's summary was correct. If the ring Ku wore could not be used against Anbari because he held the weapons to which it was tied, then Anbari could also not attack the elf. He turned his head to the side to give the impression he was going to leave the elf alone outside Draag Caverns. Then he turned back and swung his talon striking the elf in his side, the tip of his claw cutting deeply into Ku's skin. Green blood flowed from the wound as the elf flew through the air landing against a nearby tree.

The dragon slowly walked over to stand before him. Ku was grasping for breath. "How?" he asked, green blood now spitting from his mouth as he spoke.

Anbari lowered his head to be inches from his face. "The weapons could not be used against each other. You were using the ring's power against one who holds its weapons. However, I have many powers of my own, independent of the weapons. Now, if you wish to live, the weapons I hold can save you, but you must remove the ring and give it to me."

He spit blood across Anbari's face. "I will never give up this ring. I feel the power within it. It will save me." He lifted his hand as if he was going to use the ring against the dragon. "Go now. You can't take this ring from me. It is part of me now."

Anbari could see the elf was not going to use the ring against him; he was showing him the elf's green skin had grown around it. The ring had become fused with its user. He reached his talon out and lifted the elf in the air again causing Ku extreme pain, and his skin tore from the contact. His face cringed and more blood spilled onto the forest ground. "The ring isn't going to save you, Ku. You are going to die, and when you do, I will remove the ring."

"That isn't how it works, my dear friend. I have felt it. When I die, the ring will die with me. It will leave this world and whatever fool chance you believe it brings to stop Bjork will leave with it. You see, you stupid dragon, you have to save me." He coughed and a large amount of green gelatinous blood dripped from his mouth.

Anbari immediately set him down. He didn't know if the words Ku spoke were true or not, but he did recognize they could be.

The elf smiled. "You know it is how I say. Save me, dragon, or lose the ring forever."

Anbari stepped back, unsure what direction to go. He couldn't lose the ring. The powers within it were too great. How could he have trusted the elf? His poor judgement had forfeited any chance they had to succeed.

"Perhaps I could be of service," issued a voice from behind him.

Anbari swung quickly and prepared to attack and then stopped when he laid eyes on who approached. "Who are you?" he asked, staring at the strange canok before him. "I have never seen a canok that was all white with one black diamond spot."

Kirven nodded. "I do believe I am unique to our race. I have a heritage that only one other canok can claim."

Anbari refused to lower his guard and remained ready to use magic to attack. Ku began pushing himself with his feet trying to create some distance between him and Anbari. But his slow movements caused intense pain and additional blood loss with each motion. Anbari saw this but showed little concern other than he could not let the elf pass. "I don't know your intentions, canok, but I will tell you that I am not in line with the dragon direction. If you are here to assist in placing the dragon's leadership across this land, then you and I are not friends. At this point, I have no option but to claim my true direction and draw a line between us."

Kirven continued to step closer. "Then why did you bring the elf to near death only to need him alive?"

Anbari swung his eyes between the two. Ku continued to try to push away but exhaustion took over. He stopped and leaned against a tree. His appearance indicated that he only had moments to live. "I misjudged the elf. I believed he was chosen to stop this rampage. Instead, he had already made a pact with Bjork and Slayne. He was to turn the elves to the dragon way and have them follow. I gave him a tool that now will be taken with him should he pass. I can't let that happen or we will have no chance."

Through telepathy, Kirven spoke to only Anbari. "*I hear you, dragon, and I will help you, but we must fool the elf into giving us the tool. To do that, we must fight. He will not give it to you, but if he believes I side with the dragons, and that by giving me this magical tool I can save him and then help him destroy you, then perhaps he will give it to me.*"

Anbari heard the words but did not speak. Kirven now spoke for all to hear. "You are a fool, dragon. You are the one Slayne has told me about. The one who believes he can stop what is unstoppable. Step back from the elf. If he has something of such great power, then you will not be allowed to bring about his death."

"What are you saying?" asked Anbari. "You too side with the dragons?"

Kirven laughed. "I don't side with them. Slayne is my father. My mother is the one who split my race to ensure the canoks couldn't use their powers against us. I may not be able to kill you, dragon, but I can absolutely save this elf. Slayne will want him and the weapon you provided."

Anbari realized that Kirven had referred to the ring as a magical tool and a weapon. He did not even know what the elf had, yet he was still trying to gain access to it. He took a step back, showing fear at the direction. "You will never get the ring. You could never harness its power just as the elf has failed. It has fused to his hand and become one with it. The only way to remove it is if he chooses to let it go."

The canok smiled and walked slowly up to stand beside the elf. He stood hard and tall and faced the dragon as if they were about to enter into a fierce battle of magic. He leaned his head toward the elf and whispered. "Are you all right? Can you hold on longer?"

The elf's voice was still choppy and broken, but his words were clear. "I can and will."

Again, he whispered, "I don't know if I can defeat this dragon. He appears strong with magic. Can you, with this ring, provide me any assistance?"

"I can't. The dragon carries weapons that make the ring incapable of attacking. I can, however, assist with my bow."

The canok nodded understanding, but changed to telepathy again, this time with the elf. *"The dragon can't hear me. Will the ring prevent your bow from attacking? I will need your support. Remove the ring and place it on the ground. Once you do, we will attack together."*

Ku looked toward the canok who stared only at the dragon. "No. The ring cannot leave my finger. I can't give up the power."

"We will both be dead if you don't. You are not giving up the power, you are freeing yourself from being held back from it for a few moments. Together we will destroy this dragon quickly, and then you can take the ring before Slayne. I know where he is." The elf stared at the canok who turned his head back and nodded. No longer using telepathy, Kirven added, "Do it. Now is the time we attack." He turned toward Anbari and released a beam of energy causing the dragon to writhe in pain. "Now, elf, do it now!"

Ku looked at Anbari being pushed back and then he turned his eyes on the strained vision of the canok. Reluctantly, he reached his free hand over to the one bearing the ring, and although he thought it would be difficult to break free, it slid off without hesitation. He set the ring on the ground and removed his bow from his back. He knocked an arrow and began to draw back before a sharp pain erupted in his chest. He was thrown back against a far tree. He fought to stay conscious and lifted his eyes to see the white canok with the black diamond patch and the large silver dragon standing side-by-side over him.

Anbari looked down. "You are the fool, Ku. I trusted you. I believed you were the one, and you betrayed me. You could have been the hero to our world." Anbari lifted his talon up showing the ring resting inside. "You will never wear this on your finger again."

The elf coughed up more blood, his insides now even more severely damaged. "You lied to me," he stated, staring at the canok. "But I heard there were two canoks with Slayne. Two canoks with a strange diamond patch on their head. You are one of them."

Kirven stepped forward. "I was with Slayne, and in time I may be again, but for now I am going to do everything I can to find the one who can stop him. You, Ku, are not that one."

The elf had another fit of coughing. Anbari stepped forward. "Lay your head back, Ku. I believe I can ease your suffering. I believe I can save you."

"I do not wish to be saved, dragon. My elves will soon learn the truth and because I lost the ring, Bjork and Slayne will end my life sooner than I can explain. No, dragon, today is my day to die, and I harbor no ill will toward either of you for bringing it upon me. I have made many wrong decisions over the last several years and correcting them now is not possible. I pray you find what it is you are looking for." His voice was fading, and he began to tear. He reached inside his armor and removed a small pouch. In a faint and distant voice, the elf asked, "Dragon, will you please give this to Hoangis should your paths cross? It is for his eyes only." He coughed again and then removed another, much smaller pouch. "And when my time comes, will you please spread this dust across my body? It is my only chance at life, though I probably did not earn it."

Anbari took the pouches from the elf as Ku's eyes slowly closed. Kirven checked for any sound in his chest, lowered his eyes, and shook his head. Anbari said a few words and the pouch vanished to be carried somewhere inside his armor shell of a body. The second pouch he opened and with one talon reached inside and cupped a small amount of the dust it carried. He closed his eyes and spread the dust across the elf's body. A cool wind blew through the area, and slowly the elf's body vanished.

The two remained silent for a moment as they took in all that had just occurred. Eventually, Kirven turned to the dragon. "I must take the ring."

In a stern voice, Anbari replied, "That is not going to happen, Kirven. Today I almost ended any chance this world had to prevent the dragon oppression. There is no chance I am letting this ring fall into the wrong hands again."

"You have to, Anbari. You have to allow me to find the creature that will bring balance to our world. I have only bought myself time. I have not escaped the reach of Slayne and Bjork yet."

"Perhaps you need to tell me everything, canok. I have but one issue at hand. I have to destroy something that is magically prevented from me doing so. Because of that, I need to find someone who can."

Kirven stared back toward the dragon. "Then I may have the answers you seek, my friend."

The two talked in detail for a short time and then walked back out of the trees to see the crowd of humans breaking up and heading to the north.

Stoven immediately locked eyes on Kirven and walked up to him, with Hoangis in his wake. "What is your role here, Kirven?"

"I am just learning my role in many things." He paused and then added, "I am the son of Daphane and Slayne."

When he said these words, all within earshot placed their hands on their weapon of choice. Anbari was next to speak. "Kirven has given us a chance to win. He is with us, at least for now. He has a plan that may bring about the result we need. He and I are going into Draag Caverns."

Those in the area relaxed, but Stoven still stared questionably at his counterpart. "I sense a battle within you, Kirven. I pray you are strong enough to resist."

"As do I, Stoven," he replied.

Anbari turned his eyes toward the elf king. "Hoangis, I have news for you to which I must share in private. Will you join me?"

The two disappeared and Kirven knew he was going to share the information about Ku. He looked around the area and motioned to Tantis. The elf walked over to Kirven who had Stoven still standing by his side. "What is the plan for everyone here?"

Tantis pointed to the southeast as he began, "Selbee has left for the maneth camp. When I told him about the potential dragon attacks, he was worried for his camp and wasted no time. He also wished to speak to McCard about the other maneth's passing. I let him know that I believed the maneth had gone to Elvinott, but he insisted on his own path."

Kirven did not respond, but Stoven nodded understanding, as Tantis continued. "The dwarves headed back to Feldschlosschen. We have heard nothing from the mining dwarves and the specifics about division between them are also not known. They will speak with King Krystof and determine their direction." He paused, and then continued. "The humans are breaking up and headed back to their city by the North Sea. They will take the longest to return. I told them by the time they arrived, if their city remained intact, then our plan was successful." He stared down at the canok who did not show any signs of responding causing a silence that was actually uncomfortable. The elf directed his next comment toward either canok, "What are your plans?"

Stoven replied, "If Kirven and Anbari will allow me to join them, then I will return to the caverns. If not, I will follow their lead and either remain here or return to my homeland to help determine what has happened to the canoks and if it can be repaired. My path will take me near Elvinott. I will approach to see if I can be of service in defending the Elven land."

Tantis bowed his head and patted the canok on the back. "Thank you, my friend. I too will wait for direction." He spoke mostly to Kirven. "If you two wish me to join, I will stand by your side without question. If not, I will fly to Elvinott."

As he said the words, Anbari and Hoangis broke through the trees. "Time is of the essence," stated Anbari. "Kirven, we must go."

Stoven started to speak as did Tantis, but Anbari immediately cut them off. "No, Kirven and I must do this alone, but thank you for all you have done. You have given us the ability to find and destroy the Rock." He smiled. "You return to your homelands. Help them if you can. We will need all races to win this war. If we are successful today, it is but only one step."

They did not speak further, both shaking their head in understanding.

***

Geoff stared into the sky. "There they come again."

Alhize led a group of maneth away from the center of the camp. "We can't fight them, Geoff. They never come close enough for us to attack. Their fire is too great."

As he spoke, another wall of flames shot across the village. A third bank of tents burst into flames. Geoff moved quickly to his side and picked up a fallen maneth as he ran. "Alhize, we have done enough. They believe the camp was fully populated. Flee into the forests. Save all you can but don't approach the Elven village. We cannot lead the dragons there. Let them chase us until we can run no longer."

Alhize heard the words and hollered to those maneth with him. "Come everyone, this way. Don't look back and do not try to fight or engage. We have done our job. We have saved our nation, now let us save ourselves." He turned back toward Geoff and saw him lift up another fallen maneth and push him into the woods behind Alhize's group. "Geoff, aren't you coming? You will be killed if you stay behind."

"Alhize, lead them out. I will be along shortly. I will buy you some additional time." The large maneth of the Batt Line turned and darted directly back into the desolate and scorched earth making up the maneth camp. Four dragons continued their assault although there was little life still beneath them.

Geoff hid behind a large tree and reluctantly gripped a bow that Madeiris had left for him. "I can't believe I am going to use this," he said to himself. "But it does seem more practical than a club right now."

He darted from behind the tree, knocked the arrow, and let it fly at a large blue dragon that had landed to inspect the area. The shriek from the blue as the arrow struck its throat was like nothing Geoff had ever heard before. Blue dragon blood exploded from its neck showing the maneth he had somehow hit a vital spot. The other dragons in the area landed and sent walls of flame every direction. Geoff ducked behind the same tree as a sheet of fire crossed both sides of him. He could reach out and touch it if he wanted, but the heat was so intense he was not sure the trunk of the tree could withstand it. Then the fire stopped.

The maneth peeked his head around and saw a large red dragon landing behind the others. The blue he had shot had laid down on the ground. It was clearly still breathing but Geoff did not think it would be for long, as it was losing blood at a significant rate. The red dragon stared at its blue counterpart and then spoke to the others, "You have won this battle, my friends, but not without a great loss. Nothing can save our friend now."

"Several maneth fled to the trees. We should hunt them down and kill them," offered a green dragon who stood strong beside its fallen friend.

"Not this time," replied the red. "Slayne has worked a deal with another source. The maneth are no longer a threat. We need to return to Draag for further direction. The maneth in the trees are of no concern to us any longer."

The green dragon stared questionably at Draketon and then back to the fallen blue. "If they can shoot with this level of accuracy, then pursuing them now may not be the best choice. If Slayne has another plan, I agree we should hear it. The maneth are no concern to us regardless. They offered no defense and in fact, I can't believe we even considered them worth destroying."

"Aye," replied Draketon. "Let us return."

The remaining three dragons took to the air. Draketon turned his head back and stared directly at Geoff. The maneth ducked behind the tree. The red dragon roared and then telepathically sent a message to Geoff. *"Maneth, I know you are there. I am not your enemy. We will speak again someday, I hope as friends. There are dragons out there that will help, but they are few. Trust none and protect yourselves well."*

Geoff remained nestled with his back against the tree that separated him from the dragon. He didn't know if this was some trick to draw him out, so he remained frozen. He heard the deep beat of dragon's wings against the air and then all went silent. He slowly moved his head back around the tree and peeked out to the glade before him. It was empty. He let out a long, deep breath. "I need to change my armor as I think I soiled myself again." He paused and added softly, "First you say it, then you do it." He smiled to himself. "I say all this funny stuff, and nobody is around to hear it.

***

"Madeiris!" the elf shouted. "More dragons are coming."

"How can there be more?" the elf prince answered. "Bowman, open fire and don't stop until you are out of arrows." He turned to a small group standing next to him. "Flyers, take to the air and avoid one-on-one engagements, but take down any dragon you can."

A head flyer ran up to him. "Prince Madeiris, there are too many. They have cut through our enchantment. The maneth have built a wall in the forest and are engaging any we bring down, but there are too many able to fly through."

THE DRAGON OPPRESSION

The prince held up his hand. "Did I hear your correctly? If the dragons reach the ground, the maneth can defeat them?"

The flyer looked back to him surprised at the tone of the response. It was as if he had given his prince a possible solution. "Well, in most cases, yes. There are hundreds of maneth in the woods. When a dragon has fallen due to bow fire, they attack with these rudimentary clubs that for whatever reason seem to have significant impact."

"Then spread the word. Put all our efforts into bringing the dragons down. Don't worry about killing or severely injuring, just get them to the ground and let the maneth do their part."

"Aye, sir. I am on it. I will spread the word."

The elf took to the air immediately and Madeiris knocked another arrow. He saw a large brown dragon bearing down toward the village center. He let the arrow fly and instead of aiming for the throat or head that most often bounced off harmlessly, he aimed for the center of the wing. The arrow split through the skin and tore a large hole in the dragon's wing. It arched its flight and then turned wildly. It was still able to fly, but not well and immediately angled itself down into the tree line. Madeiris heard the battle screams of maneth as they attacked.

We have a chance, he said to himself. *We just need to put some fear in the dragons, but how?*

***

"Hawthorne, there are spots on the horizon," Deklan Sherblade shouted.

"I see them," she replied. "I am going to engage. Perhaps I can stop them from attacking."

"If they are dragons, we have no chance. There are too many," the human added.

Hawthorne did not reply but she believed the same. The makeshift swords and the handful of bows they had fashioned would be no match for this number of dragons. She knew she needed to stop them. *What would you do, Anbari?* she said to herself. *How can I make them listen to me?*

The spots in the sky were growling larger and larger and Hawthorne knew they saw her the same way she saw them. She did not want to engage them in battle, but if necessary, she might be able to reduce the numbers by a few before they reached the human village. She stopped in flight, angling her feet forward and her head and wings back appearing to be standing in midair. "Oh my," she whispered. "Nine dragons? We have no chance."

"What are you doing here, dragon? Did you come to join us?"

Hawthorne smiled at the blue who had spoken. "Not completely. I have been to the settlement. There are few left. Bjork wishes them to remain as servants to us at the port."

Her statement caused a stir among the nine dragons who hovered in flight in front of her, but the blue who had asserted itself as leader stared questioningly toward her. "What do you mean, Bjork wishes them to remain? It was Slayne who told me directly to level this village. Destroy it all."

She heard the tone and quickly recognized her original plan to convince the dragon of new instructions would not work. She moved closer and in a soft voice said, "Yes, but you know as well as I do that Bjork is really in charge. Slayne is simply following his lead. Bjork recognizes the importance of the North Sea. He wants to control it. How better to control it than to rule over the weak and decrepit life forms that currently inhabit it?"

"What do you mean? We can destroy it and then we will run it. We don't need those left here to do anything." The dragons behind showed their enthusiasm which only pushed this blue dragon further. "Now get out of my way, or I will simply move you."

Hawthorne smiled. "Don't take arms against me. I have been given power from Bjork himself. He will decide your fate should you test me. Do you wish to face Bjork?"

The blue stood strong, still being pushed by the others but the option to potentially face what he knew to be the most powerful dragon on Troyf caused the blue to hesitate. Hawthorne saw it.

"I see you do understand what that means," she added. "What do you think will bring you more fame? To destroy this small outpost that Bjork wants saved, or to go back to Slayne and Bjork and let them know it is left with no defense and those that remain will serve the dragons?"

The blue still showed indecision. The other dragons began to fly in small circles, the anticipation of a fight growing stronger with each moment. Suddenly, the blue turned to the others. "The attack is off. This city is to be held for control of the North Sea."

Hawthorne let out a deep breath but kept her relief hidden from those before her. She smiled and nodded. "You made a wise choice. Now go back to Draag and inform him of the direction. You will be well rewarded."

"No," the blue stated.

Hawthorne had already turned and was about to fly back when the words struck her ears. "What? We just agreed—"

She was cut off. "I agreed to delay destroying this outpost. I am not going back. I am going to land and hold it until I receive confirmation of the direction. Anyone who defies me will be killed." He leaned in closer to Hawthorne, "And that includes you."

She now leaned into him. "Are you sure you want to threaten me?"

He smiled back at her. "I suppose I am sure, since I just did."

A fire beam of immense proportion shot from her eyes and struck the blue dragon in its wing. The impact and subsequent tear of the flesh sent the dragon spiraling down to the ground. The other dragons watched as their leader crashed into the soil with a thud and lay motionless. Hawthorne turned to the others. "Do not defy me. I will destroy you the same way I just destroyed your leader. You have two choices. You may do as Bjork, our supreme leader, has stated and return to Draag and await further instructions, or you can join me in the town and assist in holding it. However, if you choose the second option, you will follow my direction to the letter. Your counterpart chose a different path and he has paid the price. Therefore, my question is, do you wish to return to Draag as heroes, or just be another dragon holding a distant seaport away from the real battlefront?"

The dragons looked at each other but none spoke. Finally, a smaller red dragon flew forward. "I will return to Draag. I will inform the other dragons that we have held the coastal city. Who can I tell them is holding it?"

She smiled. "My name is Hawthorne. Tell Slayne I am here."

The other dragons seemed comforted with this direction and quickly fell in behind. As they left, the red turned back to Hawthorne. "I don't know if this is the right direction or not, one called Hawthorne, but I do know that if it is not, I will return to see that things are set right."

"Go now, my young friend. You will find your truth soon enough."

Chapter Nineteen

"What do you plan to do?" asked Anbari.

"I don't know," Kirven replied.

"I can feel the power of the Revel Rock. We are near." The silver dragon was taking small steps to try to keep his footfalls quiet.

"I was just in these caverns, my friend. The pedestal room with the Revel Rock is just around the corner."

Anbari stopped and stared toward him. "Then I ask you again, how can you destroy it? Even with the power of the ring, which I still don't believe I will give you, only one with dragon blood can destroy the Rock. That is the enchantment placed upon it. However, no dragon can destroy it. It is the riddle with no answer."

"There is one answer to that riddle, Anbari," replied Kirven.

"But it is one you will not have a chance to offer," replied the raspy voice of Almok. "Did you really think we would leave the Rock exposed with you abandoning your family on your idealistic crusade?"

Slayne stepped out to stand beside the black canok with the white diamond patch. "Anbari, you have no idea how much of an annoyance you have become. It is time for this to end."

Anbari stepped away from Kirven. "Is this a trap, Kirven? Did you set me up? I was a fool, but not fool enough to allow you to take the ring."

Slayne's eyes opened wide. "What ring?" asked the black dragon, then his voice softened as he recognized the indecision in counterpart. "Kirven, you did well to bring him to us. Now, come join our side and we can take control of the ring."

"You traitor," Anbari stated, staring at the white canok.

Kirven's voice was calm and unmoved. "I will not stand by your side, Slayne. Your presence here will only prove to Anbari and all others that there is a movement against you. You killed my mother. You are my father. And because of that, there is dragon blood in me."

Anbari held his stare on the canok and then began to smile. "Yes, Kirven, I understand now."

The canok ignored the comment as did Slayne, whose tone was deep and confident. "You do have dragon blood in you, Kirven. My blood. You worry about your dead mother when I am standing here before you, wanting you to stand by my side. Why do you defy me? The agreement is set. We can end it now. Just move beside me, my son. Let's end Anbari's movement right now, together."

Anbari removed the ring and reached his talon out to the canok. "Daphane would be proud."

Slayne saw the exchange and smiled. "Do you think that ring will give you power? You already have power. You can't defeat the magic protecting the Rock. Only dragon magic can, but no dragon may attack it."

When Kirven took possession of the ring, his front legs buckled. He howled in pain and fell to the side. Almok stepped closer until Slayne reached out to hold him back. Anbari wanted to move to the canok but was frozen, watching what was taking place. Then, Kirven looked up, said a few words, and vanished.

Slayne laughed. "Now your failure is complete, Anbari. Kirven has stolen your ring. Now it is just you and Almok, and me."

Anbari looked on in horror. Almok and Slayne both laughed as the silver dragon lowered his head. Slayne chanted several words and balls of fire shot at Anbari. Almok moved a few steps closer and issued similar bursts. Anbari offered no defense against the attack and his body was thrown back against the cavern wall then fell to the ground. Slayne and Almok stepped closer with neither slowing their barrage of fire and energy against the silver dragon. Anbari roared in pain and lowered his head into his belly.

Slayne stopped and motioned to Almok to do the same. "Anbari, you have failed at every turn. You failed when you tried to convince the dragons to follow you instead of me. You failed when you tried to stop my movement across Troyf, and you even failed when you tried to take Hawthorne from me. Who is she going to run to now? A silver dragon that gives up with each failure, or one who rules the land. Now, you coward, you will die."

"I have not left you, Anbari, and I did not steal the ring. It is too powerful for me to master, but it did give me the power to become invisible. It is the only way I can get close enough to the pedestal room. When I act on the stone, you have to stop Almok and Slayne from attacking me. I need you to fight. We can win this."

Slayne and Almok continued to step forward but stopped when Anbari opened one eye and narrowed on them. Slayne smiled. "Ah, he wakes. It's good you are conscious, for the pain will be much greater."

The black dragon arched his neck back to release a wall of fire and heat but stopped when he saw the two great silver wings open before him. "It is over, Slayne," Anbari stated.

"Oh, you decided to come back and fight, did you? But you are still alone. You are no match for me and my son." Balls of fire dropped from Slayne's mouth with every word.

"He is not alone," stated a deep, older voice from behind.

Slayne turned in surprise. "Sabast, you old fool. You have no business here."

"I do, Slayne. I, like every dragon with any allegiance to the true way of dragons, have every business to be here. It is not your time."

Anbari roared and a wall of fire swept from his mouth across the two. Both easily defended it, but it did take their attention from the blue dragon approaching from behind. Sabast too issued an attack which caused explosions of rock all around. Almok ducked and then dove closer to Slayne. The black dragon roared in return and shot a bolt of energy into Sabast that knocked the blue dragon to its back. Then he turned on Anbari again.

Kirven closed his eyes and stared at the Revel Rock. The hum of the magical barrier grew louder but did not break. He focused his mind first on the Rock itself, then the magical barrier surrounding it. But still nothing changed. He stopped and took a deep breath. Again, he closed his eyes and focused.

"Wait!" shouted Slayne toward Almok. "I feel something. Someone is attacking the stone. Your brother has tricked us. Get to the stone, now."

"I don't think so," replied Anbari. "I may have failed at just about everything, but there is no way I am going to let you leave this cavern right now."

"And I won't either," added Sabast, now back to his feet.

Slayne stared down to Almok. "Go to the stone. I will protect you. Go and kill your brother. It is the only way we can be sure of stopping this."

A faint cloud formed and then shaped into a small tunnel that passed in front of Sabast and into the nearby room that housed the Revel Rock. Sabast tried to break through it but his attack just bounced aside. The dragon tried magic and then physical force but neither had any effect. Anbari saw the blue dragon's efforts and immediately lifted himself into the air.

Slayne smiled. "You can do whatever you want to the magical barrier I built, but it is protected the same way as the Rock. No dragon can break its barrier."

Anbari turned in flight and crashed into Slayne, sending the black dragon to the ground. Anbari used his talons and pounded him across his head. The tunnel faded and then returned, and Anbari kicked Slayne in the stomach. The black dragon curled into a ball. The tunnel faded again but returned equally as fast.

"Sabast, be ready. When it fades, grab the canok."

Anbari struck Slayne again, this time with the center of his head between the black dragon's eyes. Slayne's head fell back against the wall and he laid motionless. The magical tunnel vanished just as Almok reached the entrance to the room. Sabast reached down and grabbed the canok in his teeth. He threw him against the wall where he fell in a heap and did not move.

"Come on, Sabast. We must help Kirven." Anbari led the way into the room where he saw the white canok deep in concentration. Both dragons touched the canok trying to give Kirven more power. The surge they felt was tremendous, but still the barrier did not break.

Kirven stopped his attack on the stone and fell to his knees. In between breaths, he stated, "I can't do it. It is taking all I have, and I am having no effect. There has to be another way."

Anbari had removed the hatchet of the ring in an effort to use it against the stone, but when he saw Kirven's eyes, he knew it wouldn't work. He set the hatchet on the ground next to him. The three looked on in disbelief. "What is the secret?" asked Anbari. "We have to figure out a way."

Sabast nodded. "Maybe it is like Slayne said."

Anbari and Kirven looked at him. "What do you mean?" asked Anbari.

"Maybe his force field tunnel is exactly like the Rock."

"I don't know what you mean," inquired Anbari. "But if you know something, tell us now, for we are out of time."

Instead of attacking the force field, you attacked the source of the force field. You attacked Slayne and in turn you destroyed that which he made."

Anbari opened his eyes wider. "Yes, Sabast, yes." He turned to Kirven. "Can you feel where this force field is being created?"

"I can't for sure, but I can tell you the pedestal is generating a lot of energy."

"Focus on the pedestal, Kirven," stated Anbari. "Do it now. We will assist. When the pedestal breaks, the Rock will break free. Use your power, the power deep within you, to destroy it. As dragons we can't help you, but you are a canok. A canok with dragon blood."

Kirven smiled. "So, you realized my thoughts as well. You know, it is just a theory."

"A theory that has to be right," Anbari added.

The canok narrowed his eyes on the pedestal and spoke several words neither dragon understood. Both Sabast and Anbari placed their wings in contact with the canok again and closed their eyes. Power surged from Anbari and Sabast at first contact and Kirven's body began to shake. Slowly, however, the pedestal cracked, and small pieces broke free. Kirven remained locked on the base repeating the same words over and over and suddenly the pedestal exploded. The Revel Rock crashed to the ground, the blue aura around it still illuminating as it had before. Anbari and Sabast broke their connection and fell back. Kirven's front legs buckled under him and he crashed forward.

"Kirven, are you all right?" asked Anbari.

Sabast had recovered and took a step closer as the canok slowly pushed himself up. "I am fine," he said breathing heavily. "It took more out of me than I thought and thank you both for the support. Your powers are truly great."

The green dragon motioned to the hallway. "Slayne will be waking up soon. The field around it remains. Can you break it?"

"I don't know, but we will find out soon enough." The canok lowered his eyes and stared at the Rock. He held the ring in his paw, but it was unclear to him if any power was being drawn from it.

"Can you use the ring?" asked Anbari.

Kirven remained focused on the Rock. *"I tried when you gave it to me, but it was too strong. It protected itself from me. I believe the ring learned from Ku. It now chooses who wears it the same way the individuals choose it. It did not choose me, but it is not fighting me either. We are together."*

A beam of energy shot from the canok and exploded against the Rock's shell, but different than when it had been attacked while on the pedestal, it did not send the energy back. The canok continued his wrath forward and the light at the spot of contact grew in intensity. Anbari and Sabast both looked away, the pain causing their eyes to burn. Sound began to emit from the Rock. It was high-pitched and penetrating. Anbari tried to look but couldn't for fear the light would blind him.

"No!" shouted Slayne from the entryway. He shot a beam directly into Kirven's body but the canok refused to break his connection to the Rock.

Anbari and Sabast both swung to see Slayne moving between them. Sabast leaped in front of him with his body blocking the path. Fire shot from Slayne's mouth engulfing the fallen dragon before him. The green dragon roared in pain before issuing protection. The smell of burnt flesh bit everyone's nose when Anbari unleashed a burst of energy so strong it sent Slayne tumbling backward. Anbari turned back toward Kirven and saw white blood falling from his mouth, ears, and nose. The canok was standing tall but his legs were quivering, and the dragon could see his body was failing. He swung his head to the Revel Rock and saw the blue shell was fading, but possibly not as fast as Kirven.

A bolt struck Anbari in the back sending his head to the ground. "You have gotten in my way for the last time, Anbari." Slayne was walking slowly toward him. "First I am going to kill Kirven, my son, and then I am going to kill you."

The bolt which Slayne had used against Anbari had paralyzed his body. He was still conscious and could see and hear everything, but he was powerless to move. He could not even speak. Slayne stared at him and laughed. "You are a fool. Now watch as I destroy every chance you have of defeating me in one fatal swing."

He sent another bolt of energy into Kirven's body.

The scream was like none he had ever heard before. Anbari stared at Kirven and saw the canok still fighting to keep his attack. He looked back to Slayne and saw him doubling over, black blood flowing from where Sabast had lodged the hatchet into his belly. He removed the axe and drew back to swing again.

A second bolt struck the green dragon where he held the hatchet causing him to drop it. *"Slayne, it is too late. We have to run now, or we won't escape."*

Slayne looked back toward Almok, who stood staring back at the dragon pleading with his eyes for him to follow. Slayne turned his head back to Kirven who had stopped his attack and fallen motionless on the cavern floor. He looked over to the Revel Rock. "No!" he roared. "The Rock."

Anbari and Sabast both turned to the Rock to see it split in two on the ground. When they turned back, Slayne and Almok were gone.

Chapter Twenty

Geoff turned around and watched the red dragon fall in line behind the others. Then something unexpected happened. The dragons in front of the red turned in flight and fell. They angled hard, arched their wings, but could not maintain flight. In moments they were on the ground. The maneth watched as best he could but they were too far out of sight for him to see what happened. He wondered if the red who had spoken through telepathy to him before had done something. It must have been the case because watching them in flight, something had changed. It was as if some event had happened that made the other dragons unable to fly.

Geoff turned back to where he knew the other maneth had fled and then back in the direction of the dragons. He knew it was probably suicide, but he needed to know. He brushed off his face with his free hand and started to run to where the dragons had gone down.

As he drew nearer, he heard the dragon voices. They were much louder than they would typically be, and to the maneth's surprise, panicked.

"What is going on, Draketon? I have lost it all," the dragon stated.

"I have as well. I can't form an energy ball or beam of fire. I can barely breathe fire. My wings are weak, and although I think I will be able to fly, it will not be like before."

Draketon stepped closer to the dragons before him, his large red wings still outstretched and strong like they had been. "Something has happened at Draag. I don't draw my power from the Revel Rock. The rest of you do."

"Are you saying the Revel Rock has been compromised?" asked one of the dragons, whose look of distress almost brought tears to its eyes.

Draketon smiled slightly but did not let it show. "No, I am saying it has been destroyed. You will need to fly home. You will need to hide in the caverns until we figure this out. The dragon way has changed. Without that power, we are not the most powerful creatures in our world any longer."

"Yes!" stated Geoff to himself.

Draketon turned to where the maneth stood hidden but did not speak. Their two eyes met and then the large red dragon lifted its wings. "Come, dragons, let's go home. This attack is over."

They looked at each other and one even seemed to be struggling to lift its wings, but eventually, all broke into the air and vanished above the trees.

Geoff lifted one arm in the air and roared.

***

"Focus your attacks on the wings. Bring the dragons down to the maneth on the ground," Madeiris shouted.

Elves released a wall of arrows at the dragons still circling above them. Walls of flames were returned along with fireballs that seemed to have a magical ability to turn in flight and land directly at the source of the arrow's origin. Elves screamed in pain as the fire engulfed them but others filled in behind. It was a battle of sustainment. How many elves could continue to fall in behind to keep the support coming? Another dragon fell to the ground, and the maneth pounced with extreme force.

"Wait!" shouted Madeiris as he watched the change take place. "What is happening?"

Several of the dragons' flights changed and the attacks ceased. As the elf prince watched, other dragons followed suit. It was as if they were only just learning to fly. It was as if all knowledge they had carried had been lost with the breaking of a branch. One of the dragons actually crashed into the upper limbs of a tree causing it to then completely lose control and crash to the ground. It leaped to its feet bewildered and lost. Maneth quickly encircled but it did not fight like the others. It stared at them with a look of fear.

Madeiris shouted. "They did it. They destroyed the power at Draag. Throw everything you have at the dragons. Now, my elves. Do it now!"

THE DRAGON OPPRESSION

Every elf stepped forward and knocked arrow after arrow. At one point there were so many arrows in flight it appeared they could be walked across like a road. The dragons screamed in pain and a few returned with fire, but their reach was half what it had been and the magical balls were no longer used. One by one the dragons either fell to the ground or fled. The elves jumped and screamed as the last dragon turned and headed away.

One of the leaders of the flyers landed next to Madeiris in Elvinott's city center. "Do you wish my team to follow?" he asked.

"No, bring everyone home. This war is over." The two locked hands and twisted their wrists together, holding bows in their free hand.

"Yes, sir, I will bring everyone home." He began to take off and then stopped a few feet in the air. "And the maneth in our woods?"

"Bring them in as well, Captain. They helped save our home."

The flyer elf answered with a nod and a smile before he lifted into the air shouting direction as he did so.

***

Geoff walked back into his camp. A few maneth had returned, or never left, but their manes were burned, and their armor stained dark black. More maneth laid dead on the ground. The elation he had felt moments earlier was now absent as he looked across his desolate camp. Not one tent, table, or home remained. Even the king's tent that was reinforced with stone had been destroyed.

"Five dragons," he said to himself. "Five dragons brought us down to nothing, and one of them did not even participate. How can we ever truly be safe from these creatures?" He knelt down next to a fallen maneth he recognized. He stroked the maneth's mane and then reached out and closed his eyes. Nothing more was said.

***

"Kirven, can you hear me?" asked Anbari, shouting toward the fallen canok.

Blood still flowed from his mouth and nose. "There is nothing we can do for him. It is up to his body and power to save him now." Sabast had placed his wing across the larger silver dragon above Kirven.

"There must be someone who can help him," Anbari stated. "I am not knowledgeable about the world. Is there not a healer somewhere?"

Sabast's eyes opened. "A healer?" He paced backward and appeared deep in thought.

Anbari saw the change and stood to face him. "Do you know of someone?"

"Find McCard. He is a maneth, King of the Maneths in fact." Sabast moved across the room and used his wing to draw in the dirt. "The maneth live as nomads in the forests. Their camp is usually in this area." He drew some more showing their camp in relation to the Ozaky River. "McCard told me a story of a wizard that healed him of injuries one time. He had a strange name. I believe it was Mi-Kevan or something like that. Take Kirven there. If he survives the trip, perhaps this wizard can save him."

Anbari immediately moved to grab the canok's body and lift him onto his back but then stopped and turned back to the green dragon. "What will you do, my friend?"

"I will remain here. The dragons will be returning. You know that as well as I. They will have questions. They may not listen to me, but at least they will hear my message. Without the power of Draag and the Revel Rock, they will be lost. I don't know if they will recover or not. It may be all of us waiting for the eggs to hatch and hoping those new dragons can save our land."

Anbari nodded slowly. "I need you to care for something for me." He removed the ring from Kirven's paw and then also took back the hatchet that had been thrown on the ground. "There will be someone coming for this ring. I don't know who that will be, but they will come." Anbari said a short spell which made a box appear before him. "Only this person will be able to open this box and inside will be this ring. He will be the one to save us."

Sabast took the box and with a few words it disappeared. "I will keep it safe, my friend, until the one comes."

"Take this hatchet as well. I intended it for Claude, but I fear he has passed. I sensed something in a dwarf I met. This hatchet is to go to that dwarf. You will know when the time is right."

Sabast bowed and the hatchet disappeared as well. "I will guard them well, know that to be true. Now, go and save Kirven. His impact will be great, for his whole existence defines balance."

Anbari lifted him the rest of the way to his back. "And he has bet his life on finding the one who can do just that—bring balance." Anbari began moving quickly through the caverns. "I will find this Mi-Kevan, Sabast. Just be ready when Kirven and I find the one who will defeat Slayne and Bjork."

Sabast lowered his eyes and began walking out, choosing the opposite direction that Anbari had taken.

***

Anbari's wings beat against the wind after he broke through the skylight in the mirror room. He passed several dragons that appeared lost and confused. He did not stop and showed no concern. Their eyes were filled with wonder and locked on the dragon as he blew by. He knew they wondered how he could fly with the strength he had always carried, and they were broken down and weak. But in truth, Anbari didn't care.

"Hold on, Kirven," he stated, hoping the canok could hear. "I will find the maneth camp and find you the help you need."

There was a burst of wind that pushed the dragon slightly to the side causing Kirven to nearly fall from his back. Anbari corrected quickly, but not before the canok groaned.

"Kirven, are you awake?" Anbari asked. "You did it, Kirven. You broke the Revel Rock. The dragons have been stopped, at least for now."

Kirven again groaned but did not speak.

"I am taking you to get help—in the maneth camp. There is a healer. He can help you.."

"Anbari?" Kirven's voice was weak and cracked.

"Yes, Kirven. Don't try to speak if you are unable. I will find help very soon."

The canok lifted his head slightly. His voice was choppy and difficult to understand, but he forced the words out. "If I don't make it, you have to find the one who can stop this. We did nothing but delay the outcome. Bjork always intended to use the young to sustain his plan."

"How will we know who that 'one' is? Who can have power so great as to stop Slayne and Bjork? They become more powerful every day and never required the use of the Revel Rock. They, like me, have their power inherently within them."

"You must control who the chosen one is. Much like me, who Slayne and Bjork did not anticipate would be their undoing as a creature who was not a dragon but possessed dragon blood, we must find a dragon who does not appear as such." Kirven coughed up blood and laid his head down on the dragon's side, his last words drawing out into eternity.

"Kirven, what does that mean? Kirven?" He paused and turned his head back to the motionless body on his back. "Kirven!" he yelled, but there was no answer. He angled his wings to cut through the wind harder and pushed himself toward the area Sabast had described. "He is not going to make it," Anbari said to himself, though he was not sure he spoke it out loud or not. "What did he mean, *a dragon that does not appear as such?* A false dragon? That doesn't make sense."

Again, Kirven stirred pulling Anbari from his thoughts. "Kirven, we are almost there," he stated, but he actually didn't know if it was true or not. He simply kept flying.

After some time, he saw four dragons in flight coming toward him. He recognized them all, but one he knew well. As they arrived within a safe distance, Anbari spoke, "Draketon, what brings you here?"

The dragons stopped in midair, the ones beside Draketon maneuvering as they fought to remain in flight. Anbari saw their struggles but didn't comment further. Draketon replied, "We had gone to destroy the maneth camp, but something happened which changed the abilities of my counterparts. They no longer can draw power from Draag. We are returning to assist in repairing whatever damage has occurred. What may I ask are you doing, and with the canok?"

Anbari studied Draketon closely, looking for any sign he was not as he claimed. He saw nothing. "We were headed to the maneth homeland to assist. Because you left there, we must be close."

"I went to try to stop this massacre, and I was successful, but I need to save face with those with me. Tell me what you need to know, and I will assist."

Anbari smiled broadly upon hearing the hidden telepathic message from the red dragon. "We will continue to the maneth camp and ensure all is settled. It is critical we get there quickly though, so we can return to Draag and help recover whatever has happened. Can you point us in the right direction?"

Draketon nodded understanding. "You are very close. Just over that rise. You will see a break in the trees and what is left of the camp directly below. However, I should warn you, there is not much."

"Understood," answered Anbari. "Stay safe, my friends, and we will join you shortly."

The other dragons were completely unconcerned about the conversation and consumed by their own losses. Draketon smiled. "You stay safe as well, and when we meet again, I hope times will be different."

Both understood the comment and left without taking it further. There had been no movement from Kirven in a long time, and Anbari could only pray the canok was still holding on. He saw the clearing and landed in the center. The devastation in the area was worse than he could ever have believed. He took several steps then stopped when he felt something press into his back.

"Why are you here, Anbari?" asked Geoff, holding his club against the dragon, though he knew it would have little use. "Have you come to finish what the other dragons left behind?"

Anbari turned around and took a few steps back as he did to create some distance between him and the maneth. "I am truly saddened by all that I see. I was not nor will ever be one who would create such a travesty. If I had the power to reverse what has happened, I would."

Geoff looked questionably toward him and then lowered his club. "I believe you, but the feelings your brethren placed on my homeland will be difficult to forget. All I know is I have no strength to defend against you, even if I had to. If you are here to destroy what is left, then do so without further comment. All the maneth have fled and there are but a handful of us left."

Anbari's face turned up immediately. "Are you saying some of the maneth are safe?"

Geoff recognized the change in the dragon. "Yes, I was able to get to them before the attack. They are safe, but that doesn't answer why you are here?" He looked at the unconscious white canok on his back. "And why you have a canok on your back?"

Anbari stared hard at the maneth, but for some reason, he knew he could trust him. "This canok is responsible for stopping the dragons' progression. He singlehandedly destroyed the source of their power at Draag. However, he was severely injured. We can't help him, but one told me about a healer that King McCard knows how to find. The healer's name is..."

He was cut off by Geoff. "Mi-Kevan. You seek Mi-Kevan, but I would not call him a healer as much as an evil wizard."

"You know him?" questioned Anbari. "He is our only hope. Can you take me to him?"

Geoff shook his head. "I don't think we should do that. He gets..."—Geoff paused and then said with inflection—"uncomfortable with unknown visitors, and a dragon would definitely qualify as unknown. I will take the canok."

Anbari stepped back. "No, I must be sure. I have to accompany him."

"No, my friend. I will not let you down. I am a friend to all canoks. Although this destruction may cause my trust for dragons to be at the lowest, I will do everything within my power to save this canok. You can believe in me." There was a short pause while he let that sit. "But as I look upon him now, you need to decide quickly, for Mi-Kevan is still a bit of a trip, and I fear our friend does not have much time."

Anbari thought for a moment and then lowered his body down for the maneth to grab his friend. "I am trusting you. Please don't let us down."

Geoff smiled as he lifted the canok over his shoulder. "Let you down? For the first time in a long time, I believe I am taking a large step in the right direction. Take care, my friend." The maneth turned and began to leave. Then he turned back. "When he awakes, where can I tell him to find you?"

Anbari again thought for a moment and then answered, "The center of the South Sea. He will know where to go."

Geoff looked at him strangely, then nodded and continued without further comment.

Chapter Twenty-One

Hawthorne stared across the field and watched as the large group of humans slowly walked back toward the small village sitting on the outside of the North Sea. She could see Octavius leading the way with a white canok by his side. An instant feeling of excitement came to her.

Deklan Sherblade walked and stood next to her, creating a sight the humans still were not accustomed to seeing. "Do you believe they return because they were successful?"

"I don't know," the dragon replied, "but I hope so. I feel something has happened with Draag, but I can't place what."

"They seem to be moving at a great pace," he added.

"They do," she replied. "Would you like to ride out to meet them with me?"

Fehr grumbled. "There is not really room for…"

"Hush, my young boy. We can't head there alone, or they may take arms against us."

Deklan swung his head to her in surprise. "You mean you want me to ride on your back?" he questioned.

"I don't know any other way for you to get there with us, do you?" she answered. She did not give the human or bandicoot a chance to speak further and simply grabbed Deklan gently in her mouth and tossed him easily onto her back. He landed right next to the still grumbling Fehr. "Let's go see who approaches."

She lifted into the air and began to head toward those approaching. The human leader grabbed his sword, but when he saw that his captain rode on the dragon's back, he lowered his sword and stared at them questionably.

Hawthorne landed directly in front of them. She smiled when she spoke. "I am Hawthorne. Anbari and I decided I would stay and help defend the city. Some dragons came, but I convinced them to leave. Does your presence here mean Anbari was successful in stopping the dragon oppression?"

"I don't know," Octavius replied. "But I do know he and Kirven were returning to the caverns with a plan to destroy the rock which gave the dragons power."

"Kirven?" she questioned.

The human smiled. "A powerful white canok that brought with it something to give them an advantage. That's all I know. They told me if we arrived here and the city remained, then they were successful, but they probably did not count on you turning the dragons away, so for now, I don't think we can know for sure."

Hawthorne nodded understanding. "Well, your city is safe. I did very little, but Deklan and Fehr here," she motioned to the two on her back, "kept all in order. Thank you for allowing me to remain, but I must go and find Anbari. Don't worry, should I learn that dragons are on their way to your city, I will return to help defend it."

Octavius bowed as the dragon lowered her stance to let Deklan jump to the ground. "Thank you, Hawthorne. Though I am sure Deklan performed admirably, I am very confident your presence was much more than you described."

"And mine as well," added Fehr.

"And yours as well," Octavius repeated.

She smiled and just before taking off, she asked, "What do you call your city, if you don't mind me asking?"

He looked at her and pressed his lips together. "Well, we have not actually decided on a name. However, since it is clear we are definitely not the highest in the pecking order for the focus of the dragon attacks, I say we call ourselves, Last City."

Deklan nodded but Hawthorne tilted her head. "But you are clearly not last. If you are second in the pecking order, why not call yourself, Toopek?"

"Toopek," Octavius repeated. "I think that is exactly a perfect name." He stepped forward and placed his hand on Hawthorne's neck. "And may I say, my friend, you will always be welcome in Toopek."

She smiled. "I will always remember that, and who knows, I may return here without you even knowing."

Deklan and Octavius both smiled, but it was Octavius who answered, "Trust me, Hawthorne, if you did return here, I guarantee you we would know it." He stopped and just before the large dragon opened her wings to leave, he added, "Regarding your direction, although I know Anbari is not there, I know Elvinott was facing a brunt of the attacks and the maneth were headed there as well. It is closer than Draag."

She did not reply immediately but instead lifted into the air and then glanced back as she began to rise. "Thank you, my friends, and please always stay safe. I will go to Elvinott first, for if I can help save their homeland, my delay to Draag would be worth it." Moments later she was out of their sight and the humans were making their way back home to Toopek.

***

"Another dragon approaches," hollered and elf. "And it does not appear like the others. It still has flight."

"Archers be ready," returned Madeiris. "Wait for it to draw close enough to attack and then bring it down."

The dragon stopped just out of bow range and hovered over the village. The elf king stared at it with a battalion of elves and maneth scattered through the trees and the city center. "What is it doing?" asked one of the elves next to the prince.

"It is evaluating what has happened," answered Madeiris. "It probably expected to find our home in ruins. Keep your arrows ready. This big dragon clearly has strength. It will take us all to bring it down." He hollered to the maneth line, "Maneth, are you ready should we be able to take this dragon down?"

"We are," returned a maneth who was acting as leader.

King McCard walked up next to the elf prince. He stared at the dragon as it hovered over the trees. "What is going on, Madeiris? I thought the attacks were over."

"I thought so as well, but a lone dragon has returned and waits just beyond our reach. I believe it is sizing us up and planning its attack."

The king continued his stare and then began taking a few steps forward. "I believe you cannot assume anything during these times. This dragon does not fly with the hatred of one possessed with rule. It flies with concern."

"McCard, please stop. I can't protect you."

The maneth king turned back to Madeiris. "I don't need protection, my young friend." Then, turning back to the dragon in flight, he hollered, "We don't wish to fight. Are you here as an ally, or do you wish to follow the same direction as those dragons before you?"

Hawthorne angled her wings and dove down toward the maneth king. "I am Hawthorne. I am friend to all life in this world. I seek to learn what has happened?"

McCard outstretched his hand. "Come here, my child. Both the maneth and the elves have faced serious dragon hardships. I don't know the state of my home, but as we battled the dragons here, something changed with them. Their abilities ceased to exist, and they fled. We believe the attack on Draag was successful. We believe the Dragon Oppression is over."

Hawthorne lowered her eyes and a tear formed and dripped to the ground. "Where is your home?" she asked. "I will take you there."

Madeiris had walked up next to the king of the maneths. "There is no chance…"

McCard lifted his hand. "It would be an honor to ride on your back." He turned to Madeiris. "Is there any chance you could spare a small battalion to fly with us?"

Although Madeiris did not agree with the direction, he was not in a position to oppose a king. "I will have six flyers by your side in moments."

The king bowed. "Thank you, Madeiris. Your father would be very proud."

A female elf walked up behind him, holding her stomach as she walked. "His mother is very proud as well," she said, placing one hand on his shoulder.

"Mother? You should not be up. You are too close to my brother's birth."

She smiled. "You keep saying *brother*. Are you simply afraid should you have a sister that a female elf will be better with a bow than you would?"

Madeiris smiled. "That is a fear I will never have. Now, Mother, return to your room. I will be there shortly with a report on Father as soon as I know anything."

She waved her hand. "Nonsense. I heard there was a dragon here that was not destroying our home and I wanted to see it for myself." She looked toward Hawthorne. "Of course, you are a female. That is why you have a higher intelligence and do not attack without knowledge."

Hawthorne smiled. "I like you, Queen. I like you a lot."

"And I you," she replied. "Now go and take this war maneth back to his camp and then have everyone return; it is time for celebration. The elves will welcome all."

Madeiris smiled. "Mother, I must insist you get back to…"

"Hush. I am the queen, and I will determine when and if I return to my room. Last time I checked, a queen out-rules a prince." Those in the area smiled, all except Madeiris. She turned back to Hawthorne and the group of flyers assembled next to her. "Travel safe, my friends. Although the dragons fled from these woods, that does not mean our world is safe. Find the maneth. Bring them to us. If what we believe is true, then it is time to bring us all together."

Hawthorne nodded and just before they opened their wings to leave, the queen added, "And if you see my husband, please bring him back soon. I don't know how long I can keep this baby in place, and he promised me he would return in time."

No more words were said. Hawthorne opened her wings and took off. The flyer elves followed suit behind and McCard's eyes opened wide as they broke through the trees. He leaned down and gripped his hands underneath Hawthorne's scales.

"You will have to guide me, King."

"Continue this direction." He waved the elves forward. "Lead the way to the maneth camp. Make the straightest line possible. Several maneth are left there alone. We have to help them if we can."

***

Geoff sat outside the cave. He was not allowed to enter. He couldn't leave. He didn't know this canok, but he felt he had to stay because he gave his word to Anbari. It had been more than a day. There had been no word from the wizard. Mi-Kevan was not anyone Geoff would prefer to interact with, but this time demanded it. When he had delivered Kirven to him, the canok had not moved since Geoff had taken him. Everything about him appeared to be dead, but somehow there was still a beat. Still a breath inside him. Because of that, Geoff waited.

"What has happened?" asked McCard, approaching unseen from behind.

Geoff jumped at the voice and then bowed to his king. His eyes grew wide when he saw about ten maneth, six flyer elves, and a dragon beside him. "My King, a dragon named Anbari came to us after the battle. He brought with him a canok. A canok with grave injuries. A canok that is the reason the Revel Rock was destroyed. He asked me to find Mi-Kevan and bring the canok to him. It was his only chance to live."

Hawthorne did not give the king a chance to respond. "Did you say the dragon was Anbari, and that the Revel Rock was destroyed?"

Geoff was still not comfortable speaking to dragons, and his broken voice showed it. "I-I-I did say just that. This canok named Kirven, with the help of Anbari, destroyed the Revel Rock. When that happened, the dragons fled. They lost all power. The maneth who stayed fought bravely." He turned to his king. "We did lose some, but many survived. Our home was destroyed, but they did not pursue your trek to Elvinott. They believed they surprised us here."

McCard lifted his hand and placed it on Geoff's shoulder. "You did well, Geoff. You did amazingly well."

"Thank you, my King. I must wait here until Kirven's fate is known."

"I understand," replied McCard. "The maneth and elves with me are going to search the forests for more survivors or find those who did not. This is a time to celebrate the success and remember those who were lost. The elves have asked us to return to Elvinott to share in that celebration. If you are able, please join us when you are ready."

"I will, Your Majesty."

King McCard smiled at the response. "Please, Geoff, call me McCard, for I believe you and I will be close for a long time to come."

Geoff bowed and the king turned to leave. Hawthorne broke the short period of silence. "Excuse me for asking, but do you know where Anbari has gone?"

The maneth looked up to the dragon and nodded. "I was to tell Kirven he was going to the center of the South Sea."

"The center of the South Sea?" she repeated.

"Yes, that is all he said."

"Then I shall head that way as well. I am sure the well-being of Kirven is of critical importance to him. Please send word."

The response was odd. Geoff had no way of sending word to the center of a massive expanse of water, but he accepted the question just the same. He turned and sat on the large rock he had been on for longer than he cared to remember. He peered inside the dark cave seeing no movement, light, or any signs of life.

"I hope you are well, my friend. I truly hope you are well."

About the Author

Kenneth S. Kappelmann is a scientist by trade but began writing while living in Switzerland in the 90's. His love of reading fantasy such as the *Dragonlance* series by Weis and Hickman drove him to this genre. He used the award-winning fantasy series, *Hidden Magic*, as a launching pad to also write another award-winning crime and suspense series, *Tomas O'Malley* series.

Note from the Author

Word-of-mouth is crucial for any author to succeed. If you enjoyed *The Dragon Oppression*, please leave a review online—anywhere you are able. Even if it's just a sentence or two. It would make all the difference and would be very much appreciated.

Thanks!
Kenneth Kappelmann

Thank you so much for checking out one
of **Kenneth Kappelmann's** novels.
If you enjoy this book, please check out
our recommended title for your next
great read!

Return of the Dragons by Kenneth Kappelmann

When Kirven killed the black canok in the glade outside Toopek, he did not realize that he had just taken the first step to fulfilling Schram's destiny. At that time he did not even know for sure if Schram was the "one." He only knew that time was growing short for him to find the only one who could harness the power to defeat the dragons. If it wasn't Schram, he had wasted a long time with the human. Possibly too long for the Troyf to be saved from the dragons.

View other Black Rose Writing titles at
www.blackrosewriting.com/books and use promo code
PRINT to receive a **20% discount** when purchasing.

www.ingramcontent.com/pod-product-compliance
Ingram Content Group UK Ltd.
Pitfield, Milton Keynes, MK11 3LW, UK
UKHW040237250426
12048UKWH00040B/1555